TALES
OUT OF SCHOOL

CAROLYN WHEAT
(Photograph by Kate McIntyre)

TALES

OUT OF SCHOOL

MYSTERY STORIES BY

CAROLYN WHEAT

Crippen & Landru Publishers
Norfolk, Virginia
2000

Cover painting by Victoria Russell

Crippen & Landru logo by Eric D. Greene

ISBN (limited edition): 1-885941-47-1
ISBN (trade edition): 1-885941-48-X

FIRST EDITION

10 9 8 7 6 5 4 3 2 1

Printed in the United States of America on chlorine-free, acid-free paper

Crippen & Landru Publishers
P. O. Box 9315
Norfolk, VA 23505
USA

Email: CrippenL@Pilot.Infi.Net
Web: www.crippenlandru.com

To my many Sisters in Crime for years of sisterhood:

Abbie
Annette
Ellen
Janice
Judy
Lynn
Margaret
Marilyn
Marlys
Miyoko
Pat
Sue

CONTENTS

INTRODUCTION

I never thought short stories were my forte. I began writing them because Marilyn Wallace, in those first heady days after the founding of Sisters in Crime, wanted to publish an anthology and I didn't want to be left out. Then I started using the form to explore characters, settings, moods I had no way of integrating into my novels. I liked going back in time, switching genders, researching places and events for fiction purposes. I liked changing my identity, using language in a more conscious, almost poetic, way, compressing the work into something as dense, as rich, as a Chunky bar.

It's only now, looking back over the stories chosen for this collection, that I realize how depressing they are.

Should I say that? Is this a turnoff? Are you, Dear Reader, even now slipping the book back on the pile and skulking away — or, having made your purchase, are you now regretting having forked over the cash, wishing you'd bought that talking cat mystery instead?

What can I say? That the stories are dark because that's the way the people in them chose to behave, that they are responsible for their own fates and it's not my fault their lives are in shambles?

Or is that a cop-out?

Read and decide. And, just in case it makes you feel better, there are one or two lighter-hearted tales in this collection. Just don't expect all the cat stories to be the cute ones.

A final note — of thanks and appreciation for a great teacher. Back when I thought I couldn't write short, I gave my first mystery writing workshop in Saratoga Springs, New York. I sat in on a short story class offered by Lynn Barrett, who did me the honor of sitting in on my class as well. The very next year, her short story about Elvis won the Edgar, while I went on to improve my skills as a short fiction writer thanks to her insights into the form.

What goes around, comes around. If there's a single theme running through these tales, that's it. What begins in childhood ends in old age; we will all ride around the big carousel at our own pace. With that in mind, I organized these stories according to the age of the protagonist; we begin in childhood's confusing days, work through coming of age and loss of innocence, enter middle age. We grow older, forgetful, suspicious, set in our ways and certain only of what we do not know. We lose our dignity, our ability to control our own lives — except, perhaps, to end them.

Even the first and title story, "Tales Out of School" comes full circle in "The Metal Blessed to Kill." Justice may in the end be poetic, but it's not always pretty.

Carolyn Wheat
El Cajon, California
June 2000

The horror of this story is that it is true. Up to a point, anyway. I was told the basic tale — the "Bobby won't be in school today" part — by a cousin who couldn't understand the boy's reaction to the bloody murder scene he'd witnessed. I filled in the emotional blanks, telling a story that explained why the child didn't report the killing

TALES OUT OF SCHOOL

Randall Toller walked to school with a slow gait, dragging his feet as if to slow down time as well as his seven-year-old steps. His arm hurt. He squinched up his eyes and tried to push the pictures away. Tried to forget the rage on his mother's face as she'd grabbed his arm and yanked him out of the closet.

It was his fault his arm hurt. If he hadn't taken so long getting dressed, then she wouldn't have gotten so mad. But how was he supposed to know how long to take? Last week she'd sent him back to change his shirt because he'd put on what every boy in the world except him was old enough to know was a church shirt instead of a school shirt. She'd given him a good smack for that one; the red mark was still on his cheek when he got to school. When Miss Roth asked what happened, he said he got brushed by a blackberry bush.

He was supposed to stop by the Olson house and walk the rest of the way with Bobby, the youngest son. He didn't like Bobby, who was big and loud and bullying, just like his brothers. But Ma said it was good to get in with the Olsons since they had the biggest farm in the county, so she ordered Randall to walk to school with Bobby just as she ordered his father to play pool with Ole Olson, patriarch of the big blond clan. Randall wondered if his mother wanted Pa to lose to Mr. Olson or if that was Pa's own idea.

He dawdled and dragged his feet as he approached the big white house where the Olson family lived. It wasn't just Bobby he was afraid of, it was all the Olsons. They joked with him, played little games like asking him questions about his parents and then laughing when he couldn't answer.

Didn't they know? Didn't they know you weren't supposed to tell tales out of school?

That was the rule in his house. No tales out of school.

One time he sat at the Olson breakfast table having a glass of milk; Bobby was clowning with baby Ellen and dropped his glass on the floor. Randall had stiffened, waiting for the explosion. But Mrs. Olson just laughed, called Bobby a clumsy kid, and picked up the mess with a dishrag.

Randall supposed Mrs. Olson didn't want tales out of school; she'd probably punish Bobby later, when he wasn't there.

When he and Bobby were together, trudging through the November snow, he asked how Bobby felt knowing all day in school that his punishment waited for him at home. Personally, Randall would rather get it over with, but sometimes his mother did that. Sent him to school with a promise that when he got home, he'd pay for what he'd done that morning. He'd spend the whole day squirming in his seat, losing track of the day's lesson and making stupid answers to Miss Roth's questions, because his mind was full of the punishment that waited for him at home.

Bobby had looked at him like he was crazy. Punishment for what? he'd asked.

Randall shut up at once, new respect for Bobby filling his heart. Here was a boy who really knew the meaning of tales out of school. He wasn't going to admit to Randall that there would be a punishment.

Bobby Olson's uncle was crazy. This was a known fact and one that fascinated Randall. He asked his father what it was like to be crazy; Pa had replied that crazy people could do what they liked when they liked until they got too crazy and had to go to the County Home, which was where Lars Olson spent ten years of his crazy life.

Now he was out of the Home and living with the Olsons until he could find a place of his own.

Randall made a point of studying Lars Olson, but he really didn't seem different from other grownups. He was big like all the Olsons; he worked on the farm alongside Ole and the two oldest boys, Tom and Roger. He did have a habit of breaking into laughter over nothing, which scared Randall a little bit since he never knew when his mother's laughter would turn to sarcastic jibes and then to something worse. But Lars just laughed; nothing more. At least when Randall was around. And he knew better than to ask Bobby; no tales out of school.

Almost there. The dirt road leading to the Olson place was muddy with spring rain; violets lined the path, but not planted, just there. The tulips by the side of the house were planted, in colorful rows like toy soldiers. Yellow-and-red and red-with-white-borders and purple that was almost black.

He was going so slow he was almost walking backwards.

He wasn't exactly sure why. He just knew something was wrong today. Something bad had happened inside the Olson house. Something a stranger shouldn't see.

He stopped on the flagstone path. Stopped cold and realized why he knew something was wrong. Blackie wasn't there. Blackie hadn't run up to him and nipped at his ankles the way he always did. Bobby laughed when Blackie grabbed Randall's pants leg and shook his terrier head back and forth and Randall cried out.

"Scared of a little puppy," Bobby had jeered, but Mrs. Olson told Bobby to be quiet and put the puppy in another room while she'd poured Randall a glass of milk. Randall had buried his face in the glass, hoping to still the trembling of his lips. He'd almost cried, the puppy had scared him so much.

The puppy always ran out, barking, whenever someone came up the walk.

Where was it today?

Randall looked around. No puppy. No sounds of any kind. No milking machine noise, no tractor noise. No clinking of bottles in the shed where Tom and Roger ran the bottling machine. No telephone ringing inside, no kid noises wafting out through the half-open kitchen window.

The Olsons were a noisy family. Randall had never heard the big white house so quiet.

He tiptoed up the front steps, peered into the window, through the lace curtains. It looked as if Mr. Olson was lying on the floor in the living room. Just lying there.

Sometimes Randall's dad slept downstairs on the couch. He'd usually have his blanket folded neatly into a square before Randall got up, but once in a while Randall had come downstairs to see his father lying on the couch, snoring. He knew it was one of those things he shouldn't talk about, so he never did.

But Mr. Olson wasn't on the couch. He was on the floor, and he was lying on his stomach.

Randall didn't think Mr. Olson would want a neighbor boy to see him that way, so he tiptoed back down the porch steps and walked around to the kitchen.

That was where he saw Blackie.

Blackie was dead. Randall knew what it meant when the flies buzzed around like that. Besides, no animal could be lying in that big a pool of blood and still be alive.

His father had told him that. He'd said people have only so much blood inside and when they lose it, they're dead.

Blackie was dead.

Had Mrs. Olson killed him to punish Bobby for something, the way Randall's mother had killed his kitten when he was little?

Randall swallowed a lump in his throat as he remembered his kitten. He'd named the kitten Hopalong because of the way he jumped out at you and clawed at your shoelaces. Hoppy, for short.

It was his fault Hoppy was dead. Ma had said he could have the kitten as long as he was good, but he hadn't been good, so the kitten had to die.

Poor Bobby. He'd really loved that puppy; he was going to feel real bad if something he'd done had made his mother kill Blackie.

Randall stood on tiptoe, his old-fashioned leather shoes creaking a little. He peered over the top of the windowsill and looked inside.

The kitchen was red.

No, it wasn't. It was yellow. Yellow and blue.

But then why was there red all over everything? The table looked as if a new piece of bright red oilcloth had been spread over it, and the floor was —

Oh, no. Randall sank back on his heels and looked at the dead dog. The red in the kitchen looked just like the red under the puppy's head.

The bile came up without warning, and Randall was sick all over his shoes and the tulips.

He had to go to school. Ma would be mad if he was late and the teacher sent a complaint.

He'd have to go to school without Bobby.

The teacher would ask where Bobby was.

Should Randall lie? He gave the matter some thought as he stepped briskly out of the Olsons' yard and headed along the road to town. Should he tell Miss Roth that Bobby wasn't feeling well today?

Sometimes Ma told Miss Roth that he wasn't feeling well when the truth was Ma had hit him where it showed.

His stomach hurt. It hurt from the pain of looking at all that blood. It hurt from worrying about what to say at school. If he told tales out of school, he'd be punished for telling other people's business. If he lied, he'd be punished for lying.

He'd told his mother he never wanted another kitten.

Sometimes he was afraid she'd get him one.

In the end, all he said to Miss Roth was, "Bobby won't be in school today."

The next morning, in the teachers' room at the little country schoolhouse, Miss Roth spoke her mind.

"Did you ever hear such a thing?" she asked without expecting or desiring a reply. "He comes to school bold as brass and sits in his classes not saying a word. When I asked him where Bobby Olson was, he just said Bobby wouldn't be in school today." She paused for effect and refreshed herself with another sip of tea from the bone china cup.

"Wouldn't be in school! When the poor child was lying in a pool of his own blood, that crazy uncle of his gone clean out of his head and hacked the whole family to pieces! And all that stupid child could find to say was Bobby won't be in school today." She shook her head yet again at the wonder of it all.

"Somebody," she pronounced, "ought to take a switch to that Toller boy."

This story began with a dream. The young teenage boy and the mysterious older woman appeared in the gray early morning mist that clouds one's perceptions just before waking. I had not idea who they were or what they meant to one another until I began to write. The ending makes it, perhaps, an anti-detective story, a plea for not finding out the truth, for letting sleeping dogs slumber.

COUSIN CORA

"Now the left hand," I ordered in my official Scotland Yard voice. The most dangerous criminal in London (portrayed by my six-year-old brother Lionel) placed his pudgy little paw in mine. I rolled the fingers one by one onto the satisfying squish of inkpad, then pressed them onto a sheet of Mama's best cream note-paper. The result: a perfect fingerprint record, as guaranteed by the Hawkshaw Junior Detective Kit Company of Racine, Wis.

I gave Lionel back his hand. "Mind you don't wipe them on your knickerbockers," I warned, "or we'll both catch Hail Columbia." Lionel nodded, his round blue eyes lending the scene all the solemnity any detective could have wished.

We were in the barn, temporarily renamed 221B Baker Street. I was the great Sherlock; Lionel had taken the parts, as required, of Dr. Watson, Mycroft Holmes, several Baker Street Irregulars, Mrs. Hudson, and Toby the dog. At the moment, he was basking in the notoriety of Professor Moriarty, the effect only slightly spoiled by a smudge of fingerprinting ink on his button nose.

It was the summer the very trees seemed to sway to the Merry Widow Waltz. It was the summer my feet (which were growing at a rate that alarmed even me) began to leave the barefoot path of boyhood. It was the summer I sucked dry the bitter fruit of the knowledge of good and evil. It was the summer of Cousin Cora.

"Sa-am," a voice called in the distance. Lionel and I locked eyes, one thought in both our minds. What was the most dangerous criminal in London compared to our big sister Lucy, the most dangerous tattletale in Springfield Township?

"Sa-am, where aaare you?" Her voice was getting closer. She'd be in the barn any minute, and then she'd see Lionel's inky fingers, and then she'd spy the Hawkshaw Junior Detective Kit, and then —

It was a well-known fact that women were incapable of appreciating the Art and Science of Detection.

"Quick," I told Lionel, "scoot out the back and put your hands under the pump." He scooted. Even at six, my brother had a sound grasp of life's essentials.

I gathered up the fingerprint record of Professor Lionel Moriarty, closed the inkpad tin, and put both into the cardboard box containing the Detective Kit. Then I shoved the whole shebang into the corncrib, making sure a layer of cobs lay on top, so Lucy wouldn't see the scowling face of Hawkshaw the Detective on the cover.

I whipped my mouth organ out of my pocket and commenced to play — probably the Merry Widow, which I'd been trying to learn all summer just to get Lucy's goat. It was her favorite tune, but I didn't think she really cared for it on the harmonica.

"Sam, what on earth are you doing in this musty old barn on such a beautiful day?" My sister stood in the doorway in the stance favored by women throughout history for criticizing men: feet planted solidly apart, hands on hips, arms akimbo. Looking for all the world like an indignant milk jug.

I muttered something in which the term *beeswax* figured largely.

"What do you mean it's none of my — Why, Mama sent me to fetch you, so there."

"What for?"

"Mama's Cousin Coramae's come for a visit and Mama wants you to wash up and wear your Sunday collar to supper."

"Cousin Coramae?" My detective instincts leapt to the fore. True, Mama was Southern and therefore considered persons of the remotest connection her cousins, but why had I never heard tell of a Coramae? "And why didn't Mama say anything at breakfast?"

It was scarcely my intention to ask the question aloud, particularly of Lucy. Ever since turning seventeen and putting her hair up, she'd been impossible to live with. Putting on airs and looking down her nose at a fellow just because he was three years younger and didn't pomade his hair like the boys who went to Webley's Corners High School.

"I suppose you think Mama ought to consult you before asking her own kin for a visit," Lucy said, with a superior toss of her head. For a moment I thought her honey-blonde pompadour would shake loose from its moorings and tumble down her back, but no such luck. "And besides, how could she tell us when she didn't know herself? Cousin Coramae just turned up on the doorstep not twenty minutes ago. All alone." Lucy's eyes grew as round as Lionel's; her voice dropped into a conspiratorial tone. For a moment it was as if the bossy older sister had vanished, replaced by the pigtailed equal of former days.

"She didn't come in the hack." This momentous pronouncement was followed by another, equally startling. "And she brought no more luggage than a motheaten carpetbag and a hatbox."

This was news indeed. Mama's relations sent letters to announce their coming, telegrams to say they were enroute, and invariably arrived in the depot hack with an army of bandboxes, steamer trunks, cowhide valises, and lesser impedimenta.

Cousin Coramae was a Mystery.

I hastened to the parlor, spitting into my hand and slicking down my hair as I raced past the kitchen garden toward the back door.

The house was dark and cool, sunlight kept at bay by heavy damask curtains pulled tight so the Turkey carpet wouldn't fade. I stood a moment outside the parlor door, conducting surveillance. Mama's voice was high and fluting, the way it sounded when she was making small talk with someone she didn't know well. The voice that answered was dryly precise, with a hard Yankee edge that surprised me. Mama's kin had Southern drawls, putting a lazy, questioning emphasis on the wrong words. Not like Papa's midwestern yawp, which came down as hard on consonants as a Baptist preacher on sin. Cousin Coramae's accent was different, as though she was related to no one but herself.

I was on the verge of stepping into the parlor to pay my respects when my mother's words fixed me in place like a chloroformed moth.

"— my husband. What shall I tell him?" Mama's voice sounded like the high end of the piano. "I'd rather die than have him learn the truth."

"Tell him nothing," the Yankee voice replied. "I have come for a brief visit. That is all anyone need know."

"Brief?" Mama seized upon the word as though it meant sure salvation. "How brief, Tommy?"

I no sooner had time to absorb the unexpected nickname than the visitor replied, "Until I get the money."

Silence followed, thick as barn-dust. I crept forward, hidden by the half-closed door.

The mysterious cousin was a tiny woman. Frail, too, with bird bones and parchment skin stretched too tight over a pinched schoolmarm face. You'd have said she looked worn out, though she was about my mother's age, but there was an inner something that told me she was tough as twine.

Her hair was mud-colored and looked in need of a wash. Her skirt was travel-stained, and her high-button shoes were worn at the heels. At her throat she wore a lace jabot that looked the way my school collars did on Saturday night. My father would have said she'd been rode hard and put away wet.

She sat in the second-best chair.

The first-best chair — the green velvet plush with mahogany arms — was reserved for Grandfather Parsloe and other household gods. The third-best chairs (which had no arms) were reserved for whichever children were privileged to enter the parlor, and for Uncle Samuel, whose frequent indulgence in strong spirits no longer entitled him to chairs with mahogany arms. How did Cousin Coramae, with her pauper's luggage and her bedraggled appearance, rate the second-best chair?

I leaned in closer. Mama perched on the edge of the rose-colored chair as though afraid to lean back into its plush depths. A stranger would have thought Cousin Coramae the self-assured hostess and Mama the nervous guest.

"The money." My mother's tone was flat as an iron, hollow as an owl-tree. "And just where do you think I can put my hands on such a sum?"

"Come, Lia, you married women always have little stores put by, amounts your husbands don't know about. Am I right?"

Lia. A name I'd never heard in my life. Mama was Lillian, Lily to her sisters, Lil to Papa in a joshing mood. Never Lia.

Mama's answering sigh was a surrender. "There's the butter-and-egg money, I suppose. But I had hoped to buy Lucy a dress for graduation."

"I *need* the money, Lia."

"You don't understand, Tommy. It *isn't* money, not really." Mama's words tumbled over one another like shelled peas rolling into a bowl. "Mr. Benbow at the General Store keeps an account of what he owes me, and then gives me credit when I need something special, like the silk for Lucy's dress."

"Couldn't you ask him for cash instead?"

"He'd be mighty suspicious if I did — and he'd tell Harry for sure. Men stick together."

"I see." Cousin Coramae sat still as a barn owl, her predator's eyes fixed on Mama. "Then we must concoct a story your husband will accept. An unpaid debt? Or perhaps I stand in need of a life-saving operation."

I stood behind the door, knowing how wrong it was to eavesdrop, but unable to move. If Cousin Coramae was an owl, it was I, not Mama, who was the mouse. Sweat poured down my back; I wiped my forehead with a hand still gray with fingerprinting ink. I had plenty of chores to do before supper, including scrubbing all evidence of ink off my fingers with Papa's lye soap. Yet nothing could have moved me from my vantage point.

"Why me, Tommy?" Mama asked. "Why not one of the others?"

The mysterious visitor shrugged. "You were the closest to the College. The train station was watched, I'm sure of it, so I didn't dare travel by rail."

This was better than the dime novel I had hidden under my mattress. A mysterious woman, arriving unexpectedly, unable to travel by train. The College, I was sure, meant Springfield State Teachers' College, where Mama went before she married.

"Are you so certain they suspect —"

"They suspect a great deal more than they can prove. But the family is both influential and persistent, and I decided discretion was the better part of valor. Still, Lia, I am sorry it had to be you."

"I know, Tommy," Mama said, her voice like the soothing syrup she gave me when I was sick. "I know. And I'll get the money on Saturday, I promise. That's when Harry takes me to Mr. Benbow's store to shop for the week."

The parlor looked as it always did: Great-grandmother Hartley's silver tea service resting on the mahogany butler's table alongside the bone china cups and saucers. I'd watched Mama pour tea into those cups countless times.

Today was different. Today blackmail hung in the air, heavy as honey-suckle.

There was plenty to occupy my mind as I sat on the back porch, shucking corn for supper. I pulled each ear free of husk with a tearing sound that satisfied my soul and watched mounds of cornsilk billow to my feet. It looked as though every doll in the house had been scalped.

My first real case. No more playing Sherlock in the barn — I had a true-life female Professor Moriarty staying under my own roof. Deep secrets lay between these two strangers, one called "Tommy" and the other "Lia."

Secrets my father wasn't to know.

What could I do? Tell Papa? I stripped the last ear of corn, running my hand along the pearly golden kernels, then setting it on the pile with the others.

No — telling Papa was betraying Mama, and that I would not do under any circumstances.

Confront Cousin Coramae — if she was even Mama's cousin, which I doubted — and tell her I knew everything, like a hero in a melodrama? She had only to threaten to tell Papa the terrible secret, and I'd be back where I started.

As I carried my load of corn into the kitchen for Maisie the hired girl to put on the boil, I reflected that there was nothing in the Hawkshaw Junior Detective Kit to cover this situation. I was on my own.

It was one of Papa's town days. Although we lived on the farm his father and grandfather worked before him, Papa's real business was the Feed and Grain. He spent three or four days a week in Webley's Corners. Which meant that he was dressed for company when he walked through the front door.

We were all at the dining room table, empty soup plates resting on two layers of china before each place. My Sunday collar chafed my neck; Lionel squirmed like a tadpole. Lucy, in her new sprigged waist, sat next to me, still as a tree stump, showing how grown-up she was by her refusal to fidget.

Mama, at the foot of the table, seemed taut as a barbed wire fence. Every time there was a noise at the door, she started. She lifted her glass of ice-water to her lips every few minutes, but seemed not to drink it, for the level remained the same. Her slender fingers played with the heavy silverware.

She looked everywhere except at Cousin Coramae.

As soon as Papa's tread was heard on the porch, she jumped from her seat, jiggling the table and spilling some of her water. "Harry," she called, in the high, fluting voice I associated with nerves, "you'll never guess who's come for a visit."

They talked in the vestibule, among the umbrellas and canes. I could only hear a few words: ". . . my second cousin twice-removed . . . I haven't seen her in so many years . . . it seems the letter she sent was lost in the mail, isn't that something?"

Papa's baritone was easier to hear, though he was trying his best to mute it. ". . . can't say I do remember, Lil, but then you have so many cousins . . . Certainly she's welcome, letter or no letter. Now, let's have supper.

I'm hungry as a bear."

Papa entered the room like a bear, his big masculine presence filling space out of proportion to the actual size of his body. He wasn't a tall man, but broad-shouldered, with thick brown hair and a mustache I envied with all my heart. Would I, someday, outgrow my weedy slenderness and thin, sandy hair, becoming a real man like my father?

"Harry, I'd like you to meet my cousin, Miss Coramae Jones." Jones was not a name I'd ever heard in my mother's family. And since Mama had said "Miss," it wasn't her married name. Whoever our visitor was, I was willing to bet every marble I owned, plus my slingshot, that her last name wasn't Jones.

Supper began as soon as Papa took his place at the head of the table. Maisie brought out the soup, ladling it into the shallow bowls one by one. It was cherry soup, which I loved because it was cold and sweet and nobody else I knew had it for supper in their house.

"Cherry soup," Cousin Coramae said, her green-apple voice ripening just a bit. "This does take me back, Lillian."

Not Lia. Just then Mama said, "Remember, Coramae? We both learned to make it from that Swedish girl, what was her name?"

"Inga. Inga Gustavsen. A brain like a feather pillow, but cooked like an angel."

"I didn't know angels could cook," Lionel said. "What do they make, angel food cake?"

Papa's laugh boomed out. Mama and Lucy smiled. But Cousin Coramae exploded with laughter, as though something bottled up was being released. She pulled a dingy lace handkerchief from her sleeve and held it to pursed lips, but still the laughter came. Her eyes teared, as though the very act of laughing touched her in some deep way. Her laughter hurt, as though she'd all but forgotten there were things in the world to laugh about.

She dabbed at her eyes with her handkerchief, the tip of her nose red. She gave herself a good shake and said, "There now. I shall subside. I must apologize . . . difficult railroad journey." All at the table nodded, the notorious strain of travel upon the female sex too obvious to warrant remark. Only I knew that however Cousin Coramae had reached our farm, it hadn't been by train.

The thing about cherry soup was: Maisie had never learned to pit the cherries first. Each spoonful was a potential social disaster. Mama and Lucy ate with delicacy, gently removing each pit into their spoons and sliding it discreetly under the bowl.

I tried to do the same. Honestly, I did. But one pit got past me and slid down my throat, causing a coughing fit that sprayed red juice over my portion of the damask tablecloth. Lucy shot me a withering glance and said, "Cousin Coramae, I must apologize for my brother. He isn't really housebroken."

My face burned as though stung with nettles. I wished Lucy at the bottom of Hale Pond, which everyone knew was bottomless.

Coramae Jones fixed Lucy with a stare only an owl could have duplicated. "In my day," she began, her tone as tart as a pippin, "it was considered the height of bad manners to call attention to someone else's *faux pas*."

Lucy hung her head. Now her face looked as though it had had the nettle treatment.

Another piece of the puzzle fell into place: This woman had been a Teacher.

Stars fat as bumblebees hung low in the summer sky. I was outside, walking with Cousin Coramae. I was both afraid and curious, walking in the dark with a suspected blackmailer. There was excitement, too, in knowing that I was conducting my very first interrogation as a detective.

"Will you look at that moon!" The visitor pointed at a low point of sky, her finger twig-thin. We had passed the hitching-block and were well on our way toward the dirt road into town.

I looked; the moon was a crescent, but it lay on its side, points curving upward. "It looks like a boat," I said.

"Exactly," my companion agreed. "Like the gondolas I saw in Venice." In the pale moonlight, her weathered face took on a look of rapture.

"Have you really been to Italy?"

"Didn't your mother tell you?"

"My mother?"

"She was there too. We were a party of young ladies," she explained. "We toured Rome, Florence, and Venice. It was a very special trip for all of us."

Lia. An Italian pet-name from an Italian trip. A trip no one in the family had ever heard about.

I tried to keep my voice casual. "Did you ever visit Mama at the Teachers' College?"

"Why, yes, I suppose I must have. Once or twice." There was dismissal in the flat tone. We walked in silence for a minute or two, our shoes scuffling the summer dust. I could hear birds in the woods on the other side of the road; our side was rich-smelling alfalfa, and a little spring wheat.

My companion broke the silence. "The Hunter stalks tonight," she said.

"What?" It was not a polite reply, but I was too startled to remember manners.

"Up in the sky." The twig-finger pointed again. "There's Orion, the Hunter. See — the one that looks like an H with a crooked bar."

I found Orion without much difficulty. He was big, dominating his part of the sky the way my father dominated our dining room.

"Artemis, whom the Romans called Diana, killed him, and placed him among the stars. She was a huntress, the Virgin Goddess."

"You sound like a teacher." It was part calculated, part blurted-out, but I had to know.

"You are a very observant young man." She stated a fact, without judgment. "You notice things. You have eyes that catalogue, like an accountant. Or, perhaps," she went on, the tart-apple taste coming back into her voice, "like a spy."

It was as though the fugitive could see right into the barn, through the corncrib, under the dry cobs, to where the Hawkshaw Junior Detective Kit lay.

We passed the hollow tree where I'd seen a hoot owl the week before. The crick I fished in burbled in the distance. Up ahead was the water tower, looming over the horizon the way the Methodist Church steeple overshadowed the town.

I had to smile as I looked at the tower. There were some initials at the top I had reason to be mighty proud of.

"It takes considerable nerve to climb a tower that high," my companion remarked.

"What — what makes you think I climbed it, Cousin Coramae?"

"Please, call me Cora. I have always loathed my full given name, a fact I have some difficulty impressing upon your mother."

"Well, then, Cousin Cora," — I had been brought up never to use an adult's name without some sort of title in front of it, so Cousin Cora she became — "the truth is that one night Red Beaudine, Spider Crowley, and I climbed clear to the top of that tower and painted our initials on the back. In red paint."

"Bully for you," Cousin Cora said. "That's one peck of wild oats sown."

Even Papa, who always wanted me to be manly, wouldn't have said that. My heart warmed toward the strange visitor, and I told her things that night I'd never told another soul. How I hated farm life. How I wanted more than anything in the world to set off for the city, maybe even California.

I didn't say a word about Hawkshaw Junior Detective Kits, or the conversation I'd overheard in the parlor. I kept a few secrets. But as to the rest, Cousin Cora made no criticism. Everything I said seemed reasonable to her. Every dream I expressed she agreed could be reality if I wanted it badly enough.

As we walked toward home, our way lit by a ghostly crescent moon, I decided I'd been reading too many dime novels. This skinny spinster lady who smelled of violet water was no blackmailer.

The next morning, I was out with Papa mending fences by the dirt road. We were stringing new barbed wire and pounding the fence-posts in tighter, so they'd withstand the summer rains. It was hot, dry work and we'd been at it since sunup. My arms hurt and my shirt was soaked with sweat; Papa looked the worse for wear, but I knew he could go till sunset without a pause or a meal if he had to.

When he lifted the heavy hammer over his head, his huge arm muscles knotted and tensed as the hammer rose high into blue sky, then struck the fence-post with a force that shook the very ground. Bit by bit, blow by blow, the wood drove deeper into the caked soil.

I held the fence-posts, my hardest job being not to flinch as the hammer swung down, all of Papa's strength behind it. I wondered if the day would ever come when I could swing the hammer while Lionel held the post. Right now, it was all I could do to lift the hammer, let alone hoist it with Papa's ease.

Hoofbeats caught my attention. Sheriff Caleb Anson trotted by on Midnight, his black mare. "What say, Cal?" Papa called out. He put down the hammer and gave the sheriff a straight-armed wave.

Sheriff Cal pulled his horse up short. "Say, Harry," he said, "Didn't your wife go to the Teachers' College in Springfield?"

"You know she did, Cal."

"Well, I'd surely hate to upset Lillian, but there's been a little trouble up that way." Sheriff Cal gentled his mare, patting her coal-black neck. Still the animal fretted and stamped, eager to trot. "I'd appreciate your letting me have a word with Lillian. Seems the woman who's involved was one of her classmates. She stayed on to teach at the College after they graduated."

At the word "teach," my ears pricked like a jackrabbit's. Hadn't I already deduced that Cousin Cora had taught school?

I stood beside the fence, hoping to be taken for a fence-post and ignored.

"Involved in what, Cal?" Papa asked. He pushed back his hat, wiping his forehead with his hand.

"Not before the boy," the sheriff said. Papa edged toward Midnight; the sheriff leaned down to speak as privately as possible.

I could only overhear snatches: ". . . family very upset . . . girl died of laudanum poisoning . . ."

Papa's voice was easier to hear. "Over a lover, I suppose. That's what all these young girls get up to." I was reminded how angry he got when Eddie Ruckleshaus came to take Lucy to the church social. You'd have thought Eddie was about to start my sister on the road to ruin instead of treating her to peach ice cream at Christian Endeavor.

". . . know how it is, Harry. All-female seminary . . . women cooped up together. These things happen."

"Disgusting!" Papa gave up any effort to keep his voice low. "If you dare bring filthy talk like that into my house, Caleb Anson, I'll —"

"Could be murder, Harry." Sheriff Anson's calm tone cut through Papa's anger like a wire-cutter. "Leastwise, the Pargeters, the family of the dead girl, think so. And they've got a fair amount of influence in Springfield, so —"

"Springfield is Springfield," Papa interrupted, "and Webley's Corners is Webley's Corners."

I knew Papa in this mood: now the sheriff would be lucky to get directions to his own house from him. All I could think of were the words I'd overheard in the parlor yesterday, Cousin Cora talking about an influential family, and some reason she couldn't travel by train. Was it possible the woman I'd walked with under the stars the night before was a murderess? I should have felt excited. Instead, I felt sick.

"All the same, Harry, Lillian could —"

"Hellfire, Cal!" Papa shouted. He tore the hat from his head and slapped his thigh with it, raising a cloud of dust. The horse shied back; the sheriff pulled tight on her reins. "It's been nigh onto twenty years since Lil graduated that school. I won't have you upsetting her over something she can't possibly know anything about."

"Harry, I already told you." The sheriff's tone was patient but insistent. "This teacher, Miss Tomlin, was a student with Lillian twenty years ago. Your wife might just remember her, know where her family lives."

Miss Tomlin. Tommy. My ears buzzed, and for a moment, I could say nothing. Then I cleared my throat and said, "I never heard Mama mention anyone by that name."

"There now," Papa said. "If Sam here never heard of the woman, then Lily doesn't know her and that's a fact. She's forever going on about that school. She'd have been bound to mention this Miss Tomlin if she'd known her. Right, Sam?"

"Right, Papa." I felt dizzy, as though the sun were frying my brain. Of course Mama knew Miss Tomlin. She called her Tommy, and was being blackmailed into helping her escape.

"So there's nothing more to say, is there, Cal? You won't be coming around to bother Lily, and that's that."

The sheriff raised his palm and eased Midnight away from the fence. "Can't say as I blame you, Harry. I guess I'd do the same if it was my wife." He dug his knees into the mare's flanks and Midnight gratefully accepted the hint. Man and horse disappeared in a cloud of dust.

Papa and I finished the fence-posts in silence. I wanted him to tell me what the sheriff had said, wanted him to trust me man to man, but all he did was swing his hammer and pound wood deeper into hardpacked ground.

As soon as Papa and I finished, I made my way to the sewing room. On the wall, proudly framed in gilt, was Mama's diploma from Springfield State Teachers' College. In one corner, next to the workbasket, sat a two-shelf bookstand. The top shelf contained what I wanted: the yearbook of Mama's graduating class. I opened it, starting where I always did, with Mama's photograph.

She was Lillian Wanderley then. The face that looked at me was at once familiar as my own hand and as remote as the moon. She was my mother, but she didn't know me. Didn't know I would ever exist. Didn't know she would marry Papa and live in Webley's Corners.

She was President of the Poetry Society. Under her name was the quote: "Shall I compare thee to a summer's day?" Every time I read those words I thought how true they were. It wasn't just my mother's sun-bright hair and sky-blue eyes that made her seem summery, it was her laughter and lightness.

I turned the pages backwards, stopping at a picture of a dark-haired girl with huge black eyes in a thin face. Under the photograph was the name Letitia Coramae Tomlin. Secretary of the Poetry Society.

Papa had told Sheriff Cal the truth. Mama did go on about Springfield College, telling Lucy and me all about her friends, her teachers, the fun she'd had. I'd heard stories of every picnic, every midnight revel after curfew, every funny incident in class.

Why had I never heard of Cora Tomlin — or the trip to Italy?

The next day, I rose at five, did my usual milking and swept out the barn. As I worked, I thought about Cousin Cora, and what I ought to do. It was wrong to let Cousin Cora take my Mama's money, wrong to let her go without telling the sheriff where she was, wrong to let her escape.

On the other hand, there was the terrible secret — whatever it was Mama was so desperate to hide. I remembered what Sheriff Anson and Papa had talked about. What if Cousin Cora really had killed the Pargeter girl? Could I let her go, knowing what I knew?

I needed more evidence. As I passed the corncrib, I took out the Hawkshaw Junior Detective Kit and hid it under the bib of my overalls.

It was just as well I did. On the way out of the barn, I met Lucy, dressed in a gingham skirt with a matching ribbon in her hair. "Going to town with us, Sam?" she asked, tossing her head. Practicing for the Webley's Corners beaux.

"Don't know," I replied. It was Saturday, the day Papa took Mama to Benbow's General Store. The day Cousin Cora would get her butter-and-egg money.

"Your sweetheart will be leaving today," she teased. "Mama says Cousin Coramae's taking the four-fifty to Chicago this afternoon. Don't you want to be there to say good-bye?"

"Not specially." I stuck my hands in my pockets and began to whistle, hoping to discourage conversation.

Nothing discouraged Lucy when she was bent on talking. "I don't know what you find so fascinating about Cousin Coramae," she said. "She's just a dried-up old stick, if you ask me." When my continued whistling convinced her she'd get nothing more out of me, Lucy flounced toward the kitchen door.

I thought Lucy wasn't wrong: Cousin Cora was like one of those stick-insects that looked like a twig and then scared the bejesus out of you when it started to move.

The guest room looked as though no one had slept there for years. The bed, with its rose satin coverlet, was neatly made, the bolsters propped against the cherry headboard. The dresser, with its hand-embroidered scarf, was empty of Cousin Cora's personal belongings. The only evidence that she had ever occupied the room was the hatbox and carpetbag sitting beside the door.

Mama's Singer whirred in the sewing room next door. I was glad; no one would hear me with that noise going on. I pulled the Hawkshaw Junior Detective Kit out from under my overalls and opened it. Inside I had fingerprint powder, an insufflator, and special tape to lift latent prints.

There were plenty of surfaces in the room that ought to have given me prints: the top of the dresser, the night-table, the wash-stand. None did. Every time I puffed away the excess powder with my insufflator, there was nothing there. The room had been wiped clean. Either Maisie had suddenly become the perfect housemaid, or Cousin Cora had erased all traces of herself.

I was so busy working I didn't notice at first that the sewing machine had stopped. I froze. Was Mama about to come into the guest room? What would I tell her if she did?

Then I heard the sobs.

I crept down the hallway toward the sewing room. The door was open, but I didn't go in. Mama sat in the rocking chair, her head in her hands, her shoulders heaving. On her lap was the yearbook.

"Mama?" My heart thudded inside me like Papa's hammer striking the fence-posts. I could count on the fingers of one hand the number of times I'd seen my mother cry.

"Sam." Mama raised her tear-streaked face and gave me a watery smile. "I was just looking through my book, and so many memories came back. So many memories." She wiped her cheeks like a child, without benefit of handkerchief.

"Are — are you all right, Mama?"

"Yes, Sam. Please just let me be." She attempted a smile. "I was just reminiscing, that's all. You'll understand when you're older."

"Mama, I know the truth," I began.

"And what truth is that, Sam?"

I stepped over to where she sat and knelt beside the rocker. "I know about the dead girl at the College and about Cousin Cora's not being our cousin but being Miss Tomlin instead. And," I finished boldly, "I know you mean to give her money and let her get away."

Mama turned her gaze toward the window, where the last lilacs drooped on the bush. They were brown-edged now, but still filled the sewing room with a fragrance that reminded me of Mama.

"If you know that much, then you know I have to, Sam. I have no choice."

"But, Mama, couldn't we —"

"*No*, Sam." Her voice sharp as sewing-scissors, she cut off my words. "Please, for my sake, don't ask any more questions. Just let it be."

I left her turning the pages of her yearbook. When she thought I was out of the room, she bent her head. A tear fell onto the page, and then another. I crept away quietly, as though from a sickroom.

What would Sherlock Holmes do? Find the truth at all costs. What would Papa do? Protect Mama at all costs. What was I to do?

I went back to the guest room. I didn't know what I wanted, the truth or comfortable lies or if I wanted to turn back the clock so that Cousin Cora had never entered our lives. I only knew that whatever I wanted, the truth was what I had to have.

I opened the carpetbag. Inside, among the neatly folded clothes smelling faintly of violet, was a small packet of letters tied with a black velvet ribbon. I drew them out, and recognized my mother's elegant penmanship.

Love letters, to someone not my father. Some were four and five pages of thick vellum, others were just notes. On the back of one of Mama's engraved calling-cards: "I so loved our picnic by the river, Dear One." On monogrammed pink notepaper: "How do I love thee? Let me count the ways." On a torn-out sheet of school tablet paper: "I dare not ask a kiss, I dare not beg a smile."

I felt like a fence-post on the receiving end of Papa's hammer. I was face-to-face with the terrible secret, the hold Cousin Cora had over my mother. Mama had had a lover when she was at the Teacher's College, a lover who received letters with poetry in them. Letters signed "Lia."

Someone besides Cora Tomlin had known my mother by that name. Someone she had met in Italy? And how had Cousin Cora come to have the letters?

The last note said only: "Since there's no help, come let us kiss and part."

It was when I put the letters back that I found the vial of laudanum.

I drew it out, turning it in my fingers. Cousin Cora, blackmailer, using Mama's letters to her lost lover as a weapon to extort money. Cousin Cora, murderess, using laudanum to poison a girl at the College. Had Cousin Cora blackmailed the dead girl, too, then killed her to prevent her telling anyone?

There was only one thing I could do. It felt like betrayal, and yet with murder at stake I had no other choice. Besides, Papa would understand. He often joked with Mama about the beaux she could have had back in her Virginia home town. I took the letters out of the bag and put them in the pocket of my overalls.

Papa was in the bedroom, standing before his shaving-glass, straight razor in his hand. His face was lathered, except for the precious mustache. Ordinarily, I loved watching Papa shave, taking mental notes so that I could handle the razor with ease when I had enough whiskers to worry about. I came straight to the point. "Papa, there's something I have to tell you."

It was as though an anarchist's bomb went off in our little farmhouse. Papa exploded out of the room, lather still on his face. He made straight for the guest room, picked up Cousin Cora's bags and tossed them out the front door. He ordered Maisie to tell Cousin Cora, who was out strolling in the woods, to high-tail it off his property at once.

Then he marched to the sewing-room. I hid behind the stairwell, feeling as though I was weathering a tornado. Papa's angry shouts filled the air, followed by Mama's tearful replies.

". . . phony cousin. Wanted by the police, of all things."

". . . don't understand, Harry . . . not murder. The poor child took her own . . . wasn't Tommy's fault."

"Tommy! Is that what you call the creature?"

Lucy came down from upstairs, her face anxious. When she saw me behind the stairwell, she whispered, "What's wrong?"

"Not sure," I lied. But I couldn't look at her. Whatever was happening behind that closed door was my doing.

I felt even worse when Lionel came out of the kitchen, one half of a gingerbread boy still in his hand. He looked as scared as he had the day he nearly fell into the well.

"How could you, Lily?" Papa asked. It was a plea, a prayer.

"I was so lonely," Mama answered. "Away from home for the first time. . . . Tommy was good to me. I didn't understand at first, and then — I was in love."

"Love! You call that love?" Papa's voice sounded wrenched from him. "It's a sin, Lily, a sin against nature." His words ended with a sob.

The air felt heavy, the way it had when the baby died. Mama had been betrayed, but not by Cousin Cora. I'd wanted to protect her, but it was me she'd needed protection from.

The last I saw of Cousin Cora she was walking up the dirt road, back straight, carrying her carpetbag and hatbox in either hand.

Nothing was ever the same again. We never had cherry soup. Mama's sunshine nature faded like the lilacs. Papa worked later and later in town, sometimes staying over at Mrs. Hepwhite's boardinghouse. He never again called Mama Lil.

As for me, my detecting days were done. I swapped my magnifying glass to Red Beaudine for a pea-shooter and three immies I didn't really want. The rest of the Hawkshaw Junior Detective Kit I burned behind the woodshed. As the flames curled around the scowling face of Hawkshaw the Detective on the cardboard cover of the box, I decided hell was the right place for anyone who caused that much pain.

At the time I wrote this story, I was working for the New York City Police Department, and I was very conscious of police officers and the practical and moral choices they made on a daily basis, The title came to me first and rattled around in my brain for a long time before the story followed.

FLAKE PIECE

He came outa nowhere. I swear to God. One minute I'm walkin with my partner, tryin to say somethin he won't rag me about later. Night's as calm as a warm bath. Next thing I know, this kid comes flyin out of the alley. Nearly knocks my partner over. The Hairbag looks at me; I look at him. He's got thirty years and fifty pounds on me, so guess who chases the kid.

I start running. Behind me, I hear yelling, Spanish and English. Sounds like some lady in the tenement got broken into.

Kid runs down Avenue A, then takes a sharp right on East Seventh, right below the park. His sneakers skid on the cobblestone street. I puff along behind, my heavy cop shoes pounding the pavement. It feels like we'll run that way throughout eternity, him just ahead, me just behind, forever and ever amen.

"Stop!" I shout at the top of my lungs, but all that comes out is a winded croak. I yell it again. "Stop, goddamn it. I'm a cop." Voice is louder this time, kid's gotta hear me. He's gotta. I just can't run no more. Stitch in my side and I'm breathing like an eighty-year-old with asthma.

Kid disappears. *Where the hell —*

My head swivels. *I can't lose him. I was so close.* A vacant lot on the corner. Has to be. Kid has to be there.

I run toward the emptiness. It's dark as hell. Real hell, the kind Father Fahey used to scare us shitless with at the ten o'clock Mass. Slippery, too. God knows what kind of filth people throw in here.

My breath sounds like a steam radiator on a below-zero night. I hear his too, but hearing's all I can do. There's no light at all.

Ice-cold sweat pours down the inside of my tunic. Gun hand's wet and shaky. I point at God knows what.

A movement. I feel it, I don't see it until the kid steps into the streetlight glare. His heel slides and he catches himself. He's into a half-crouch and suddenly I see the glint of metal in his hand.

A gun. Oh Jesus, a gun. Freakin kid's carryin. I'm gonna die I'm gonna die. Oh Mama I'm gonna die.

My finger jumps on the trigger, pulls back like my whole body energy was pumped into that one place. I hear noise. Could be one shot, could be more. Could be mine, could be his.

Kid crumples. Like a freakin house a cards the kid crumples to the ground. He writhes a minute, then lays still. Too goddamn still.

I feel weird. Breath gasping like a landed fish. I'm shaking like I'm having a fit. My crotch is wet, just like that time in second grade. Oh, Mama look at the hero, shoots a kid and pisses on himself.

I walk toward the kid. Big red hole in his stomach. BIG freakin red hole. Oh God I don't wanna look I hafta look. Kid is not alive. No way he's alive with a hole like that in his —

You stupid little turkey, why did you make me kill you?

My eyes move toward the kid's hand. The hand with the gun. It takes me a minute but finally I see what's in front of me. No gun.

No gun. Christ, let my legs hold me up don't let me fall. No gun. There's gotta be a gun for God's sake please there's *gotta* be a gun.

There's no gun. No metal in the kid's hand at all. Freakin kid's unarmed. Sweet Jesus, don't let it be true. I *saw* metal in his hand. I wouldn't shoot an unarmed kid. I'm not that kind of a cop.

I drop to my knees. There's shit all over the lot — garbage, dog crap, discarded rubbers, used needles. I don't care. I paw through all of it. I need that gun. There has to be a gun Goddamn it there has to be a gun there has to be a gun *there has to be a gun.*

My breath's coming in sobs. I'm on my knees in the crud of the city. My hand touches a furry dead thing and I jump back with the willies. Christ, what the hell was that it's only a dead puppy. Coulda been a rat. *God what am I doing here?*

Freakin kid shouldn't of turned on me, metal gleaming in his hand.

What could I think? What could I do? I saw my death coming. I had no choice. I had *no* choice.

I see the headline:

COP SHOOTS UNARMED BOY

His mother cryin on the six o'clock news. My mother cryin on the eleven. I'm in the Grand Jury beggin for time to talk to my lawyer before

I answer the next question. Me, a cop, jerking the system around just like the lowlifes I'm always bustin. And when it's all over, the best that can happen — the *best*, goddamn it! — is that I get a rubber gun and ride a desk. No more street cop. No more me.

I seen it happen before. Guy named Garrigan, in the Five-Four. Dropped a kid in a shootout in an abandoned building. Got to where he spent more time in hearing rooms than he did on the job. Worst part was even guys that knew him, guys that shoulda stood by him, walked the other way when he came by. Like he had AIDS or something. Like he wasn't in the family no more.

There has to be a gun. Freakin kid coulda threw it. I reach deeper into the garbage. A whole potful of burned rice. A bloody tampon. A rotten banana. The pizza I had at Sal's rises in my throat. I swallow it back and sit on my heels. I look down at myself and realize I've been wiping my hand on my pants leg for I don't know how long. Little pieces of rotten banana cling to the blue serge.

No gun. No freakin gun. I shot an unarmed kid. I might as well put the gun in my mouth and pull the trigger.

I'm rockin back and forth in the garbage, thinkin about how bad it's gonna be and pretty soon the blood's pounding in my head and it hurts like hell, only behind the pounding I'm starting to hear words. Slap slap, jack him up. Slap slap, jack him up. Slap slap, *jack* him up. Slap slap *jack him up, jack him up, jack him up.*

My first week in cop school. Too freakin green to even be a rookie. Guy giving the lecture asks what wouldja do if a loudmouth drunk come along and started cursing you out, calling you names. He's not breaking the law or anything, just acting like an asshole. What would you do, Cadet Petrizzo?

Vic thinks about it. In the back of the room, Holmesey, whose brother's in the Four-Six, starts the whisper. He slaps his hand into his palm like he's got a blackjack and he says, real soft, jack him up. Pretty soon there's three or four guys doing it. Slap slap, jack him up. Slap slap, jack him up. Slap slap, *jack* him up, *jack him up.* By the end, everybody's doin it.

Jack him up, jack him up, jack him up. Even the lieutenant teaching the class grins as he gives us the standard bullshit about jacks being illegal and drunks having rights like everyone else. His grin says, I gotta say it but nobody says you gotta listen.

The only guy not slapping his palm and sayin *jack him up* is me. When Holmesey asks me about it after class, I shrug and say I'm not that kind of a cop. He laughs but not like he means it and says that's fine in the classroom, shithead, but whatcha gonna do on the street? *You're a cop not a freakin social worker.* When he walks away, he shakes his head in disgust.

On the street, it's the same. My partner's this old hairbag with more time on the job than God. His first advice to me: check out the places where it's okay to eat on the arm. His second: get a flake piece.

I'm not that kind of a cop, is what I said. He said, oh yes you are. You're either that kind of a cop or you ain't a cop at all and you goddamn well better decide which it's gonna be, kid, cause nobody's gonna want you for a partner if you ain't a standup guy.

What's bein a standup guy got to do with carryin an extra gun around just so you can plant it on some dude and say he tried to shoot you, I ask.

The Hairbag shook his head like Holmesey and said I'd learn sooner or later and he personally was hoping it wouldn't be on his tour of duty.

I'm not that kind of a cop, I said as he walked away. I didn't say it real loud, but I said it. And I meant it.

The thing is, I've got the piece.

I didn't mean to keep it. I took it off a smartmouth kid who found it in the subway. I saw that story on *60 Minutes* about the five-year-old who shot his sister, so I decided I couldn't let that kid keep the gun no matter what. I was gonna take it to Property but I worked overtime Tuesday and then Thursday was the funeral for the sergeant from the Seven-Six who never got outta the coma, God rest his soul, so I hadda get my dress uniform from the cleaners and I never did get the freakin piece to Property like I said I would so it's in my back pocket and nobody knows I've got it. Not even the Hairbag, since I was off duty at the time. The kid won't say anything, and the punk who dropped it in the subway won't be showing up to put in his claim neither.

It's a perfect flake piece. Put it in the hand of the kid with the big red hole and I'm golden. Well, maybe not golden. There'll still be a helluva stink, lots of questions, but at least I'll have a chance of somebody believing me when I say I had to shoot to save my life. Just wipe my prints off and put the gun in the kid's hand.

I'm not that kind of a cop.

Slap slap, jack him up.

Slap slap, *jack* him up.

Slap slap, *jack him up, jack him up, jack him up,* JACK HIM UP, JACK HIM UP, JACK HIM UP.

Voices are so freakin loud. Pounding in my head. Head hurts so bad. I'm not that kind of a cop *just shut up* the voices are getting louder *shut up you bastards* I'm not that kind of a cop. I'M NOT THAT KIND OF A COP.

It's quiet now. I look up like I'm seeing everything for the first time. The garbage, the ghost-light from the streetlamp behind me, the dirty brick wall behind the kid. Wind whips through me, hitting the cold spots. My underarms, my crotch. I shiver, then stand up. I holster my gun, then watch my hand go toward my pocket, pulling out the other one. I go over to the kid with the big red hole. I wipe it off with my handkerchief and bend over.

I look down at the kid with the big red hole and the black gun in his hand. I don't have any memory of putting the gun there, but there it is. Just as if he'd really pulled it on me. The sound of cop shoes running is heard in the distance.

The Hairbag puffs his way along the street. He runs like an old lady tryin to catch a bus, little shuffling steps and no wind.

"What . . . happened?" he asks between gasps, bending over like he's just broken the marathon record.

I can't believe how steady my voice is. "I followed the perp into the alley. He pulled a piece on me. I hadda shoot. I think he's dead."

The Hairbag stumbles toward the body. His breath is still coming in ragged gulps. He looks down at the kid, then turns back to me. There's a funny look on his face. A cold trickle runs down my back. Something's wrong.

"Not . . . the perp," the Hairbag says, panting between words. "Russo and . . . Johnson picked . . . him up at the . . . corner."

I look into the mud-gray eyes of the partner I've despised for eight months, the partner I would have given anything not to be like. *I'm not that kind of a cop*, I said to myself a hundred times listening to his stories of the old days, the good days, the freewheeling days before Serpico and the Knapp Commission and college degrees. Those eyes are like a mirror now, a tarnished mirror with the silver all but washed away by time.

I *am* that kind of a cop.

This story came out of the same cop-oriented period of my life and resulted directly from my attendance at the Crime Scene Unit's lecture to new detectives. The gory pictures of dead and mutilated bodies, the wisecracks meant to deflect unwanted emotion, the wry wit and unflinching realism of these cops caught my attention and shaped the story.

CRIME SCENE

Police Officer Toni Ramirez stood in the doorway of the East Side apartment, one regulation brogue resting lightly on top of the other. Her stance was exactly the same as that of the barefoot child who had stood in the doorway of her uncle Rafael's butcher shop in San Juan fifteen years earlier. Now, as then, she prayed not to be noticed, for to be noticed was to be shooed away. Now, as then, there was the rich smell of blood.

There were four cops in the room: Monelli on prints, Olivera on pix, Jacobs bagging evidence, and Gruschen drawing the floor plan. They each worked alone, yet the combined effect of busily moving hands and task-directed bodies was pure ritual. A High Mass, perhaps, or a bullfight.

The squat detective with the polyester hairpiece sprinkled fingerprint powder on the dark polished surface of the coffee table. "You shoulda seen it, Manny," he said, as though continuing rather than starting a conversation. "Broad was hacked up like gefilte fish."

"Like this one, you mean?" Detective Olivera gestured toward the body, sprawled like a broken doll on the parquet floor. He held a camera in his hand, ready to photograph the corpse.

"Nah," Monelli replied. "Worse'n this, *amigo*. This here's just a little slice and dice. Somebody got one a them Vegematics for Christmas and hadda try it out." He opened his vinyl bag and took out the kind of big soft brush women use to put on blusher. Plying it with the delicacy of a makeup artist, he smoothed away the powder around each fingerprint. "The one I'm talkin' about needed a duplex coffin."

Toni bit her lips as a nervous giggle rose from her stomach. This was her first homicide, and so far she'd taken it like a cop. No tears, no hysterics, no tossed cookies. She'd hustled the shocked neighbors away, called the detectives, and secured the crime scene until their arrival.

She had always been curious. Her dark eyes opened wide and her mind overflowed with questions whenever something unusual crossed her path. In the new world of Nueva York, where her family moved when she was eight, her saving grace had been her willingness to learn new ways, new words. Her curiosity led her at last to the Police Academy, where she graduated with honors.

Now she was learning the street. The body was just another lesson. And thanks to the crime scene detectives, she was seeing first-hand the way real cops reacted to violent death — with humor that etched like acid, turning thin skin to thick scar tissue.

"Remember that stiff in the Four-four?" Manny Olivera directed his remarks at the fingerprint man, but Toni's female instinct told her that at the same time he was showing off for her. Of the four cops in the room, only he seemed to see her in the doorway. Only he exchanged glances with her, spoke as though she could hear. Now he looked at her with a distinct gleam in his eye, the look that told her he'd want her phone number before the day was over.

She smiled back. She liked his lean, swarthy face, his swaggery walk, his cynical smile. It would be fun to sit in a cop bar with a crime scene detective and listen to war stories.

"Which one?" Monelli moved from the table to the doorknob of the French doors in search of more prints. In the china closet, the gold rims of the dinner plates gleamed in the sunlight, while crystal goblets glittered like diamonds.

"You know, where the guy was out up in quarters, like a steer or something. We only found one of the two lower halves, remember?"

"Yeah," Monelli replied, grunting as he knelt on one knee. He placed cellophane tape over the knob where he'd already dusted and brushed, lifting the prints with the precision of an eye doctor handling a contact lens. "Just another half-assed case, right, Manny?"

Toni's laugh exploded with a little snort. The jokes were terrible, but they helped in a way she couldn't explain. Helped to calm the jumping nerves and sweaty palms, the prickly feeling under her skin. Helped her look at the rusty-black pools of dried blood caking the pink terrycloth robe.

"At least McCarthy ain't here," Monelli said. There was a sly smile on his face that told Toni he was baiting Olivera.

"Thank God for small favors," Olivera replied. He left the body, walking over to the pool of blood where the cleaver lay, obscene in its crusted blackness.

"I mean," Monelli went on, "most people if they're gonna cry, they save it for weddings. They don't cry at crime scenes."

"Sentimental Irish bastard." Olivera snapped pictures as he talked, moving around the cleaver like a fashion photographer taking closeups of Christie Brinkley. Unlike a model, the cleaver didn't tease the camera. It just lay flatly on the gleaming parquet floor, amid splatters of blood.

"McCarthy's still the best, Manny," Detective Arlene Jacobs murmured absently, as though she'd made the assertion many times before. She circled behind the body, walking toward the coffee table. "You shoot these?" she asked Olivera, waving a beautifully manicured hand at the teacup and saucer resting on the edge of the table. "I want to bag them."

Toni fixed her eyes on the coffee table, noting the way the patina gleamed in the sunlight. She focused on Detective Jacobs' long, violet nails, on the delicate thinness of the bone china cup and saucer. Anything to keep from seeing the bloody cleaver, the broken body at the other end of the room.

"Yeah, I got 'em, Arl," Olivera called over his shoulder. He knelt on one knee, leaning closer to the blood spatters around the cleaver. Toni's jaw clenched; she turned away.

Detective Jacobs took out a handkerchief, lifted the cup gingerly and placed it into a plastic evidence bag. She jotted her initials on the bag, just as Toni had learned to do at the Academy, then turned her attention to the saucer.

Toni was so engrossed in the synchronized activity of the crime scene unit that she jumped when she realized there was someone behind her. She raised herself to her full five feet three and prepared herself for a dressing-down. She should have been back on patrol half an hour ago. Her job at the crime scene was over the minute the detectives arrived.

"At ease, Officer," a soft voice said. Toni edged her gaze to the left, noting a gray-blue tie with what appeared to be yellow spermatozoa imprinted on it. Raising her eyes, she saw a wrinkled white shirtfront, a shiny gray suitcoat, a thick neck, and a face that could only belong to a cop. Toni remembered McCarthy from his lectures at the Academy, where he'd showed slides the police cadets labeled "New York's Goriest."

She interpreted his nod as an invitation to stay. He walked past her into the apartment, ignoring the technicians, stopping inches from the blood spatters on the shiny floor. He bent his head, in an attitude almost of prayer.

McCarthy was a shabby mountain of a man, at least six feet tall, with a shambling walk and cracked black shoes. Fifty-odd years of living, of eating and drinking and looking at corpses were stamped on his ruddy face. Like a run-down boardinghouse in a decaying neighborhood, his sagging body looked as though it had outgrown his spirit some years before.

There was the distinct sound of sniffling. "Oh, Christ," Olivera said under his breath.

McCarthy reached his hand up and put his fingers to the bridge of his nose. If Toni hadn't heard the detectives' conversation, she never would have realized he was crying. The gesture would have passed for a tired man rubbing his eyes.

Detective Arlene Jacobs stepped over to where Olivera knelt.

She stooped down and with deft fingers lifted the bloody meat cleaver off the floor, swiftly placing it into a plastic bag. She sealed the bag and wrote her initials on it for identification.

"Officer — ah, is it Rodriguez?" a diffident voice asked.

Toni started, then answered quickly, "Ramirez, sir." The face she turned toward McCarthy was the carefully controlled mask she'd learned at the Academy to present to superior officers.

"You found the poor girl, didn't you?"

"Yes, sir. I was on patrol when I was approached by the super of the building. He said the tenant in 5C hadn't picked up her mail and he was worried. He opened the door with a key, and I — I" she broke off, swallowing hard.

Memory hit in pictures, quick, vivid images that churned her stomach and burned her eyes. The cheerful, heart-shaped welcome mat in front of 5C's door, the homemade wreath of straw twined with cornflowers and a lace-trimmed blue ribbon. The sun pouring in through sheer peach curtains, making golden squares on the parquet floor, where death lay waiting.

McCarthy's voice, softly insistent, seemed to come from far away. "Tell me, what did you feel when you saw her lying there?" He pointed to the contorted figure in the pink terry robe. Obscene splashes of red blotched the front, which opened to reveal a naked, mutilated young woman.

"Feel, sir?" Toni asked, her lips stiff. Feeling was not something for which you gained points in the Department. Was McCarthy trying to trick her, to show her up as a rookie?

"I — I tried not to feel anything, sir," she faltered. "I knew I had to contact my C.O. and the Crime Scene Unit, so I went to my radio and did that. And then I waited."

McCarthy nodded, sighing heavily. "You followed the Patrol Guide perfectly, Officer Ramirez," he said. "And it's true the Patrol Guide doesn't say anything about feelings. Or about tears," he added in a near-whisper. The pink in his cheeks could have come from embarrassment or whiskey.

"How old are you?" he asked softly. "Not more than twenty-one, I'd guess. And how old do you think that poor child was?" When Toni didn't answer, he went on: "Her driver's license puts her at twenty-three. She's had two more years of life than you, Officer. Two more years of sunshine and chocolate-covered peanuts at the movies and lilacs in the spring and waking up between clean sheets in the morning. And now it's over. It's over forever and it ended in agony. And so I ask you again, what did you feel when you saw her lying there in her own blood?"

Blood. Uncle Rafael's shop, with its dead Easter lambs. Lambs like the white woolly ones in her picture book, frolicking in green fields. Only these lambs hung from the hooks in the *carneceria,* their wool matted with rusty blood. She had cried for the dead lambs, their frolicking life drained out of them.

The sob burst from her like a pressure cooker overflowing. Before she knew it, a strong arm enveloped her and guided her out of the apartment. She crossed the heart-shaped mat and leaned her forehead against the cool hallway wall. As she wept, McCarthy's meaty hand worked her shoulder; a handkerchief the size of the flag of Puerto Rico found its way into her hand.

"Let me tell you a story," the old cop began. "I was about your age. As new and green a rookie as ever stumbled over his regulation clodhoppers. I came upon my first dead body. A baby it was, about nine months old."

Toni blew her nose, then looked at McCarthy. The blue eyes seemed to turn as cold and gray as a steel gun. "It was covered with blood," he said. "And there were welts and old yellowed bruises and half the tiny head was dented in from the force of a blow. And I stood there, all nineteeen years of me, and I cried. I tried not to let the others see, brushing the tears away so they wouldn't notice what a pansy-ass I was, but the tears wouldn't stop, no matter what I did."

McCarthy drew in a huge breath. Even now, his red-rimmed eys threatened to overflow. "And as I cried, the pictures started coming. I saw a hand reaching out toward that soft smooth skin, ready to strike. I noticed the reek of whisky and felt the terror that baby felt whenever that smell filled the house. I was wiping my nose on my sleeve when up comes my sergeant and bellows, 'What are you, bawlin'? McCarthy, we need *cops* here, not mollycoddles. We know who did it,' he goes on, 'all we have to do is find the kid's father and we can close this one out.' "

"I turned as red as a brick wall," McCarthy went on, a sheepish smile on his face. "As soon as the tears stopped, so did the pictures. The baby was just a piece of meat, like a leg of lamb. Just a job.

"Then one of the detectives called me over. Roth his name was. A real tough guy with a mug like a baseball mitt. Wore a fedora, like they all did in those days. Looked like he'd been born in the goddamn thing. I figured I was in for another lecture, so I went all stiff — just like you are now, Ramirez." McCarthy gave a throaty chuckle that ended in a cough. Toni relaxed her mouth into a wan smile.

" 'You know, kid,' Roth said to me, 'I never see a stiff without crying inside. It don't show, but I cry just the same. And you know something, kid,' he said, 'there ain't a homicide dick worth jack who don't do the same. You don't cry for the victim, you don't care enough to nail the bastard who killed him. So don't listen to your sergeant, kid. You go ahead and cry and maybe someday we'll see you in Homicide.' "

Toni stood motionless, spellbound by the quiet, insistent voice and the mesmerizing blue eyes. She was close enough to see silver stubble on the old man's pink cheeks, and to smell the reek of tobacco that clung to him like perfume.

"Then Roth said to me, 'What happened here, kid?' I closed my eyes and saw pictures again. I felt the tears starting, but I didn't care anymore. I remembered the washed bottles in the dishrack and the vaporizer under the crib. I remembered the fresh diaper. I blurted it right out: 'Somebody loved him, and somebody else killed him.' "

" 'Good,' Roth says. Like he already knows, and he's glad I know too. 'Go on.'

"I close my eyes again. Something about the diaper strikes me. It's clean and it's pinned nice, but it's all bunched up. It would take a strong hand to force pins through the knot of fabric. Then I think back to the ashtray next to the glass of whiskey. Half-smoked cigarettes with red lipstick stains on the filters.

" 'Holy shit!' " I burst out. It's almost like a sob, maybe because I just buried my own mother in Greenwood Cemetery. " 'It wasn't the father. It was the mother,' I tell Roth. 'The drunken bitch mother killed her own baby.' "

McCarthy shook his head slowly. He sighed. "I was right," he said. "It was the mother. We found her body in the airshaft. When she got sober and saw what she'd done, she took a dive. And that's why when I get to a crime scene, I let my experts roam all over, taking pictures and prints and picking up souvenirs, while I just look at the body and let myself feel everything I can. I refuse to wear the shell of cynicism the Department issues its officers along with the dress blues. Does this make sense to you?"

Toni nodded.

"My people in there," McCarthy went on, "are good cops. They do one hell of a job. But they don't use all the equipment they were born with. They use hands and eyes and brains, and most of the time that's good enough. But once in a while it helps to use the heart."

McCarthy put his arm around the rookie's shoulders. "Would you care to look at the body again?" he asked gently.

As if in trance, Toni walked through the doors of apartment 5C. She was hyperconscious, aware of the smells of Jacobs' perfume and Gruschen's cigar underneath the smells of blood and excrement from the body. She willed herself to ignore irrelevancies, walking straight to the corpse on the polished floor. She stared a long time at the honey-colored hair with the dark roots just starting to show, at the coral-painted toenails, at the thin gold ankle bracelet. This time she didn't turn away from the blood-soaked pink terry-cloth robe.

As she looked down at the dead woman, Toni felt herself becoming the girl in the pink robe. She was wiping her makeup off, getting ready for bed. Under her bare feet, the wooden floor was cold, yet she hated slippers. She moved toward the kitchen, to make her nightly cup of herbal tea.

Teacup in hand, she walked toward the comfortable green-and-peach chair in the living room and set the tea on the coffee table. She turned on the television, taking a videotape from the library of tapes in the woodgrain rack. Settling herself in the flowered chair, she tucked her legs underneath her and pulled her robe a little tighter.

A wave of loneliness hit Toni. How many nights had the dead girl sat in her cozy chair, wearing her fuzzy pink robe? How many nights had she spent alone, with only the TV for company? Toni's eyes traveled toward the large color TV on its wheeled stand. A tape lay on top of the VCR. It appeared to have been played halfway through.

Things nagged at Toni. A tiny silver object on top of the TV console. She looked more closely — a loose nut. On the lower shelf beside the VCR sat a tiny jeweler's screwdriver.

She closed her eyes and became again the girl. She was watching her video, tea cooling in the thin cup. The picture on the screen stopped. She reached for the remote control box, then hunted for the instruction book. Finally, she went to the phone.

Toni took a ragged breath, bringing herself back to the reality of now, of the girl dead on the floor. She looked at the VCR. Its digital clock read "12:00," yet Toni knew it had to be at least 3:30. She stared at the green numbers, her ears hearing sounds that came from the past.

A knock at the blue-wreathed door. The padding sounds of the girl's bare feet as she crossed the parquet floor. The scraping of locks as she undid her elaborate security system to let in her always-helpful super. Laughter and joking, an offer of tea. Warmth and gratitude in the girl's voice, turning to fear and terror as she realized the kind of payment he expected.

"Oh, God," Toni murmured, closing her eyes. She felt faint. "Don't. Please don't." A shudder ran through her, shaking her slight body with a violence she didn't expect. "I just wanted the VCR fixed," she whispered.

Toni closed her mind, shutting out the rest. She felt McCarthy's warm, steady hand on her shoulder, heard him say, "Tell Homicide to check out the super."

She opened her eyes, and looked down at the slight, still figure on the floor. "We'll get him, *chica*," she promised softly.

This is the first story in which I deliberately attempted humor. As a recovering cat lady, I was amused at the idea of a cop with ten cats, and I liked the idea that this cop's rookie partner might misunderstand the older cop's negotiations with neighborhood businesses. In a way, this story is the comic version of "Undercover," which is included later in this collection.

ON THE TAKE

Ten — count 'em — ten. He'd never meant to have ten.

Who the hell did?

But there they were, all ten of them, meowing and swirling around him, rubbing up against his legs, getting their fur all over his blue uniform pants, and you know what, it was kinda nice having living creatures glad to see him when he opened the door. Happy that he was home instead of bitching that he was late again and what did he mean stopping off at Hanratty's for a coupla beers with the guys, and was he sure that bimbo Shawna Taylor hadn't come on to him again?

Ten cats beat the hell out of one wife. Especially a wife who'd started out as a cop groupie herself, so she knew from personal experience how the girls at Hanratty's went after the married guys.

But ten. You could live down one or two, maybe. Three — not so easy, but you could pass off three as halfway normal. Ten was way the hell out of range. Dooley down at the station house — oh, he could hear Dooley now. "Ten freakin' cats in a freakin' studio apartment, what the hell's that all about? That the only pussy you're gettin' these days, Perkie?"

You couldn't even say Don't call me Perkie. Ten cats, you couldn't say nothin'.

Fernandez would start in, too. Where Dooley led, Fernando followed. Evil twins, separated at birth, even if Dooley was a big black linebacker and Fernando a little Puerto Rican with more mouth than muscle.

He sighed at the injustice of it all, then reached down and patted the head of the animal nearest his leg. He'd named them all, but it took a minute to recall that the orange one with the amber eyes was Linda. He'd named them after old girlfriends, and the sad thing was that he had maybe two names left. Three more cats and he'd have more of them in his apartment right now than he'd ever had women in his whole life.

Linda arched her back and leaned into his hand, purring loudly. She swished her tail flirtatiously and turned around, coming back toward him for more.

If only the human Linda had behaved the same way instead of brushing off his roving hands, pushing him away when all he wanted was a little loving.

The cats never pushed him away. They loved the feel of his strong hands on their silky fur.

He had to get rid of them. Well, six of them, anyway. Four wouldn't be completely out of line. He could maybe keep four and survive the station house.

But where could they go? It wasn't like there were a lot of farms around here, ready to take in a couple more barn cats. There were farms upstate, but upstate was a big green world of Unknown as far as he was concerned. Born and bred in Brooklyn, he'd just about barely been ten miles from Greenpoint, and he didn't know any farmers.

His mother? Would she take in a cat or two? Old ladies liked cats, didn't they?

Ha. In books, maybe. But Anthea Rose McKechnie Perkins wasn't an old lady in a book, she was a beer-drinking, bingo-playing baseball fanatic who'd screw up her face and say, "You bring them dirty moggies over 'ere, I'll give you such a clip on the ear'ole." Fifty years Anthea Rose had been out of Liverpool, but her tongue remembered the old country all too well. And so did the hand that had clipped him on the earhole so many times he still had a ringing on the left side of his head.

So Mum was out. Where else could he take his pets, the ones he couldn't keep?

Not the shelter. He looked into the sad green eyes of Betsy, the first one he'd brought home, and thought of them putting her into a little cage and then a little oven and suffocating the life out of her sinuous little black body, and it made him feel as if he was the one about to die from lack of oxygen.

No, not Betsy. No matter what, Betsy had to stay.

But the others had to go.

If only he knew where.

"Hey, kid," Dooley called out as the rookie entered the station house, two cardboard containers of coffee in his hands, "You bringin' Perkie coffee now? You gonna clean up his desk for him, too? Make him breakfast like a good little wife?"

The kid was very young and very fair, which was why Dooley loved riding him. His blush started at the nape of his neck and climbed, inch by visible inch, up to his forehead. Even his scalp under short blond hair glowed red when he was embarassed — which was pretty much most of the time.

Fernandez made a salacious remark about other things good wives did for their husbands, and the kid's blush deepened to a near-purple.

"You seen my partner?" The kid turned to Olivetti, the oldest guy in the squad, and the only one besides Perkins who treated him with a modicum of respect.

"In the can," Olivetti said, shifting his cigar from one side of his mouth to the other.

The kid set the coffees down and opened one up. It was so light it looked like hot milk; he opened four sugar packets at once and emptied them, then stirred the sweet mess with a red plastic stick.

"Hey, thanks, Randy." Perkins stepped to the desk, picked up his coffee, popped a little hole in the plastic top, then drank it straight. The kid wondered whether maybe you started out drinking it milky and sweet and as you got older, more experienced, you gradually cut down the sugar and milk and you finally drank the black, oily-looking mess that looked as if it belonged in your car instead of your stomach.

He wondered if he'd ever grow the hell up.

Their first stop was a bodega on Seventh Avenue. Nice little place, open practically all night, and Perkins knew they had a little book going in the back room, which was why he and Randy were there. Every four months or so you had to write up a place like that. You'd never shut it down, and maybe you didn't really want to, truth be told, but you had to write them up, give them a fine to pay.

The idea hit him as soon as he crossed the threshold. Stores had cats in them all the time. Well-fed, friendly cats who sidled up to the customers or sat on bags of rice, sunning themselves in the windows.

Just what Linda and Heather and Tiffi needed: good jobs in the neighborhood. They'd be well cared for, and the best thing was, he could still see them when he wanted to, still reach his hand down to their level and feel the soft welcome of their furry bodies against his rough skin.

But how to get the idea across without the kid hearing? He liked Randy, even if he was the wettest-behind-the-ears rookie he'd ever seen, but you had to admit, the kid's baby face gave away everything. If he found out about the cats, it would take a Manhattan minute for Dooley and Fernandez to catch on, and from that moment on, his life would be a living hell.

So he put his hand on the store owner's arm and gently eased him into the back room, saying he had to talk to him alone. He asked Randy to stay outside and wait for bettors to come in with their betting slips.

Hector Rosario didn't like the idea. "No *gatos*" about summed it up. "I don't like no *gatos* in here. This is a clean place."

"Yeah, but it could be cleaner if you didn't have mice. Cats can help with that," Perkins said in his most persuasive tone.

"I don't got no mice," the bodega owner protested, his mustache quivering with indignation. "I don't got no mice, and I don't got no cats. No *animalitos* nohow."

"Yeah, but you could have cats. I mean, one or two cats in here, make the place homey. Make the customers feel at —"

"Two? Whaddaya mean two?"

"One it is," Perkins cut in before the man could change his mind. "I can have her here by eight tonight."

The little man's eyes narrowed shrewdly. "And what do I get in return for taking this cat off your hands?"

Perkins sighed. He'd known this was coming, although why he had a hard time fathoming. Surely giving a home to his beloved Linda ought to be reward enough in itself. But it was a hard world, and you had to give in order to get.

"Well, you're lucky this time, Mr. Rosario. I don't see any evidence of gambling this time around. But I'll be back in another four months, and I'd better not find any betting slips in your till."

Rosario smiled, his gold tooth flashing, as he hefted a huge bag of kitty litter from the shelf.

The kid couldn't believe it. Oh, he'd learned all about it at the Police Academy; he wasn't stupid. He knew there were cops on the take in the old days, but he'd thought those days were long past.

But here was his partner, his own partner, a guy who hardly even cursed on the job, he was so squeaky-clean, taking a bribe to look the other way.

That bodega was dirty. Randy knew it and Perkins knew it, and yet they'd walked out of there without writing the guy up. No search of the cash register for betting slips, no arrest, and Perkins taking the guy off into the back room for a private chat.

It added up to just one thing: corruption.

And he, Randy Piasecki, was in it up to the bright-red tips of his ears.

The same scenario, more or less, played itself out four more times. Two of the store owners actually seemed to like the idea of acquiring feline employees, which made Perkins feel good, but at least the others said yes in the long run.

"For you, Officer Perkins, I could maybe take in a cat," Leventhal the butcher said. "A tiny little *katz*, not a big fat *mamzer* eats so much it never wants to catch the mice."

Greek Tony the shoemaker growled a little about the price of milk, but when the fire code violation in back of the store was mentioned, he gave a gruff assent to letting Andrea move in with him. The pizza guys agreed to take two, which really made his day, and made him glad he'd thought of pretending he'd seen a mouse run from their rest room to the storeroom in the rear of the pizzeria. Heather and Jeri would feast on mozzarella and anchovies, and he could stop by and pet them when he picked up his pie every Thursday, which he did like clockwork.

The one place he didn't ask was the Chinese restaurant.

But all in all, it had been a good day. Five cats placed. One to go. And the kid none the wiser, which meant he'd kept his secret from Dooley and Fernando.

When a good cop goes bad, he goes real bad. That was the wisdom Randy had been taught at the Academy. It might start with a free cup of coffee, but corruption was a slippery slope, and pretty soon you had cops with summer houses in the mountains and fancy cars and boats, even.

They'd stopped at a lot of little businesses, and in each and every one, Perkins had taken the owner for a private consultation where Randy couldn't hear, and they'd left each and every store without writing up any tickets even though violations were jumping right out at them from every corner, and after they'd left Perkie had a smile as big as the Bronx on his homely but pleasant face.

It was exciting in a horrible sort of way.

Horrible because Perkie was a good guy and a good partner and you didn't rat out your partner no matter what he did, and besides, Perkie never made him blush. At least not on purpose.

Exciting because he felt like Serpico. The fate of the entire NYPD rested on him, an untried rookie. He could go along with the corruption, ask for a cut of the take, and become a grizzed old veteran with cynicism oozing from every pore.

Or he could be a hero. Blow the whistle. Turn his partner in and let the world know that he wasn't cut from the same dirty cloth.

He didn't yet know which road he would take, but the very fact of knowing there was a road and that his next steps would determine not only his personal future but affect a lot of other people thrilled him to the core.

Dooley and Fernandez wouldn't mess with him if he was Serpico. They'd scorn him as a man who turned on his partner, but they'd be scared of him at the same time. Scared of what he might find out about them.

If only it was Dooley instead of Perkie who was on the take. It would be easy then; he could ruin Dooley's miserable life without a second's hesitation.

But Perkie was different. He liked Perkie. He didn't want Perkie to be a dirty cop.

But he was. Randy had seen it with his own eyes.

Five cats and one cat carrier.

First you had to chase the cat you wanted, and of course all the others ran too, hiding under the bed or jumping onto the kitchen counter. Annie made it onto the top of the refrigerator even though he'd decided to keep her.

Finally he had the right cat inside the little suitcase with holes in the side. The captive howled in protest, sounding like a cross between a banshee and a little kid whining "Mommy, I don't want to go to camp." He'd march down the steps anyway, determined to follow up on his day's work by delivering his darlings to their new homes.

They were scared at first. All of them. Piteous meows and hiding in corners and Perkins felt like an executioner turning around and going back home for another one. But they'd get used to their new surroundings, and he'd made it very clear that the cats had better be looking healthy and happy the next time he stopped in for a visit.

Finally it was done. Five gone, five left at home. He was going to a West Indian roti stand tomorrow; that would be perfect for Tiffi, who had a taste for spicy food.

He'd been up all night. Tossing and turning in the bed, then padding to the fridge to finish that carton of Ben and Jerry's, then explaining to Ma why he wasn't sleeping so good and finally convincing her it wasn't because he'd seen a particularly grotesque murder the day before. Try as he might, Randy could never quite convince Ma that after a whole three months on the job, he wasn't Columbo and hadn't yet stumbled across his first dead body.

He didn't tell her about Perkie. He couldn't. He'd already convinced her that Officer Perkins practically walked on water, and he couldn't shatter her illusions. It was, after all, a man's job to shelter his women from the harsher side of life, so he sighed and carried the increasingly heavy burden of his suspicion all by himself.

What should he do?

The options were clear in his mind. There was no ambiguity. He just didn't want to do any one of them. He didn't want to go upstairs and talk to the sergeant, who would call internal affairs and wire him for sound so he could bring down his best friend on the force and resign himself to nineteen years and nine months of isolation from his fellow cops, none of whom would ever talk to a snitch ever again. All he'd ever wanted to be was a cop, and ratting on his partner would kill that dream dead.

But if he went along with it, if he closed a blind eye — what then? Someday, sometime, someone else would start to suspect. It might start small, but after a while, after Perkie started driving a new car and talking about vacations in the mountains and when he finally announced that he had a boat — well, everyone knew what that meant. You had a boat, you were going down. No two ways about it.

And since he, Randy Piasecki, was Perkie's partner, he'd go down too, even if he never so much as spent a minute on that boat.

It wasn't fair.

How could Perkie do a thing like that to him?

So, okay, with a heavy heart and all that, he'd go to the sarge and tell what he'd seen. And the sarge would pick up the phone and —

Or would he? What, after all, had Randy seen? Trips to back rooms, that's all. No money changing hands, no deals being made. Just private conversations and no tickets written.

It wasn't enough.

But it was suspicious.

The answer hit him as he buttoned his blue uniform pants. He had his own little tiny tape recorder, a present from his uncle Julius last Christmas. Why Jule thought a cop needed a pocket tape recorder was anyone's guess, but it turned out he was right, because that was just what Randy needed today. He'd wire himself, get the evidence on tape, and then decide what to do with his information.

If he had it on tape, the sarge would have to listen. And if, by some miracle, he was wrong about Perkie, he could destroy the tape and go back to business as usual.

He sighed with relief as he slipped the recorder into the inside pocket of his blue uniform jacket.

One more to go. One more cat placed and he could relax. Four was okay. A little over the line, maybe, but he'd promised Annie the night before and he couldn't disappoint her. She was a feisty little thing with emerald eyes and a snarling hiss that scared felines twice her size into backing down.

He smiled as he remembered her staring down at him from the top of the refrigerator.

One more. Tiffi, short for Tiffani, and although he liked the cat well enough, the real-life Tiffi had skipped out of the Valentine's dance at PS 211 with Ricky Mogelescu, leaving him to wander disconsolately through the crowd like a total loser. So Tiffi was the one he had to place today; the Jamaican roti guys were pretty laid-back and he didn't foresee any problems.

Until he parked his car on Nineteenth Street, behind a white van. He put his cop placard in the window and locked up, then walked along the street toward the bodega on the corner, prepared to stop in and see how Linda was doing in her new home.

But out of the alleyway between the brownstone and the brick apartment house, there came a little mewing sound. A tiny, tiny sound that cracked his heart wide open, because he knew at once what it was and that it was up to him to do something about it.

The kittens were about a week old. Four of them. Cute as bugs, splattered with orange and gray and white as if a painter had shaken his brushes at them. One had a little smudge on her nose and another had a bright orange tail and —

He was in love.

Purely and simply in love.

All the other cats he'd found in the neighborhood had been grown, or nearly grown. They'd been dirty and hungry, so thin you could feel their ribs when you petted them. Scared of people, and for good reason. He'd had to coax them, leave food for days at a time, then bring the cat carrier and make his capture.

But the kittens tumbled toward him without fear, their tiny pink tongues exploring his hand, their needle claws digging into his skin but so delicately that he felt nothing. Their little noses enchanted him, and their huge eyes sucked him right into their world.

He had to have them. And Mama Cat too, if she wanted to come. She was either dead or out hunting breakfast.

"I'll be back," he promised them. "I'll get the carrier and come back for you. Just wait here until I'm off duty."

Four and four make eight. If Mama showed, nine.

He was almost back to square one.

Randy hated the hot roti shop. Not the music, which was a nice bouncy reggae, or the guys with their giant knitted hats. It was the smell, which was bad because it was goat and now he knew it was goat. The smell hadn't, in truth, bothered him before he knew, but now that he knew, he pictured a little goat with little horns on its head, turning on a spit. Which wasn't what you saw because roti was sort of ground up, but still.

Goat.

The place wasn't open yet, so only the cook was there. Perkie motioned him into the back room, telling Randy to stand watch outside.

But Randy didn't. He edged toward the beaded curtain that separated the two rooms and slipped his hand into his pocket, fumbling for the buttons on his recorder. Finally, realizing he couldn't be seen, he took the thing out and turned it on, then held it up so that the microphone faced the doorway.

What he heard chilled him to the bone.

"You've got to help me out here," Perkie said. "I'm a desperate man. I need you to take at least two, maybe three."

Take?

Take what?

Wasn't it supposed to be the other way around? Wasn't the roti man supposed to give something to Perkie? Something like money?

Unless —

Oh, no. Not that. Not drugs. Not Perkins the squeaky-clean using the storefronts to push dope. Making semi-honest businessmen peddle crack or heroin or —

Why else would the roti man take something?

Why else would Perkins be so desperate? Some big drug dealer had Perkie by the shorts and now Perkie had to strongarm the shopowners into pushing the product?

This was big. Big and dirty and disgusting and pretty exciting, too. Because he, Randall James Piasecki, Junior, had it all on tape.

He'd be on the news. HERO COP BUSTS DRUG RING

He was blushing already.

Hero cop.

The beaded curtain swung open and the roti man came back into the front part of the shop. Randy nearly dropped the recorder, and was fumbling with his jacket pocket when his partner stepped in front of him.

"You won't be needing that," Perkie said, and Randy nearly wet himself. Had Perkins seen the recorder? Was this the part where the honest cop got wasted by the drug dealers?

But Perkie added, "We're not writing any tickets here. I didn't find any *ganja* in there. For once." The roti shop was well known in the neighborhood as the best place to score a fat joint.

So unless Perkie was being incredibly cagy, he really thought Randy was trying to get his ticket book out instead of trying to put his tape recorder in.

Outside, on the street, Randy considered his next move. Should he try to get a little more on tape? Get Perkie to admit he was dirty? He slipped his hand into his pocket and pushed the record button.

"Y'know, I kinda heard a little bit of what you were saying back there," he began in a tentative tone.

"Oh, Geez, man, you don't know what a relief that is." Perkins let out a long sigh; some of the tightly-wound tension in his shoulders relaxed. "I mean, at first I didn't want you to know, but now, I need your help, partner. I need it bad."

"Help?" Try as he might to control his voice, it squeaked into the adolescent register Fernandez loved to mimic. "You want me to help you shake down the businesses on our beat?"

"Well, shake down is kinda strong," Perkie objected. "I'm only asking them to do something that will be good for them in the long run."

"Good for them? I mean, like I hear what you're saying, but is money everything? Sure, they'll make money in the short run, but in the long run, they could wind up dead. And so could you. I don't want any part of this."

"Dead? Money?" Perkins stopped dead in the street, earning a glare from a nanny wheeling a stroller. "What are you talking about?"

Oh, no. Perkins knew. He understood that he was being taped, and now he was getting cagy. Randy considered how to say what he had to say without actually using the words. If he said it flat out, Perkie would continue to stonewall, but if he hinted, maybe he could slide an admission out of his partner.

"I mean, people like going into a store and seeing a cat in the window. They like stopping to pet it, hearing it purr." Perkie smiled as he warmed to his subject. "You sit in that pizza place, eating alone, it's nice a cat comes over and rubs your leg, maybe even jumps into your lap. You can feed it some cheese — but not pepperoni. Too spicy."

Randy's face went beet red and he sputtered as he said, "Don't pull this crazy act on me. Don't treat me like a kid. I know what I know and I heard what I heard. You forced that guy back there to take two, and he didn't even want to take any. You're making these guys sell dope for you and I don't want any part of it. Got that?"

"He's taking cats," Perkie said with a bewildered air. "My cats. I — well, the truth is, I got these cats. A lot of cats." He hung his head and now the blush crept into his face, even if he was old enough to drink black coffee and like it.

"I picked them up in the neighborhood," he explained. "They looked so sad, so hungry. I never meant to keep them, just feed them and maybe find them a home, but that's not easy, you know."

"Cats."

"Cats. I had ten yesterday." Perkie's blue eyes pleaded with Randy. "You know what Dooley and Fernando would have to say about ten cats?"

"Oh, yeah. I got that picture clear. Ten?"

"Ten. So I got five placed, and today I was gonna hit up the roti guys and it would all be over, but then I found these kittens in the alley, and now I'm back to nine, only the roti guy said he'd take two, so that makes it eight, but that is definitely four too many, you know what I mean?"

"Kittens."

"I'll show you."

And he did, and when Randy Piasecki saw the four little guys with their big sparkling eyes and cute little button noses and whip tails and baby claws, he was in love too, because any guy who hated to think about a goat turning on a spit was bound to fall for kittens, so it turned out all right in the end. He took two and Perkie took two, and they managed to place three others with the pharmacy and the deli and the bakery.

But not the Chinese restaurant.

The character's first name is Nikki, an homage to Nikki Porter, Ellery Queen's secretary. The cats are my own feline Gang of Four and the story was first conceived as a BePuzzled jigsaw-cum-mystery that never became a puzzle. Since I'm now a defelined cat lady, I turn to this story when I want to remember my beloved, if rambunctious, little cat family

THE BLACK HAWTHORNE

I love cats. And I like to help my friends, so when Mrs. Simpson-Phelps, my next-door neighbor, asked me to cat-sit for her, what could I say but yes? Little did I know that the job would entail the skills of a private detective — which I most decidedly am not, though I do read what my husband refers to as "those stupid mysteries."

I know her cats. Everyone in our Georgetown neighborhood knows her cats. We see the curious Tigger in her backyard, acting like his Winnie-the-Pooh namesake, all stripes and bounces, peeking under the fence, jumping at squirrels. We see Paddington, the Fred Astaire of cats, graceful, slender, impeccably dressed in a sleek black fur tuxedo with a white patch at his throat, walking along the back fence, delicately stepping over each picket. We see Arthur, the Mighty Hunter, stalk through the tall summer grass, on the prowl for a mouse, a bird, anything he can capture and crow over. Once he "caught" a charcoal briquette from my barbecue, and meowed as loudly and as proudly as if it had been the biggest rat in the world.

You have to be a very close neighbor of Mrs. Simpson-Phelps to see her fourth cat. Little Orphan Annie, who's very shy, likes nothing better than to bask in the sun, preferably on a self-made cushion of newspaper or a grocery bag. She views the world through grass-green eyes that see everything and register surprise at nothing.

Mrs. Simpson-Phelps and her feline family welcomed me to the neighborhood when I first moved in three years ago. I was a newlywed, she newly widowed. We started chatting over the back fence, the way neighbors do, and soon I was picking up one or the other of her straying pets and handing him over the fence. She handed me homemade scones, perfectly toasted crumpets dripping real butter, lemon-curd tarts — all the delicacies of her native England.

Mrs. Simpson-Phelps was Violet Simpson of London's East End till she met a handsome GI named Harry Phelps and became a war bride. Now she wanted to go home again. But what to do about the cats? That was where I came in.

". . . just couldn't trust an agency, so impersonal. And my dear niece, Wanda, lives all the way in Fredericksburg, so it won't do to ask her, though I know she'd oblige if she could. She's a doctor, you know, very busy. She suggested I board them with a vet, but I can't bear to think —"

"Of course I'll take care of them, Mrs. Simpson-Phelps," I said warmly. I'd said it once already, but my neighbor's anxiety about leaving her pets seemed to have affected her hearing. After all, I reasoned — already mentally making my case to Bud, my skeptical husband, who would no doubt call me a pushover — how hard could it be? I'd open cat food cans, empty the litter pan, let them sit on my lap and purr for a while, and that would be that. Just because Bud called our neighbor's cats The Wild Bunch didn't mean they were really —

"*No*, Arthur," Mrs. Simpson-Phelps said firmly, as Arthur made a gigantic leap into the air, going after a low-flying blue jay. Arthur plopped down on the brick patio and licked his white paw furiously, as if to show he had no interest whatsoever in creatures of the avian persuasion.

We were in our usual conversational mode: standing on either side of the whitewashed fence that separated our tiny backyards. Around us, forming a square, were the rear entrances of townhouses, their warm Georgian brick lit by early spring sun. My apricot tree was in full creamy bloom; Mrs. Simpson-Phelps's weeping cherry was just budding in pink.

"I'm so pleased, Nikki. Thanks ever so, love. With you looking after them, I know my darlings will be in good hands."

She clasped her own beringed hands to her breast.

Mrs. Simpson-Phelps had one of the few clotheslines left in our rapidly gentrifying neighborhood. She did her own hand washing and often hung lace dresser scarves and linen tea towels out to dry in the sun, proclaiming electric dryers the ruin of good Irish linen. I noticed a clothespin dangling from the line; whatever it had secured had fallen to the ground.

"Look, I think Annie has —" I began, but my neighbor had already noticed; she made a beeline for the white-and-tabby cat. Annie was busily kneading the tea-towel into a cushion, getting it ready for her plump little body.

"Annie, love, please give me that nice clean towel," my neighbor cooed, deftly pulling the now-dirty scrap of linen from under the cat's white feet. Annie meowed indignantly and stalked, tail high, into the house through the open French doors.

"Oh, dear." Mrs. Simpson-Phelps looked at me ruefully. "They *are* rather a handful, aren't they?"

I was beginning to have second thoughts about cat-sitting The Wild Bunch, so I changed the subject. "When was the last time you were in England?" I asked.

"Oh, not for years and years. I believe little Prince Charles was just being christened the last time I was home. Oh, dear, I shall have forgotten everything I ever knew about getting round London, I know I shall."

"But why haven't you gone back?" I asked, my head filling with romantic stories about her family cutting her off with a shilling because she dared to marry an American soldier.

"Because of my kitties, of course. England has the *most* barbaric quarantine laws, and I just couldn't bear to leave my darlings home for so long." Mrs. Simpson-Phelps gazed fondly at Paddington, who glided along the back fence with the graceful balance of a tightrope walker.

"Before I had this lot, there were other cats in my life," she explained. "Let me see — there was Bunny Brown and his sister Sue, Alice in Wonderland — she was a sweet little thing, pure white and deaf as a post. And Mole and Ratty and Mr. Toad — the fattest ginger tom you ever did see. I never could bear to part with them, or to have them quarantined for six whole months. But now," she said, her face clouding, "with my sister Mavis ill, I really must go over. No more excuses."

"Oh," I said. I explained my melodramatic picture of family opposition to her American husband, and she laughed.

"No, it was nothing like that, love." Her chuckle was as rich as Devonshire cream. "My family adored Harry, really they did. The only thing my father wanted was that I keep the family name, which was why I go by Simpson-Phelps. As though my old dad was a duke instead of a pubkeeper. In return, he gave us The Black Hawthorne as a wedding present."

She said the words in capital letters. I had to ask what The Black Hawthorne was, and she responded by inviting me to "come round at once and be educated."

It was my first entry into my neighbor's house. For all our good-natured back-fence chatting, we had never been inside one another's homes. I had to admit I was curious; it's always instructive to see how others choose to live.

When she opened her front door to let me in, Tigger bounced at me and twined himself around my legs, mewing pitifully. "Shush, you awful Tig," my neighbor said, her voice tinged with a mixture of mock annoyance and shameless indulgence. "You'll have Nikki thinking I never feed you, when the fact is you're positively stuffed with tinned mackerel."

The front parlor — Georgetown houses have front and back parlors instead of living rooms — was a little piece of England tucked away in the capitol of the colonies. A Victorian sofa of hideous proportions occupied the place of honor across from the fireplace, and vases of dried weeds with peacock feather accents sat in corners on dark, carved tables with marble tops. The walls were festooned with family photographs in oval frames, along with pallid watercolors.

"There," my hostess said proudly, pointing to the mantel, "that's The Black Hawthorne."

I had no trouble seeing why she spoke so respectfully of her heirloom. It was a Chinese ginger jar, slightly taller than a cat, of a deep rich black with a twisted-tree design on it. Very graceful, very old, very valuable.

"The Black Hawthorne was brought from China by Captain Hosea Simpson in 1869," my hostess explained. "My nephew, Gerry, says it's worth a small fortune, though it is only Ch'ing instead of Ming. Whatever that means," she added with a laugh.

"Such a shame I shall be going to England just when Gerry is visiting over here, but it can't be helped."

The words burst out of me before I could stop myself. "But Mrs. Simpson-Phelps, Violet, you can't just leave a thing like that on an open mantel! What about the cats? Don't you worry that one of them will —"

"Nonsense, Nikki," my neighbor said complacently. "My darlings know how important The Black Hawthorne is to me. They would never knock it down. Would you, pets?" Since only Annie was in the room, sitting this time on a real cushion, the objet d'art, perched on the mantel with the Toby jugs and the seashell-statue that said "Souvenir of Brighton 1943," was probably safe, at least for the moment. Wherever Tigger had disappeared to, his temporary absence gave the precious object a reprieve.

I stayed long enough to drink what Mrs. Simpson-Phelps proudly called "a proper cup of tea" and to eat two of her melt-in-the-mouth scones. Just as I was finishing the last few crumbs, Tigger bounced back into the room, dragging a shopping bag after him. I laughed as he shook his head from side to side, trying to free himself from the handle, which had wrapped itself around his neck.

"Nikki, it isn't a bit funny," my neighbor scolded as she caught Tigger and lifted the twine handle over his head while the cat squirmed and squealed with fright. "He might strangle on one of these carry bags. I should never have them in the house. And before I go, I intend to get rid of every one I have, even the lovely Christmas ones from Lord and Taylor's."

I apologized for laughing and promised once again to take good care of The Wild Bunch. I eyed The Black Hawthorne on my way out of the parlor. One more thing to worry about during the three weeks Mrs. Simpson-Phelps would be away. I wasn't just a cat-sitter any more; I was a ginger jar-sitter as well.

Still, The Black Hawthorne had survived The Wild Bunch and their predecessors for lo these many years; why should three more weeks put it in danger?

I put the ginger jar and my neighbor out of mind for the next week. It was getting closer and closer to April 15, when my office, the dreaded Internal Revenue Service, would be swamped with last-minute tax returns. I worked late every night and so waited till the last minute to shop for a birthday present for my sister in St. Louis. On my lunch hour, I crossed Constitution Avenue to the massive gift shop at the Smithsonian's Museum of American History. That's the home of the real ruby slippers and has more gift ideas than a whole raft of catalogues. Acres and acres of everything from replicas of Egyptian gold earrings to place mats with American advertising logos. Paper dolls of the First Ladies and Japanese playing cards. Rice-paper kites and Civil War soldiers and scarves with stained glass designs and dominoes with pictures of Presidents and make-it-yourself cardboard White Houses — and that's just the first floor.

The ginger jar sat on a glass shelf along with marble bookends in the form of lions. "Reproduction Ch'ing Dynasty ginger jar in unusual black lacquer with hawthorne pattern," the printed label read. "While primarily produced for the export market," it burbled, "these vases are among the rarest of their period. Add a touch of Oriental elegance to *your* home with this reproduction of the real thing."

I bought Susan a silk scarf with purple irises and a silver iris scarf-pin. But I couldn't get the ginger jar out of my mind; its image followed me onto the bus for the ride home to Georgetown. Had Mrs. Simpson-Phelps made up the story about her sea-captain forbear, passing off a museum reproduction as a valuable antique? Did that explain her willingness to leave the ginger jar within easy reach of feline tails, or did she really own the genuine article — and have an extraordinary faith in the kindness of cats?

Either way, the ginger jar would become my responsibility in the morning. Should I leave it in its place of honor on my neighbor's mantel, or should I take it to my own home for safekeeping while she was away? I pondered both sides of the question as the bus made its way into the picturesque narrow streets of Georgetown. I continued thinking about it as I walked along the brick sidewalk toward my town house.

I had no clear answer as I rang the next-door bell the next day. I found Mrs. Simpson-Phelps in a state of pre-travel panic. "Oh dear, where *is* my passport?" she asked, rummaging through a kitchen drawer. "Do you think I've bought enough cat food, love?" She pointed to a mountain of canned gourmet meals for felines.

I never had a chance to say yes. "And on top of everything, Gerry and Wanda — Harry's brother's oldest girl — have been quarreling over The Black Hawthorne. They've each asked me to leave it to them in my will. As if I could think about something as trivial as a will at a time like this!"

She was putting her hat on as we spoke, but that didn't stop her telling me, for the fifth time since asking me to cat-sit, how Annie hated liver but Paddy doted on it and how Arthur was not under any circumstances to be allowed outside.

"I'd worry myself sick thinking he might be lost, you see," she explained. "Which reminds me. At least Wanda has some appreciation of my feelings. She promised to take good care of my darlings if anything ever happened to me. In return for The Black Hawthorne, no doubt. But that's more than Gerry offered. He can't stand cats, made no bones about it when he came to see me. 'Keep them away from me, Aunt Violet,' he begged. 'Especially that black one!' As if my Paddy wasn't the gentlest creature alive," she finished indignantly.

The doorbell rang. I went to open it, since my neighbor was proving her point by cuddling the black cat, murmuring endearments into his oversized ears.

The woman at the door was about my age, tall, with blonde hair cut short and sculpted to her head like a cap. A Valkyrie with a Vidal Sassoon haircut. "I'm Wanda Phelps," she explained, offering me a hand to shake. The other hand held a handsome wine-colored doctor's bag.

"I'm driving Aunt Violet to the airport," she said. Ms. Phelps looked meaningfully at her aunt as she added, "I'll probably pop in on the weekends to see that everything's all right. I see patients at a free clinic on Saturdays and it's on my way. But I couldn't make the trip every day, so I'm really glad you're taking care of her cats."

"Oh, it's no trouble," I said lightly, noting that Tigger was about to make a giant leap from the back of the sofa to the top of the china closet. Arthur stood at the French doors, meowing to be let out into the sunny summer day.

Mrs. Simpson-Phelps put Paddy down and stroked Annie's white fur. "Oh, I must go, mustn't I?" she asked Wanda in a plaintive tone.

Turning to me, she said, "Here are the keys. *Do* pet them for me, will you?" Her eyes filled with tears.

"Yes, of course I will," I said, impulsively grasping her plump hand in mine and giving it a farewell squeeze.

It's hard to leave your children in someone else's hands.

As the door closed behind Wanda's hand-knit pink sweater and Mrs. Simpson-Phelps' good traveling hat, I looked at The Wild Bunch and said, "It's up to you, guys. You can be good kitties or you can break an old lady's heart. Which is it going to be?"

Despite the full bowls of food on the kitchen floor, all four felines ran to the mountain of cat food cans and begged as though they hadn't eaten in a week. I sighed.

Nevertheless, the three weeks my neighbor was gone passed smoothly. I opened can after can of gourmet cat food, cooked liver for Paddy, changed litter box after litter box, picked up hairballs, and generally made sure things were all right in the Simpson-Phelps menagerie. Each Saturday morning Dr. Wanda Phelps's white Volvo pulled into a parking space on our narrow street and the tall blonde navigated the cobblestones, her wine-colored medical bag in her hand.

The day before Mrs. Simpson-Phelps was due to arrive home from her native land, I opened the door to chaos. I looked first at Paddington, perched on the mantel licking his paw. Then I saw what lay on the floor beneath him. I looked at Arthur, batting something around the floor while Tigger poked his head out from inside a shopping bag with twine handles. Finally, I looked at Annie, curled up on a bundle of pink stuff she'd managed to knead into a cushion.

Any other cat-sitter would have gotten out the broom and cleaned up the mess.

I called the police.

"Just what is it you think happened here?" the stalwart, skeptical, just-the-facts-ma'am detective — who also happened to be my husband — asked for the third time.

I took a deep breath and started in again. "Bud, I've already told you. We're supposed to think Paddy broke The Black Hawthorne," I explained. "When I came in, he was on the mantel, licking his paw. And, as you can see, the jar's in pieces on the floor."

My hand waved at the shards of black lacquered porcelain that lay on the parquet. "But Paddy's the most graceful cat I've ever seen. There's no way he would have been clumsy enough to knock that thing down."

Detective Bud Parker raised a single eyebrow. Apparently the gracefulness of cats didn't qualify as admissible evidence.

"If your men do a thorough examination of the mantelpiece," I went on, "I think they'll find traces of liver. Cooked liver that someone put up there to lure Paddy onto the mantel."

Now the other eyebrow went up. I'd seen this expression before, and it did not denote acquiescence to my point of view.

"Liver," he said. He sighed. "Was this on *Murder, She Wrote* or something?"

"And then there's Tigger," I said, ignoring the comment. The fact that the hour between 8 and 9 p.m. on Sunday evening was as sacred to me as the Super Bowl was to him had no bearing on the facts at hand.

I pointed to the colorful shopping bag with the dangerous twine handles Mrs. Simpson-Phelps had been so concerned about. "It's from Harrod's. That's in London," I added helpfully. "A place our neighbor hasn't visited in donkey's years. Which means that someone who *had* been in London recently came and left it here. What's more," I said, going for the clincher, "I know Mrs. Simpson-Phelps got rid of all her shopping bags because she was afraid Tigger would get his head caught in the handles. So that bag was brought here while she was away."

I sat back on the velvet-covered sofa, which was just as uncomfortable as it looked, waiting for Bud to catch up with my thinking. "Mrs. Simpson-Phelps has a nephew who lives in England. He's here in Washington right now — and he had his eye on his aunt's valuable antique."

Bud nodded. His eyebrows were back in their normal position; he was clearly more comfortable discussing human rather than feline psychology.

"Look at Annie," I continued, pointing to where the green-eyed cat sat in sphinx pose on a hand-knitted pink sweater. Even the arrival of several heavy-footed police officers hadn't moved her from her comfortable seat.

"See what she's sitting on?" Without waiting for an answer, I went on. "I last saw that sweater on Wanda, Mrs. Simpson-Phelps' niece. You remember, I met her just before Mrs. Simpson-Phelps left. And she had designs on the vase, too. That's why she came every Saturday, to show her aunt how much she cares for the cats, so Mrs. Simpson-Phelps will leave her the ginger jar in her will."

"So you think Wanda is behind all this?" Bud asked. "You've seen her enter the house; the pink sweater is hers — maybe she tried to steal the vase and broke it instead."

"No," I answered. "It was Gerry who stole the real vase. Then he broke this reproduction so his aunt would think it was destroyed forever."

"How do you know it was him instead of the niece?"

"Because of Arthur," I replied.

"Arthur? Who's he?" Bud demanded. "Another nephew?"

I laughed, then pointed at the gunmetal gray cat with the white peninsula on his clown face. "That's Arthur," I said. "And if you'll look at what he has between his paws, you'll see what I mean about Gerry."

Bud hoisted his bulk out of the blue velvet sofa — which clung to its sitters like the sea to its dead — and walked to where Arthur guarded his captured prey. "Hey," he said, picking up the object, "this is a charcoal briquette. What's this cat doing with —"

"That's what I mean," I said triumphantly. "Arthur's been outside. Mrs. Simpson-Phelps specifically told me he wasn't to go out while she was away. Somebody disobeyed her and let him out. You remember the Adzakians' barbecue last Sunday — Arthur must have captured a briquette from their grill."

"So why couldn't Wanda —"

"Because she loved the cats," I said triumphantly. "She wouldn't have let Arthur go outside. And she'd never have left a shopping bag where Tigger could get his head caught in the handles. It's my guess Annie made a cushion of her sweater and Wanda left it so that her aunt would see it and be touched by her kindness."

Again Bud gave me the two-eyebrow treatment. I plunged ahead anyway. "But Gerry, unlike Wanda, dislikes cats. In fact, he's afraid of them. So it's natural he'd open the French doors while he was here in hopes that at least Arthur would go out and leave him alone. He brought the bag because it contained a replica of The Black Hawthorne from the Smithsonian gift shop. He took the real vase, then smashed the replica and put liver on the mantel so Paddy would climb up and get blamed for the broken ginger jar. He figured his aunt would never know he'd taken the real one. If you move quickly," I suggested, "you can probably catch him at Dulles Airport. He'll have to go through Customs, after all."

I allowed myself to preen a little when Bud called an hour later to say that Gerry Simpson had been arrested. I may have allowed references to Jessica Fletcher to pass my lips when Bud reported that Gerry had declared a black hawthorne ginger jar as a souvenir.

I lost my complacency when Dr. Adzakian, chairman of the Chinese Art department at the Smithsonian and unofficial advisor to the D.C. police department, declared the ginger jar a fake.

The only thing that made up for my chagrin was what Bud described as the very real dismay on the face of Gerry Simpson.

"He really thought we were putting him on," Bud said, tucking into the leftover goulash I'd microwaved for him. "He thought he had the real thing, I'm sure of that."

"Which means," I began slowly, wary of making another blunder, "that somebody substituted ginger jars before Gerry made his move."

"I still think the old lady did it herself," Bud said. This was a theory he'd propounded more than once during my three weeks of cat-sitting. "I know if I had a valuable ginger jar and a houseful of cats, I wouldn't just leave the thing on the mantel."

"But you aren't Mrs. Simpson-Phelps," I argued. "She loves her cats and she loves her vase and she doesn't see any problem with —"

"Okay, so what happened, Sherlock?" Bud challenged.

"Wanda."

"When and how?" This was said through a mouthful of goulash.

I remembered the wine-colored doctor's bag. What reason could she have had for carrying it from her car into her aunt's house — except as a convenient receptacle for The Black Hawthorne?

Bud woke up a District of Columbia judge, got a search warrant signed, and had the ginger jar — the real one, this time, according to Dr. Adzakian — before Mrs. Simpson-Phelps's plane landed the next day. Since Wanda was in custody, I drove to Dulles Airport to meet my neighbor's plane.

After she'd heard everything, she leaned back in the bucket seat of my little red Honda and said, "Thank goodness you were there, Nikki. I can't thank you enough for what you've done for me. I don't know how I can ever show my gratitude."

"Oh, there's no need —" I began, but Mrs. Simpson-Phelps cut me off with a sudden cry of inspiration.

"I know," she said triumphantly, "I shall change my will and leave *you* The Black Hawthorne!" She turned to me, her face radiant, "And the cats, too, of course."

I was living in San Diego when Carole Nelson Douglas asked me to write a story about Marilyn Monroe. I read every book about Marilyn I could find; the letter she wrote to a friend on Hotel Del Coronado stationery, in which she misquoted the line from Yeats and drew a stick figure of herself drowning in the surf, led me to choose filming of Some Like It Hot *as the background for my story. A group of mystery writers performed an edited version at Left Coast Crime 8 in San Diego.*

LOVE ME FOR MY YELLOW HAIR ALONE
(32 Short Films about Marilyn Monroe)

only god, my dear
could love you for yourself alone
and not your yellow hair

— w.b. yeats

1. The watcher:

The Hotel Del Coronado squats on the silver strand of beach like a fat, aging duchess. Huge, sprawling, its rust-red roof like a giant mushroom cap, it dominates the Coronado oceanfront.

The woman sits on a beach chair, her face upturned to catch the rays of the sun she professes to hate. She is blonde and pale; sun will dry and wrinkle her skin, she says often. Yet she inhales the sun's heat, she revels in the languorous feeling it spreads through her body. She undulates in her beach chair, shifting her perfect anatomy to expose more skin to the blinding light. She disdains the hat her companion proffers, waving it away with an impatient hand whose fingernails are meticulously manicured but unpainted. Not Hollywood hands, but the hands of a secretary or a bookkeeper.

The companion is a middle-aged woman with a soft, lived-in look. She wears a shapeless black dress; her feet are encased in support hose and orthopedic sandals. A Jewish housewife, thinks the man with the binoculars. He knows her husband is the high priest of Method acting, but he does not know that the Jewish housewife is herself an accomplished actress, a woman who is not permitted to work because of the blacklist. He thinks the high priest has sent his wife to baby-sit the temperamental star.

2. *The extra:*

And, boy, was she ever temperamental! She never, but absolutely never, got to the set on time. Once she showed up at noon for a nine o'clock call, and the minute she got there, Mr. Wilder picked up his megaphone and called "Lunch."

I was an extra on that movie, one of twenty Coronado kids who got to sit around on the beach and get our pitchers took, as my Okie grandfather said with a cackle when I told him about my summer job.

We were military brats, my pals and me. We grew up surfing before anybody in the rest of the country knew what a surfboard was. We bummed around on the beach and took jobs at the Del for pocket money, clearing tables or carrying suitcases and waiting for the day when we'd take the ferry to San Diego and start college and never come back to boring old Coronado where there was nothing to do.

Johnny Benson told me about the movie coming. You remember Johnny — his dad was Navy all the way and Johnny was supposed to go to Annapolis, only he didn't want to. His idea of heaven was MIT; kid was great at math and science. Only his dad thought scientists were pointy-headed weirdos who were either Jewish or faggots or both, and he was god-damned if any son of his was going to —

Well, you get the picture. So that was Johnny, and you wouldn't think a kid like that would care much about the movies or even about Marilyn Monroe, but you would be wrong because Johnny was seriously in love with Marilyn and the minute he heard that movie was coming, he decided he had to meet Marilyn. Really meet her, not just sit on the same beach as her, watching her through binoculars like all the other goofballs on Coronado.

3. *The private eye:*

I was a Rita Hayworth man myself. That long, red hair, those full lips. Plus, she could dance. I'm not much of a dancer myself, but I love a woman who can dance. Marilyn, you could see she'd had to take a lot of lessons before she danced on screen, but Rita was a natural.

But a job is a job is a job, to quote that dyke writer in Paris. And besides, I always had a soft spot for Joltin' Joe. So he was divorced from her, that doesn't mean he can't take an interest? He can't hire a guy or two to keep an eye on her, he knows she's in some kind of trouble?

I wouldn't of taken the job if I hadn't believed I was working for DiMaggio. Honest. I would have turned that money down cold, even though making a living as a p.i. in San Diego was no picnic in those days. America's Finest City was fine, all right — too fine to need a lot of guys wearing gumshoes.

But I wouldn't have taken the money if I'd of known.

Honest.

4. *The director's assistant:*

Mr. Wilder was so patient with her. Like a father with a fractious child, he told her over and over again just what he wanted. He'd say the same thing twenty different ways, trying for the one phrase that would connect and bring out a performance. The other actors, Curtis and Lemmon and Raft, all they needed were one or two takes and they'd have it right. But Marilyn would shake her head and her lip would tremble and a tear would fall down the perfect face and then Makeup would have to come over and do her up again.

I'd stand there in the hot sun, holding an umbrella over Mr. Wilder's head so he wouldn't get heatstroke, and I'd watch her stumble over a line and stop, demanding another take.

Even when she got the lines right, she wasn't satisfied. "I need to do it again," she'd say in that baby voice. "It wasn't right."

Mr. Wilder would lean forward and whisper in her ear. I'd have to lean forward too, so the umbrella would shield him. She'd shake her head and wave him away. "I need to think," she'd say. "Don't talk to me, please. I'll forget how I want to play it."

As if she could know how to play the scene any better than Mr. Wilder did! As if she were some kind of genius and Mr. Wilder was nothing more than a ham-handed amateur who might screw her up.

The nerve of that little bitch, I thought, gripping the umbrella with white-knuckled hands.

Until I saw the rushes. Until I saw the tiny, subtle differences between the scene as Billy had instructed her to do it and the scene the way she felt it from within.

She was magic on the screen. Even Mr. Wilder said so. Later. Much later.

5. *The hotel maid:*

He was always in the room. Whenever I came to clean, there he'd be, sitting on one of the wicker chairs on the balcony or writing at the desk by the window. He'd nod politely and tell me to go ahead even though I always told him I could come back when it was more convenient. That was what the management wanted us girls to say, so I said it. Some rooms the maids didn't get to clean until 5:00 in the p.m. on account of the movie people kept pretty strange hours.

"My wife's on the set," he'd say. I'd nod as if to say, where else would the star of the movie be?

But she wasn't on the set. Everybody knew Mr. Wilder and the other actors were going nuts because Marilyn didn't show until afternoon. Everybody knew except Mr. Miller. Except the husband.

The husband is always the last to know.

6. *On the beach:*

"She's just a *pretend* lady," the chubby little boy with the potbelly confided.

"I know," the little girl replied. She was an inch shorter than the boy and her hair was the exact same baby blonde as the real lady's hair.

"She's a man dressed up like a lady," the boy went on. "For the movie."

"I know," the little girl said again. She walked toward the approaching waves; she stood on the hard sand and waited for the cool water to lick her toes. When the wave washed over her feet, she jumped and squealed, then ran back to the soft sand.

The lady who wasn't a lady walked funny. She wobbled and her heels buckled under her and the people crowding around laughed.

The little girl wasn't sure why the people laughed when the pretend lady walked. The real lady wobbled when she walked, too, only the people didn't laugh.

Once she wobbled so much she fell down on the stairs. If the pretend lady had done that, everyone would have laughed. But nobody laughed when the real lady did it.

7. The New York journalist:

> "Hollywood," quips Bob Hope, "where every Tom, Dick, and Harry is Tab, Rock, and Rory." And where a white-trash California girl named Norma Jean Baker transformed herself into the most glamorous sex symbol of her time.
>
> California is the edge of America. It's where you go to reinvent yourself, where you can leave behind the person you were and become someone new, shedding the past like a worn-out snakeskin. You expect the freeways to be littered with crackling, near-transparent carapaces of dead selves.

I gotta cut that last bit. Too goddamn literary for this rag. Maybe I can pull it out and reshape it for a piece in the *Times.* Yeah, the *Times*'ll eat that crap with a spoon. But for the *Mirror,* I need a little dirt.

She's late on the set. She's always late, they tell me, but this time it's different. This time she's not in Hollyweird; she's at this godforsaken hole near San Diego. So what the hell's she doing every morning instead of showing up for work?

She's not doing the horizontal mambo with her hubby, that's for sure. She leaves the room, but she doesn't go down to the set.

Miller thinks she's with Wilder; Wilder thinks she's with Miller — and the whole thing smells to me like a nice big fishy story. A story I can clean up a little for the *Mirror* and spice up a little for *Hollywood Confidential.* In this business, there's nothing better than getting paid for the same story twice.

Three times, if I can toss in enough bullshit for the *Times.*

8. The watcher:

He trains his binoculars on the silver strand of beach. The prop men from the movie have strategically placed several wicker beach chairs that wrap around the sitter like a cocoon. In the movie, Tony Curtis, dressed like a Twenties playboy, will sit in one of the chairs and Marilyn will mince past him and strike up an acquaintance.

He thinks it would be interesting if someone walked past the wicker cocoon and discovered that the person sitting inside, facing the ocean, had been dead for some time.

9. *The private eye:*

This thing is a security nightmare. I can't believe Wilder lets everyone and his twin brother watch the shooting on the beach. They put up ropes to hold back the crowds, but any nut could pull out a gun and shoot Marilyn where she stands. Hell, someone with a good aim could pot her from a passing boat — and a lot of boats go by, people training binocs on the shore to get a glimpse of the stars.

Wilder's there in his white cloth cap, a cigarette dangling from yellowed fingers. He looks like a cabbie, not a famous director.

Lemmon's wearing a girl's bathing suit from the Twenties. He's standing next to Marilyn, and they're both laughing. I can't hear what they're saying, but I have a good idea why Lemmon, at least, is enjoying himself.

He doesn't have to wear high heels on the beach.

10. *The drama student:*

I saw him on Orange Avenue this afternoon. I don't know why, but I thought he was taller. And I definitely visualized him wearing a suit and tie. But he had on a pair of slacks and a striped t-shirt and a baseball cap. He looked like a father on his way to his son's Little League game.

The most famous American playwright of our time, and he was walking along Orange Avenue just like anybody else.

He walked faster than everyone else; he kept moving around other people. I guess they walk a lot in New York City.

He's here because of Her, of course. I don't imagine a man like him would even step foot in California if it weren't for being married to Her.

How can he write with all the distractions She brings into his life? How can a man of his genius be content to play second fiddle to a silly movie star? Why doesn't he realize that she can bring him nothing but pain, that he needs a woman of high intellectual attainment, a woman who will devote herself to nurturing his art, not pursue her own meaningless career?

11. *The actor:*

You do the work. Forget this self-indulgent bullshit about being ready or not ready. Forget this Method crap about getting in touch with your inner feelings. You show up, you hit the marks, you say the lines — hell, first you *know* the lines; you don't show up three hours late and ask for cue cards.

She was just off a movie with Larry Olivier. Can you feature that? I've been in the business since I was younger than Marilyn and nobody ever let me get close to a movie with Olivier, and that no-talent blonde gets a movie with him and screws it up.

I'm a character actor; you could see this movie nine times and still not really notice my performance. Which is another way of saying it's a good performance, since I'm not supposed to be noticed.

Her husband, now, he understood what professional was. He was a writer, he knew how to produce. He knew that you have to put your keister in the chair and pound away on the typewriter every day whether or not you feel like it. He wanted Marilyn to act like a pro, to give a damn about the other people on the set. Every time she threw one of her tantrums or burst into tears, he died a little. You could see it; he'd grimace like a father whose kid is acting bratty at the officers' club.

12. *The acting coach:*

I know what they call me on the set: the wicked witch of the East. They hate Easterners out here, which is amusing, really, because so many of them are from the East themselves. But they've gone Hollywood and I haven't.

The sun gives me terrible headaches, which is why I dress like a Bedouin, and yet I sit with Marilyn on the Ocean Terrace, going over lines and working on the scenes. I pass on bits of wisdom from my own acting days, spiced with little sayings from Lee, from the Studio.

"A scene is like a bottle," I tell her. "If you can't open it one way, try another."

She mumbles something I have to ask her to repeat.

"Maybe I should just throw the bottle away," she says in her wispy voice, which almost but not quite gets swept out to sea by the strong breeze.

13. *The cameraman:*

You know how they say in Hollywood that the camera loves somebody. It sounds kind of stupid when you say it; I mean, how can a camera love anyone? But it's true. You take Marilyn, now. All I do is point the camera at her and she lights up. Her face plays to the camera, tilting ever so slightly to catch an angle of light. Or she widens her eyes and the camera zooms right in on her baby blues. She tosses her head and the camera records the swirl and fall of fine, golden hair.

We're shooting black-and-white, remember. And yet the camera catches, somehow, the precise shade of her blonde hair, the wide blue eyes. She is going to look wonderful on screen, lit from within like a Japanese lantern.

We're shooting black-and-white because of the boys. Wilder says if we were doing the movie in color, the drag bits wouldn't work; the makeup would be too garish.

He's right. The studio bitched at first, said nobody would ever pay good money to see a black-and-white picture again, color was here to stay. But for this movie, they'll pay. Curtis is great, Lemmon is greater, and then there's Marilyn.

The camera loves her, and I think I do too.

14. *The local reporter:*

I can't believe this quote! Little old me from sleepy little San Diego with a quote that's going to make headlines around the world.

TONY CURTIS ON MARILYN: "KISSING HER LIKE KISSING HITLER."

Can you believe my luck in being actually in the room when Tony Curtis tells the world his glamorous co-star is really more like the hated dictator?

Of course, I go on to explain in the article that what he really means is that in her relentless drive for perfection in every little thing she does, Marilyn sometimes drives her co-stars to distraction. But rest assured, I intend to tell the movie-going public, the results on screen will be worth it! They always are with La Monroe, aren't they?

15. *The studio doc:*

You don't get rich in Hollywood by saying no to big stars. And Marilyn was one of the biggest. When she was in a picture, everyone on the set lived on Marilyn time. The stars, the extras, the director all sat around waiting for Her Highness to show up. On a good day, she made it before the lunch break. On a bad day, she didn't make it at all.

She lived on champagne, caviar, and Nembutol. Once, I tried to tell her she needed to taper off, not use the pills every night, especially if she was serious about wanting a baby. She looked at me with her beautiful, bleary eyes and said, "What night? My life is one long, goddamned horrible day that never ends."

I shut up and wrote another prescription.

16. The continuity girl:

That last picture she made with Wilder, she didn't even have a name. Her character was called The Girl. That's all, just The Girl, as if any bubble-headed blonde in the world could have walked in and played the part.

That's what Wilder really wants from her. That she play The Girl, not a real person.

I'm forty-two years old. I've been in the picture business since I was nineteen. When I started, I *was* a girl, I guess. But now, it sounds pretty silly when people introduce me as "the continuity girl." Not bothering to find out my name, just calling me "the girl."

Just like Marilyn in *The Seven-Year Itch.*

I know where she goes in the mornings. I've seen her. I know I should tell Mr. Wilder. And I will — the first time he calls me by my name.

17. The drama student:

He's writing a movie for Her. The greatest playwright of the twentieth century, and he's wasting his time writing a stupid movie.

I can't believe it. I can't believe he's that besotted.

If only I could talk to him. If only I could make him understand that he has a duty to his art. He needs to know there are people like me, who love him for what he's done. He needs to know he doesn't have to prostitute himself.

I have to talk to him.

18. The psychiatrist:

It was a classic case of Electra complex. Marrying an older man, a father figure. And of course, there was already a father figure in Lee Strasberg, not to mention her way of playing bad little daughter with her directors. She craved their approval, and she refused to earn it by behaving properly.

Classic.

Classic, and tragic. By the time she was making that movie, any competent therapist could have told her the marriage was coming apart at the seams. Anyone could have told her nothing would save it; certainly not a baby.

19. *The Hairdresser:*

Sweetie, this movie is going to be a *hoot.* You haven't *lived* until you've seen macho Tony Curtis mincing around in high heels! The poor boy looks *so* uncomfortable. I'd just die if one of his butch friends like Kirk or Burt came on the set and saw his Cupid's bow lips. Honey, he's the *spitting image* of Clara Bow!

Oh, all right, I'll lay off the camp. Just for you, sweetcheeks.

Oh, don't be such a closet queen. I won't tell your Navy buddies who you like to kiss on weekends, so just relax, will you?

What's she like?

The truth? She's like a poisoned bonbon, beautiful to look at, but, oh, Mary, don't —

All right.

She's like a child. A mean little child who'll do anything to get her own way.

God, what hets go through for a little taste of sex on the silver screen!

20. *On the beach:*

"Here comes the lady," the boy said. He squatted on the sand next to the sand castle he'd made with his pail and shovel. It was a simple castle; all he'd done was turn over a pailful of hard, wet sand and dig a little moat around it for the water to run in.

The little girl kicked at the shell and drew her foot back with a cry. "It hurts," she said. "It's too sharp." She picked up the offending object and threw it as hard as she could into the water. It landed with a plop about three feet away.

The lady came every morning. She walked along the beach in her bare feet, but she wore pants instead of a bathing suit. And she wore a scarf over her blonde curls. It was a funny way to dress for the beach, the little girl thought. Her mother wore a bathing suit and a white cap with a rubber flower on the side.

Maria turned the pages of her book. It was a book with pictures, and it was written in Spanish. She watched the approaching woman with an expression of indifference. She knew the blonde lady was in the movie they were making at the big hotel, but it would never have occurred to her that the pasty *gringa* with the capri pants and the head scarf was *La Magnifica* herself.

The blonde scuffed her feet in the water, sending salt spray up in little fountains.

"Hi," she said as she got closer. "Catch any fish today?"

"How could we?" the boy replied with a crowing laugh. "We don't have any fishing poles."

"Oh, you don't need poles," the lady said with a shake of her head. "All you have to do is want the fish, and they'll swim right over and ask you to catch them."

"That's silly," the boy retorted.

"Would the fish die if we caught them?" the little girl wanted to know. "I wouldn't like it if they died."

"Oh, no," the lady answered. "That wouldn't be nice at all. The fish wouldn't die. They'd swim into your little moat here and you could scoop them up and take them home and put them in a glass bowl and watch them swim around."

"You still need poles," the little boy pronounced. He walked over to his sand castle and began to kick it with his tanned bare feet. "I saw the men fishing on the pier, and they all had poles."

"The fish I'm talking about are called grunions," the blonde lady explained. Her forehead creased as she talked, like someone who really wanted them to understand. "They swim very close to shore, and you can really catch them in a bowl if you want to."

"Do you have any little girls?"

The lady stood very still. She looked toward the place where the sun would be if the fog weren't so thick. One hand touched her tummy very lightly and she said, "I hope I'm going to. Very soon."

She smiled, and the smile was like the sun breaking through the Southern California morning fog. "Very, very soon," she repeated.

21. The extra:

If Johnny had just kept his mouth shut, he might have gotten away with it. But then, if he had, nobody would have believed him, so what would have been the point?

The whole point was that he had to kiss Marilyn and all the guys on Coronado had to know he kissed her. That way, his father couldn't get away with calling him a faggot on account of he wanted to go to MIT instead of Annapolis.

He started out just wanting to meet her, but all the guys razzed him when he talked about it, so he bet Carl Rasmussen that he wouldn't just meet Marilyn, he'd kiss her.

He'd kiss her right in front of the Del.

And Carl could watch, and then Carl could pay up, 'cause he, Johnny, was going to do it, and when he said he was going to do a thing, that thing was as good as done.

Which I could have told Carl was the truth because I was there that time in seventh grade, which Carl wasn't, being as his father was stationed in Hawaii that year. And I knew that if Johnny Benson said he was going to kiss Marilyn Monroe, then she was going to get kissed, come hell or high water.

What I didn't know was exactly how much hell there was going to be.

22. The director's assistant:

"When Marilyn Monroe walks into a room, nobody's going to be watching Tony Curtis playing Joan Crawford."

That's an exact quote, I can assure you. I was in the room when she said it, right to Mr. Wilder's face. She made him reshoot the opening, said she wouldn't finish the picture unless he —

Yes, she said Joan Crawford — and isn't Miss Crawford just going to die when she sees that in print? I mean, I can't look at Tony in his costume any more without thinking of Joan.

Did I hear what Mr. Wilder said about doing another movie with Marilyn?

Well, yes, but I don't think I really ought to —

Well, since you already know, I guess it won't hurt to —

He said, "I've discussed the matter with my doctor and my accountant, and they tell me I am too old and too rich to go through this again."

Yes, that's what he said. But please don't quote me.

23. *The studio doc:*

You've had two tube pregnancies, I reminded her. And then I had to explain for probably the fifteenth time exactly what that meant. You have two Fallopian tubes, Miss Monroe, I said. And what they're supposed to do is carry your eggs down to your womb so that if you get pregnant, the baby can grow in your womb like it's supposed to.

Understand?

I was using words I'd use to explain menstruation to a slow thirteen-year-old, and the look I'd get from her was as if I was trying to explain Einstein's theory. No comprehension.

Your trouble is that your eggs don't travel all the way to the womb. They stay in the tubes, so that when the sperm fertilizes the egg, it starts growing in the tube. This is called an ectopic pregnancy, and it won't work. The baby can't grow that way.

Your chances of having a normal pregnancy, Miss Monroe?

Slim to none, I'd answer. With your history, slim to none.

24. *The private eye:*

This job is pointless. I've got a film of Unguentine on my face so thick it traps gnats, that's how long I've been out in the sun watching Monroe. And so far, nobody's come close to her except a couple of toddlers, only it was her got close to them instead of the other way around.

If something doesn't happen by the end of the day, I'm off this job. Money or no money, DiMaggio or no DiMaggio.

25. *The drama student:*

He wouldn't listen. He wrote me an autograph and said I should keep studying. He said he'd write me a recommendation to the Yale Drama School if I wanted him to, but he wouldn't listen.

I looked up into his face, all white and drawn with suffering, and I knew what I had to do.

I was wrong trying to talk to him. He's too noble and good to betray the woman he loves. The woman he thinks he loves.

Next time I'll talk to Her.
Only I won't just talk.

26. *The extra:*

Johnny had it all planned. He needed a diversion, he said. Just like in
the war. He needed somebody to help distract the people around Marilyn
so he could step in and make his move.
He didn't mean any harm.
Honest.
He was just a kid who wanted to impress his buddies.
So we started by tossing a flying saucer back and forth on the beach.
You know, those round disks you throw and somebody catches them?
Anyway, Tug Murphy had one and we tossed it around, getting pretty close
to where the grips were setting up the next shot. One of the grips yelled at
us to move away, but we hollered and pretended not to hear. So the grip
steps over to Tug and says something and Tug said something back, and
pretty soon a lot of grips were walking over to straighten things out.
Marilyn was just standing there, in this funny bathing suit that didn't
show nearly enough of her attributes, if you know what I mean. She was
shivering on account of it was breezy out there by the shore. Nobody from
the movie was standing near her. It was weird, like none of them wanted to
be close to her. The funny old lady with the big black hat was sitting in one
of the canvas chairs, watching like a hawk, but she was too far away to do
anything.
Which was why Johnny made his move. He ran out of the crowd and
made straight for Marilyn.

27. *The drama student:*

I was watching in the crowd, waiting for my opportunity. I'd been there
the day before, and the day before that, and there hadn't been an
opportunity, but I was certain that today was the day my luck would change.
And it did.
It was a boy, a stupid boy. He ran out of the crowd toward Her as if he
was going to catch her in a flying tackle.
She screamed and her hand flew to her mouth and she jumped back. She
jumped back toward me. Toward where I stood in the crowd with my knife

at my side, waiting for my opportunity.

Waiting to liberate the greatest playwright in the English language from his stupid mistake.

28. *The private eye:*

Like everybody else, I saw the kid. Like everybody else, I reacted — only, being a professional, I reacted a little faster. The trouble was, I was reacting to the wrong threat. I didn't see the girl until it was too late.

Until the little bitch raised the knife and screamed like a banshee in heat and lunged at Marilyn.

I had the kid in a wrestling hold I learned in high school, but I let him go and went after the girl.

But the kid was young and strong and I was getting beerbellied and slow. He got there first — and so did the knife.

By the time the cops came, I had her under control and the knife in my hand.

But the kid had been cut. Cut bad, too, judging from the amount of blood seeping into the white sand.

28. *The extra:*

Johnny saved her life. At least that was what she said.

All around her, people were yelling and screaming. Some of the women ran backwards, screeching as if they'd seen a hundred mice. The big guy grabbed the girl around her waist and took the knife away from her, but she wouldn't stop crying that she was going to kill Marilyn and nobody was going to stop her. Johnny and the big guy already had stopped her, but she didn't recognize that.

With all the yelling and running, you'd have thought Marilyn would take off for safety, run over to the old lady in the black hat or something. But she didn't. She just stood there while everyone else went crazy and then she knelt down in the sand and picked up Johnny's head and put it in her lap.

And when the guys with the stretcher came pushing through the crowd, she bent down and kissed him on the lips.

Which is when I turned to Carl Rasmussen and told him he'd better pay up or else. I didn't spell out what the or else was going to be because my voice was shaking so bad I thought I was going to cry.

Which was pretty weird on account of all that happened was that Johnny did what he said he was going to do.

29. *The cop:*

Sure, the movie people hushed it up. Can you blame them? The kid was okay — well, okay if you think thirty-eight stitches in the shoulder is okay, but you get my point. Nobody died or anything. They took the girl over to the state hospital, but this kind of publicity the movie didn't need, so they asked us all to keep it as quiet as possible.

And no, this isn't Hollywood, it's Coronado, but have you ever been anyplace where money doesn't talk?

Well, I haven't. So when the Chief said the whole thing never happened, I saluted smartly and said, What never happened, sir?

You'll go far, boy, the old man replied. And he was right.

30. *The actor:*

Three words of dialogue; sixty-five takes. Sixty-fucking-five. That's the story of this picture in a nutshell. Wilder's going nuts, the actors are going nuts, the crew's loving the overtime, and this picture may sink into the ocean like a chunk of cliff in an earthquake.

31. *The letter:*

She sits at the little round table in her room. There's a piece of Hotel Del stationery in front of her, and a powder-blue typewriter in a plastic case.

She smiles at the paper, picks up a pencil, and draws on the hotel's logo at the top of the page. It shows the sprawling building, with its distinctive mushroom rooftop, beside the beach. She makes a quick stick-figure drawing of herself in the billowing waves and writes the word "help" next to it, as if the figure were drowning.

Then she slips the paper into the carriage return, smartly maneuvers it to a space below the logo, and types in the date: September 11, 1958.

The letter is to a friend in New York. She tells him that the boat she is on is sinking and refers to the Straits of Dire.

She adds that she has nothing to worry about as she has no phallic symbol to lose.

She smiles wryly, then hits the carriage bar several times to leave room for the oversized signature she intends to write. Another thought strikes her, and she adds:

PS "Love me for my yellow hair alone"

32. The local doctor:

"I asked for a doctor, not a nurse," the tall man with the dark-rimmed glasses said when he answered my knock.

I've heard this before; female doctors are not usual, even in the field of gynecology. "I am a doctor," I said, keeping my tone even. "May I see your wife, please?"

He stepped aside and let me in.

"She's in the bathroom," he said. There was an edge of disgust in his tone; he turned abruptly and made for the door. "Tell my wife I'm going down to the set to tell the director that she's too sick to film today." He was speaking loudly enough for the woman in the bathroom to hear, and he pronounced the word "sick" with quotation marks around it. I had the distinct feeling I had been summoned as a witness to the fact that Miss Monroe was feigning her illness.

I'd heard the rumors; I'd even read a movie magazine or two. I knew Marilyn's reputation as a difficult actress, and as a woman who ingested pills the way other people chewed gum.

So I stepped into the bathroom with a brisk, businesslike air, expecting to see a spoiled star with a barbiturate hangover.

She squatted on the toilet seat, her head between her knees. She groaned weakly and sobbed as I approached. Her arms hugged her stomach; on the floor next to the commode lay a silk slip soaked in blood.

Post-script:

Marilyn Monroe, who had all but completed shooting the new Billy Wilder comedy *Some Like It Hot*, was hospitalized today in Southern California. Doctors announced she had suffered a miscarriage; Miss Monroe is married to Pulitzer prizewinning playwright Arthur Miller. Mr. Miller, emerging from his wife's bedside at an undisclosed hospital, declined to be interviewed.

— *New York Mirror*

Ghost stations do exist in the New York City subway system, old abandoned stops with dirty tiles; you can see them flash by as your train goes through without slowing down. I loved the name and the image, and working for the NYPD put me in touch with transit cops, so the idea grew into this story.

GHOST STATION

If there's one thing I can't stand, it's a woman drunk.

The words burned my memory the way Irish whiskey used to burn my throat, only there was no pleasant haze of alcohol to follow. Just bitter heartburn pain.

It was my first night back on the job, back to being Sergeant Maureen Gallagher instead of "the patient." Wasn't it hard enough being a transit cop, hurtling beneath the streets of Manhattan on a subway train that should have been in the Transit Museum? Wasn't it enough that after four weeks of Detox I felt empty instead of clean and sober? Did I *have* to have some rookie's casually cruel words ricocheting in my brain like a wild-card bullet?

Why couldn't I remember the good stuff? Why couldn't I think about O'Hara's beefy handshake, Greenspan's "Glad to see ya, Mo," Ianuzzo's smiling welcome? Why did I have to run the tape in my head of Manny Delgado asking Captain Lomax for a different partner?

"Hey, I got nothing against a lady Sarge, Cap," he'd said. "Don't get me wrong. It's just that if there's one thing I can't stand . . ." *Et cetera.*

Lomax had done what any standup captain would — kicked Delgado's ass and told him the assignment stood. What he hadn't known was that I'd heard the words, and couldn't erase them from my mind.

Even without Delgado, the night hadn't gotten off to a great start. Swinging in at midnight for a twelve-to-eight, I'd been greeted with the news that I was on Graffiti Patrol, the dirtiest, most mind-numbing assignment in the whole Transit Police duty roster. I was a Sergeant, damn it, on my way to a gold shield, and I wasn't going to earn it dodging rats in tunnels, going after twelve-year-olds armed with spray paint.

Especially when the rest of the cop world, both under and above ground, was working overtime on the torch murders of homeless people. There'd been four human bonfires in the past six weeks, and the cops were determined there wouldn't be a fifth.

Was Lomax punishing me, or was this assignment his subtle way of easing my entry back into the world? Either way, I resented it. I wanted to be a real cop again, back with Sal Minucci, my old partner. He was assigned to the big one, in the thick of the action, where both of us belonged. I should have been with him. I was Anti-Crime, for God's sake. I should have been assigned —

Or should I? Did I really want to spend my work nights prowling New York's underground Skid Row, trying to get information from men and women too zonked out to take care of legs gone gangrenous, whose lives stretched from one bottle of Cool Breeze to another?

Hell, yes. If it would bring me one step closer to that gold shield, I'd interview all the devils in hell. On my day off.

If there's one thing I can't stand, it's a woman drunk.

What did Lomax think — that mingling with winos would topple me off the wagon? That I'd ask for a hit from some guy's short dog and pass out in the Bleecker Street Station? Was that why he'd kept me off the big one and had me walking a rookie through routine graffiti patrol?

Was I getting paranoid, or was lack of alcohol rotting my brain?

Manny and I had gone to our respective locker rooms to suit up. Plain clothes — and I do mean plain. Long johns first; damp winter had a way of seeping down into the tunnels and into your very blood. Then a pair of denims the Goodwill would have turned down. Thick wool socks, fisherman's duck boots, a black turtleneck, and a photographer's vest with lots of pockets. A black knit hat pulled tight over my red hair.

Then the gear: flashlight, more important than a gun on this assignment, handcuffs, ticket book, radio, gun, knife. A slapper, an oversized blackjack, hidden in the rear pouch of the vest. They were against regulations; I'd get at least a command discipline if caught with it, but experience told me I'd rather have it than a gun going against a pack of kids.

I'd forgotten how heavy the stuff was; I felt like a telephone lineman.

I looked like a cat burglar.

Delgado and I met at the door. It was obvious he'd never done vandal duty before. His tan chinos were immaculate, and his hiking boots didn't look waterproof. His red plaid flannel shirt was neither warm enough nor the right dark color. With his Latin good looks, he would have been stunning in an L.L. Bean catalogue, but after ten minutes in a subway tunnel, he'd pass for a chimney sweep.

"Where are we going?" he asked, his tone a shade short of sullen. And there was no respectful "Sergeant" at the end of the question, either. This boy needed a lesson in manners.

I took a malicious delight in describing our destination. "The Black Hole of Calcutta," I replied cheerfully, explaining that I meant the unused lower platform of the City Hall station downtown. The oldest, darkest, dankest spot in all Manhattan. If there were any subway alligators, they definitely lurked in the Black Hole.

The expression on Probationary Transit Police Officer Manuel Delgado's face was all I could have hoped for. I almost — but not quite — took pity on the kid when I added, "And after that, we'll try one or two of the ghost stations."

"Ghost stations?" Now he looked really worried. "What are those?"

This kid wasn't just a rookie; he was a suburbanite. Every New Yorker knew about ghost stations, abandoned platforms where trains no longer stopped. They were still lit, though, and showed up in the windows of passing trains like ghost towns on the prairie. They were ideal canvases for the aspiring artists of the underground city.

I explained on the subway, heading downtown. The car, which rattled under the city streets like a tin lizzie, was nearly riderless at one a.m. A typical Monday late tour.

The passengers were one Orthodox Jewish man falling asleep over his Hebrew Bible, two black women, both reading thick paperback romances, the obligatory pair of teenagers making out in the last seat, and an old Chinese woman.

I didn't want to look at Delgado. More than once, I'd seen a fleeting smirk on his face when I glanced his way. It wasn't enough for insubordination; the best policy was to ignore it.

I let the rhythm of the subway car lull me into a litany of the AA slogans I was trying to work into my life: EASY DOES IT. KEEP IT SIMPLE, SWEETHEART. ONE DAY AT A TIME. I saw them in my mind the way they appeared on the walls at meetings; illuminated, like old Celtic manuscripts.

This night I had to take one hour at a time. Maybe even one minute at a time. My legs felt wobbly. I was a sailor too long from the sea. I'd lost my subway legs. I felt white and thin, as though I'd had several major organs removed.

Then the drunk got on. One of the black women got off, the other one looked up at the station sign and went back to her book, and the drunk got on.

If there's one thing I can't stand, it's a woman drunk.

ONE DAY AT A TIME. EASY DOES IT.

I stiffened. The last thing I wanted was to react in front of Delgado, but I couldn't help it. The sight of an obviously intoxicated man stumbling into our subway car brought the knowing smirk back to his face.

There was one at every AA meeting. No matter how nice the neighborhood, how well-dressed most people attending the meeting were, there was always a drunk. A real drunk, still reeling, still reeking of cheap booze. My sponsor Margie said they were there for a reason, to let us middle-class, recovery-oriented types remember that "there but for the grace of God . . ."

I cringed whenever I saw them, especially if the object lesson for the day was a woman.

"Hey, kid," the drunk called out to Delgado, in a voice as inappropriately loud as a deaf man's, "how old are you?" The doors closed and the car lurched forward; the drunk all but fell into his seat.

"Old enough," Manny replied, flashing the polite smile a well-brought-up kid saves for his maiden aunt.

The undertone wasn't so pretty. Little sidelong glances at me that said, *See how nice I am to this old fart. See what a good boy I am. I* like *drunks, Sergeant Gallagher.*

To avoid my partner's sly face, I concentrated on the subway ads as though they contained all the wisdom of the Big Book. "Here's to birth defects," proclaimed a pregnant woman about to down a glass of beer. Two monks looked to heaven, thanking God in Spanish for the fine quality of their brandy.

Weren't there any signs on this damn train that didn't involve booze? Finally an ad I could smile at: the moon in black space; on it, someone had scrawled, "Alice Kramden was here, 1959."

My smile faded as I remembered Sal Minucci's raised fist, his Jackie Gleason growl. "One a these days, Gallagher, you're goin to the moon. To the *moon!*"

It wasn't just the murder case I missed. It was Sal. The easy partnership of the man who'd put up with my hangovers, my depressions, my wild nights out with the boys.

"Y'know how old I am?" the drunk shouted, almost falling over in his seat. He righted himself. "Fifty-four in September," he announced, an expectant look on his face.

After a quick smirk in my direction, Manny gave the guy what he wanted. "You don't look it," he said. No trace of irony appeared on his Spanish altarboy's face. It was as though he'd never said the words that were eating into me like battery-acid AA coffee.

The sudden jab of anger that stabbed through me took me by surprise, especially since it wasn't directed at Delgado. *No, you don't look it*, I thought. *You look more like seventy.* White wisps of hair over a bright pink scalp. The face more than pink; a slab of raw calves' liver. Roadmaps of broken blood vessels on his nose and cheeks. Thin white arms and matchstick legs under too-big trousers. When he lifted his hand, ropy with bulging blue veins, it fluttered like a pennant in the breeze.

Like Uncle Paul's hands.

I turned away sharply. I couldn't look at the old guy anymore. The constant visual digs Delgado kept throwing in my direction were nothing compared to the pain of looking at a man dying before my eyes. I didn't want to see blue eyes in that near-dead face. *As blue as the lakes of Killarney,* Uncle Paul used to say in his mock-Irish brogue.

I focused on the teenagers making out in the rear of the car. A couple of Spanish kids, wearing identical pink T-shirts and black leather jackets. If I stared at them long enough, would they stop groping and kissing, or would an audience spur their passion?

Uncle Paul. After Daddy left us, he was my special friend, and I was his best girl.

I squeezed my eyes shut, but the memories came anyway. The red bike Uncle Paul gave me for my tenth birthday. The first really big new thing, bought just for me, that I'd ever had. The best part was showing it off to cousin Tommy. For once I didn't need his hand-me-downs, or Aunt Bridget's clucking over me for being poor. *God bless the child who's got her own.*

I opened my eyes just as the Lex passed through the ghost station at Worth Street. Closed off to the public for maybe fifteen years, it seemed a mirage, dimly seen through the dirty windows of the subway car. Bright color on the white tile walls told me graffiti bombers had been there. A good place to check, but not until after City Hall. I owed Manny Delgado a trip to the Black Hole.

"Uh, Sergeant?"

I turned; a patronizing smile played on Delgado's lips. He'd apparently been trying to get my attention. "Sorry," I said, feigning a yawn. "Just a little tired."

Yeah, sure, his look remarked. "We're coming to Brooklyn Bridge. Shouldn't we get off the train?"

"Right." *Leave Uncle Paul where he belongs.*

At the Brooklyn Bridge stop, we climbed up the steps to the upper platform, showed our ID to the woman token clerk, and told her we were going into the tunnel toward City Hall. Then we went back downstairs, heading for the south end of the downtown platform.

As we were about to go past the gate marked *No Unauthorized Personnel Beyond This Point*, I looked back at the lighted platform, which made a crescent-shaped curve behind us. Almost in a mirror-image, the old drunk was about the pass the forbidden gate and descend into the tunnel heading uptown.

He stepped carefully, holding on to the white, bathroom-tile walls, edging himself around the waist-high gate. He lowered himself down the stone steps the exact replica of the ones Manny and I were about to descend, then disappeared into the blackness.

I couldn't let him go. There were too many dangers in the subway, dangers beyond the torch killer everyone was on the hunt for. How many frozen bodies had I stumbled over on the catwalks between tunnels? How many huddled victims had been hit by trains as they lay in sodden sleep? And yet, I had to be careful. My friend Kathy Denzer had gone after a bum sleeping on the catwalk, only to have the man stab her in the arm for trying to save his life.

I couldn't let him go. Turning to Delgado, I said, "Let's save City Hall for later. I saw some graffiti at Worth Street on the way here. Let's check that out first."

He shrugged. At least he was being spared the Black Hole, his expression said.

Entering the tunnel's blackness, leaving behind the brightly-lit world of sleepy riders, a tiny rush of adrenalin, like MSG after a Chinese dinner, coursed through my bloodstream. Part of it was pure reversion to childhood's fears. Hansel and Gretel. Snow White. Lost in dark woods, with enemies all around. In this case, rats. Their scuffling sent shivers up my spine as we balanced our way along the catwalk above the tracks.

The other part was elation. This was my job. I was good at it. I could put aside my fears and step boldly down into murky depths where few New Yorkers ever went.

Our flashlights shone dim as fireflies. I surveyed the gloomy underground world I'd spent my professional life in.

My imagination often took over in the tunnels. They became caves of doom. Or an evil wood, out of *Lord of the Rings*. The square columns holding up the tunnel roof were leafless trees, the constant trickle of foul water between the tracks a poisonous stream from which no one drank and lived.

Jones Beach. Uncle Paul's huge hand cradling my instep, then lifting me high in the air and flinging me backward, laughing with delight, into the cool water. Droplets clinging to his red beard, and Uncle Paul shaking them off into the sunlight like a wet Irish setter.

Me and Mo, we're the only true Gallaghers. The only redheads. I got straight A's in English; nobody's grammar was safe from me — except Uncle Paul's.

I thought all men smelled like him: whisky and tobacco.

As Manny and I plodded along the four-block tunnel between the live station and the dead one, we exchanged no words. The acrid stench of an old track fire filled my nostrils the way memories flooded my mind. Trying to push Uncle Paul away, I bent all my concentration on stepping carefully around the foul-smelling water, the burned debris I didn't want to identify.

I suspected Delgado's silence was due to fear; he wouldn't want a shaking voice to betray his tension. I knew how he felt. The first nighttime tunnel trek was a landmark in a young transit cop's life.

When the downtown express thundered past, we ducked into the coffin-sized alcoves set aside for transit workers. My heart pounded as the wind-wake of the train pulled at my clothes; the fear of falling forward, landing under those relentless steel wheels, never left me, no matter how many times I stood in the well. I always thought of Anna Karenina; once in a while, in my drinking days, I'd wondered how it would feel to edge forward, to let the train's undertow pull me toward death.

I could never do it. I'd seen too much blood on the tracks.

Light at the end of the tunnel. The Worth Street Station sent rays of hope into the spidery blackness. My step quickened; Delgado's pace matched mine. Soon we were almost running toward the light, like cavemen coming from the hunt to sit by the fire of safety.

We were almost at the edge of the platform when I motioned Delgado to stop. My hunger to bathe in the light was as great as his, but our post was the shadows, watching.

A moment of panic. I'd lost the drunk. Had he fallen on the tracks, the electrified third rail roasting him like a pig at a barbecue? Not possible; we'd have heard, and smelled.

I had to admit, the graffiti painting wasn't a mindless scrawl. It was a picture, full of color and life. Humanlike figures in bright primary shades, grass green, royal blue, orange, sun yellow, and carnation pink — colors unknown in the black and gray tunnels — stood in a line, waiting to go through a subway turnstile. Sexless, they were cookie-cutter replicas of one another, the only difference among them the color inside the black edges.

A rhythmic clicking sound made Delgado jump. "What the hell —"

"Relax, Manny," I whispered. "It's the ball-bearing in the spray-paint can. The vandals are here. As soon as the paint hits the tiles, we jump out and bust them."

Four rowdy teenagers, ranging in color from light brown to ebony, laughed raucously and punched each other with a theatrical style that said *We bad. We* real *bad.* They bounded up the steps from the other side of the platform and surveyed their artwork, playful as puppies, pointing out choice bits they had added to their mural.

It should have been simple. Two armed cops, with the advantage of surprise, against four kids armed with Day-Glo spray paint. Two things kept it from being simple: the drunk, wherever the hell he was, and the fact that one of the kids said, "Hey, bro, when Cool and Jo-Jo gettin here?"

A very black kid with a nylon stocking on his head answered, "Jo-Jo be comin with Pinto. Cool say he might be bringin Slasher and T.P."

Great. Instead of two against four, it sounded like all the graffiti artists in New York City were planning a convention in the Worth Street ghost station.

"Sarge?" Delgado's voice was urgent. "We've gotta —"

"I know," I whispered back. "Get on the radio and call for backup."

Then I remembered. Worth Street was a dead spot. Lead in the ceiling above our heads turned our radios into worthless toys.

"Stop," I said wearily as Manny pulled the antenna up on his hand-held radio. "It won't work. You'll have to go back to Brooklyn Bridge. Alert Booth Robert 221. Have them call Operations. Just ask for backup, don't make it a 10-13." A 10-13 meant "officer in trouble," and I didn't want to be the sergeant who cried wolf.

"Try the radio along the way," I went on. "You never know when it will come to life. I'm not sure where the lead ends."

Watching Delgado trudge back along the catwalk, I felt lonely, helpless, and stupid. No one knew we'd gone to Worth Street instead of the Black

Hole, and that was my fault.

"Hey," one of the kids called, pointing to a pile of old clothes in the corner of the platform, "what this dude be doin in our crib?"

Dude? What dude? Then the old clothes began to rise; it was the drunk from the train. He was huddled into a fetal ball, hoping not to be noticed by the graffiti gang.

Nylon Stocking boogied over to the old drunk, sticking a finger in his ribs. "What you be doin here, ol man? Huh? Answer me."

A fat kid with a bushy Afro walked over, sat down next to the drunk, reached into the old man's jacket pocket, and pulled out a half-empty pint bottle.

A lighter-skinned, thinner boy slapped the drunk around, first lifting him by the scruff of the neck, then laughing as he flopped back to the floor. The old guy tried to rise, only to be kicked in the ribs by Nylon Stocking.

The old guy was bleeding at the mouth. Fat Boy held the pint of booze aloft, teasing the drunk they way you tease a dog with a bone. The worst part was that the drunk was reaching for it, hands flapping wildly, begging. He'd have barked if they'd asked him to.

I was shaking, my stomach starting to heave. God, where was Manny? Where was my backup? I had to stop the kids before their friends got there, but I felt too sick to move. *If there's one thing I can't stand, it's a woman drunk.* It was as though every taunt, every kick, was aimed at me, not just at the old man.

I reached into my belt for my gun, then opened my vest's back pouch and pulled out the slapper. Ready to charge, I stopped cold when Nylon Stocking said, "Yo, y'all want to do him like we done the others?"

Fat Boy's face lit up. "Yeah," he agreed. "Feel like a cold night. We needs a little fire."

"You right, bro," the light-skinned kid chimed in. "I got the kerosene. Done took it from my momma heater."

"What he deserve, man," the fourth member of the gang said, his voice a low growl. "Comin into our crib, pissin on the art, smellin up the place. This here *our* turf, dig?" He prodded the old man in the chest.

"I — I didn't mean nothing," the old man whimpered. "I just wanted a place to sleep."

Uncle Paul, sleeping on our couch when he was too drunk for Aunt Rose to put up with him. He was never too drunk for Mom to take him in. Never too drunk to give me one of his sweet Irish smiles and call me his best girl.

The light-skinned kid opened the bottle — ironically, it looked like it once contained whisky — and sprinkled the old man the way my mother sprinkled clothes before ironing them. Nylon Stocking pulled out a book of matches.

By the time Delgado came back, with or without backup, there'd be one more bonfire if I didn't do something. Fast.

Surprise was my only hope. Four of them, young and strong. One of me, out of shape and shaky.

I shot out a light. I cracked the bulb on the first shot. Target shooting was my best asset as a cop, and I used it to give the kids the impression they were surrounded.

The kids jumped away from the drunk, moving in all directions. "Shit," one said, "who shootin?"

I shot out the second and last bulb. In the dark, I had the advantage. They wouldn't know, at least at first, that only one cop was coming after them.

"Let's book," another cried. "Ain't worth stayin here to get shot."

I ran up the steps, onto the platform lit only by the moonlike rays from the other side of the tracks. Yelling "Stop, Police," I waded into the kids, swinging my illegal slapper.

Thump into the ribs of the kid holding the kerosene bottle. He dropped it, clutching his chest and howling. I felt the breath whoosh out of him, heard the snap of rib cracking. I wheeled and slapped Nylon Stocking across the knee, earning another satisfying howl.

My breath came in gasps, curses pouring out of me. Blood pounding in my temples, a thumping noise that sounded louder than the express train.

The advantage of surprise was over. The other two kids jumped me, one riding my back, the other going for my stomach with hard little fists. All I could see was a maddened teenage tornado circling me with blows. My arm felt light as I thrust my gun deep into the kid's stomach. He doubled, groaning.

It was like chugging beer at a cop racket. Every hit, every satisfying *whack* of blackjack against flesh made me hungry for the next. I whirled and socked. The kids kept coming, and I kept knocking them down like bowling pins.

The adrenalin rush was stupendous, filling me with elation. I was a real cop again. There was life after Detox.

At last they stopped. Panting, I stood among the fallen, exhausted. My hair had escaped from my knit hat and hung in matted tangles over a face red-hot as a griddle.

I pulled out my cuffs and chained the kids together, wrist to wrist, wishing I had enough sets to do each individually. Together, even cuffed, they could overpower me. Especially since they were beginning to realize I was alone.

I felt weak, spent. As though I'd just made love.

I sat down on the platform, panting, my gun pointed at Nylon Stocking. "You have the right to remain silent," I began.

As I finished the last Miranda warning on the last kid, I heard the cavalry coming over the hill. Manny Delgado, with four reinforcements.

As the new officers took the collars, I motioned Manny aside, taking him to where the drunk lay sprawled in the corner, still shaking and whimpering.

"Do you smell anything?" I asked.

Manny wrinkled his nose. I looked down at the drunk.

A trickle of water seeped from underneath him; his crotch was soaked. *Uncle Paul, weaving his way home, singing off-key, stopping to take a piss under the lamppost.* Nothing unusual in that, except that this time Julie Ann Mackinnon, my eighth-grade rival, watched from across the street. My cheeks burned as I recalled how she'd told the other kids what she'd seen, her hand cupped over her giggling mouth.

"Not that," I said, my tone sharp, my face reddening. "The kerosene. These kids are the torch killers. They were going to roast this guy. That's why I had to take them on alone."

Delgado's face registered the skepticism I'd seen lurking in his eyes all night. Could he trust me? He'd been suitably impressed at my chain-gang of prisoners, but now I was talking about solving the crime that had every cop in the city on overtime.

"Look, just go back to Brooklyn Bridge and radio —" I was going to say Captain Lomax, when I thought better "—no, call Sal Minucci in Anti-Crime. He'll want to have the guy's coat analyzed. And make sure somebody takes good care of that bottle." I pointed to the now-empty whisky bottle the light-skinned boy had poured kerosene from.

"Isn't that his?" Manny indicated the drunk.

"No, his is a short dog," I said, then turned away as I realized the term was not widely known in non-drunk circles.

Just go, kid, I prayed. Get the hell out of here before —

He turned, following the backup officers with their chain gang. "And send for Emergency Medical for this guy," I added. "I'll stay here till they come."

I looked down at the drunk. His eyes were blue, a watery, no-color blue with all the life washed out of them. Uncle Paul's eyes.

Uncle Paul, blurry-faced and maudlin, too blitzed to care that I'd come home from school with a medal for the best English composition. I'd put my masterpiece by his chair, so he could read it after dinner. He spilled whiskey on it; the blue-black ink ran like tears, and blotted out my carefully-chosen words.

Uncle Paul, old, sick and dying, just like this one. Living by that time more on the street than at home, though there were people who would take him in. His eyes more red than blue, his big frame wasted. I felt a sob rising, like death squeezing my lungs. I heaved, grabbing for air. My face was wet with tears I didn't recall shedding.

I hate you, Uncle Paul. I'll never be like you. Never.

I walked over to the drunk, still sprawled on the platform. I was a sleepwalker; my arm lifted itself. I jabbed the butt of my gun into old, thin ribs, feeling it bump against bone. It would be a baseball-sized bruise. First a raw red-purple, then blue-violet, finally a sickly yellow-gray.

I lifted my foot, just high enough to land with a thud near the kidneys. The old drunk grunted, his mouth falling open. A drizzle of saliva fell to the ground. He put shaking hands to his face and squeezed his eyes shut. I lifted my foot again. I wanted to kick and kick and kick.

Uncle Paul, a frozen lump of meat found by some transit cop on the above-ground platform at 161st Street. The Yankee Stadium stop, where he took me when the Yanks played home games. We'd eat at the Yankee Tavern, me wolfing down a corned beef on rye and a cream soda, Uncle Paul putting away draft beer after draft beer.

Before he died, Uncle Paul had taken all the coins out of his pocket, stacking them in neat little piles beside him. Quarters, dimes, nickels, pennies. An inventory of his worldly goods.

I took a deep, shuddering breath, looked down at the sad old man I'd brutalized. A hot rush of shame washed over me.

I knelt down, gently moving the frail, blue-white hands away from the near-transparent face. The fear I saw in the liquid blue eyes sent a piercing ray of self-hatred through me.

If there's anything I can't stand, it's a woman drunk. Me too, Manny, I can't stand women drunks either.

The old man's lips trembled; tears filled his eyes and rolled down his thin cheeks. He shook his head from side to side, as though trying to wake himself from a bad dream.

"Why?" he asked, his voice a raven's croak.

"Because I loved you so much." The words weren't in my head anymore, they were slipping out into the silent, empty world of the ghost station. As though Uncle Paul weren't buried in Calvary Cemetery, but could hear me with the ears of this old man who looked too damn much like him. "Because I wanted to be just like you. And I am." My voice broke. "I'm just like you, Uncle Paul. I'm a drunk." I put my head on my knee and sobbed like a child. All the shame of my drinking days welled up in my chest. The stupid things I'd said and done, the times I'd had to be taken home and put to bed, the times I'd thrown up in the street outside the bar. *If there's one thing I can't stand . . .*

"Oh, God, I wish I were dead."

The bony hand on mine felt like a talon. I started, then looked into the old man's watery eyes. I sat in the ghost station and saw in this stranger the ghost that had been my dying uncle.

"Why should you wish a thing like that?" the old man asked. His voice was clear, no booze-blurred slurring, no groping for words burned out of the brain by alcohol. "You're a young girl. You've got your whole life ahead a you."

My whole life. To be continued . . .

ONE DAY AT A TIME. ONE NIGHT AT A TIME.

When I got back to the District, changed out of my work clothes, showered, would there be a meeting waiting for me? Damn right; in the city that never sleeps, AA never sleeps either.

I reached over to the old man. My fingers brushed his silver stubble.

"I'm sorry, Uncle Paul," I said. "I'm sorry."

*The very first time I attended a meeting of the San Diego chapter of
Sisters in Crime, a woman volunteer with the canine rescue unit talked to us
about cadaver dogs and showed off her Bouvier. It was my first introduction
to this gory but necessary subset of rescue work. Fascinated, I took notes and
a scant four years later, got a short story out of the lecture. Fast is not my best
thing.*

SHOW ME THE BONES

"He doesn't look like a bloodhound," the little girl said. Her hair was
dirty and so was her sharp little face and so were her bare feet.

What was the mother thinking, bare feet on this hard desert ground,
with spiky plants and lizards and scorpions and God knew what else? I had
on my day hikers, the hightops, and two pair of socks under that. But then
I intended to walk as far as the track would lead me, and the kid meant to
stay in her mean little yard, among children's toys left out so long their
bright colors had faded long ago because it hardly ever rained out here.

"He's not a bloodhound, honey," I said in a syrupy tone I barely
recognized as my own. Why I invariably called all kids honey or sweetie or
some other cotton-candy nickname I couldn't say. Except, I suppose, that
they made me nervous with their direct little eyes and blunt questions. "He's
a Bouvier, and his name is Polo."

"Can I pet him?" She edged her dirt-smudged hand with its bitten nails
toward Polo's curly black head. Her thin wrists were scarred, I hoped from
cactus and not abuse. The long red-tipped tendrils of ocotillo had sharp
thorns; maybe she'd reached in to touch the flowers and torn her skin on the
long needles.

"Do you think he'll find my sister?" The little girl's voice sounded
squeezed through a thin tube, and she directed her gaze toward the ground
instead of looking at me with her intense blue eyes.

God, I hope not, kid.

See, I never actually told the families what Polo was. They saw a dog,
they figured "rescue." They figured tracking meant hunting for a living
person on the move through the scrub. They didn't know Polo was a cadaver
dog, trained to forget the living and find the dead.

I cleared my throat and said, "He's a good dog. He'll do his best, and so will I."

"Dogs always find lost people, don't they?" Now she gave me the full force of those blue eyes, gazing at me with a luminous innocence that pushed the breath out of my lungs. She looked both hopeful and scared to death, as if in some part of her eight-year-old brain she knew her sister wouldn't be found alive.

The ten-year-old had been missing five days now. Five long days and nights. The trackers worked all night; you didn't stop if you thought you might find a living child in need of medical care. But if you were looking for a body, you waited for first light.

There were four of us Sheriff's Department K-9 dog handlers gathered in the inky blue early morning. Devon had Kali, her black lab, on a long canvas leash. Kali roamed the perimeter, sniffing at each prickly pear, every cactus and bush, then looking back at Devon for confirmation that she was doing a good job. I always had the feeling the dogs were perpetually surprised to realize that their humans didn't actually smell the same things they did.

Scout, Jen's golden retriever, waved her feathery blond tail and sniffed the people instead of the bushes. Ruth's Daisy, the Doberman, wanted to do the same, but the child edged away as the dobe headed toward her with a determined expression in her doggy brown eyes. Poor Daisy; she was as sweet as her name, but the Doberman reputation preceded her, and people often looked deathly afraid when all she wanted was to lick their faces.

We were waiting for one more team, and finally the metallic blue van with Nancy and Toby skidded into the dirt driveway. I even said to the kid, "Here comes a bloodhound," as if to reassure her that we were really taking her sister's disappearance seriously.

Blood drained from the child's face as Nancy slid open the door of her van and Toby bounded out. "A real bloodhound," she whispered.

"Do they smell the blood?" I had to strain to hear the words, then realized that in her ears, the word *bloodhound* carried sinister overtones.

But how to answer? How to say, Well, no, it's not blood so much as the scent of a decaying corpse. Not exactly a reassuring reply.

Before I could formulate a suitable response, a deputy walked toward me and said, "We ready to get this show on the road?"

There were cops all over the place. The sheriff's vans and cars were parked further along the dirt road, and they'd made a makeshift headquarters in the workshop at the rear of the little frame house. Radios crackled and guys milled around aimlessly while pretending to be incredibly busy. The real work was in the backcountry and everyone knew it. The cops who were still here were just waiting for news from the desert, news that would have them summoning an evac helicopter and a medic — or a crime scene team.

As the days and nights passed, the evac helicopter seemed less and less likely.

I didn't like being so close to the family of the missing child. I preferred law enforcement to keep itself separate from the grieving and the wailing, but out here in the middle of absolute backcountry nowhere, Ocotillo Wells, California — which called itself a town but was in reality a gas station, a hamburger joint, fourteen houses, and thirty mobile homes — there was nowhere to go that would insulate us from the little girl's devastating blue eyes.

Toby lived up to her expectations. She watched with undisguised fascination as the big brown animal loped along the hardpacked dirt, snout to the ground like a living vacuum cleaner, sniffing up every trace of scent. At one point, he stopped, threw back his head, and emitted his mournful howl.

The cops stopped talking. Jen and Ruth, who'd been gossiping in low tones, went silent, too, although they'd heard Toby's war cry a hundred times before. Something about that sound went right through a person, brought back tales of banshees and spirits of the dead crying from the grave.

The little girl burst into tears and ran toward the house. I wanted to stop her, to call out something that would reassure her, but I had no words. We were out here to find the body of her sister, and no sugar-coating was going to soften that blow.

It was time to get moving. Toby was ready, and that meant the rest of us were too. All the dogs were straining their leashes, eager to hit the trail and do the job they'd been trained for.

The sergeant broke us into smaller units. Each dog would accompany a sheriff's team heading in a different direction; we'd cover the backcountry near town first, hoping the child hadn't been abducted by a car and driven to El Centro.

Most of the other teams got into cars to be driven to a point of origin, but Polo and I would walk from the hamburger joint at the edge of town, right off Interstate 8. I would be with two deputies, one male, one female, both young and eager.

"First time you've worked with dogs?" I knew the answer by the way they eyed our animals, but I wanted to open conversation. They nodded in unison and introduced themselves as Don and Sarah.

When we reached the hamburger stand, which wasn't open for business but still emanated a strong odor of cooking grease, Polo bounced on his bearlike legs and jumped on me. "No, babe, not now," I said. "We're going to work, Polo." I leaned in close and spoke directly into his tiny black ears with a deep-voiced seriousness that Polo had been trained to recognize as meaning business.

"Find the bones, Polo. Find the bones." Polo leapt and gave a single bark to tell me he understood. I unhooked his leash and let him race into the brush.

Bones. Saying "find the bones" instead of "find the body" made it sound clean and bloodless. But the kid was gone only five days, and that meant whatever we found, it wouldn't be nice clean bleached bones like the skulls in a Georgia O'Keeffe painting. It would be messy and bloated and there would be flies. And the dogs would love it.

I liked this job, in a strange and horrible way. I liked being out in the wilderness and I liked giving Polo a job. Dogs were meant to work; they went a little crazy if all they were expected to do was entertain their humans. And I liked being of help to people, which finding bodies was when you thought about it. People needed to know the truth about their missing children or parents or whoever, and they needed the comfort of bodies recovered and buried according to their rituals.

Polo and I were trained for tracking the living as well as the dead, but somehow it was the cadaver searches we were assigned to the most. Toby, on the other hand, almost always worked living cases, but Nancy had been out of town when this child went missing, so she wasn't available for the early search teams, and Toby had to make do with bones instead of sniffing the kid's sweater.

See, living people all smell different, and you use an item with a person's individual scent on it in order to set the smell, get the dogs familiar with the exact scent they're tracking. But dead people all smell alike. So all you have to say is "find the bones" and the dogs will let you know when they find any dead human.

It was the finding-the-body part I didn't like very much, and the main reason for that was that the dogs loved it as much as I hated it. Polo loved it on a pure animal level, reveling in the smells and the grue, rolling in the human goop caused by a badly-decayed body, trying to eat the flesh and, in one memorable instance, carrying a decapitated head in his wide maw. I loved my big black bear of a dog, but it was hard to pet him for a little while after that, and if his tongue touched my flesh, I washed immediately.

But I was back on the trail the next week, with a Sunday morning training stint in between. The work had to be done, had to come before my distaste.

We walked a good five miles, mainly in silence on my part, although Don and Sarah talked in low tones. It was as if the kid, the little sister, walked with me and I didn't want to seem frivolous in the face of her loss.

Polo raced ahead, plunged into the brush, sniffed everything, and then ran back to me, urging us to move faster. At one point, he lingered over a cholla cactus wound around with jimson-weed; I stepped gingerly into the desert tangle and made my way toward him, only to find a very ripe jackrabbit corpse.

"Polo," I said, deliberately sharpening my voice, "those are not the bones. Find the bones, Polo. Show me the bones."

He was reluctant to leave his prize, but he really did know the difference between lunch and his job, so he trotted away, albeit not without a few fond looks back at the dead jack. The deputies gave one another surreptitious glances that said, Boy are we wasting our time out here with this big ragmop of a dog. Wish we had the bloodhound.

Well, Polo and I would show them.

I hoped.

The morning sun popped up over the horizon with incredible swiftness, and the desert took on a new and colorful persona. Wildflowers bloomed in profusion, thanks to recent rains; cactus flowers were an improbable fuschia and there were poppies and desert lilies and yucca flowers standing straight as sentries, over six feet tall.

The heat was growing by geometric proportions. I'd drunk half my water already and soaked my bandanna in it to keep the back of my neck cool.

The desert plants didn't care about the heat. They didn't care about anything, with their prickles and their leather skins, the gray-green not-quite-leaves that didn't even look plantlike. There were wildflowers smaller than your tiniest toenail and big yellow blooms on the barrel cacti and the long red-tipped ocotillo. Hawks circled overhead, and for a minute I wondered if we waited long enough, would we see turkey vultures and then we wouldn't even need Polo, we'd just follow the carrion birds to where the child's body lay.

We were going to find a body. I knew it. The hollow place in my stomach knew it. Five days out here; the kid wasn't alive. She couldn't be.

The sound of rapid, joyous barks from up ahead stopped my musing and had me running toward the ironwood tree. Polo bounded up to me and circled me, bumping against me to move me faster. Bouviers are herd dogs, but instead of nipping at the heels of their cows, they push the animals into compliance, as Polo was trying to do now, to me and the deputies.

"He found her?" Don asked, his voice carrying a world of skepticism.

"That's what he's telling us," I replied, moving as quickly as I could in the oppressive heat.

"Show me the bones, Polo," I said, the little shudder of anticipation turning into a full-fledged tremble. "Show me the bones."

Polo skidded on the edge of the wash and headed down the steep incline. I leaned over and had a look. The body lay at the bottom of the arroyo, sprawled in a posture no living creature could have tolerated. Polo barked and pawed the ground, circling the body in a gruesome dance of triumph, crowing over his find and nuzzling the body with his snout.

It was a man. A Mexican, probably an illegal trying to make it into the U.S. His black hair was matted with blood. There were flies all over the place and a smell you didn't have to be canine to recognize.

I stood in stunned silence, then reacted like a handler, reaching into my vest pocket for the goody box. I made my way with slow carefulness down the slope and joined the deputies at the body. I opened my tupperware box and took out a dog treat.

"What are you doing?" Sarah's gray eyes were wide with disbelief. "You think this is a good time to feed your dog?"

"I'm not feeding him," I replied. I leaned as close to the stinking corpse as I could, and held the dog treat in my open hand. Polo bounced and snatched it, then did another circle dance of triumph. "Good dog," I said with forced brightness. "Good Polo. What a good dog. You found the bones, Polo."

I turned back to Sarah. "I'm rewarding him. He has to associate treats with the scent of bodies if he's going to be a good cadaver dog."

"But it's the wrong body."

"He doesn't know that."

I could hear the crackle of Don's radio; he was calling our find in to headquarters.

104 Tales Out of School

Polo jumped up on me. "Oh, you good dog. Oh, you perfect and beautiful beast," I crooned, resolutely keeping my eyes locked on his sweet black face instead of looking at the dead man. I didn't want to see more of what I'd already seen — the horrible movement of the body, which meant that insect life was taking over inside the rapidly decaying corpse.

I was trying to breathe as little as possible; Sarah reached into her vest pocket and pulled out a tiny jar of Vicks. She scooped some out and pushed it under her nose, then handed it to me. I took it with a nod of gratitude and filled my nostrils with the strong scent of menthol, hoping to block out the overpowering odor of human rot.

Don's orders were to remain with the body while Sarah and I made our way back to Ocotillo Wells. We'd make a circle, continuing to search as we headed west.

I had to pull Polo away by brute force; every instinct in his body told him to stay with the dead man, to examine him fully and to — God forbid, but he was a dog, and dogs will be dogs — eat some of him. This I didn't explain to Sarah, somehow becoming as protective of her as I'd felt toward the little girl back at the frame house.

I walked for a while without giving a new order, letting Polo adjust to the fact that he was now heading away from 'the bones' instead of toward them.

I saw the child's guileless blue eyes before me. *Will you find my sister?*

"Sarah?" I stepped up my pace until I strode next to the deputy, who was moving with angry swiftness. "Any news from the base?"

"You mean was the kid at her grandmother's eating cookies and milk? Not hardly. They're sending a helicopter and two more dog teams. Anybody finds that kid, it won't be us. Thanks to that damn body in the wash."

I nodded. I'd known that had to be the case; if there'd been news, Don would have said so. But the little ghost girl walking next to me had to hear it for herself.

I didn't even know her name, yet she was as clearly part of the expedition as Polo and I. The missing girl was Melissa Sue. Ten years old. The child at the base was about eight, although I wasn't much of a kid person, so she could have been seven or nine.

Why didn't I know her name? Why hadn't I asked?

What the hell was I going to say to her if — when? — we found her sister.

I didn't have to say anything. That was the cops' job. But I knew that this time I would. This time I couldn't just load Polo into the van and head home for a much-needed hot shower, leaving the body and the search behind me. Pretending to myself that this had been no more than a practice run, with Body in a Bottle instead of the real thing.

It was time to give Polo his new command. I bent down and spoke into his tiny ear; he reeked of creosote bush and cadaver. "Find the bones, Polo. Go find the bones for me, boy."

He gave his yelp of understanding and bounded into the brush. He was matted with cactus fishhooks and spine clusters and his paws looked as if they hurt from the hard ground, but he set off with an enthusiasm that put Sarah and me to shame. We were spent, demoralized by the body in the wash, and more than ready to pack it in — but for the need to bring the little girl home for her final rest.

We passed mesquite and pencil cactus, sun-wilted evening primrose and century plants, huge feathery palo verde trees at the edge of arroyos, prickly pears six feet tall with giant red balls ready to open into fleshy blooms..

Some people thought the desert was beautiful. I thought it was scary as hell, a dangerous place where only the strong survived, and I felt about as strong as a pillow.

How in God's name was a ten-year-old going to survive out here, even if she was born and brought up in Ocotillo Wells?

We were approaching the town. I could tell because I heard the Interstate's low hum and caught a glimpse of dust rising from the dirt road behind the hamburger joint. More sheriff's cars, I supposed, come to join in what the newspeople would call the massive manhunt. Or maybe the newsvans themselves, each local channel out to get a sound bite for the evening report.

Massive girlhunt.

Where would a little girl go around here? This wasn't like my Michigan girlhood, where there were creeks and parks and trees to climb, secret places only your best pals knew about. There was simply no shade anywhere, no honest-to-God trees to shelter you and let you climb into green, leafy hideaways.

My face was bright hot red despite the slathers of sunscreen and my straw hat. I was out of water, having given most of mine to Polo. We'd been out here five hours, and already we were ready to pack it in.

And Melissa Sue had been missing five days.

There was no way she could have carried five days' worth of water, and despite the recent rains, there weren't enough streams with drinkable water for her to stay alive.

Polo looked discouraged, too. He still sniffed the mesquite and the cactus, rubbed against the desert mistletoe and poked a very cautious nose into the ocotillo, but he moved more slowly and his tongue hung from his mouth as his craving for water grew more intense.

We had to stop. Sarah looked more than ready to take a shade break, and I didn't think there was much point in continuing the hunt. By now the town was in view; I could see the red roof of the hamburger place that was the town's only landmark.

Polo raised his head and sniffed the air. He stood, only his head moving this way and that, clearly trying to capture an elusive scent.

"Can't he hurry up?" Sarah's voice was sharp with fatigue and disappointment.

"I think he's on scent," I replied. "He may have something."

"Oh, come on, we're practically back at base. Every inch of this place has been searched already. It's probably another jackrabbit."

I ignored her and said, "Show me the bones, Polo. Show me the bones."

He gave his yelp of understanding and moved in the direction the scent led him.

You know the expression, being led around by the nose?

That's precisely what Polo looks like when he's on an elusive scent. His nose sniffs the air and he follows it. That simple; the shiny black nose catches a tiny whiff and he moves his head this way and that to make sure he's following the strongest odor.

Scent flows like water. If we could see what dogs smell, we'd see eddies and streams, scents blown on the air like twigs on top of a stream.

He was moving slowly. I liked that; it meant he had something and was being as careful as he could be to track it to the source.

"Show me. Show me the bones."

"There aren't going to be any damn bones."

I didn't usually tell sheriff's deputies to shut the hell up, but this was going to be an exception.

Polo barked. A single, sharp bark, and then he took off running toward a palo verde tree in the distance. I followed at the swiftest pace I could muster, while Sarah brought up a sullen rear.

He circled. He twisted his big black body and wagged his stub of a tail. His ears flattened and he bounded ahead, kicking up dust with his big bearlike paws.

"Find the bones," I called, which was pretty stupid because he was doing just that, but I wanted him to know I understood and appreciated.

Next to the palo verde stood an abandoned well. Polo circled it, then pawed the ground next to it.

"Oh, my God," I cried, racing toward the stone structure. "The kid's in the well."

Polo barked and pawed, lowering his muzzle to the dirt and then pawing again. His unmistakable signal that he'd found the bones.

The child's body was at the bottom of the long stone tunnel. Alice caught in the rabbit-hole, forever in Wonderland.

Sarah called it in on her radio, her voice swelling with triumph, naively pleased at being the one to find the body. In this, she resembled Polo, who did his victory dance, although he was disappointed at not being able to get really close to the corpse. I took out my goody box and went through the reward ritual while I pondered the best way to break the news to the little girl back at the frame house.

And then I saw the jack.

Not a jackrabbit, but a little metal jack, the kind you scoop up after you bounce a rubber ball. I didn't know kids still played with jacks, and there was nothing to indicate how long the jack had lain in the gray desert dust, but the truth stabbed me like a pencil cactus thorn.

The child hadn't been hoping the bloodhound would find her sister. She'd been deathly afraid the bloodhound would unearth the truth. She knew where her sister was, but she'd been afraid to tell her parents.

Two little girls in the desert, playing wherever they could, using the thin shade of the palo verde and the stone well as their special place.

Had the child died instantly from the fall, or had she lain inside, calling for help?

And why hadn't the little sister told her parents? Was the household so abusive that she was more afraid of the punishment than she was of her sister dying? Or was she simply too young to understand the consequences of falling into the well?

I would probably never know. I would go back into town and let Sarah do her cop duty, let the wheels of law enforcement turn with excruciating slowness.

I would put Polo in the back of my van, drive home and give both of us a long, scented bath to wash away the sweat and the smells, and I would write up my report and move on to the next search, the next body.

But I didn't think I'd ever go out tracking again without the little sister at my side, her blue eyes wide, her face pinched with the fear that the dogs would reveal hidden truth she was too afraid to face.

"Good dog, Polo," I said again, but it was hard to praise him for finding out what I hadn't really wanted to know.

This one came out of an experience I had as an administrative law judge, listening to an old woman ramble on about people coming to her house and pushing their way in despite her protests. She wasn't complaining, really, just sort of mentioning the fact that she wasn't strong enough to keep people from walking into her living room and taking what they wanted from her. I found myself for a brief, horrified moment looking at the world through her eyes and realizing how awful it would be to have so little control over one's home and possessions. Then I wondered how it would feel to empathize with such a woman while defending at trial the man accused of ripping her off.

THREE-TIME LOSER

It was my own personal first day of spring. Forget the calendar, forget that forsythia was just starting to bud and the morning still held a lot of winter chill. For me, spring had sprung. I felt like a kid, when choosing red or blue Keds for summer was one of life's great decisions.

The sneakers on my feet were leather Reebok, not red Keds (I always chose red, in spite of Mom's inevitable protest, "But Cassie, blue goes with everything.) And I wasn't back in Ohio playing beside the creek in muddy blue jeans, I was walking across the Brooklyn Bridge, on my way to try a case in Manhattan Supreme Court.

It didn't matter. I felt like a kid, bouncy and light, ready to jump rope, play hopscotch, ride my bike across the county line. My cross-examination suit, my leather briefcase, jury selection notes — none of these got in the way of my feeling like a frisky ten-year-old.

I mounted the steps of the walkway, taking in the full grandeur of the bridge. Gothic arches, massive as cathedral walls, ropes of cable crisscrossed in an intricate web of silver that reflected the pale sunlight. I took a deep breath of East River scented breeze (all right, it was a strong wind), and thought of the creek back home, of the innocent child I'd been.

I know a lot more about innocence now. I just don't see much of it. I'm a criminal lawyer.

It started slowly. First I noticed that the Lower Manhattan skyline, seen through cable webbing, looked as if it was behind bars. Then the huge granite pylons that reached deep underwater and lifted high into the sky, seemed made of cold gray prison stone. The final straw was gazing out at the sweep of harbor, taking in the pewter-colored bay, Governor's Island, Lady Liberty.

Liberty. Something my client, Buckley Carlisle, wasn't likely to have much longer. He was a three-time loser, if you watched old Warner Brothers movies, a persistent felony offender if you didn't.

I hate trying a case I'm going to lose.

But I had to. I was a grownup, with no red Keds and someone else's freedom in my hands.

When I got to the courthouse, I stopped at the ladies' room, changing my Reeboks for red heels that matched my Chanel-style jacket. I untangled my windblown hair, put on crimson lipstick, and transformed myself from tomboy to trial lawyer.

Buckley was already in the hallway, as usual. Not once in our seven-month attorney-client relationship had I ever gotten there first. An uncle in Jamaica had posted bail and paid my fee; I'd frankly expected Buckley to take the next flight to Kingston.

I almost wished he had.

Buckley scared the hell out of me. The guilty ones are easy; you do your best, go home to a hot bath and a cold drink, and forget about them. The innocent you never forget.

Was Buckley innocent? I didn't know. I only knew he didn't act guilty.

Most of my criminal clients come to court — when they *do* come to court — two hours after calendar call, wearing T-shirts with obscene comments and seven earrings in each ear. All they know about the law is that they ain't did nothin' and if I'm supposed to be their lawyer, how come I can't get these charges squashed?

Buckley Carlisle showed up for every appearance, his shoes shined, his nails filed and buffed, smelling vaguely of patchouli, a scent that took me back to Indian print skirts and love beads. He dressed for court in well-cut suits, always with a touch of tropical color in the tie, the handkerchief, like a splash of paint on a cinderblock wall. He always carried the thick paperback lawyers call the "gray book" — a combination Penal Law and Criminal Procedure Law. He looked more like a lawyer than most of the members of the bar who hustled for clients in the hallways of 100 Centre Street.

If Buckley lost this case — if I lost this case — he'd do ten-to-twenty, minimum.

It was time for the spiel.

"Look, Mr. Carlisle," I began, "I know we've been over this before, but I want to be sure you understand what it means if you're found guilty."

"Why you don't call me Buckley today?" My client's face, dark and smooth as a buckeye, settled into a mock pout. "Have I done some thing to offend you, or — " the pout dissolved into a grin of immense charm "— is it that you must call me Mister Carlisle because we speak on such a momentous topic?"

We were leaning against marble walls the color of used chewing gum. Around us, lawyers, defendants, distraught families bustled past, looking for their courtrooms in the maze of Supreme Court.

"Hey," my client urged, spreading out his arms, "like the man say, 'Don' worry, be happy.' "

In spite of myself, I smiled back. "We need to talk seriously."

"And so we must be serious. All right," Buckley conceded, firming his face into a frown of concentration. "I will suppress my natural high spirits and become attentive to your every word. But first, you must let me give you a present in honor of the spring." He brought his arm from behind his back like a small boy hiding a gift from his mother and handed me a red rose in a plastic cylinder.

"Buckley, I —" It wasn't often that words failed me. Words were my medium, my tools. I owned them, the way I owned the hallways and courtrooms I spent my life in. But no client I'd ever represented had thought to give me anything. Most of the time, I didn't even get a thank-you. And now I had a rose. It made what I had to say to Buckley even harder.

"I don't know what to say." To my annoyance, my voice wavered. The rose inside its plastic cage reminded me all too clearly of Buckley behind prison bars: a living thing entombed, the appearance intact, the essence embalmed.

"Say nothing," Buckley advised blithely. "Just smile."

I hate it when men order me to smile. But for Buckley, I smiled. I lifted the rose to my face, drinking in the familiar scent. It wasn't real, of course. Roses in plastic cages lose their true smell and have to be enhanced by essential oils.

I put the rose on top of my briefcase, which rested on the windowsill. "And now to business."

Buckley struck a pose. "Give it to me straight, doc. I can take it."

I hoped he could; this was my last chance to appeal to reason before the jurors were marched in.

"I just want to remind you that you've got two priors on your record, and the DA's out for blood. He's offering three-and-a-half-to-seven on a plea, which is a lot better than the ten-to-twenty you'd get if we blow trial. I know you were just a kid when you took the burglary rap, but the trouble is, the judge didn't give you Youthful Offender treatment. If he had, it wouldn't count against you now. But he didn't, and it does. As to the second crime —"

"As to the second conviction," my client interrupted, "that was a mis-understanding. I'm an 'ardworkin' man with a respectable occupation. I accept the plea of guilty because I am new in this country and am afraid to litigate."

"Even so," I continued, feeling more desperate with every minute that passed, "those prior convictions make you a three-time loser."

"But Cass," Buckley said, his voice pleading, "I done this lady no wrong. I was in jail once, for three long years, and it was like a curse on me. I was like a wild bird lock up in a cage, wings clipped. Are you tellin' me to go back to that?"

"I'm telling you that the DA's got a witness who made a positive ID, who says she saw you in good light for at least fifteen minutes. You say you were home alone, reading a book. I believe you, but that means you have no alibi. Even a Manhattan jury —" Manhattan juries are notoriously liberal, thank God "— may find it hard to acquit."

"Now don't be underestimating my intelligence, Miss Jameson." Carlisle held up a cat-black hand with long, bony fingers. "I am very well aware of the precarious position in which I find myself. But I have no choice. I must go all the way, and I have every confidence in you as my barrister."

"I'm not a barrister —"

"Court's in session," a friendly court officer warned. I stopped into the courtroom in time to hear the bailiff open the court day with the time-honored words: "All rise."

While my client and I had been talking, the courtroom filled with the necessary personnel: judge, assistant district attorney, clerk, and court officers.

The jurors were black, white, Hispanic, Chinese. They were teachers, housewives, one accountant, two postal workers, and a host of other occupations. In an odd way, they were enjoying the performance of their civic duty, like kids on a field trip to the museum.

If I'd been the one on trial, I'd have done anything to keep from putting my fate in their hands. But then the lawyer was never born who truly trusts a jury.

Why did Buckley Carlisle trust them? Why hadn't he flown to Jamaica and hidden out in a cane field? Wasn't that the real reason the rich uncle had posted his bail — to give him a chance to escape?

Buckley had to be innocent — or stupid in the first degree.

"Mrs. Mildred Eldridge," the clerk called out, and a wizened old black woman, leaning on the arm of a court officer, hobbled into the room. Her legs were thin as pipe cleaners; she could hardly have weighed a hundred pounds.

On the one hand, she was one hell of a sympathetic witness. On the other hand, she looked around the courtroom, blinking like a mole. Around her neck, she wore a black cord attached to thick glasses.

The State's chief witness took her oath in a voice that shook as badly as her palsied hand. Her fingers were bent from arthritis; she hunched like a crone.

I glanced at Buckley. "A small smile lifted his lips. "Mrs. Eldridge is one very old lady," he whispered. "Her sight is none too good, you know. I expect you will make a point of this in your cross-examination."

My spirits rose. There was hope after all.

Direct was short and sweet. Just what I'd have done if I'd been the D.A. Put the witness on, let her tell the story, and hope to hell she didn't have to endure too much cross.

The story was sad but simple. Mrs. Eldridge had been at home — she was always at home, tending her twin brother, who was dying of cancer in the only bedroom. In fact, he had died since the crime, making her the only witness the people had.

Her doorbell rang. She ignored it. In her Harlem neighborhood, ignoring the doorbell was the best policy. It rang again, persistently. She went to answer, knowing how her brother hated noise.

There was a man at the door. A black man. A young man, well-dressed and well-spoken, in a singsong Jamaican accent. He told her he had a delivery for an upstairs neighbor. She didn't know what neighbor he was talking about, and she didn't want to let him in, but the next thing she knew, he was in.

He was in, standing at the door, showing her the beautiful quilt that had been delivered to Mrs. Jacquard on the fifth floor. Mrs. Eldridge didn't know Mrs. Jacquard well; how could she talk to someone who only spoke Creole

French? But she knew the name and said, yes, she'd hold the delivery for her neighbor.

The young man was so friendly, so willing to hold the quilt open for her to see, that she almost considered buying it herself. The young man said she could, said the quilt was cash on delivery, and if Mrs. Jacquard wasn't interested enough to be home when it came, why it could be sold to anyone who'd pay the fifty dollars.

Fifty dollars. That was the rub. She finally told the young man she couldn't spend that kind of money, not possibly, and saw him fold the colorful quilt back into a thick square, then step out of her doorway. He'd decided not to leave it after all, but to give Mrs. Jacquard another try.

When she went into the bedroom to give her brother his medicine, she noticed the missing jewelry box. The little TV she'd bought him with her Social Security money was gone too, and so was the silver frame with her parents' pictures.

"I felt like the biggest fool in the U-nited States of America," Mrs. Eldridge said. "Gawking at that there quilt while all the time he was holding it up so some thief could crawl behind it into the bedroom and steal me blind."

The blanket scam. One of the oldest cons in the world.

The climax of her testimony was ADA Bernstein's asking her if she recognized anyone in the courtroom. Mildred Eldridge stood up, grasped the railing of the witness box with one hand, and pointed her twisted finger at Buckley Carlisle.

"That's him," she said, her voice stronger than at any other point. "That's the man who done kep' me at the door, talking that West Indian trash, while the other one rob me. Took the onliest treasures I had left in this world. My opal ring my Mama give me when I wasn't but fifteen years of age. My pearls from Aunt Ruby, she died after I come up North."

I objected. It wasn't a popular move. Juror number five glared as though I'd slapped the old woman. It wasn't even a legal objection; I just wanted to detour the witness' trip down memory lane.

Not only was I overruled, but the witness kept on going as though I hadn't said a word.

"How could you take them pictures?" She asked Buckley directly, as though they were the only two people in the room. He stared back blandly, his face an ebony moon. "They *my* folks, not your'n. I expect you pawned the frame, which don't make no never-mind to me. But if you could see your way clear to letting me have my pictures back, I'd be very much obliged, thank you kindly." Her voice had taken on a feisty edge that had juror number seven, a black postal worker, giving her a surreptitious grin.

I glanced at the ADA. Whatever Saul Bernstein's original intention, he wasn't about to stop his witness while she was winning over the jury.

"Your Honor," I pointed out, "this witness isn't answering questions, she's giving a speech."

"Sustained." A technical victory. Bernstein immediately put another question to his witness.

"Were those the only photographs of your parents in your possession?" he asked. It was leading as hell, but I didn't dare object. I'd asked for a question; I'd gotten a question.

"Yessir, they was. Since my albums that I brought all the way from Alabama was stole in a burglary, I disremember how long ago. All my family was in them albums, people been dead fifty year and more. Gone now, all gone."

At another time, in another place, I'd have felt sorry for Mildred Eldridge. There was no doubt that somebody — and in her long, hard life, maybe more than one somebody had taken from her things she loved. But it wasn't Buckley. That was what I had to keep my eye on. It wasn't Buckley.

"And how much did you say you paid for the television set you bought your brother?"

She'd already said it once, but Bernstein was on a streak and he knew it; the jurors were eating it up.

"I done told you that already, mister. Ain't I said I bought it from Honest Kareem's House of Appliances on Hundred-Twenty-Fifth Street? Ain't I said he give me the special senior citizen discount, so's it only come to a hundred-eighty-nine dollars and sixty-four cents? And that was two Social Securities, which I didn't mind giving up on account of I had my late husband's benefits and I knew how much poor Amos would enjoy that little set. Wasn't no bigger than a picture postcard, but he could see all his stories and the Hour of Power on Sunday."

Finally, the words I'd been dying to hear: "No further questions."

I rose, thinking fast as I walked past the prosecution table to about the middle of the jury box. The direct had been interesting for what hadn't been said: no description of the man beyond the fact that he was tall and spoke with a West Indian accent. How much had the nearsighted old lady really seen of the man who kept her talking at the door?

One of the choices a defense lawyer makes is how long the witness stays on the stand. Given this one's ability to win points with the jury, I decided to hit Mrs. Eldridge with a few questions, hardball her about her eyesight, question her ability to observe and remember, and sit down.

"Mrs. Eldridge, did you call the police after the robbery?"

She nodded. "I did. And it took them a whole hour and fifteen minutes to come. I could have been dead on my kitchen floor all that time for all they cared."

"And when the police came, did they ask you what happened?"

" 'Course they did. They wasn't stupid."

"And what did you tell them?"

"Told them what I told this here court. Told them the truth, as God is my witness."

I preferred to leave God out of this, so I stopped warming up and threw the pitch.

"Did you describe the man to the police?"

She nodded. It was the first time she hadn't given an answer in words, usually more than the question called for. "Did you tell them how tall he was?"

Another nod.

"And didn't you say he could have been anywhere from five feet seven to six feet tall?"

This time the judge ordered her to stop nodding and give her answer in words. She grunted a grudging "yes."

"And you told the police he spoke with a West Indian accent, is that right?"

"Yes."

"Isn't it true, Mrs. Eldridge, that those details were the only ones you were able to give the police?" I'd seen the police reports, so I knew how meager her description had been.

ADA Bernstein's objection was sustained. Good. That meant I could mention one by one all the details that should have been in a good description and show the jury they'd been missing in Mrs. Eldridge's.

"Did you tell them how old the man was?"

"I said he was maybe twenty, maybe thirty. Hard to tell with young peoples."

"Maybe twenty, maybe thirty. That's a big difference, Mrs. Eldridge."

Bernstein's objection was drowned out by his witness' answer: "To you, maybe. You still a young girl. When you gets to my age —"

"And how old is that, Mrs. Eldridge?"

"Be seventy-six next birthday, if the Lord spares me —"

"Did you tell the police how long the man's hair was?"

She stared at Buckley. "Short, just like now."

"But you didn't tell that to the detectives, did you, Mrs. Eldridge? You said you didn't remember how long his hair was, isn't that right?"

"I only know he didn't have them dirty dreadlocks, like most of them has."

"When you say *them,* Mrs. Eldridge, who do you mean?"

"You all know who I mean. Them peoples from the Islands what come up here to New York and lay around all day smokin' reefer."

I looked over at Buckley, ready to stop any outburst he might make. He sat calmly, his neatly manicured hand resting on the gray book as though it were a Bible.

Juror number ten, a thirtyish woman who'd answered my *voir dire* questions with a marked West Indian accent, frowned.

I decided the point had been made, and moved on. "I notice you wear glasses, ma'am. Do you need them all the time, or just for reading?"

"I needs them all the time." The answer was so low the judge asked her to repeat it. "They bifocals. For far-away and close-up both."

"And just how far away was this man you say spent fifteen minutes talking to you?"

"He closer than you is now."

I started walking slowly toward the witness box. "Stop me," I told the witness, "when I get to where he stood."

One giant step. Mother, may I? Two giant steps.

"Stop," the witness ordered. I was three feet away. I said so to the court reporter, and the distance was stipulated into evidence.

"Three feet away. And yet he could be twenty or thirty? Five feet tall or six feet?" Before Bernstein could object to my giving my summation during cross, I asked, "Mrs. Eldridge, you said you wear your glasses all the time, is that right?"

She nodded vigorously, on solid ground again. "All the time."

I went in for the kill. "Then why are they on a cord, ma'am? Isn't that so you can take them off, the way you have now?"

Bernstein was on his feet, objecting, but I had the jury hanging out of the box, so I kept talking.

"What kind of light do you have in your kitchen, Mrs. Eldridge?"

"One of them flourescent lights. Like a ring."

"And was the light on?"

"It was on." Her old eyes shifted away from mine, hiding something. I didn't know what, but I knew it could be important. Dangerous, too. Rule Number One in cross is never ask a question you don't know the answer to.

I decided to break it. "Do you know how many watts that flourescent bulb is, Mrs. Eldridge?"

"How'm I supposed to know something like that?"

"Is there a window in the kitchen, or was the bulb the only light?"

"There's a window on the airshaft."

She was still hiding something. Her mumbled answers and averted eyes told me as much. But what?

I glanced at Buckley. He leaned forward in his seat, eyes firmly fixed on Mrs. Eldridge. When he saw me looking, he began to blink, slowly at first, then faster. Nerves, I decided. No wonder, the time he was facing.

I'd had a flourescent light in my kitchen in Greenwich Village, before I moved to Brooklyn. I remembered how annoying it was when it started to burn out, the way the light blinked brightly, then darkened.

"Mrs. Eldridge," I said, my voice sounding more confident than I felt, "that flourescent light was burning out, wasn't it?"

She hung her head and mumbled an answer I couldn't hear.

"May I remind the court that the witness is under oath." I said it softly, but it got the desired result.

Mildred Eldridge raised her head, looked me in the eye, and said, "It's the truth. That light was flickering something awful. Like the oil lamps down South when I was a child. Nobody to fix it, what with Amos laid up and that super no damn good."

Bingo — bad description, bad eyesight, bad lighting. All I needed were a couple more questions to nail it home to the jury, and Buckley was as good as free.

"Mrs. Eldridge, when you first opened the door to the man, he said he had a delivery for your neighbor, is that right?"

"Yes, and I knew right off he was trouble, on account of it ain't the kind of building where peoples get deliveries. The elevator usually broke, so nobody want to come all the way up the stairs to the fifth floor."

"But this man did?"

"He say he took the steps on account of the lift was busted. He meant the elevator, I suppose."

A tiny bell went off somewhere in my head. *Lift,* not *elevator.* Just as Buckley had called me a barrister instead of a lawyer. I brushed the thought aside. Didn't most West Indians use some British expressions?

Mrs. Eldridge continued. "He asked me to take the quilt for the lady. Not that I didn't want to be neighborly, but you don't never know who be coming into your house. But there wasn't nothing I could do," she said with a sigh. Her eyes filled. "It wasn't the first time they got in on me. Last year some mens come, said they from the in-surance. They wasn't from no insurance, they just got in to rob an old lady. Year before that, I was broke into, they got my wedding ring and everything."

"Move to strike, Your Honor." Desperation play, but what else could I do? "Not responsive to the question."

"Your Honor," Bernstein protested, "counsel opened the door She just doesn't like what walked in."

"Overruled," the Judge said with a smile. The smile was for me; that was *my* line Bernstein had used.

"You don't know how it is," Mildred Eldridge went on. "How it is to live in that house with a dying man — and before that, it was my second husband Prescott lying in that selfsame bed, coughing his lungs out — and knowing that any time they wants to peoples can come and push they way in and take anything because you ain't got the strength to stop them."

"Your Honor!" I was practically shouting. "Move to strike. There's no question before this witness."

His Honor granted the motion. Big victory. The jury had heard every word and weren't about to forget the image of old Mrs. Eldridge alone in her apartment, waiting to be ripped off.

The trouble was, neither would I. Who was the three-time loser in this case — Buckley Carlisle or Mildred Eldridge?

I went back to my strong point. "Mrs. Eldridge, isn't it true that the only things you remember for sure about the man in the doorway is that he was tall and spoke with a West Indian accent?"

"I don't appreciate nobody coming into my house and taking what's rightly mine, especially when they ought to have stayed where they belong, not come up from the Islands to rob decent folk. Ain't they enough crooks in this city without we bring in more?"

"Mrs. Eldridge, that's no answer to the question." I spoke loudly, wondering whether the old woman's hearing was as bad as her sight.

"And he smelled funny, too." Juror number ten didn't like that at all. ADA Bernstein looked as though he couldn't wait for the one o'clock lunch break. Knowing Judge Rodriguez, it would come any minute now. He'd been known to break for lunch in mid-sentence if the clock struck one.

"He smelled like that sweet oil the Muslims sell in the subway," Mildred Eldridge went on. "Like incense."

Like patchouli. Like Buckley Carlisle.

It suddenly struck me that the blinking eyes he'd shown me during my questions about Mrs. Eldridge's flourescent light had nothing at all to do with nerves. He'd blinked to lead me into asking the very questions that had set the seal on my successful cross. He'd known that bulb was flickering, and he'd known it because he'd been the man in the doorway, holding the quilt.

I was still dazed, my mind unable to form another question, when the judge called the lunch recess.

Don't get me wrong. I've represented guilty clients before. It's a part of the job I've learned to accept. But not this time. Not with the picture of Mildred Eldridge opening her door to men she knew would take from her, yet having no choice but to let them in.

I had no choice either. I had to win this case for Buckley Carlisle. I had to continue grinding Mildred Eldridge into tomato paste, destroying her credibility with the jury, so Buckley could go free. It was my job. My grownup job.

I walked back to the defense table, taking my place next to Buckley without looking at him, staring straight ahead as the young ADA helped Mildred Eldridge off the stand, as the bailiff led the jurors to the jury room, as the judge left the bench.

The smell of patchouli that clung to my client's clothes sickened me; it no longer reminded me of innocent flower children.

There was a lot I wanted to say to Buckley. I said none of it.

My client had no such reticence. "Cass, your cross-examination was most satisfactory," he said, his smile wide and welcoming. "I especially liked the way you asked her about the glasses."

Sure he did. Buckley had chanced trial not because he was innocent, but because he'd known Mildred Eldridge was an old lady who couldn't make her identification stick any more than she could keep thieves out of her house. Even worse, there was no rich uncle in Jamaica; Buckley Carlisle's bail had been posted out of the proceeds of his ripoffs. Mildred Eldridge was paying my fee.

"I'll see you after lunch," was all I answered.

Lunch was a walk to City Hall Park, where I tossed the plastic-caged rose into the first garbage can I saw.

I knew how Mildred Eldridge felt — like the biggest fool in the U-nited States of America. Buckley Carlisle's charm, his smile, his plastic rose had flim-flammed me into thinking him an exotic tropical fish instead of a killer shark.

I sat on a beach next to an old man feeding pigeons, watched a group of pro-day-care demonstrators march around City Hall, and thought long and hard. Long and hard and without result. All I got was cold — it still wasn't really spring — and hungry. No brilliant ideas came to me.

I didn't want to win this case. I had to win this case. Not only was it my job, but Buckley's familiarity with the gray book meant he'd know if I fudged. He'd have grounds for appeal if his lawyer didn't defend him with all the vigor he was entitled to under the Constitution.

I believe in the Constitution. It's what keeps me going through all the guilty pleas, all the suppression hearings, all the sentencings of my work life. But I also believed in Mildred Eldridge.

Back in the courtroom, it took a while to round up stray jurors, and get all the players back into position. While we waited, Buckley showed me some notes he'd made.

"I want you to ask this woman how it is she can be so certain I am the man who robbed her," he said. His tone was firm; there was none of the jokiness of our morning talk.

His skeleton hand rested on the gray book. I wondered how I could have seen its presence as a token of innocence. If I hadn't been snowed by his charming smile and smooth British talk, I'd have known it for what it was: the sign of a jailhouse lawyer.

"Buckley," I began patiently, "that's the kind of question a freshman in law school knows better than to ask. It's too openended. The witness could say anything."

"I want you to ask her. She's an ignorant old woman. She picks on me because I am Jamaican, don't you know? She say all Jamaicans lay about smokin' ganja day and night. She is rotten with hate, like a mango in the sun. Ask her why she thinks it is me. Ask her."

There's a story every law student learns in evidence class. Two men had a fight. One bit off the other's nose. A witness was asked several questions about the event, all of which he answered by admitting he hadn't seen the nose bitten off. The defense lawyer made the fatal mistake of asking One

Too Many Questions: "If you didn't see him bite the nose off, how do you know he did it?"

The classic answer: "I saw him spit it out."

Buckley Carlisle was begging me to ask One Too Many Questions.

If I held firm, refused his request, we'd win the case. If I did as he asked, I ran the risk of snatching defeat from the jaws of victory.

I did it. I rose to my feet, approached the witness box, and asked Mildred Eldridge how it was she could be so certain Buckley Carlisle was the man who kept her in the doorway.

"It was his hands, Miss. You can always tell by they hands. See, I used to be a manicurist before my own hands done twisted up so bad." She looked down at her fingers, gnarled as roots, then back up at me.

"I notices hands. How long the fingers is, how well they be kept, how big the half-moons in the nails are. In the old days, when I worked at Bethea's Beauty Shop in Harlem, I used to put polish on the girls' fingers and leave the half-moons white. That's the way they liked it in them days. So maybe I couldn't tell you about his hair or nothing, but I could tell you them hands right down to the fingernails."

She proceeded to do so. I objected, of course, telling the judge the answer wasn't responsive. Once again, Saul Bernstein, grinning broadly, reminded me that I'd opened the door.

The jurors got to inspect Buckley's hands. They probably also smelled the patchouli. Anyway, they were out less than two hours before they came in with a conviction.

It was tough hearing the click of handcuffs on Buckley's wrists. That's when you know it's final, when you hear that click.

He asked me to slip the gray book between his hands as they led him away. I had no doubt he'd be boning up on appellate practice very soon, and that the first point he'd raise was incompetence of trial counsel. The record would show I'd asked Mildred Eldridge a monumentally dumb question; it wouldn't show my client begged me to ask it.

Some days it's hard being a grownup.

I was thrilled to be asked to impersonate John Watson by writing a story about Sherlock Holmes in Holmes for the Holidays. *I was living in Northern California's wine country, so the idea of a California connection appealed to me. The Irish defense lawyer recalls John Dickson Carr's* Patrick Butler for the Defence; *I hope to bring him back in another story some day, with or without Holmes and Watson. I did have the honor of writing a second Holmes story for the companion volume,* More Holmes for the Holidays.

THE ADVENTURE OF THE ANGEL'S TRUMPET

"Really, Watson," Sherlock Holmes exclaimed in a deprecating tone as he peered over my shoulder, "the affair you have chosen to chronicle can scarcely be termed an adventure. I did little more than sit in a draughty courtroom listening to an interminable series of lies. Indeed," he went on, "my brother Mycroft could have solved the case perfectly well without ever leaving his chair at the Diogenes Club."

"But, Holmes," I protested, "without your presence in the case, an innocent young woman would surely have hanged. And the fact that you managed to clear her name even though you were not called in until the eleventh hour is the most remarkable fact of all. Surely such circumstances qualify as an adventure of a particularly intellectual sort."

"Perhaps you are right," my friend agreed with a sigh. "I fancy I played a small part in the satisfactory outcome of the affair of the angel's trumpet. And the case itself was not without points of interest and even of instruction."

The events that precipitated Miss Charmian Carstairs' trial for the murder of her grandfather began in December and culminated in the week in which Christmas festivities were at their height. During that time, Holmes and I were engaged in a most delicate business on the Sussex downs; we knew little of the events which would later catapult my friend into one of the most bizarre cases of his distinguished career. Thus it was not until some six months had passed and the young lady stood in the dock facing a charge of murder that the affair thrust itself onto his consciousness.

"Yes, Watson, you are correct," Holmes remarked, seemingly apropos of nothing. My friend and fellow-lodger lounged upon the sofa in an attitude of extreme languor, wearing his purple dressing-gown and smoking a pipeful of the most unpleasantly aromatic tobacco ever imported from Virginia. I had lately finished reading the morning papers, which lay scattered at my feet.

"It is a terrible business," he went on, speaking in low, drawling tones, as if the very formation of words was too much for him, "this murder of a grandfather by his newly-discovered granddaughter. One would think the natural bonds of filial piety would overcome even the most mercenary motives, and yet we see the young woman in the dock."

"But, Holmes," I protested, "I have said nothing concerning the case in question. However did you know I was contemplating that horrible business?"

"You had lately put down the morning-paper, which carries a very full if only marginally accurate account of the affair. You then directed your gaze at the miniature of your own grandfather, which reposes upon the secretary. You proceeded to heave a sigh. Surely the meanest intelligence could ascertain that you were thinking of the Carstairs case and wondering how any grandchild could be so unnatural."

"Yes," I admitted. It seemed absurdly simple now that Holmes had explained the reasoning behind his remark. "It appears a wholly cut-and-dried affair, does it not? There appears no room for doubt that Charmian Carstairs poisoned her grandfather immediately upon being informed that she was to be his sole heir."

"No room for doubt indeed, Watson, and yet I fancy the barrister defending Miss Carstairs will exert himself to the utmost to obtain an acquittal."

"Mr. O'Bannion is celebrated for his eloquence," I remarked. "Some call him the Great Defender."

"He is equally well-known," my friend amended, with a touch of acerbity, "as 'that confounded Irishman.'"

I have seldom attempted to duplicate my amazing friend's ability to deduce facts from the most insignificant of details, but I attempted a foray into such a deduction on this occasion. "You have had dealings with Mr. O'Bannion, I take it."

"Excellent, Watson," Holmes replied. "I have not wasted my talents on your education after all. Yes," he continued, his face becoming grave, "I had the misfortune to be in the witness box when Mr. O'Bannion was counsel for the defence. I gave my evidence in a most straight-forward and logical manner, while he proceeded to twist and obfuscate and generally obscure the truth. In the end, he was responsible for the acquittal of the most accomplished jewel thief in London."

"Well," I replied stoutly, "he will have his work cut out for him if he intends to do the same for Miss Carstairs."

The doorbell rang. As it was still quite early in the morning, I raised an inquiring eyebrow. "A client, at this hour?"

"Pray instruct Mrs. Hudson to send the visitor away, no matter what his name or how urgent his errand," Holmes said in a voice that brooked no disagreement. "I have worked night and day for the past fortnight and am disinclined to exert myself on another case at the moment."

Mrs. Hudson led the visitor into the room. His curly brick-red hair and humorous face marked him an Irishman; his severely-cut black coat and trousers marked him a professional man.

"Mr. Holmes," the visitor began, "You must help me. A young lady's life depends upon it."

"And you are —" I inquired, drawing myself up and glaring at the man who would command my friend's services without so much as stating his name.

"Why, Watson," Holmes cried, "I cannot believe your obtuseness. Surely you recognize our visitor from the accounts you have lately read in the *Globe-Dispatch*. For he is none other than the legal pettifogger who succeeded against all reason in convincing a jury of twelve good men and true to disregard my testimony, the man who held me up to ridicule before that same jury, the man who holds the fate of Charmian Carstairs in his dishonest hands."

The Irishman bowed as if Holmes' words were the most fulsome compliments. He smiled broadly and finished   the introduction.

"Kevin O'Bannion, at your service, sir," the Irishman said, turning his attention to me. There was but a hint of brogue in his speech; he had taken a first at Oxford and could speak when he chose with an accent worthy of the Archbishop of Canterbury.

"At my service, indeed," Holmes scoffed. He waved the visitor away with a petulant hand. "Pray remove yourself from my doorstep at the earliest opportunity, Mr. O'Bannion. I have neither the time nor the inclination to bandy words with you."

"I've not come here to bandy words, Mr. Holmes," the barrister cried, his florid face reddening. "My visit here is a matter of life and death to the young woman I have the honour to represent."

"Life and death, indeed," Holmes replied. He jumped from the sofa with remarkable agility for someone who had appeared so lacking in energy, and stood before the fire, rubbing his hands. "Your client will most assuredly hang if she is convicted of murdering Sir Wilfred."

"Mr. Holmes, she is innocent," O'Bannion replied. He placed a large hand over his heart and repeated the words in thrilling tones that would have done justice to an organ. "She is innocent, sir, as God is my witness."

"Well," Holmes replied briskly, "that must make a nice change from your usual clientele."

The Irishman's ruddy face fell with comic swiftness. "You must help me, Mr. Holmes. Only you can unravel this tangled skein of evidence and help me prove that Miss Carstairs did not poison her grandfather."

"You seek my help?" Holmes inquired in a tone of injured acerbity. "You seek the help of a man you described to a British jury as 'an interfering, meddling amateur'?"

O'Bannion had the grace to blush. As he was very fair of skin, the blush was a deep rose that suffused his entire face. Although he dressed like a Regency dandy, his features and build were those of a common hod-carrier.

"Mr. Holmes, I beg of you," he said earnestly, "do not refuse Miss Carstairs the aid she requires because of ill-feeling between us."

Holmes raised a single eyebrow. "Ill-feeling? Do you think permitting a criminal to go free rouses in my breast nothing more significant than ill-feeling, sir?"

The Irishman waved away Holmes' words and said, "Come, Mr. Holmes, all I ask is that you and Dr. Watson attend the trial and listen to the evidence. I confess I can make nothing of it that will help my client, and yet I am convinced that she did not poison her grandfather."

"She is the sole beneficiary of her grandfather's will," Holmes pointed out. "He had but lately altered that will in her favor, disinheriting his other relations. She alone had the motive to poison Sir Wilfred."

"Mr. Holmes," the barrister proclaimed, "I would stake my not inconsiderable reputation on the fact that that pure, sweet angel did nothing of the kind."

It did not require the powers of a Sherlock Holmes to deduce that the celebrated barrister had fallen victim to the spell of the fairer sex. I found myself looking forward to meeting the object of O'Bannion's admiration.

Holmes knotted his brow in thought. "I will admit," he said at last, "that the case presents some features which are not entirely devoid of interest."

"But, Holmes," I cried, "the trial begins this very morning. How is it possible to conduct a proper investigation six months after the murder?"

"There is, I fear, no question of an investigation, Dr. Watson," the Irishman explained with an air of apology. "I daresay I should have sought your assistance sooner, but only now do I realize the overwhelming extent of the evidence against my client. I urge you to come to court and hear the testimony, to suggest lines of questioning I may pursue on cross-examination, and to assist me in conveying to the jurors a true explanation of the baffling events that occurred on the night of December 22d last."

"Do you mean to suggest," I inquired, my breast swelling with indignation on my friend's behalf, "that Holmes investigate this crime six months after it has occurred, with no opportunity to visit the scene of the crime or to interrogate witnesses directly?"

O'Bannion had the grace to look abashed. "I agree the case is a difficult one," he began, "but under the circumstances —"

"Difficult?" I repeated. "It is more than merely difficult, man. It is impossible!"

Holmes turned his attention from the fire; for the first time since the unsatisfactory conclusion to the curious affair of the Cypriot banker and the seven pug dogs, the light of battle gleamed in his dark eyes.

"Impossible, Watson?" he echoed. "Surely nothing is impossible where human intelligence is applied."

Less than an hour later Holmes and I sat in a draughty room in Holloway Prison. Seated across from us at the plain wooden table was a spirited young woman with glossy black hair and speaking gray eyes. She wore a shapeless gray smock and was without adornment of any kind, yet her face was as exotically lovely as a tropical flower growing against all odds in an English garden.

"Miss Carstairs," Holmes began, "I have agreed to place my small talents at the disposal of your attorney." He nodded at O'Bannion, who stood in a corner, arms folded, having agreed with bad grace to remain in the background while Holmes questioned his client. "But before I undertake to examine the evidence against you, I wish to hear your story from your own lips."

The young woman nodded. "It is a story well-known to the newspaper-reading public by this time, I believe," she said, "but I will recount it as briefly as I can."

Her voice was low and well-modulated, marred only by her American accent, which tended to flatten the vowels and elide some of the consonants. "I was born in California," she began, "but my father came from England. He was the son of the late Sir Wilfred Carstairs, but he and my grandfather quarrelled, so he emigrated to America when he was a young man. He traveled extensively and held a great number of jobs in the West. Sowing his wild oats, Mother always used to say."

"Your mother was an American?" Holmes inquired.

Miss Carstairs nodded. "Her people were French," she explained. "Her name was Madeleine Duclos, and her father owned a vineyard in the Sonoma Valley. When my father married her, he went to work for Grand-pere in the winery. Papa was very fond of growing things, and became great friends with Mr. Burbank in Santa Rosa."

The expression on Holmes' face was one of disappointment. "Then your father had nothing to do with gold mining?" he inquired. We had but lately made the acquaintance of a lady from San Francisco named Hatty Doran, and Holmes had been quite taken with her accounts of claim-jumping in the American West.

"Really, Mr. Holmes," Miss Carstairs replied with evident amusement, "you have formed the most outlandish ideas about my homeland. I live in a fertile valley studded with lovely little towns and criss-crossed by farms and vineyards. There may be gold in the mountains," she went on, "but for us the gold is on the vines. California will someday produce the best wines in the world."

Holmes said nothing to this extraordinary boast, but a quirk of his mouth indicated serious doubts about the young lady's knowledge of vintage wines.

The dark Mediterranean eyes took on a faraway cast. "I miss my home," she said with a simplicity that touched me deeply. "I miss the scent of redwood trees at night. I miss the sunshine gleaming off the grapevines. I miss the blue skies and the cool mornings and the misty fog between the hills. I don't know how you can bear to live in this damp, gloomy place — but then, of course, you have never seen California."

As the only place on earth that might be considered damper and gloomier than England was Kevin O'Bannion's native land, I doubted the Irishman's evident infatuation with his client would bear fruit unless the man was willing to consider expatriation.

"Your father never renewed contact with his family, Miss Carstairs?" Holmes asked, bringing the conversation back to the terrible events of December 22.

The young woman shook her head. "No," she replied sadly. "It was the dearest wish of his life that he would someday be reconciled with his father. Indeed, he talked of it often, particularly during the Christmas season. He told me all about the grand Christmas feast his family prepared every year. All the servants and tenants would be invited into the dining hall, where glasses of wine would be poured and a toast drunk."

The girl's face glowed when she talked of her father. "Papa loved California," she said, "but he was always a little bit melancholy at Christmas-time. He wished more than anything else for a real English Christmas like the ones he'd known as a child."

"Your father did not live to fulfill this wish," Holmes said with deliberate bluntness.

Charmian Carstairs shook her head. "My parents died when their carriage plunged off a narrow road into a cañon near our home," she explained.

"When your parents died, you wrote to Sir Wilfred," Holmes continued. His elbows rested on the scarred table between us and the young lady; his slender fingers were steepled. "Pray tell me what made you do that."

"I thought my grandfather should know that his son was dead," the American said. "And I was curious. I wanted to know my father's family in the same way I knew my mother's. I suppose I was searching for a part of myself."

"Sir Wilfred's reply to your letter included an invitation to visit him in London," Holmes prompted.

"Yes," the young woman replied. "I was to stay a month, through the Christmas holidays."

"It would appear you and your grandfather became quite fond of one another," remarked Holmes.

The pale face lit with pleasure. "Oh, yes, Mr. Holmes," she said with enthusiasm. "We took to one another at once. He loved hearing me talk about Mr. Burbank's work and about the interesting plants we have in California. And I enjoyed spending time in the conservatory with him."

"You brought him several treasures from your native land," Holmes said. "That was most kind of you."

"I brought dates and dried figs and walnuts — I could not bring fresh fruit, of course. And I brought cuttings and seeds from Mr. Burbank."

"There were seeds from the plant known as 'Angel's Trumpet,' were there not?"

The young woman nodded. "Its botanical name is *datura sacra*. It is, strictly speaking, not a native of California. It was introduced from Mexico, and it is very showy. The blossoms are quite large and they hang from the branches like great white trumpets. Grandfather particularly requested that I bring him seeds so that he could grow his own Angel's Trumpet in his conservatory."

I entered the conversation for the first time. "The seeds are quite poisonous," I remarked. "Were you aware of that fact when you brought them from America?"

"Of course," she replied. "Any competent horticulturist knows the properties of the plants she works with. Angel's Trumpet is related to jimsonweed and nightshade. The entire plant is toxic, but the seeds are particularly so."

Holmes turned to the barrister and explained, "The toxicity of *datura sacra*, commonly known as sacred datura, results from the presence of the alkaloids hyoscyamine, atropine, and scopolamine."

O'Bannion nodded. "The celebrated Dr. Hopgood is expected to testify for the prosecution," he replied glumly. "I do not anticipate that his testimony will be favorable to the defence."

"He is England's premier toxicologist," I remarked. "I shall be quite interested in what he has to say."

"The symptoms of datura poisoning are particularly horrible," Holmes remarked, in a manner that might have been considered callous by one who did not know him. "The sufferer feels a dryness of mouth, and a great thirst. The skin reddens, the pupils dilate. The patient suffers hallucinations and disturbed vision. The pulse races, the patient grows increasingly delirious and may appear insane. The final stages involve convulsions and then coma and death."

The young lady's face paled; she swayed slightly, but did not flinch. "Mr. Holmes," O'Bannion cried, abandoning his post in the corner and rushing to his client's side, "kindly remember that you are speaking to a lady."

The lady in question was made of sterner stuff than her defence counsel believed; she waved away his protests and said in a calm tone, "Indeed, the plant is called *datura sacra* because the natives of Mexico use it in their rituals. Taken in minute quantities, it produces visions. Taken in larger quantities, it produces death."

"It is a horrible way to die," I remarked.

"It is a death no man should endure," Holmes replied. His eyes remained fixed on Charmian Carstairs' beautiful, exotic face.

"It is a death I did not cause," the young lady said with calm firmness.

"And yet you profited from it," Holmes persisted. "You were your grandfather's sole heir, and you were aware of that fact because the late Sir Wilfred announced the change in his will to all at the dinner table the night before he died."

"He said something of the kind, but I didn't believe he really meant to do it," she protested. "I thought if I talked to him, he might change his mind. I had no need of his money; my father left me well-off and my Grand-pere in California promised me a share in the family vineyard as my dowry when I marry. So I had no need of Grandfather Carstairs' money, and I was sorry to see the true heirs cut out of the will."

"Were you, Miss Carstairs?" Holmes asked with palpable disbelief. "Had Miss Letitia Carstairs and Mr. Cyril Carstairs been so good to you that you felt obliged to intercede on their behalf?"

"No, on the contrary, they were horrid to me, as you well know," she replied with a show of that spirit one associates with the daughters of the former colonies. "Miss Carstairs referred to me as 'a baggage' and Mr. Carstairs called me an 'Amazon from an uncivilized country.' But they had lived with Grandfather for years and had expectations of him, and I didn't think it was right for them to be left with nothing."

"But before you could discuss the matter with your grandfather, he died by poisoning," Holmes retorted. His tone was so palpably skeptical as to border on the offensive. O'Bannion, who stood next to his client in an attitude of protectiveness, bristled but remained silent.

"Yes, but I had nothing to do with his death!" the young woman cried. Tears sprang into her eyes; she turned her face away and said, "If you do not believe me, then leave me alone to face my fate in the courtroom. I can endure this questioning no longer."

"Mr. Holmes, this is enough!" the barrister cried. "I did not invite you here to badger my client but to help her."

"And what of the box, Miss Carstairs?" Holmes inquired with deadly gentleness. His eyes bored into Charmian Carstairs' face; he ignored totally the indignant Irishman.

"What then of the box and the things it contained?"

The lovely oval face paled and the large dark eyes widened as the young woman gazed earnestly into my friend's face. "As God is my witness, Mr. Holmes," she said in a low, thrilling voice, "I knew nothing of that box, nothing at all."

"And yet you brought it to your grandfather," Holmes persisted.

"I brought it," the young lady whispered at last. "I brought it, but I was ignorant of its contents. I did not know what that box contained until the morning my grandfather's body was discovered in the study. And even now, Mr. Holmes," she continued, her eyes pleading for understanding, "even now that I know what items were in the box, I still do not know what they mean."

"And what of the legend on the box itself?" Holmes persisted. "What of the letters O.G.D., which appeared on the cover? What do they signify?"

The Irishman could stand it no longer. He drew himself up and signalled his client to say nothing. "Mr. Holmes," he said in ringing tones that resonated through the bare room, "it is clear from your cross-questioning technique that the bar lost a valuable asset when you chose to exercise your talents elsewhere. You would have made a fine prosecuting counsel. But the fact remains that my client will have to answer such questions as Sir Bartholomew Anders chooses to put to her when she testifies in court. I will not have her subject to cross-examination twice."

Once again, O'Bannion's client refused to shield herself behind her defender's skirts. "I had never seen the box before," she explained. "I found it among my father's effects, along with a letter indicating his desire to send the box to his father should they ever reconcile. And so I brought it when I came from America." She drew a ragged breath. "Please, Mr. Holmes," she begged, "find the meaning of the things in the box and I have no doubt you will find the person who killed my grandfather. But as God is my witness, I did not know, Mr. Holmes. And I did not kill my poor grandfather, whom I had grown to love very much."

"Not the most promising of defences, Mr. O'Bannion," Holmes commented as we stepped into the misty spring air after leaving the prison.

O'Bannion said nothing, but his expressive face indicated a profound gloom. "Mr. Holmes," he said in a tone heavy with irony, "I thank you for a most instructive morning. I now feel the case against my client is even more daunting than I believed before I enlisted your aid."

He stepped into the street and raised his hand as a signal to passing cab-drivers. Holmes followed; the three of us piled into a hansom.

"You need not continue with this case," O'Bannion said, "since it is obvious you have no belief in my client's innocence of the charges against her."

"My beliefs signify nothing," Holmes replied in a mild tone. "It is the evidence and the evidence alone which should be examined. I have every intention of continuing with this case, and of hearing that evidence from the mouths of the witnesses."

The Irishman appeared less than pleased by this intelligence, but he instructed the driver to take us to the Old Bailey with all possible speed.

The first witness for the prosecution was our old friend Lestrade. He took the oath with an air of pompous determination, as if to say he was a plain man who would speak plain truth no matter what questions fancy Irish lawyers might think up to ask him.

Sir Bartholmew Anders, an impressive figure in his silk gown and immaculate white wig, elicited from Lestrade the particulars of his career in the Metropolitan Police Force. He then asked Lestrade to elaborate upon his part in the events of December 22d last.

"I was called," Lestrade said, warming to his subject under the prosecutor's friendly interrogation, "to the house of Sir Wilfred Carstairs by the butler, who said his master had been locked in his library since the night before. I proceeded to assist the butler in opening the door, which had been locked from the inside."

There was a stirring in the crowd at these words; next to me, a man leaned over and murmured something, then pointed a bony finger at the prisoner in the dock. Charmian Carstairs stood still as a statue, dressed in her plain prison gown, regarding the events in the courtroom with a detached air, as if watching the trial as a mere spectator.

"When we succeeded in opening the door," Lestrade continued, "I saw the body of Sir Wilfred lying on the floor beside his desk. He appeared to have died in a horrible convulsion," the inspector intoned, "and so I arranged for a doctor to be sent for. The doctor said it looked like poison, so I instructed the servants to give an account of the events of the night before, with particular emphasis upon what was eaten and drunk in that house."

Beside me on the hard pew of the first row of spectators, Holmes leaned forward intently. He seemed to make a mental inventory of the testimony, and nodded with satisfaction when Lestrade stated, "In the opinion of the Chief Toxicologist, the poison was administered in a cup which sat on a small table next to Sir Wilfred's desk."

The cup itself sat on a corner of the table used by the prosecuting attorney. It was a large silver cup of medieval design, almost a chalice, of a type rarely seen in our modern age. But Charmian Carstairs had spoken of an old-fashioned Christmas with ceremonial toasts; perhaps this cup was a family heirloom used to drink the health of the season.

Lestrade was permitted, over O'Bannion's vigorous objection, to testify that the means of death was a little-known plant poison whose Latin name was *datura sacra*.

"And was there a time when the seeds of the *datura* were found in the house where Sir Wilfred died?" the prosecuting counsel inquired. He directed his gaze at the prisoner as he spoke, as if silently accusing her with his eyes.

"I obtained a warrant and searched the whole house from top to bottom," Lestrade replied. "In the bedroom occupied by the accused I found a box containing *datura* seeds along with a note and a picture," he went on.

Holmes pulled a small notebook from his pocket and sat poised to take notes; there had been speculation regarding the contents of the mysterious box in the newspapers, but none of the accounts had contained a definitive list of the items therein.

Crown Counsel handed Lestrade a piece of paper; he identified it as the note he'd found in the box in Charmian Carstairs' room. It was marked and entered into evidence; Lestrade was asked to read its contents into the record.

The tension in the courtroom was palpable. Lestrade held the piece of paper in his hand and in ringing tones read the words thereon: "When the Angel's Trumpet sounds, then shall you cross the abyss."

There was no sound in the crowded courtroom; all who heard the words were struck by their ominous intent. Sir Wilfred Carstairs had ingested those poisonous seeds and he had indeed 'crossed the abyss' from life to death.

"And the picture?" Sir Bartholomew persisted. "Can you describe for the jury the picture you also found in the box that contained the seeds and the note?"

"It was of the Last Trump," Lestrade said. He shifted in the witness box; he had been standing for the past half-hour.

Beside me, Holmes drew in a sharp breath. "I must see that picture," he muttered. "And the note as well."

"It showed the Archangel Michael," Lestrade explained, "blowing a golden trumpet and summoning the souls of the dead to judgement. Under the picture was the single word: Judgement."

Once again all eyes in the courtroom turned to Charmian Carstairs. Once again, she stood immobile as a marble effigy, her beautiful, exotic face expressionless.

The picture was marked and entered as well, then passed among the jurors. One or two of them handled the small rectangle and passed it along, but most looked up from the pasteboard to the young woman in the dock, shaking their heads as if in no doubt as to her guilt.

Charmian Carstairs claimed to have no knowledge of the items in the box she had carried from California, but to the jurors, as to everyone else in the courtroom, the contents of the box signified a Day of Reckoning for past wrongs. And the young woman on trial was the daughter of a man disinherited by his father, a man who might well have imbued his child with the desire for revenge and instructed her in the means to take her grandfather's life.

At a signal from Holmes, O'Bannion rose and requested a recess. It was granted; within moments we sat in a small paneled conference room with the barrister, who paced the floor with ill-concealed impatience.

"I must see the picture in question," Holmes began. O'Bannion nodded and dispatched an assistant to fetch it. "And I have questions I should like answered."

"Have you an idea, Mr. Holmes?" the Irishman asked with an almost pathetic eagerness. "Have you discerned a pattern in this seemingly incomprehensible testimony?"

"I have a glimmer," Holmes replied. "I feel it is imperative to know the exact contents of Sir Wilfred's study. Were there objects besides the fatal cup on the small table next to the desk? And what lay upon the desk itself? Was there a book, and if there was, what did it contain?"

O'Bannion drew in a long breath and regarded Holmes as one might a dangerous animal. "Mr. Holmes," he began, "the putting of questions to a witness on cross-examination is considered an art in my profession. One does not ask questions in order to obtain information, particularly information which may be detrimental to one's client."

"Mr. O'Bannion, I assure you," Holmes replied, his tone grave, "the answers to these questions could be vital to the discovery of the truth."

"The truth?" O'Bannion's voice rose in disbelief and his words took on the rhythms of his native land. "Is it the truth you're after wanting, Mr. Holmes?" He pulled a white handkerchief from the sleeve of his gown and mopped his brow. "It was a dark day indeed when I sought help at your door, Mr. Holmes," he muttered. "The truth, is it? God help me and my poor young lady now."

The assistant returned with the picture of the Last Judgement. Holmes studied it; I looked over his shoulder. It was an ordinary picture, with bright colors and crude lettering.

"I hadn't realized the late Sir Wilfred was a Roman Catholic," I remarked, hoping to hear a word or two of praise from Holmes for my deduction. The picture was not one a worshipper of the Church of England would have carried in his Book of Common Prayer.

Holmes grunted. "This card is no relic of the Church," he replied, his tone grim.

"Do you recognize it, then?" I asked.

"Is it important?" O'Bannion demanded.

"It is of the utmost importance," my friend replied. "Indeed, its significance cannot be overstated."

The butler, Reginald Bateson, was the next to testify. He attested to the fact that there had been a small, intimate gathering at Sir Wilfred's house on the evening of December 21. In celebration of the Christmas season, a toast had been drunk, with Sir Wilfred raising the medieval cup to his lips. The house had been decked with holly and ivy; it was truly the old-fashioned English Christmas Charmian Carstairs had been promised.

On cross-examination, O'Bannion asked the butler about the curious items on the table next to Sir Wilfred's desk.

"A queer lot, they were, that's certain," the butler replied. "There was a sword that usually hung over the mantelpiece, along with a stick and the drinking cup and a gold coin."

"Let us," O'Bannion suggested, "take these items one by one, shall we. Please tell the jury about the sword, Mr. Bateson."

Crown Counsel objected, but his Lordship permitted the question. The butler puffed himself up like a turkey cock and proceeded to satisfy the court's curiosity.

"It was a family heirloom," he explained. "A sword from the time of Cromwell, it was. Hung over the mantelpiece from the time I first came into service, it did. And the day after Sir Wilfred died, there it was on the table with the other items."

"And the stick?" O'Bannion continued.

"A walking-stick," the butler stated. "A plain staff, such as a man might take on a tramp through the woods. Brought from the country, I daresay, though I'd never seen it before that morning."

"Can you describe the cup, Mr. Bateson?"

"Old-fashioned, it was," replied the butler. "Like something out of the Middle Ages. A heavy metal cup with no handle. Never seen the like, myself, but there it was on the table with the other things, plain as day."

"Please tell us about the coin," O'Bannion urged.

"Well, now, I'm not altogether certain it was a coin," the man said, shaking his head. Next to me, Holmes leaned forward in the pew, his eyes alight.

"What do you mean by that?" O'Bannion asked. There was a slight frown between his eyes. "It was either a coin or it wasn't, Mr. Bateson."

"I mean it wasn't money, not proper English money, any road," the butler retorted. "It was gold, right enough, just like a sovereign, but no picture of our Queen on it. Just a queer design, a star, like."

Holmes leaned forward in his place with a suddenness that had one of the bailiffs rushing toward him. He held up a warning hand, then pulled a piece of paper out of his breast pocket and scribbled a note. He handed the note to the bailiff and pointed toward O'Bannion. The attendant took the note and walked to counsel table.

O'Bannion had all but finished his questions, but he read the note and raised his eyes to the bench. "If I might ask one more question, Your Lordship?" he asked.

His Lordship glared, but nodded assent. "Very well, Mr. O'Bannion."

"How many points did the star have, Mr. Bateson?"

The butler frowned. "It had five points. Five, but there was something queer about the star. It was crooked-like."

O'Bannion thanked the witness, but it was clear to me he had no idea what the man had said that was important. Yet next to me, Holmes nodded and smiled as if he'd just heard the name of the true murderer.

The next witness was the deceased's nephew, a foppish young man who claimed to have taken his uncle's change of will with equanimity.

"Where there's life, there's hope," Cyril Carstairs said jauntily. "He couldn't very well change his mind and put me back into the will once he was dead, now could he?"

Holmes stirred in his seat, then stood and made for the door. I followed.

"We must visit the house where Sir Wilfred died," Holmes insisted. "I cannot confirm my hypotheses without a glimpse of the study where the events took place."

"But, Holmes," I protested, "we shall miss the testimony."

"That young man knows less than Miss Carstairs about what happened," Holmes replied with some acerbity. "No, Watson, we shall do our client more good by going to that house than we could by any other means."

Sir Wilfred's London house was a large, airy Georgian mansion situated near Green Park. In the absence of the butler, the door was opened by a housekeeper, who invited us to enter. Holmes asked to be directed to the library; the housekeeper inclined her head and led us along the hallway in silence.

The library was crammed with leatherbound volumes, some of which looked to be of great antiquity. Holmes ran his slender fingers along the leather bindings. Then he gave a cry and pulled a volume from the shelves. "Here it is," he cried, brandishing it aloft in triumph. "I knew I should find it. We must take it to O'Bannion at once."

"What is it, Holmes?" I asked. "What single book could possibly explain these bizarre events?"

"It is called *The Book of Thoth*," Holmes replied. "It was written by a man called Aleister Crowley, and it is the Bible of an organization known as the Order of the Golden Dawn."

"O.G.D.," I said, repeating the letters on the cover of the box Charmian Carstairs had brought from America. "Then O.G.D. stands for Order of the Golden Dawn. But what is this Order, and how is it connected with the murder of Sir Wilfred?"

"It has nothing whatever to do with his murder," Holmes answered, "but it has everything to do with his death."

There was a japanned box on top of the desk, next to an elaborately decorated inkwell with a design on it of a cross with a rose in the center. Holmes opened the box and drew out a square object wrapped in black silk. He lifted the silk away with a flourish and revealed an oversized pack of cards.

"I hadn't realized Sir Wilfred was a gambler," I said. "Perhaps he was murdered by someone to whom he owed money."

"These are not playing cards, Watson," my friend said. He turned over the deck; instead of ordinary suits and numbers, these pasteboards were painted with bizarre designs. The one Holmes showed me was of a man hanging upside down, a golden aureole around his head. It was a grotesque image, but its horror was soon surpassed by the other images Holmes revealed in the deck: a man lying face-down with ten swords sticking out of his back; a woman with a blindfold holding two crossed swords; a tower struck by lightning. The most unnerving card of all portrayed Death on a black horse.

"What do you think you are doing here?" an imperious voice said. I looked up, startled, to see a formidable woman standing in the doorway. She was of an age with the late Sir Wilfred, and the way she bore herself told me she must be the deceased's sister.

"Miss Carstairs," Holmes began, "I must apologize for presuming to enter your brother's study. I had thought you were attending the trial, or I should have begged your housekeeper to make you aware of my presence."

"If you had, Mr. Holmes," the old woman replied stiffly, "I should have had her deny you access. My home is not a place where riffraff may come whenever it pleases to satisfy its curiosity."

"I am here for a far different purpose than that, Miss Carstairs, as you must suspect if you know my name," Holmes replied in a tone that might almost have been called gentle. "I am in search of evidence that will support the defence contention that your grand-niece did not murder your brother."

The old woman sniffed. "Then you have come on a fool's errand, Mr. Holmes, for no such evidence exists. That girl killed my poor brother and no amount of fiddling by that Irishman is going to help her escape the fate she so richly deserves. She will die on the gallows, Mr. Holmes, and justice will finally be served."

"You did not approve of your brother's change in his will, did you, Miss Carstairs?"

"I make no secret of the fact that I considered my brother besotted on the subject of his granddaughter," the woman announced. "She had no manners whatsoever, no pretense to gentility. I sincerely hoped my brother would recover from his infatuation with this uncivilized young woman who was the product of the most ill-advised union two people ever entered into."

"What about the gathering on the night your brother died, Miss Carstairs?" Holmes inquired, changing the subject with an abruptness that caught me by surprise. "You were the hostess, I believe."

"It was a gathering in honor of the season," the lady replied dismissively.

"Yes, but which season were you celebrating, Miss Carstairs?" Holmes persisted.

"I do not know to what you are referring, Mr. Holmes," the woman replied, but there was a spark of fear in her eyes.

"I refer to the season," Holmes said. "I refer to the reason for your gathering. I refer to the night upon which your brother died. It was a celebration, and the house was decorated with the traditional holly and ivy, but was it in point of fact a celebration of Christmas?"

The old woman raised a trembling hand to her throat; she fingered a brooch which fastened her collar. In the center of the brooch was a rose, and in the center of the rose, a small cross. The design was similar to the one on her brother's inkstand.

"You will leave my home at once," she said in a shaking voice, "or I will summon the police."

"I shall leave, Madam," Holmes answered with a bow, "but I shall take with me this book and these cards, for they are vital pieces of evidence that must be laid before the court without delay."

"There are one or two points to which I should like to draw your attention," Holmes said. We sat in the small panelled conference room, the japanned box and the *Book of Thoth* resting on the table between us.

"I should be grateful if you did, Mr. Holmes," the barrister replied, "for a less promising series of accounts I have seldom encountered."

"Have you ever heard of the Order of the Golden Dawn?" Holmes asked. O'Bannion shook his head; it was clear he was as much at sea as I myself.

"It is a branch of the Rosicrucian sect," Holmes went on. I parsed out the meaning of this new term, and a chill went through me as I realized Rosicrucian meant "rose cross." I remembered the brooch the elder Miss Carstairs had worn at her throat, and the strange design on Sir Wilfred's inkwell. Both were variations on the theme of cross and rose.

"The Order of the Golden Dawn, which is an offshoot of the Rosicrucians, bases its belief system upon the Tarot. Those were the cards we found in Sir Wilfred's desk, Watson."

"And the curious items on the table, Holmes?" I cried. "What can they have to do with this strange business?"

Holmes set the deck of gaily painted cards on the table and spread them in a fan-shaped array. He reached in and pulled one out, then held it up for us to inspect.

The card showed a young man wearing a red robe, holding one hand aloft and standing before a table. On the table were four items: a stick, a sword, a chalice, and a coin.

I shivered; the table in Sir Wilfred's study was an exact duplicate of the table depicted in the strange card.

"This is the Tarot card known as The Magician," Holmes explained.

"The four items on the table represent the four suits of the Tarot deck: swords, wands, cups, and pentacles."

"The five-pointed star!" O'Bannion exclaimed. "The gold coin with the star was a pentacle."

"Precisely," Holmes agreed.

"But what is the meaning of all this?" I cried. "Why should Sir Wilfred place such objects on his table?"

Holmes answered my question with a question. "Watson," he asked, "what was the exact date upon which Sir Wilfred died?"

"Why, early in the morning of December 22," I replied, astonished that my friend should have forgotten so elementary a fact. "Three days before Christmas."

"No, Watson," Holmes admonished, with a shake of his head. "Sir Wilfred did not die three days before Christmas. He died instead on the holiday he had chosen to celebrate in its place: the winter solstice, which occurs between December 21 and December 22. He hid the pagan symbols of that holiday beneath the trappings of an English Christmas, but the true meaning of holly and ivy precede the Christian era in England. He invited others of his sect to partake of the holiday, and when they left, he embarked upon his own initiation as an adept, setting forth the items on the table and ingesting the sacred seeds."

"Then there was no murder after all?" O'Bannion exclaimed.

"There was no murder," Holmes repeated. "The late Sir Wilfred was an Adept of the Order of the Golden Dawn, and as such, he aspired to an even higher state of spiritual knowledge and power. He prepared his study for a ritual that would take him, in the words of the note, 'across the abyss.'"

"Then the Abyss does not refer to death, Mr. Holmes?" O'Bannion inquired; the relief in his voice was almost comical.

"In a way, it does," Holmes answered. His face was grave. "Do you know why the Angel's Trumpet is known as the sacred *datura*?" he asked. I shook my head, as did O'Bannion.

"Because it produces a type of mania that is believed to be conducive to spiritual visions."

Holmes stood and began to pace the small room. "I have read accounts of shamans who have ingested the seeds of the sacred *datura*," he went on. "They fall into a deep trance and appear to be dead. Then they rise from the dead and claim to have witnessed extraordinary visions and to have obtained occult knowledge. It is my belief that Sir Wilfred took the seeds of his own

free will, seeking to 'cross the abyss' from worldly to otherworldly knowledge. The note was indeed written by Miss Charmian Carstairs' father, but
it was not a symbol of revenge, but of a spiritual bond between father and
son."

"But what of the angel, Holmes?" I cried. "Surely the angel with the
golden trumpet must be a Christian symbol?"

Holmes shook his head. He lifted a slender hand and moved the Tarot
cards about. At last he lifted one and showed it to me. It portrayed an
archangel blowing a trumpet while gray figures emerged from their coffins.
Underneath the card was written the single word Judgement.

"It is a card of the Tarot deck," Holmes stated. "Lestrade had never seen
it before; he assumed it was a Christian picture."

"But, Holmes," I protested, "the brooch Miss Letitia Carstairs wore was
of a rose and cross; do you mean to imply that she, too, was a member of this
Golden Dawn? And if she was, why did she not come forward and make the
truth of the ritual known to the police?"

"That question is easily answered, Watson," Holmes replied with a grim
smile. "Mr. O'Bannion can tell us what happens to an heir who is convicted
of murdering the testator."

"She would be disinherited," O'Bannion explained, "and the inheritance
would pass to the residuary legatee."

"I think you will find that Miss Letitia Carstairs occupies that position in
her late brother's will," Holmes said. "She not only hated her grand-niece,
she intended to keep her brother's fortune for herself by refusing to explain
that Sir Wilfred took the *datura* seeds of his own free will."

The testimony of Sherlock Holmes in the trial of the American heiress
was a nine-day's-wonder. Kevin O'Bannion's motion to dismiss all charges
against his client was granted amid much clamour in the courtroom. The
headlines in the morning-papers trumpeted the news of The Great
Defender's latest courtroom triumph to an admiring public.

To Kevin O'Bannion, she was always *the* woman.

Or perhaps not. Holmes and I attended the opera last night (the
incomparable Goldini was singing), and who should we see in a box but the
Great Defender himself, escorting a lady whose raven hair and large gray
eyes were reminiscent of the California poppy he had defended with such
skill. But a closer look revealed her to be a pale copy of her American
predecessor, who I later learned had taken the first boat for New York as

soon as she was released from prison.

We received a case of wine only last week. It bore a label showing rolling hills and the name Duclos Winery, Sonoma Valley, California. Holmes proclaimed the vintage, which bore the improbable name *zinfandel*, undrinkable (without actually tasting it), solely on the grounds that no vintage produced in the New World could possibly please an educated European palate. I, on the other hand, sampled a glass with last night's chop and found it most satisfactory, if a trifle young and forward, a quality that renders it not unlike the daughters of the great Republic from which it came.

This story represents one of those times in my writing life where I woke up with the story in my head. The "voice" of this old-time cop retired on disability just filled my brain as I made my way from the East Broadway F train stop to One Police Plaza, where I then worked. I also had another story percolating, and somehow the two stories merged into one.

UNDERCOVER

You can get away with murder if you don't mind copping to something worse. I learned this life truth from Mr. Carlucci. I learned a lotta things from Mr. C. You might say he made me what I am today.

What I was was a cop. 1952 I graduated the Academy with a hundred other Micks hungry for the street. Last year — can it really be 1967 already? — I got the three-quarters and a bum knee. And nothing to do for the rest of my life but limp around like an old fart.

Chick Dunahee, outta the old one-nine, always starts in on how three-quarters is one thing for a guy who's shot, but anything less is just goldbricking.

I say, you gonna grudge three-quarters to a guy gave his whole life to the Department? Who sat around shootin the shit after his tour was over on account of the precinct was more like a home than his home? Who spent more time in a black and white than he ever did in his own Chevy it took him seven years to pay for? It don't make no difference how the guy bought it, a shotgun blast or a lousy little fenderbender put his knee out permanent.

That accident was the best damn thing ever happened to me is what I tell everybody. I slap the stupid bitchin knee and say, I got all the time in the world.

Yeah. Time. Time for a third cup of coffee at Klinger's deli, for a fourth beer down to Hanrahan's. Time to play another hand of gin with Harve Petrovich and Chick Dunahee.

Time. Time to sit on a park bench with all the other old farts who don't know what the hell became of their lives. Time to drink too much and time to think too much.

I miss the gun. I can't hardly believe it; I mean, I never fired the damn thing the whole time I was in uniform, except on the firin range, but the weight of it being gone is like having one less arm. Without the gun, I'm nothin. Worse than nothin.

I decide to look up Mr. Carlucci. Notice the *Mister*. You talk about a mutt, you don't call him Mister. You call him Jones or Hey, You or slimebucket, but you don't call him Mister. He's just a mutt, he don't deserve no respect. But Mr. C, I don't care how much dope he deals, or how many hookers he's got on the street, or how many guys took a swim in the East River on account of him. He's a gentleman, Mr. C.

I used to stop by the restaurant when I was a rookie hoofing a beat. God, I loved the beat. I loved the feeling that the streets belonged to me, that I was there to take special care of my blocks, my people.

So one night I dropped in to Carlucci's, just to see that everything's A-OK. What I seen was an underage busboy carrying a drink to a table. Now, it goes against my grain to hang up a nice place like that over a petty beef, so I call the maitre d' over and mention it, casual-like, just so he knows for next time. But the guy's a wiseass, one of your smooth types with patent-leather hair. He starts givin me grief, daring me to write him up, tellin me his boss has a hook with the State Liquor Authority. I'm about ready to bust the place when I suddenly see the guy's face go gray. Next thing I know this tiny little man with silver-white hair and sharp blue eyes is looking up at me. He don't look like no Italian, but he says he's Mr. Carlucci and what's the trouble here?

I tell him. I don't even look at Patent Leather Hair, it's like he's gone even though he's still there. Mr. C whispers a few words to the monkey suit and he goes about his business.

Mr. Carlucci apologizes. Not like he's scared or nothin, more like he's pained that I should be treated bad in his place. Like he invited me to his house and somebody insulted me. Then he takes me over to his own personal table, the one with the red carnations in the middle. I sit down. It feels good to take a load off my feet. He snaps his fingers at a kid in a white coat and next thing I know I'm sittin in front of the biggest plate of spaghetti bolognese you ever saw. A big glass of vino joins the pasta and so does a basket of breadsticks, the kind with the little seeds all over.

Some cops always eat on the arm, never open their wallets the whole time they're on the job. Other cops are regular Mr. Cleans, never take so much as a cookie. Me, I was somewhere in the middle. I never took food from nobody I didn't think could afford it, and I never took from nobody I didn't respect.

To me, Mr. C was just trying to make up for the grief his maitre d' give me. He was being a gentleman. So I reached for the cut-glass dish of fresh-grated Parmesan and ladled it on thick.

It got to where I stopped in once, twice a month. Not too often, not like I was takin advantage, but just enough to let Mr. C know how much I liked the food and appreciated the hospitality. In six months I put on ten pounds and hadda get new uniform pants. Nothin worse for a cop than a beat with good food.

Course, I heard the rumors. How Mr. C was a lot more than just a guy made great manicott'. But I never seen him bring that side of things into his restaurant.

About a year later, I got transferred to the Four-Four. It was a real Bronx zoo up there, let me tell you. And nothin to eat but cuchifritos and Shabazz bean pies. I lost the ten pounds, and then ten more.

I haven't gone there since I got the line-of-duty.

But I gotta take the chance. So I hitch up my pants and pull on the fancy brass door handle.

As I walk through the carved wooden doors, I think of that first plate of pasta. The old decor's gone now — no more hand-painted scenes of Napoli, no more red napkins on starched white tablecloths, no more red carnations. The place has real class: peach-colored napkins folded into goblets like Chinese fans. More forks than a guy could use in three dinners.

I liked it better before, but I'd never tell Mr. C. I wouldn't want to hurt his feelings.

There's a new maitre d'. I tell him I want to see the boss, but then I start feeling ashamed. What if Mr. C thinks I'm there just to cadge a free meal? I start to mumble something about coming back another time.

Before I can turn my stupid leg around to walk out the door, he's there. Mr. Carlucci in person, his hair just as white and his eyes just as blue and sharp as they ever were. He puts out his hand; I shake it. It feels good when he says, "Officer Sweeney. It's been too long, my friend."

Just like he done that first time, Mr. C. ushers me over to his private table. There are peach-colored flowers, real exotic-looking, in the cut-glass vase that used to hold carnations. Like always, his bouquet is bigger and fuller than the ones on the other tables. And none of his flowers are brown at the edges, neither.

I sit. It takes a minute to get the freakin knee under the table. Mr. C. looks the other way, like the gentleman he is, and then sits down next to me.

He waves a waiter over and orders for both of us.

I'm no Italian, but I know better than to talk business right away. So I tell Mr. C how I busted up my knee and he shakes his head and says it's a shame. We talk about the old days, what happened to Klinger the deli owner, how the blind newsie on the corner got robbed again. How nothing's the same since Kennedy was shot.

When the food comes, we stop talking. Fettucine alfredo, veal piccata, and escarole sauteed in garlic butter. Dessert is expresso coffee with a jolt of anisette. Mr. C takes the tiny slice of lemon peel and rubs it around the rim of his cup. He takes a sip, then leans back in his chair with a sigh of contentment.

That's my signal. Business can now be mentioned.

I come into the restaurant a defrocked cop. I leave a bagman.

I coulda kidded myself. I coulda bought Mr. Carlucci's kind words as he walked me to the door. I can always use a good man, he says, in my business. His business. He don't mean the restaurant and we both know it. We both know what I am, but he's too much the gentleman to say the word.

He proves it when I go out the first time. He pours me a glass of red wine and gives me my instructions in person. I know for a fact he never done that with the other guys who collected for him. They take orders from Vinnie the Fish.

When I leave the restaurant and start walkin up the street, it's like I'm breathing brand-new air. It's like spring came overnight, even though I still see patches of dirty snow in the gutter. I belong again. I own the streets, I have my blocks and my people.

First thing I do, I buy a new suit. Like I was starting a new job, only I never had to buy a suit for a job before. I always had the uniform. Funny thing is, I buy a blue suit. Some things never change.

My first collection is from a skinny little Greek who sells fruit and vegetables. He tries to offer me some avocados, free, but I shake my head. Taking them would break both my rules.

Next stop: a Puerto Rican social club. Only thing he offers me is a hard-eyed stare, but it don't make no never mind to me. I get the bag.

Same result at the Jewish dairy restaurant and the jazz joint with a soul food smell so good I almost break the rule. The black mama in the kitchen gives me a big Aunt Jemima smile and says she loves to see a man enjoy his food. I smile back, but I know better than to trust her. The minute my back is turned, I'll find her kitchen knife between my ribs, the lard not even washed off. So no smothered pork chops. Just the bag.

Sometimes I feel bad. But, hey, if it's not me, it'll be somebody else, just like if it's not Mr. C, it'll be somebody else. They probably had bagmen in the Old Testament. It's keeping me off the park bench is all I know. All I want to know.

It starts to go wrong about the time the trees in the park behind the courthouse start blooming. All these little pink buds, real nice, like looking through rose-colored glasses. Then the rain comes and the buds fall off and stick to your shoes and who needs it?

It starts with little things. But, hey, I'm a cop, or I was before I got the line-of-duty, and I know how little things can add up until finally you're up crap creek and somebody stole your paddle.

So even the first time I don't see Mr. Carlucci before I go out to collect I get a funny feeling. Vinnie the Fish tells me Mr. C's home with the flu, and maybe he is. So okay, I take my orders, but I let him know I don't like it and the next week there's Mr. C and no sign of the Fish.

It was the Fish gave me the new stop on my route. It's a fag bar at the ass end of Christopher Street, which is in the Village, which figures. I start to object; I don't want to go to no fag bar, but Mr. C says these fruits are givin him a hard time, refusing to pay up, and the place needs special handling.

I walk down Christopher as fast as I can, cursing the limp for slowing me down. There's fag bars all over the place; I can tell even though they gotta be careful. I pass one called Stonewall that I know is run by the mob so there's no trouble about them paying up.

I'm practically in the Hudson River before I reach the joint I'm supposed to collect. It's called Christopher's End and it's next to the West Side Highway; there are trucks parked on the cobblestones under the road. Skinny guys in black leather jackets and Greek sailor caps lounge around by the trucks. I get the shivers just looking at them, knowing what they're waiting for.

Inside, I expect wall-to-wall fruits. But it's afternoon, and there's only a couple guys sitting at the bar and a foursome playing pool. None of them look faggy; if I hadn't of known, I might not have guessed. The bartender's got muscles like Gorgeous George and a USMC tattoo on his right arm. Hired muscle. No wonder the fags think they can defy Mr. C.

I walk up to the bar. Real quick, before the bartender starts to think I'm there for the wrong reason, I mention Mr. C and say I'm here for the pickup.

The bartender fixes me with the kind of hard blue eyes only an Irishman can have and says, "We're not paying."

Cold, flat. Just like that. I get my Irish up and say, "Who do you think you are, you don't have to pay? Just because the fruits that run this place hire some muscle means they're different from every other fag bar on this street?"

"Hell, yes, we're different," the bartender says. Leans over the bar and gives me an evil grin. "See, I'm not hired muscle. This is *my* bar for *my* friends and I'm not paying anybody to stay in business. Got that?"

I sit there stunned, like I been hit with a ball-peen hammer. The man was a Marine! A United States Marine turned fruit. I can't hardly take it in.

He talks about how hard it is to be a fag, what with cops keeping tabs on who comes into the bars, writing down license plate numbers of cars parked nearby, then running a make. He says why should guys get a jacket just for going into a bar? He also says why should they have to pay Mr. C to stay in business?

I turn my head away, thinking what to say next. I look at the guys playing pool. There's this one kid, well-built, with dark hair. Never take him for a nellie, the way he eyes the ball, places his cue. Shoots like a master, makes his shot, then grins into the glare of the green-shaded light over the table. White teeth in a tanned face. An actor's face. He catches my eye and gives me a victory salute. Like he wants me to applaud or something.

I turn back to the bartender. "Bad things happen to guys who cross Mr. C," I remind him.

"We'll take our chances," he says. He turns his back on me. I want to say more; hell, I want to rush the bar and beat the shit out of the bastard. The queer punk bastard. Only he ain't no pansy; he's got ten years and twenty pounds on me and his is muscle, not flab.

So there's nothing to do but go. For now. I turn and hoist my leg off the barstool. As I slide off the leather seat, the kid with the actor's face is standing next to me. I get a noseful of Brut as he whispers, "Can I buy you a drink?"

I run out of the place as fast as my gimpy leg will let me.

As I walk back down Christopher, I look for the cops the bartender talked about. Sure enough, hidden around the corner on Washington there's a beat-up '59 Chevy the Department thinks nobody knows is an unmarked. There's one guy behind the wheel, another with a notebook in his hand. Prominent, like they want people to see they're there.

I can't have them gettin the wrong idea. What if it came back to Chick

Dunahee that Biff Sweeney was seen comin out of a fag bar? I walk over to the unmarked and start thinking fast.

By the time I get the recorder's attention, I got a story all ready. About how I do a little private investigation now I'm retired, about how this father came to me real upset, said his son was hangin around with queers and he wanted it stopped. About how I only went into the bar to see if the bartender knew the kid.

Nothing about collecting for Mr. Carlucci.

They stare at me with blank cop eyes. I got no idea whether or not they believe me. I open my mouth to add to the story, then realize that would really make me sound like a mutt tryin to talk himself out of a jam. So I shrug and walk away.

When I get back to the restaurant, the Fish is not happy. Mr. C is not happy. How can a man with Mr. C's rep let a bunch of fairies push him around?

He can't. I have to go back, make noises about how places without insurance have been known to burn to the ground. With people inside. Owner-type people.

But one thing I make clear: any damage to the bar has to be done by somebody other than me. I may be a bagman, but I'm no hitman. I'm still too much cop for that.

The Fish starts to say I'll do what I'm told, but Mr. C cuts him off. "I understand," he says. Always the gent.

This time I learn the bartender's name is Mick Hennessey. Not just a Marine but an Irishman. Go figure. He feeds me a drink. I take it; hell, I need a drink to sit in a place like this, the way I feel about fags.

We talk about fire. I talk about fire. About how dangerous it is, how it can trap people inside and burn them to bacon before they knew what hit them.

Mick talks about sports, about how someday the football leagues are gonna get together and have a big playoff game. Which'll never happen, you ask me. Why should the NFL bother with a bunch of farm teams like they got in the AFL? You think a team calls itself Dolphins can take on the Green Bay Packers?

I don't say none of that; I keep talking about fire. I keep drinking. Things are getting blurry when I smell Brut and turn to see the kid from the pool table sitting next to me. He says his name's Darius. Darius Kroeger. Only he uses the name Cooper when he goes for auditions.

"I knew you was an actor," I tell him. "You got the face for it."

He smiles. That's all, just a smile. But his eyes reach into mine the way no guy's eyes are supposed to reach into another guy's.

I'm drunk. I mean I'm as plastered as I ever been in my life. That's the only way it could've happened. I had to be drunk outta my face. I hadda be.

I wake up the next morning with a large furry animal in my mouth. I think it's my tongue. My head feels like — ah, hell, you ever had a hangover, you know how my head feels.

But that's not the bad part. The bad part is what I think happened between me and Darius.

I lay in bed with the cold sweats, with shakes so bad I can't lift a glass of water to my mouth to pop an aspirin. But it's not the booze; it's the memory.

I never felt like that before. I never knew I could feel like that. Even Monica O'Shea, who gave the best handjob in Hell's Kitchen, never made me feel like that, and every guy at Sacred Heart knew what she could do with those long white fingers of hers.

Oh, I used to brag, just like the other guys. How horny I was, how much I needed a woman. Then I'd go to Monica, get what I came for, and tell my buddies it was great. But I was just blowing smoke; it was okay, but that was all. Just okay.

Same thing with the Times Square hookers we used to bust. They'd offer freebies to stay on the street. You hadda take it once in a while. The other cops would talk about how Crystal or Bobbie Jo, how they did stuff the cops' wives never even *heard* of and wouldn't do for a million bucks. Me, I figured they was okay, but nothing special.

Darius was more than okay. Much more.

I was drunk. I was drunk, I lost my head, and it'll never happen again.

Once doesn't mean you're a faggot.

Does it?

The phone rings. It's as loud as the Last Trump, and it scares me as much.

I'm right to be scared. It's Mick Hennessey; he asks me how Darius and I got along last night.

He knows. He fucking knows. I didn't think I had any more sweat left in my body, but there's a cold stream trickling down my back.

He knows.

He also knows there will be no fire at Christopher's End.

I put the phone back in the cradle and try to stop shaking.

It rings a second time. I pick it up. What could be worse than what I just heard?

The Fish, that's what.

"So, you're too high and mighty to torch a place for the Boss," he says, his voice slimy with self-satisfaction. "The truth is you don't want to hurt your fag buddies, do you, *faggot?*"

He spits the last word; it practically jumps through the phone and wets my face.

"You think Mr. C's dumb or something, *faggot?* You think he doesn't watch his back at all times? Well, there better be a nice big bonfire at that fag bar or everyone in the NYPD's going to know you like it with boys. Got that, *faggot?*"

I lean over the bed and throw up on the floor, with Vinnie the Fish on the other end of the line listening to every retch.

I can't believe Mr. C will let this happen. He's too much the gent. But when I ask to talk to the Boss, the Fish says, "He's taking a shave. Besides, he's got no use for faggots. Except to collect from fag bars, which is all you're gonna be doing from now on. *After* you light that fire."

"I won't —" I croak, but the Fish chops me off.

"You *won't?* You forget, we own your ass. At least," he sniggers, "we own whatever's left over after your pretty boyfriend gets through with it. So you *will* light that fire and it will cause great damage to life and property. Won't it, faggot?"

The fire. The fire that will cook Christopher's End and Mick Hennessey and Darius Kroeger-Cooper and burn the memory of last night to the ground. To the ground.

Darius. I think about last night, about how he made me feel, and I realize I been under cover my whole life. Thinking it was like this for all guys; that they bragged about women but didn't really like it all that much. But it wasn't them; it was me. It was me that was missing something, and now I found it and I gotta burn it up. I gotta burn it up or be called a faggot the rest of my life.

I seen plenty of fairies on the job. Guys in skirts beat up when the john getting the blowjob realized what they had between their legs. Guys caught in mens' rooms copping some boy's joint, begging the cops not to book them or the wife'll find out.

I never in my life thought that I —

Once!   Once doesn't make you a faggot.   Anybody can make one mistake.

I clean up the mess on the floor and start thinking about the fire. How I have to plan. How it has to go smooth as silk, nothing coming back to me.

I think about Mick Hennessey, how talking to him was no different from talking to Chick Dunahee or any other ex-cop. I think about Darius, his white smile, his smooth dark face. I remember the way his hands caressed my .38; he said he used to go target shooting with his dad. He liked guns; he liked that I was a cop.

I think about burning him to bacon.

It takes me a week to set things up right. To get my alibi in place. To case the joint, working out where the fire should start. How I can get to the site without being seen hefting a can of gasoline through the streets. How I can get away without being spotted.

Every night I dream of Darius, waking with an ache in my groin.

There's only one way I can do this. I gotta become a cop again in my head. I gotta think about it like I was writing up a 61 on a torch job some mope already done. In my mind, I start dictating a police report.

At 1500 hours, the perpetrator approached the location. Male White, 6', 185 pounds, no limp or other identifying characteristics. Carrying a duffel bag.

It's a half hour after closing. I've got the gasoline can in the duffel bag. My leg's wrapped tighter than hell in an ace bandage so's I can keep from limping. One less thing to be identified by.

I peer through the windows, just to make sure. There they are, taking a drink together. The two guys I need to eliminate if I'm going to have peace in my life.

The fire originated at the rear exit. Source of the fire was garbage bags ignited by means of an accelerant later identified as gasoline.

I stop a minute before lighting the matches. This is wrong. Everything in my life tells me how wrong. It's like all the priests and nuns I ever knew, all the sergeants I answered to, even my dead mother are standing over me, telling me they're ashamed they ever knew me.

But I have to do it. I have to.

After four tries, I get a match lit and toss it onto the garbage bags. Flames jump at me right away; the gasoline is that ready to burn.

Perpetrator ignited a second fire at the front entrance to the location by dousing the wooden door with accelerant.

I slip around the corner and duck into an alley. It's back streets all the way, and a quick subway ride. The duffel bag's ash now, along with the garbage. So's the watch cap. I leave the pea jacket in the subway; it'll be gone by morning.

I can't believe I did it.

I need a drink to steady my hands, settle my stomach.

I walk out of the subway. The ace bandage is killing me; my leg feels like a blimp. But I force myself to walk straight, no limp, past my own car, toward the light pouring onto the pavement from the window of my destination.

I have a report to make.

I open the door and walk in.

"Is it done?"

I nod.

"To a crisp," another voice says. Darius slides off the barstool and walks over to me. Embraces me in a cloud of Brut, his lips brushing my cheek. Mick Hennessey pours me a drink.

We toast Darius for his acting job. Thanks to him, the cops watching Christopher's End have my license plate number and a description of a man in a trenchcoat and fedora limping into a fag bar at the same time Carlucci's Ristorante went up in flames.

Who's going to believe a cop set up a phony alibi in a fag bar? Nobody, that's who.

I lock eyes with Darius; we both know how the night will end.

Like I said, you can get away with murder if you don't mind copping to something worse.

I don't mind. I've got a new beat now, and I don't mind at all.

Another foray into humor — I hope. Coincidentally, I was asked to write a story set on a cruise ship before taking an actual three-day cruise with my family. The assignment enhanced the trip for my niece and nephew, since the three of us explored the ship with a view toward the best site for a body, and I found myself gazing at the water slide with a very strange expression on my face when I realized its possibilities. My nephew, who is contemplating a career in filmmaking, is a chip off the old aunt.

THE TIME OF HIS LIFE

"Not much curb appeal," Margot said, her green eyes peering over the tops of her oversized sunglasses. "But could make someone a nice fixer-upper."

"Margot," the younger woman in the next lounge chair said with a giggle, "you can't talk about him like that. He's a man, not a house." The two basked in the sun on the Lido deck of the Mayan Princess, having staked out their spot right next to the Sea Breeze bar, the one with the cutest bartenders.

The object of the women's scrutiny sat in the Jacuzzi, his bald head leaning back over the rim, taking in the sun's blistering rays. He'd be pink as watermelon by the end of the day, and he'd wear his sunburn proudly, tangible evidence that he was having the time of his life.

That was, after all, the motto of the Festival Cruise Lines.

"You'll have the time of your life," the perky honey-blond spokesmodel promised as she danced the macarena with her morning-show co-star on the deck of a Festival ship. "Whether you choose three fun-filled days on the Mayan Princess or a three-week scenic adventure on the Eskimo Princess, whether you dance to a calypso beat on the Jamaican Princess or learn the hula on board the Hawaiian Princess, we guarantee you'll never forget your Festival Cruise."

Margot's whisky-deep, cigarette baritone replied, "Sure I can, hon. It's the same principle exactly. When you're young, you want flash, you want to impress people. You get a little older, a little wiser, you'll settle for comfort instead of style. You'll put more work into it, keep it a little longer. Renovate what you've got instead of trading up."

Her companion giggled again. "So who do you see him with?"

She pointed a pink-nailed hand in the general direction of the bar. "That fat woman with the umbrella in her drink?"

Margot's answering frown was all in her voice, not on her face. No need to invite wrinkles. "We in the industry prefer the term *'zaftig.'* "

"Oh, is that French for porky?" Sherri ran her manicured hand over the tan flesh of her exposed belly. A belly that sported a neat gold ring in the button, which even the bald man in the hot tub thirty feet away could see was an outie.

"Warning, hon. We don't talk that way about our clients, even when they're not listening. The key to success is respect. R-E-S-P —"

"I know how to spell it," Sherri said with a pout the bald man found extremely sexy. "I heard that old song about a million times. Besides," another sip of the strawberry daiquiri found its way into Sherri's pink-lipsticked mouth, "she's not our client. She doesn't even know we exist. And neither does he."

"Yet," was Margot's response, which Sherri dutifully echoed.

"Yet."

The woman at the bar wore sunglasses too. Old ones that turned up at the end like cats' eyes and had rhinestones on them. The kind teenagers liked to wear when they were goofing on Grandma, but she wasn't wearing them as a hoot. She'd always liked sunglasses like these, and she was going to wear them. Besides, they'd been a present from the only man she'd ever loved, and so what if she'd loved him in the fifties and these were the nineties?

She sipped her piña colada and sat back in her seat with a small sigh of satisfaction. How lovely it was to be on a cruise once again. Something about shipboard life just called out to her, begged her to leave her little condo and take to sea. She loved the organized leisure of it, the decadent pursuit of enjoyment that stretched from the morning breakfast of exotic tropical fruit garnished with flowers to the last after-dinner drink after the last whirl around the ballroom with Pierre, the dancing teacher.

Pierre was such a nice boy. So smooth and sleek and polite. Not like so many men these days, too busy making money to take time with a woman. Not like her Herb, who had taken her along on all his business trips.

"I feel like a matzo ball," the bald man said, but he made no move to step out of the Jacuzzi. Instead, he lay with his head back, lolling in the sun like a big tomcat, except of course that no tomcat worth the name liked getting wet.

He was as hairy as a tomcat; he'd have no worry about burning the skin on his arms or chest because the sun was in no position to penetrate the dark mat of hair that covered him like a coat. Only his head was deficient in the matter of hair, and it would look like a pomegranate by evening.

"Yes, isn't it heavenly?" The petite blonde had just immersed herself in the tub, one gorgeous inch after another, in a slow motion ballet he'd found quite entertaining. Good thing her old bag friend was still over on the lounge chair; he had the blonde all to herself.

She lifted a smooth, shapely leg and watched the water drip from it with an air of amused detachment, as though it were a phantom limb belonging to someone else.

"I had the world's worst cramp sitting over there, and I just knew a dip in this tub would make it all better." She rolled her foot in the air; he watched her calf muscles contract and flex. Her toenails were painted a faint shell pink. The color matched exactly her wisp of a bathing suit, which made a nice contrast with her tanned skin.

He was glad the water was steamy hot. He had a sudden vision of himself sucking those toes, one by one, to the music of her delighted giggle-squeals. The heat disguised the resulting blush. Why would a cute little dish like this let an old fart like him —

Well, there you had it. When was the last time you heard anyone call a girl a cute little dish? Hell, that kind of talk went out with the forties. *It's not like I'm really old enough to talk like that*, he thought; it's just that — well, somehow girls like the little blonde sent him back to childhood, when his older brothers had talked like that, and it had won them girls like her to go to football games with and take to dances and even marry.

Oh, yes, Eddie had married a girl like that. Old Eddie, his second brother, the one with the dimple, had married a cute little blonde with a giggle and the longest, reddest fingernails in Sheepshead Bay. His mother had had a great deal to say, he recalled, on the subject of those nails.

And she hadn't been wrong. While Eddie was fighting for his country — or at least baking for his country; he'd been a pastry chef in the Navy — Cora Jean had gone and had a kid by a Marine on leave. A Marine who looked nothing at all like Eddie, so that the olive-skinned, curly-headed little boy she named Nicky was a constant reminder.

The funny thing was, Eddie didn't seem to mind. He put Nicky on his lap and tickled him and bought him a baseball glove and tossed the ball with him every night just as if it didn't matter. There was never another kid, so Nicky was all he had. Eddie and Cora Jean and Nicky were just about the happiest family he'd ever seen; the brothers who married nice girls who went to Mass every Sunday were miserable, but Eddie was blessed.

"What are you looking at?" The words could have been a challenge, but she asked them with a playful, flirty quality that took the edge off.

"You," he said with a smile. "You remind me of someone."

More flirty glances from under mascaraed eyelashes. "Someone nice, I hope."

"Someone very nice. Someone I think I was a little bit in love with once."

Her face fell. "Just a little bit in love? Not a whole lot in love?"

"She was married to my brother at the time. Still is, actually. I was a kid, and she was my first crush."

"Oh. That's different, then. I remember my first crush like it was yesterday."

"Sweetie, in your case, it probably was yesterday."

His foot jerked; something had touched it unexpectedly. Something touched it again. Something began teasing the hairs on his leg, playing with them, sliding up and down and causing delicious tingles.

Her foot. Her delicate, pink-toed foot was making its way up, up, up his leg.

All the way up. All the way up to his boxer trunks, all the way up to —

Her giggle had nothing on his, once her foot reached its destination.

Margot's smile was not without humor. Rueful humor, to be sure, but humor nonetheless. When she'd first started in the business, it was her job to cozy up to the mark. She was the one with the bikini and the sweet, seductive smile and the very active little foot.

There hadn't been that many hot tubs back then. Back then, you sashayed into the cocktail lounge and stood at the bar, waiting for the mark to come over and light your cigarette. Nowadays, he not only wouldn't flip a lighter open for you, he'd tell you in a snarky voice that he was allergic to smoke.

Chivalry is dead, hon. It died when the Surgeon General put that first warning on the pack.

Sherri was okay. Bubbly; guys liked those champagne blondes who went to their heads and made them silly as geese. They liked her petite fragility and the little-girl quality that contrasted so nicely with her healthy appetite for sex. Margot had been more of a Jane Russell type in her day. Big and buxom and brunette and brazen.

Another rueful smile. Mention Jane Russell to Sherri and the most you'd get is, "The bra lady? Isn't she, like, really old?"

Still, Margot reflected, it could be worse. She still had her figure, not like that old gal at the bar. The one with the weirdo glasses and the too-pink skin. She smoothed more suntan lotion on her arms and moved her head ever so slightly to catch more of the conversation in the Jacuzzi.

Sherri was dangling the hook.

The mark was ready to bite.

She had work to do.

Wasn't it a coincidence? Not only were Sherri and Stan both dining in the West Wind Dining Room at the first sitting, they were at the very same exact table. And not only were they both going into Puerto Vallarta the next morning, they had chosen the exact same excursion, the one that cost a bit more but promised authentic Mexican artifacts and the best margaritas in town at a little cantina off the tourist beaten track.

Some coincidence, Margot thought with a slightly sour air as she made her way to the dining room. She'd paid a handsome price to the young man at the accommodation desk for the last-minute change. She'd always had better luck at the late sitting herself, but Stan was an earlybird, so Sherri would eat her dinner at 6 and like it. And go into Puerto Vallarta and walk around the dirty little tourist traps in her espadrilles and hang on Stan's arm and laugh at his jokes until she had him eating out of her hand.

And then —

Then came the fun part. The part where money changed hands.

Stan was no fool. He knew a cutie like Sherri wasn't making up to him because he'd suddenly turned into Tom Cruise. She figured he had money, and she figured right. But, hell, what good was that money doing him if it couldn't buy him a couple nights of sitting next to a cuddly blonde who giggled at his jokes and slid her tanned legs close to his under the table?

"I'm in cement," he said to the guy across the table. He wished the guy would shut the hell up so he could get to know Sherri better, but the guy was playing the usual social game of 'whose is bigger?' and that was a game Stan sure as hell hated to lose.

"Biggest cement dealer in Southeast Florida," Stan went on. "You need something built, you call Stan the Man. And what do you do, Mr. —"

"Actually, it's Doctor," the guy said, which figured. He looked like a guy never actually did a day's work, just made money by knowing things and making people pay for what he knew.

Stan grunted; it was his social duty to ask the next question, to nudge the guy into telling all about his specialty, but he didn't want to know. He didn't want to waste his time with anyone except the cuddly blonde. Hell, he was here for the time of his life, wasn't he? He wasn't going to have that listening to some goofus talking about podiatry, or whatever.

Dr. Feigenbaum was not a podiatrist. He was a heart specialist. He talked about triple bypasses and heart transplants and artificial hearts until even his wife stopped beaming with pride and started nudging him in the ribs to shut up so someone else could get a word in edgewise.

"My late husband Herb died of heart failure," the plump little woman sitting next to Stan said. She pulled an honest-to-God lace hankie out of a straw bag and dabbed at her eyes under her rhinestone glasses.

That shut the doc up at last. Stan turned his full attention to Sherri, who was biting the tails off her shrimp cocktail with such sensuous enjoyment that Stan felt a stirring in his Bermuda shorts.

Puerto Vallarta was colorful and noisy. Solid little Mexican women wearing four layers of clothing in 90 degree temperatures hefted huge armfuls of blankets and displayed them before the tourists with impassive Mayan faces. Sherri clung to Stan's arm with a proprietary air that amused him; overnight they had turned into a couple.

Behind them, a discreet distance away, Margot followed unobtrusively. When Sherri turned to her and glared a warning, she took an immediate and profound interest in a window display of Oaxacan animals, intricately carved and brightly painted.

The plump older woman from the ship stopped also. "What a cute little toothpick holder," she said in a breathless voice. "I wonder why the tooth-picks are such a strange color?"

Because it's not a toothpick holder, you ninny. It's a porcupine and those are its quills.

She decided the woman would make a good cover in case Stan suspected he was being followed. So she swallowed her annoyance and explained the animal carvings, pointing out that many of them were of mythical animals like the dragon with red-orange flames coming out of its mouth.

When she moved to the next window, the little woman, who introduced herself as Rose, followed with more questions. Why were there so many images of the sun and moon? Why so many snakes? Weren't all the skeletons morbid?

"I've heard they even make candy skulls," Rose said in her breathy voice. "I can't believe any parent would let a child eat candy in the shape of a skull. It doesn't sound nice at all."

Mexico, my dear ninny, is many things, but nice isn't one of them.

"The Day of the Dead is very important in Mexico," Margot said. She was aware that she sounded like a tour guide, but what the hell — she might as well play the role so long as Sherri and Stan were still in view up ahead.

"Families honor their dead here; they take picnic lunches to the cemetery and have a party among the gravestones."

"Well," Rose replied, drawing herself to her full five-foot height, "all I can say is, we don't do things like that in St. Louis."

"Oh, look, isn't that one cute?" Sherri pointed her pink-nailed finger at one of the Day of the Dead tableaux. They were all three-sided boxes with figures inside. Musicians played instruments and dancers danced and one showed a judge sentencing a prisoner and another showed a couple getting married and each and every single one of the figures inside the boxes were skeletons. White skeletons with clothes on and big empty eye sockets and death's head grins.

"What a wonderful Halloween present." Sherri picked up one of the boxes and thrust it in Stan's face. "Doesn't this look just like the ship?"

Stan nodded. The artist who'd made this scene might have copied it directly from the Lido deck of the Mayan Princess. There was the salt-water pool, where skeleton-children swam in painted blue water. There was the spa, a painted blue circle with two skeletons enjoying the hot water. A twisted bit of cardboard mimicked the waterslide; one skeleton with its bony arms and legs outstretched came down the slide while two others waited on the ladder to take the plunge. Paper umbrellas covered tiny plastic tables, and the skeletons in the dollhouse plastic chairs held little tiny tropical drinks in their skeleton hands.

The image struck him as a lot of things: spooky, weird, sicko, off-the-wall, unnerving, and just plain wacky.

It was not cute.

He bought it for her anyway. He'd have bought her the Mayan Princess if she'd asked him for it.

And he could have done it, too. With cash.

"You know what would turn me on?" she whispered in his ear between the appetizer and the pasta course at dinner that night. "Making love on the deck. Under the stars." Her hot breath licked his ear.

His Bermuda shorts felt tight, and it wasn't from the massive amount of food he was putting away. The vision of him and Sherri on a deck chair roused him in a way that nothing had in a long time.

He'd been busy making money. Too busy to have a good time.

But that was about to change; he was going to go out on that deck as soon as the moon rose, and find a secluded place and he and Sherri were going to —

"More fettucine, sir?"

He nodded, not really having heard the question. A huge blob of white noodles landed on his plate.

"On the slide," she whispered, and this time more than her breath licked his earlobe.

"What did you —"

"On the water slide. Won't that be exotic? We'll be up on top and then, just when we're ready to — well, let's just say we'll come down the slide together."

She put heavy emphasis on the word 'come.' He almost did.

The next morning, Margot stepped onto the Lido deck wearing her lime green stretch pants and tank top, a purple straw hat that matched her sandals shading her from the sun. She registered the tiniest of frowns when she saw Sherri sitting alone at the table next to the Sea Breeze bar.

"Where's your escort this morning?" She slipped into the chair next to Sherri but perched on the edge, ready to leave as soon as she spotted Stan's boisterous Hawaiian shirt.

"We were supposed to meet here at nine," Sherri said with more than a hint of pique in her voice. "I've been waiting at least an hour. I hope he hasn't had a heart attack or anything."

Margot's lip turned up slightly. Had she ever been so young, so innocently self-assured that she believed the only reason a man would miss an opportunity to be with her was that he was dead?

"Did you think to check with his room steward?" The minute the words left her mouth, Margot realized her mistake. No question that began with the words "Did you think" was likely to produce an answer she'd be happy with.

Sherri tossed her blonde curls. "Well, I didn't want to look like some kind of slut. Like I was being too eager or anything. You said yourself that the buyer has to be the one who moves the sale."

"Right. He's on the Riviera deck; I'll just go below and —"

The opening of the salt-water pool to eager swimmers wasn't the high point of either woman's morning, as a rule. But today, when the deckhands removed the netting and the waterslide was turned on, something slid down the chute and hit the water with a loud splash.

It was Stan. Very naked and very dead. Very like the skeleton on the slide in Sherri's Day of the Dead tableau. Very like the way Sherri had suggested they make love the night before.

There was a ship's doctor, of course. Dr. Suchat, in due course — with the pool cordoned off and the passengers herded into the Sailors' Rest bar on the Promenade deck for an impromptu macarena contest — pronounced Stan dead. He concluded the man was the victim of a massive heart attack, probably brought on by an unseemly display of sexual athletics following a particularly cholesterol-laden dinner at the early sitting.

"He insisted on going to the Grand Buffet last night," a tearful Sherri confessed. "He said he was only going to look at the fancy ice carvings, but I knew he couldn't resist that Death by Chocolate."

Saying the name of the dessert brought on a fresh flood of tears. Margot handed Sherri another tissue from a box she'd found under the bar.

She felt like crying herself. She and Sherri stood to make a nice fat bundle from old Stan, and he'd gone and eaten himself to death before they could capitalize on their investment.

"Will you," Sherri said between gusty sobs, "will you bury him at sea?"

"No, no, do not think about that," Dr. Suchat said in his best bedside manner. "We have a policy in these matters and there is no need for you to —"

"What he means," Margot cut in, "is that they'll pack the poor SOB in ice like a red snapper. I'd order my drinks straight up from now on, hon. You ask for ice, you could be drinking a little piece of Stanley."

Dr. Suchat glared at her. She glared back.

Then a new voice made itself heard.

"I wondered if you might be able to use my help."

"Sir, this area is closed to the passengers at the moment," one of the white-coated stewards said. "If you'll just step this —"

"Dr. Feigenbaum," Sherri said, "thank you so much for coming. I'd feel so much better if you had a look at him."

Dr. Feigenbaum introduced himself to the ship's doctor, whose face wore an expression of mingled relief and pique. On the one hand, it was clear he didn't welcome an outsider looking at his body; on the other, if there was heat to be taken, it would be good to share it with someone else. Dead American passengers, in his experience, meant heat. And an American specialist would carry much more weight with American authorities than a doctor from Thailand.

"I would welcome your professional courtesy, Doctor," Suchat said with as good grace as he could muster.

After ten minutes of poking and prodding, opening orifices and peering inside, Dr. Feigenbaum proclaimed that the deceased had succumbed to — a massive myocardial infarction.

"Oh, thank you, Dr. Feigenbaum," Sherri said, her eyelashes working overtime, "I feel so much better now."

"That is the same thing as a heart attack," Dr. Suchat muttered, as much to himself as to Margot. "The man is agreeing with me. Why can he not just say so?"

Margot was only half-listening. Most of her brain was engaged in speculation. Was it too late, she wondered, for Sherri to turn her attention to the tall, skinny Texan with the bad toupee and the five-million-dollar tire business?

Was he at the early sitting in the West Wind dining room or the late sitting in the East Wind? Was he booked for a sightseeing tour in Ensenada, or was he going snorkeling?

Perhaps Sherri could arrange to sit next to him at the ten-dollar blackjack table. That talented little foot could work its way up his skinny calf, and they might go home winners after all.

But the skinny Texan had heard all about Sherri's pursuit of the late Stanley, and he made it clear he wasn't interested in a trip down the water slide. Neither was the insurance broker from New Jersey or the bowling alley owner from Rhode Island.

"That," Margot said over her third Gibson, "may have been my lowest point in this business. To be turned down by a man whose claim to fame is that he invented the Suds 'N' Strikes combination laundromats and bowling alleys."

"It's not my fault he saw me and Stanley making out on the bus from Puerto Vallarta," Sherri whined.

One more whine and Margot was going to leave her ashore next time, cuddly blonde or no cuddly blonde. She wasn't so old herself that she couldn't pull in a mark if she put her mind to it. In fact, she'd try it right now. She'd get right up this minute and sashay over to the Sea Breeze bar and take out a cigarette and wait for that distinguished-looking man with the blistered nose to light it for her.

"Oh, God, here comes a smoker," the blister said in a loud voice. "I'm off to seek refuge in the civilized air of the Jolly Roger. That's the only smoke-free lounge on this tub."

By the time the ship reached port and was pushed into its berth by a tiny red tugboat that somehow reminded Margot of the little pink woman with the cat's eye glasses, she and Sherri were no longer speaking. They walked down the gangplank separately, moving carefully even in the crush so as to avoid any possible physical contact. They each made for the direction of their luggage, grouped by color according to the deck they'd slept on, without exchanging a word.

Margot picked up her imitation leopard-skin cases and marched off toward a waiting taxi she'd arranged before the trip.

Never again, she thought as she gave the driver the address — in a much less fashionable section of Los Angeles than she'd led Sherri to believe. Never again would she go to sea with a total neophyte. Never again would she teach the tricks of her trade to an ungrateful little bitch who had no more sense than a shih tzu. Never again would she —

Unless, of course, she could reach Joyce. Joyce was a natural. And the Jamaican Princess sailed in four days. With good connections, they could meet in Boca and —

She leaned back in the cab with a smile of satisfaction.

Sherri stood at the curbside, her matching pink leather suitcases spread out on the sidewalk. She looked forlorn, as if she'd been abandoned by her only friend.

"Is someone picking you up, dear?" A chirpy, breathless voice sounded in her ear; she turned to see the plump lady from the boat, the one with the pointy glasses.

"No," she replied. "I was going to call a cab, but —"

"Oh, don't bother, dear. I can give you a ride as far as the airport. I think I heard you say you had a plane to catch."

Sherri smiled and thanked the lady profusely. As the porters piled their luggage into the roomy trunk, she stepped into the late-model El Dorado with the tinted windows and settled herself into the real leather upholstery with a sigh of relief.

"You did very well, my dear," Rose said as she guided the huge car out of the pier parking area. "I'm extremely pleased with your performance. You are a natural, if I do say so myself."

The breathy quality had left her voice; she sounded very much like a boss lady complimenting a subordinate.

And Sherri sounded every inch the subordinate as she replied, "Coming from you, Mrs. Ballantine, that's a real compliment. Of course," she went on, "it was just sheer luck that Dr. Feigenbaum showed up when he did. I was afraid the police wouldn't listen to that Thai doctor. If they'd held the body for autopsy —"

Rose allowed herself the slightest of deprecating coughs. "Nothing in this business is 'sheer luck,' Sheryl Anne. You should know that by now. Dr. Feigenbaum was a dear friend of my late husband's, even if he wasn't able to save Herb's life with that last bypass."

"You mean you knew Dr. Feigenbaum would be on board?" Sherri laughed. "If I'd known that, I wouldn't have missed two nights' sleep worrying about the doctor finding digitalis in his bloodstream. I was afraid Dr. Suchat would see that puncture wound on his thigh and get suspicious."

"Oh, he saw it, dear. I noticed him frowning when he examined the body."

"Then why didn't he say anything? Don't tell me he's on the payroll too?"

"No. That would become so expensive we'd have no profit from our little enterprise. Dr. Suchat is a man who wants to keep his job. He won't keep it if he tells his superiors they have a murder on board. No, a heart attack after — or perhaps during — a bout of unwise sexual congress is one thing, but murder does tend to discourage tourism."

"During?" Sherri blanched as she realized the little brown doctor had known all along that she'd been present when Stan breathed his last.

The smile on Rose's pleasant face wouldn't have looked out of place on

Margot's. "And then, of course, there was that awful woman you were traveling with. Dr. Suchat knew very well what she was up to, and since you were working with her, he assumed that the late unlamented Stanley meant a great deal more to you alive than dead. I was counting on that, of course, when I sent you to her for 'instruction.' "

Another thought struck Sherri. As the brown California hills sped by outside the noiseless white carriage, she said, "I couldn't believe it when I saw that Day of the Dead box with the skeleton coming down the slide. I know you had it made and placed in the shop for me to find, but wasn't it incredibly dangerous? What if someone had made the connection?"

"Ah, my dear," Rose replied, her voice carrying a wealth of nostalgia. "It was your first job, and I wanted you to have a souvenir. Something that will always remind you of your professional debut. I still have my souvenir from that first outing with Herb, and I treasure them still."

She fingered the rhinestone sunglasses and a teary smile spread across her pink lips.

"And now," she said a minute later, all business again, "we must plan your next triumph. I'll give you all the details regarding the target at the airport; I've booked you on the Jamaican Princess out of Boca Raton."

When Nancy Pickard called to ask about doing a First Lady short story, I begged for Abigail Adams because of her proto-feminist ideas. I dearly love Gore Vidal's gossipy historical fiction, so I tried to emulate him in constructing my story of political deceit and betrayal in the election of 1800. Since the Adamses were all prolific letter writers, the epistolary form seemed perfect for this tale of very early Washington, D.C The nasty crack about Georgetown is authentic Abigail, as is the coinage "newsliars."

"A" IS FOR ADAMS

November 26, 1800
New York City

The little man with the big voice spoke as if to the small circle of men around him, but his words were intended for a larger audience than that assembled in the courtyard of Fraunces Tavern, the chief watering place of New-York's political class.

"As a true Federalist," he declaimed in a tone more suited to the meeting-hall, "I could wish for nothing more ardently than the re-election of a President of my own philosophy." He paused and clasped his hands behind his waist, thrusting one stocking-clad leg before the other in a belligerent stance.

The orator's voice dropped a full octave as he finished in a low, thrilling tone, as if confiding a terrible secret, "But as a patriot, there is nothing on this earth I desire less than the re-election of that usurper. He shall have no support from this quarter, sir, not even if my worst enemy should win the prize instead."

Shrewd smiles and knowing nods said that everyone present recalled the last election, when Aaron Burr's support contrived to exalt that same enemy, Republican Thomas Jefferson, to the post of Vice-President under the Federalist Adams.

"Aye," an old man with the piercing blue eyes and ruddy face of a seaman said, "We didn't topple King George from his throne only to exalt King John in his place, sir."

A tall man wearing the new fashion of trousers instead of knee-breeches, spoke up. "Ah, but will the prize fall to Mr. Jefferson, sir, or will it go to another who even now intrigues for a greater place than the voters intend him to have?"

"That remark can have but one meaning, sir," Hamilton said, his tone dangerously calm. "What intrigue is Burr up to now?"

The red-faced seaman answered with a coarse laugh. "Hadn't you heard? He's going to marry his way into the presidency."

"What the gentleman means," the tall man said, with only the tiniest emphasis on the word *gentleman,* "is that Burr's daughter is engaged to marry South Carolina in return for its votes supporting him as president and relegating Jefferson to vice-president."

"Aye, the prospective son-in-law is on his way to Monticello even as we speak," a small man in a large hat explained, "bearing a letter which conveys Burr's absolute and total loyalty. And you know, sir," he added with a snigger, "what that portends."

Hamilton's answering smile was not a pleasant sight. "Yes, Mr. Burr is always at his most treacherous when he is swearing fidelity, is he not? What, after all, can be expected of a man who served under Benedict Arnold in the late war?"

This sally, while shopworn with age and overuse, never failed to produce a murmur of approval from veterans of the war for independence.

"What would happen if this letter failed to reach its intended recipient, I wonder," Hamilton ruminated. "What, indeed, would happen if the writer's true intention were to be made plain?"

The tall man in trousers gave a single nod. He and Hamilton stepped away from the crowd and sat together in a dim corner of the tavern. By the time the innkeeper shut for the night, they had their plan.

A substitute letter. A letter revealing Burr's true mind. A letter which would be found on the person of young Mr. Alston — for that was the South Carolina bridegroom's name. A letter to be 'discovered' by accident and circulated intentionally in the circles where it would do the most harm to Burr — and the most good to Hamilton.

What Fraunces Tavern was to the Federalist Party, the newly-formed Tammany Hall was to the Republicans. There Aaron Burr, de facto leader of the party, held court at the table nearest the fireplace. He sat at his ease, a long clay pipe in one hand and a glass of madeira in the other.

"Adams is finished," he proclaimed. "The Federalists' day is over, and the Republicans' day is dawning."

"All the same, Mr. Burr," a large man in a dirty waistcoat said, "do you not fear the Virginia junto as much as the Massachusetts faction?"

"Mr. Adams has no faction, sir," Burr replied with a laugh. "Mr. Adams is far too contentious a man to attract sufficient following to constitute a faction. What he does have —" and here the speaker paused, with the sure instinct of a born orator, waiting for the curiosity of his listeners to mount — "what he does have, that our late, lamented first President lacked, is a son. A son worthy of a dynasty."

Brows knit. Throats rumbled. "Adams made his own son envoy to Prussia," one man said with a firm shake of the head. "General Washington never would have done that. Never."

All agreed that General Washington, who had just been laid to rest at his beloved Mount Vernon, was the one and only model of a President, and that the present incumbent was a poor substitute.

But what of the son? What of John Quincy Adams, that limb of Satan, that Prince Hal with a Harvard education?

"I tell you, sir," Burr declaimed, "it is plain as day that young Mr. Adams has his sights firmly set upon the same house his father now occupies with such a notable lack of distinction. It will do our cause little good," he went on, letting his dark eyes roam the circle, bringing the men under his spell, "to rid the country of Mr. John Adams so long as Mr. Quincy Adams is permitted to run free."

More nods and murmurs of agreement. Men who had never given one second's thought to the existence of John Quincy Adams were now determined to prevent his rise to the presidency.

"No," he continued, raising his voice once again, "the Federal City must be cleansed of Adamses, purged of the New England disease, scoured from top to bottom like a milk-jug permitted to sour. Not a cat belonging to that family shall remain in the capital when I've finished."

This pronouncement was greeted with loud laughter, some applause, and many offers to buy Mr. Burr a small beer. He sat back in his chair with a self-satisfied smile on his saturnine face. He would do it, too; he would scotch the budding political career of the Adams brat, who was even now basking in the glow of a successful treaty with the Prussian king.

But how? That was the question.

Letters, he decided over a friendly pipe with one of his sycophants, an actor from Crumley's Theatre on Maiden Lane. Letters were the life-blood of the Adams family. How ironically pleasant, how poetically just, it would be if a letter were to be the downfall of Adams the Younger.

November 30, 1800
Washington City

My dearest John Quincy,

I have but lately arrived in the place everyone calls the Federal City, but it is a City in Name only. Such mud I have not seen since that Spring in London, when the sewers overflowed and their contents spilled into every drawing-room in Mayfair. I only hope that if there is ever a City named for your Father it will boast finished streets instead of rutted lanes stinking of horse droppings.

Of the President's mansion, the less said the better. It is a castle of a house and will doubtless be a fine dwelling once it is staffed by the twenty or so servants it requires. As I have but five, you will draw your own conclusions as to our Style of living. The rear yard is a sea of mud; I have therefore chosen the East Room as the perfect place in which to dry the laundry. It will someday serve as an assembly hall, but at the moment it is hung with bed linens and table cloths, which even a constant fire in the grate cannot render dry enough to use.

Your father has chosen a rather odd egg-shap'd room as his office. The room above it is designated the Elliptical Saloon, and would be a charming location for my Tuesday afternoon levees, but for the fact that the plaster on the walls refuses to dry. There is also the trifling matter of the absence of a staircase between the first and second floors, but no doubt the guests could shinny up a pole if need be.

I need not tell you, dear Quincy, that these private jests are not to be repeated. We are well aware that this is a House built for the Ages and not for the convenience of the Adams family. Whenever anyone here asks how I like the house, I smile and reply — and quite truthfully, too! — that the situation is remarkably fine. It has become such a habit with me that when your father and I both ran across the muddy yard to the outdoor privy — oh, how I miss my modern water closet in Philadelphia, dear John Quincy! — he said, "Oh, but Abby, think of the situation. Consider the situation, my dear." And so we both commenced to laugh, which is the only sensible thing to do when living in a completely intolerable state.

All is not well with your brother Charles. Indeed, I brought little Susan with me — she is four years old and knows all her Goody Goose by heart. I cannot help but fear I shall never again see my Bonny Prince Charlie, and that the dear child will never again see her father.

I shall close for now, but will always remain,

Your loving mother, Abigail Adams

The actor sat at the writing-desk in the common room of Tunnicliff's Hotel, the only habitable hostelry in the raw, unfinished capital. He regarded his handiwork with a smile of satisfaction.

The letter was complete. It resembled to an uncanny degree the one Burr had given him to use as a model. The language was that of a scholar, flavored at intervals with a foreign phrase. He shook his head as he sprinkled sand over the parchment to dry the ink. These Adamses were just as bad as Mr. Burr had said; true Americans didn't use fancy French and German to express their honest sentiments.

He read the lines over again, holding the candle so close it was like to light the parchment and render it to ashes. Yes, he decided, the letter would do. It would convince anyone who read it that young Mr. Adams had made a lucrative financial gain from the treaty with Prussia.

There was but one more touch which would confirm the authenticity of the letter and seal Prince John's fate.

The actor smiled at his pun. For what he needed was John Quincy Adams' personal seal for the wax. One look at that seal and anyone would believe the letter genuine, for how could you sit in a tavern in Washington City and forge a letter using the seal of a man in Berlin?

You could do it if you had a duplicate seal.

And by tomorrow night, a duplicate seal was exactly what he would have.

December 1, 1800
Washington City

Dear John Quincy,

We have this Evening entertained a Visitor from your part of the World. Count Rupert von Hohensteiner presented his compliments at the Tuesday levee and was most Effusive in his Praise of your excellent Conduct of affairs in Berlin. We were most gratified to hear news of you, dear Quincy, and so we invited Count Rupert to a private supper.

My residence in this City has not served to endear the world to me. I am sick, sick, sick of Publick Life and desire nothing more ardently than a return to my beloved Braintree. This happy event will not be long in coming, for your Father is certain that he will not be re-elected. For my own Part, I am content, though I think it a Shame that a man who has given so much to his country should be thrown on the Ash-heap when that country has finished with him.

You will say, no doubt, that as a Woman I have no right to meddle in Publick affairs. If a woman does not hold the Reins of Government, I see no reason for her not judging how they are conducted. You will recall that when we lived in Philadelphia, I often visited the Senate to watch your Father preside over that contentious body. If I do not do so here in Washington City, you must attribute my absence to the immense amount of work to be done in the house, and not to a Want of Interest.

I remain, ever your loving,

Mother

It was the best trick of all, pretending to be a Prussian aristocrat, fawning over John Quincy Adams before his doting parents even as he contrived to slip away and secure the twin tokens of their ambitious son's downfall. The actor whistled as he walked to his hotel, and his fingers caressed the signet ring he had taken from the president's desk drawer.

Back at the hotel, he ordered a glass of the best port and settled himself at the writing-desk in the common-room. He would have preferred privacy, but the sleeping chambers in the hotel were so sparse, so barren of even the most rudimentary furnishings, that he had no room to complete his business there. Besides, who would take notice of a man at a writing-desk putting the finishing touches on a letter?

He reached toward the candle atop the secretary, and used its flame to light a stick of wax in the exact shade of green favored by young Mr. Adams. He dripped several drops of wax on the folded halves of the parchment forgery, then carefully set the signet ring atop the melted circle. Quickly, he lifted the ring and placed the thimble on top of the still-soft initials. It was delicate and careful work; the resulting mark must look as if it had been made by a single seal.

The two impressions — the initials JQA from the signet ring, and the laurel wreath embossed on the thimble — together constituted the insignia on the seal used by John Quincy Adams.

The actor waited for the wax to dry, then stuffed the letter into his coat pocket and set out again into the raw November night.

A tall man in trousers leaned forward from his wing chair in the rear of the common room. He leaned forward just far enough to catch a glimpse of the signet ring and the resulting impression in the wax. The letter A stood out like a beacon, calling to him from across the room.

He was to wait for a man named Alston, who would stop at Tunnicliff's Hotel in Washington City on his way to Monticello. A man who carried a letter that must be replaced with another letter of far different import.

And here was the man, bold as brass, sitting in the publick room at his hotel, writing that very letter he was to obtain at all costs. Rising from his seat and setting forth into the deserted city at this ungodly hour when no one with a lawful purpose was to be seen abroad.

The trouser-clad man rose with a fluid motion and followed his quarry into the chill night air. He quickened his step and soon fell in behind the man with the letter.

He lifted his arm and, with the help of a stocking filled with sand, delivered a crushing blow. The man bent forward and fell with a heavy thud.

As he reached toward the man's coat to remove the letter, he realized his victim had struck his head on a rock and lay very, very still. He touched the man's neck and felt no pulse. He placed a hand over the man's mouth; no air went in or out.

He was dead. Alston was dead.

Hamilton hadn't wanted the man dead. He had only wanted the letter replaced.

And replaced it would be. The letter Hamilton had forged would be found on Alston's body, and the world would believe he had been set upon by highwaymen.

The trousered man reached into the dead man's coat pocket and pulled out a parchment rectangle.

He gave it a cursory glance, expecting to see the seal of the Alston family. Instead, he recoiled in horror.

The initials on the seal contained the JA that one would expect for Joseph Alston, but there was an additional Q in the center.

Q for Quincy. JQA for John Quincy Adams.

He had killed the wrong man.

December 2, 1800
The President's House

It was bright and shiny. Susan loved things that were bright and shiny. She loved her little locket that Aunt Nabby gave her for her birthday. But Cousin Louisa wouldn't let her wear it now. Cousin Louisa said she had to wear a horrid black necklace instead, just as she had taken Susan's nice blue dress away and made her wear a heavy, starchy black frock that caught under her slippers when she ran.

Cousin Louisa said she wasn't to run, either. Little girls whose fathers were dying weren't supposed to run.

She was sorry Papa was sick, but she didn't see how running would make him feel any worse.

The sun glinted off the bright little thing, which peeked out at her from underneath a leaf next to the outdoor privy. Susan knelt down and picked up the shiny object.

It was a thimble. A thimble Susan recognized as Gran's because it had a circle of leaves on its top.

She ought to take it to Gran at once. Gran would want to have it back.

But it was so pretty, and it shone like fire in the sunlight.

Gran wouldn't want her to prick her finger when she did her sewing lesson. Gran would want her to have the thimble. She was sure of it.

Susan slipped the bright object into the pocket of the huge black skirt, but then remembered that Cousin Louisa had a nasty habit of asking her to turn out her pockets. She'd hide the thimble in her special place, under the little pile of firewood, where no one would find it. She'd put it next to the other treasure she'd found that morning, the gold ring with an A on it.

"A," she chanted aloud as she skipped to the woodpile, "is for Apple. A is for Ant, and A is for Adams." She slipped the thimble under the log, setting it beside the A is for Adams ring. Then she went inside to ask Cook for a slice of bread and treacle.

December 3, 1800
Washington City

My dear John Quincy,

We have had a Most Disturbing Turn of Events at the President's house, but one that you shall not read about in the Publick Press. I thank God for the Sedition Act; if it were not in place, I shudder to think what the newsliars would make of it. They are as false as Hell — or as false as the English, which is worse.

I shall endeavor to set forth the Facts as they Occurred. First, Mr. Ingleby, our butler — he is a Virginian to the core and shows open Disdain for our New England ways — announced that there was a dead body in the privy. Your father insisted upon being shown the corpse, and was dismayed to recognize it as Count Rupert von Hohensteiner.

Such is the State of Disarray in the Federal City that even President Adams had no earthly idea as to whether there were Local Authorities who ought to be summoned. The City has no mayor, and even the lowly office of Town Watchman has yet to be filled. Mr. Ingleby mentioned that the only place in town with a sufficiently large Ice-house to keep the body fresh was Tunnicliff's Hotel. A servant was dispatched and Mr. Tunnicliff himself attended upon us within the hour.

Imagine our Surprize and Consternation when he identified the corpse as that of Jeremiah Hazlitt, late of New-York City — an Actor!

Why an Actor should impose himself upon the President and his Wife by impersonating a foreigner is unknown at present, but Mark this Well, John Quincy: the man did not pretend to be a Frenchman or a Hindoo. He acted the part of a Prussian aristocrat and he claimed a connexion with you.

Your Father believes the mischief to be the Work of Aaron Burr, who is a constant schemer and will stop at nothing to insure high office for himself. I have no Opinion on the Matter, although the Venality of a Man as Licentious as Mr. Burr is not to be underestimated.

My chiefest fear, dear Quincy, is that this affair will somehow recoil upon you and your work in Berlin.

I remain your Devoted and Ever-Vigilant
Mother

December 4, 1800
Alexandria

Dear Mr. Hamilton:

It is with mixed emotions that I greet you and render an Account of recent Events of Interest to us Both. Due to a circumstance entirely beyond my Control, I found myself staring into the Eyes of a Dead Man and realizing I had dispatched the wrong man to his Maker.

I could not leave the body in the Street, for it was too near the hotel, and I might be remembered there. No, I reasoned, the body must be moved. But where?

A cunning, wicked, low thought struck me at that moment. I bent down and lifted the body, then hefted it over my shoulder and carried it to the president's house, where I propped it up in the privy behind the mansion.

Let King John make what he can of that, sir, I said to myself as I sauntered away.

I have no doubt that you will thank me for a good night's work in spite of my little mistake. I am even now on my way to Monticello to meet the real Mr. Alston.

Your Devoted Servant,
Brutus

Post scriptum:

The dead man carried a letter on his person, along with a note saying the letter contained proof that John Quincy Adams is a corrupt betrayer of the publick trust. I considered that this Letter might serve as a Benefit to you, sir, and so I placed it into Hands that would disseminate it as widely as possible. I slipped it under the door for Mr. Adams' butler to find. He is no friend to the Federalist cause, and will use the letter to make much Mischief, if I am any judge.

December 6, 1800

My dear Sister,

I write this letter in a state of Perplexity and Confusion. I know you will have reason to understand my Situation, as your son William was once embroiled in a financial scandal that was not of his making.

Of all my children, John Quincy worried me least. He was always a helpmate to his father and me, and never gave Trouble in any way. You more than anyone know how Charles grieved me with his drinking and Thomas with his want of steadiness and Nabby with her marriage. Only John Quincy seemed above any possible danger.

Now that danger has come upon him, and it is a bitter pill indeed. I do not know whether he is aware of it, but Washington City talks of little else. I journeyed to George Town today — which is the very dirtyest hole I ever saw for a place of any trade — and overheard a fish monger remarking that "some people's sons were born to disappoint them." He said the words just loud enough for me to hear, and when I stared him down, he blushed and turned away.

That my son, my successful and brilliant son, should be spoken of in a derogatory manner by a fish monger raises a gust of anger such as I have not felt since John was in Philadelphia at the Continental Congress and I feared we should capitulate to England! My very Soul rebels at the thought that John Quincy could act in a manner unbefitting to his station and his Name.

A letter has been shown round Washington City, passed from hand to hand like a scurrilous ballad. It purports to prove that John Quincy's treaty with Prussia was negotiated for his own financial benefit and not the Good of the Nation.

I contrived to procure a copy of the letter. The writing and phrasing are similar to John Quincy's, which signifies only that it was made by a competent forger. This alone would be damning, but the truly incriminating fact is that the letter was sealed with an insignia containing the letters J, Q, and A intertwined within a border of laurel leaves.

There may be many such seals, I do not know, although these are far from common initials. What I do know is that I ordered a seal of this exact description to be made for my son on the occasion of his appointment to the Berlin post.

There is not a single particle of my being that believes John Quincy capable of writing such a letter. Yet I cannot explain the presence of his seal on the forgery. Surely the writer did not travel to Berlin for the purpose of sealing a faked letter.

This has something to do, I am certain, with the dead actor in the privy.

Though vexed and concerned, I remain,

Ever your loving Sister,
Abby

Susan dashed across the yard, now hard and dry after the first frost, to her cubbyhole under the woodpile. She scrabbled under the log and pulled out her locket. She might not be able to wear it, but she could open it with her tiny fingers and gaze upon the miniatures of her mother and father. She wasn't sure what dying meant, but she knew she would never see her Papa again, and Mama was far away.

Perhaps Cousin Louisa would let her carry the locket with her, if she asked nicely.

She reached back inside the hole and fished around for the thimble. She knew she ought to take it back to Gran. But her hand touched something hard, something that hadn't been there before. She pulled it out; it was a stone. A plain gray stone. She hadn't put it there. She wouldn't have put it there.

She frowned and thrust her hand inside the hiding place, determined to make sure all her treasures were accounted for.

But they weren't. The ring was gone. The ring with the letter A for Adams was gone, and this ugly little stone left in its place.

She remembered a story her mother had told her, about the fairies carrying away a child. She'd thought for a moment that she'd like to be taken by fairies; their lives sounded so much more interesting than her own. And the fairies, Mama said, always left something behind in place of the baby. A cabbage or a rabbit or a magic lamp.

The fairies must have taken the A for Adams ring and left her this plain old pebble instead.

Susan sighed as she put her things back into their hiding place. Next time, she thought, I hope the fairies leave me something better than an old rock.

December 8, 1800

My dearest Betsy,

I know, my much loved Sister, that you will Weep with me over the Grave of a poor unhappy Child who cannot now add another pang to those which have pierced my Heart for several years past.

Poor Charlie's tormented life ended last Week. He was the gayest of my children, and the one who was quickest to win hearts. John Quincy is the match of any man in the Republic for honor and depth of understanding, and Thomas is a shrewd lawyer, but Charlie was a man at whom everyone smiled. I do not know if it is Charlie the man I shall miss, or if memories of his golden boyhood fill my mind more completely at this moment. I only know that a light has gone out of my life.

It is both Pleasure and Pain to have little Susan with us at this time. Pleasure, because her childish laughter warms this great Barn of a house, and Pain, because the sight of her playing Horsie with her Grand-papa brings back memories of Charlie as a little lad, and also calls to mind my own little Susanna, dead these many years.

At least two of our mysteries have been Cleared Up. The dead man in the privy seems to have been murdered by highwaymen; this Federal City is in the midst of wilderness and so such Occurrences, while Deplorable, are only to be expected.

As to the letter supposedly written by John Quincy, I have divined how the seal was counterfeited. You may recall that it was formed of his initials, which I copied from a signet ring he used to wear, and a wreath of laurel leaves like the one on the silver thimble Grandmother Quincy left me.

What could be more simple than to obtain these two items, and so create a wax impression the spit and image of the seal? And what better way to gain entrance to the president's house than to pretend Acquaintance with his son?

I hastened at once to search for the ring and the thimble, and I am both dismayed and pleased to have had no results. Pleased, because this means my Theory is Sound; the ring and thimble must have been stolen by this very Actor whose Body we discovered in the privy. And dismayed, because without the ring and thimble to show how the trick was done, my protests will sound Hollow indeed.

John takes the View that we should be above politicks, which after all is a mere catch-penny, but I cannot be so Sanguine, as it is my son's Character which is at stake.

Your truly affectionate but afflicted Sister,

Adams

"Where *is* that thimble?" Gran poked her hands into the sewing basket and rummaged until the threads and ribbons lay on the floor in a colorful heap. It was the fifth time she had turned out the entire basket, but she refused to accept the notion that the thimble would never be found.

Susan stared into the fire, hoping no one would notice her. But then Cousin Louisa said, her voice as sharp as Gran's scissors, "Child, do you know where your grandmother's thimble is?"

"I didn't steal it, Gran," Susan protested. "I found it in the yard and I kept it because it was so pretty and shiny, but the fairies came and changed it into a buckeye."

"That child and her stories!" Cousin Louisa looked as though she wanted to slap Susan, who began to cry in anticipation.

"It's true, Gran," she protested, throwing herself upon the mercy of the older woman. "I put it in my secret place, only the next time I went there, it was gone and there was a buckeye instead. It was the fairies, Gran, truly it was."

Louisa murmured something about the path to Perdition, but Gran said, "Let us go see this remarkable buckeye."

Susan led the way, her heart sinking. What if the buckeye was gone? What if the fairies changed it back into a thimble? She smoothed her black skirt behind her, as if anticipating the sting of a switch on her tiny rear end.

Under the wobbly log in the woodpile, they found one child's locket, a spray of dead flowers, a broken fan, a doll's hat, a comb with no teeth, a round pebble, and a fat, shiny buckeye.

Susan sighed with relief and said, "You see? That's where I put the thimble."

"Stuff and nonsense," Louisa said. "I daresay we shall find the thimble in the child's room."

Susan picked up the pebble. "It used to be the A is for Adams ring, but then the fairies came and took it and left this in its place."

Gran frowned.

Susan blanched. Was there going to be a spanking in her future after all?

"What do you mean, child, A is for Adams?"

"I found it," Susan protested. "I didn't steal it out of Grand-papa's desk drawer. I didn't."

"How did you know it was in your grandfather's desk drawer if you didn't —"

"Hush, Louisa. Are you talking about a ring with the letter A on it, Susan?"

" 'A is for apple, A is for Ant, and A is for Adams,' " Susan chanted. "That's what Papa used to say."

A look of sadness came over her grandmother's face. It seemed as if everyone who talked about her papa did so with sadness now.

Louisa looked at her aunt as if she had lost her celebrated mind. "Aunt Abigail, all we need do is search this child's room, and you shall find your thimble. And, I daresay, a great many other things that have gone missing."

"I may be the President's Lady, Louisa," Abigail Adams replied, "but I am a farmer's wife at heart. And I think we will have better luck finding what we seek if we look in that hollow tree behind the privy."

December 12, 1800

Dearest Johnny,

I hope this form of Address does not Offend, but sometimes a Mother must surely be permitted to remember her Son as he was before he Attained his Exalted Position in the World. Perhaps it is Charlie's passing that makes me sentimental. Or perhaps the sight of little Susan sitting on her grandfather's knee and blowing soap-bubbles through his favorite pipe brings me in mind of my children when you were Young.

You will no doubt Remark that if you or Nabby had ever done such a thing, your Father would not have chuckled indulgently, but the World has long known that Grandfathers are far more lenient than Fathers when it comes to the little ones.

I write to set your Mind at Rest concerning the Late Excitement regarding a counterfeit count. The matter has been most satisfactorily resolved, thanks to a small gray mammal known as the trade rat.

I had already divined that the seal purporting to be yours was contrived by the use of a signet ring and Grandmother Quincy's thimble. Both, however, were missing — and little Susan proclaimed that they had been stolen by Fairies. Something she said convinced me that in essence she was correct: the items had been removed and something else left in their place.

You will doubtless recall the Incident of the Missing Salt Cellar. I was overly Severe to a young maid, whom I believed had misplaced our silver Salt Cellar that came down to us from the Boylstons. I cannot now recall whether it was Charles or Thomas who discovered the Salt Cellar in a hollow tree, along with other Interesting Objects hoarded by a trade rat, so called because he seldom takes one object without leaving another.

A thorough search of the trees in the yard behind the President's House uncovered the rat's nest, in which we found both thimble and signet ring. I quickly used them to make an impression in wax, which proved identical to the one on the fraudulent letter.

The end of it all is that while your Father will surely be sent packing by an Ungrateful Electorate, your reputation remains unstained by any Hint of Scandal. As you make your way in Publick Life, you shall have the satisfaction of knowing that you were spared by the efforts of your loving mother and a rat. My only uncertainty is as to which of us performed the greater service, but since he lost both home and treasure, I must own that the rat made the greater sacrifice and is therefore entitled to a larger measure of gratitude than

Your loving
Mama

It is probably no surprise to the reader that this began as two separate stories, one about Avery Nyquist, Wall Street hotshot, and the other about an elderly woman on a death penalty jury. But neither story really got off the ground until I put them together, juxtaposing the two women's experiences in dealing with a difficult case headed for the Supreme Court.

CRUEL AND UNUSUAL

New York City, November, 1994

It was a typical Ambrose, Jeffers file: thick as the Manhattan telephone directory, every page neatly aligned, color tabs for the sixteen exhibits at the end. Avery Nyquist had thumbed through hundreds of case files in her seven years as an associate with the prestigious firm, read thousands upon thousands of legal documents, digested millions of words designed to throw a cloak of legalistic obfuscation over the simplest fact.

Never had she read, or even imagined reading, the words of Petitioner's Exhibit "A". They lay before her, their coal-hard reality sending a chill through her. It was as though a black widow spider had walked across the pristine surface of Avery's designer desk.

"... there to be taken to a place determined by law, to be subject to execution by means of the electric chair, until he shall be pronounced dead by a duly authorized coroner of the state of Wyoming."

A death warrant. She was looking at a death warrant. A piece of paper, duly signed, stamped, and filed with the county clerk, a piece of legal paper just like all the thousands of papers she'd read in her legal lifetime. Only because of this paper, a boy would die.

She had been asked to do many things since her first day at the most prestigious law firm on Wall Street. Work from eight in the morning until midnight, then show up bright and eager for more at seven the next morning; argue a major securities fraud appeal before the Court of Appeals in Albany, then dash to a top-secret merger negotiation on Maiden Lane that evening — and be fully prepared for both, facts, figures, and legal precedents at her polished fingertips; visit a hapless junior arbitrageur at the Metropolitan Correctional Center, then go to an elaborate sushi lunch with Japanese bankers and know just the right things to say to both.

But this was too much.

Avery stared at the file for a few more minutes, considering her options with the same cool detachment she brought to her clients' affairs. Could she afford to say no? And if she could, how should she do it?

At last, sighing, she ran a hand through her shoulder-length blonde hair, pushing it back from her forehead in a gesture her colleagues would have identified at once as signifying Decision Mode. She pushed herself back from the polished desk and hefted the file. Heavy. Too heavy.

She marshaled her arguments as she strode down the hall toward her mentor's office. Harrison Jeffers III had always supported her at the firm, had always recommended her for the tough assignments other partners doubted she was ready for; he had run interference for her on those few occasions where her suggestions fell on deaf ears. Surely he would see how absurd it was to waste her valuable time and talent on a case more suited to a Chambers Street criminal lawyer.

It took all of thirty seconds for Avery to see that her optimism was unfounded. The deep wrinkle between Hal's eyebrows became a canyon as he listened to her carefully worded reluctance to handle the case.

"Avery," he began, in the near-condescending tone he'd used when she first arrived at the firm, a bright-eyed, eager law graduate. "I wouldn't have assigned you the case without good reason."

His ice-blue eyes looked into hers. She was supposed to lower her lashes, defer to his masculine authority, agree that of course he was right and she'd been a fool to question his wisdom.

But that was not how she'd earned the respect of one of the sharpest minds on Wall Street.

She kept her eyes locked with his. "I am probably the best securities fraud litigator in this country," she said. "I know more about the Securities and Exchange Commission's rules than people who've spent twenty years at the SEC. I know Blue Sky Law better than the people who deal in speculative stocks. I have the complexities of civil RICO at my fingertips." She paused to let her words and her air of confidence sink in. Then she went for the jugular of her argument.

"So what am I doing representing a berserk teenager who killed his family with a shotgun? In Wyoming, no less?" She softened the challenge with a smile and a shake of her head. She could afford a touch of femininity so long as she didn't let it detract from her edge.

"You're fulfilling this firm's commitment to *pro bono* litigation." Hal leaned back in his custom leather swivel chair, puffed on his pipe, and waited for her comeback. He was, as usual, enjoying the verbal tennis match.

So was she. Leaning back in the client chair, which was three inches closer to the ground than Hal's, she copied his pose of leisured ease. They had all the time in the world, and she was his equal. Those were the messages her body language sent across his uncluttered ebony desk.

She crossed expensively stockinged legs. "I know what *pro bono* means. It's the legal equivalent of Mobil Oil sponsoring a public television program on the environment. It's the WASP version of Yom Kippur: one day's atonement for a year of sins. I understand all that. What I don't understand is why this case isn't being handled by a two-year associate hungry for litigation instead of one with a desk already piled with matters that should have been conferenced yesterday."

"For one thing, you've already been to the Supreme Court," Hal said. He took the predictable three puffs on his pipe before continuing. "I want someone who can go before the Court and *argue*, not sweat bullets because he's finally made the big time. Someone who won't be awed by just being there. Someone who —"

Avery raised a weary hand. "All right," she conceded. "Understood. You want experience. So why not let me supervise one of the younger associates from here, then fly down to D.C. on the day of argument? That way, you'll get the benefit of my experience and I'll still have time for my important cases."

Hal raised an eloquent eyebrow. "A young man is about to be electrocuted by the state of Wyoming, and that's not an 'important' case?"

"You know what I mean," she retorted. "Important to the firm."

"Important to your career," he countered, but his tolerant smile took the sting out of the words.

"That's always been the same thing," Avery argued. She abandoned her pose of leisured ease and leaned forward in her chair. "What's good for the firm is good for my career, and vice versa. That's the way it should be. And that's why this is different: it doesn't matter to the firm, and it could even damage my career by taking me away from cases I should be prioritizing."

She didn't bother to add what they both knew, that it could damage her career if she didn't win in court. And the odds of winning a death penalty case in the present political climate were very low indeed.

Hal sighed. He laid his now-cold pipe on the marble ashtray that flanked his left arm. "I had hoped never to hear you use language like that, Avery," he said, more in sorrow than anger. "There is no such word as 'prioritize'."

Avery grinned. This was the Hal she'd always loved to do battle with — the nitpicker, the elitist, the world-weary cynic. Surely descending into a discussion of syntax meant she'd won her point. Her shoulder muscles relaxed in anticipation of victory; she considered asking her mentor if he wanted to share a late lunch at Fraunces Tavern.

"The thing is, my dear," Hal said, his tone one of patient finality, "I made a promise to a friend. A very old friend. I said I would send my best lawyer on this case. And that, I'm afraid — or rather, I am not afraid, I am in fact pardonably proud to say — is you."

Cody, Wyoming, June 1987

Mr. Farkas was a practical man. He kept saying so, over and over, in a louder and louder voice, as if no one else in the jury room could come close to him in the matter of practicality.

Mr. Dundee didn't care how practical Mr. Farkas was. He was tired of being bullied, and his weariness showed in the droop of his eyelids and the cutting edge of his tongue. "Give it a rest, Farkas. We all know where you stand. Give someone else a chance to talk, will you?"

Farkas grunted. "If they say something worth listening to," he grumbled.

" 'Something worth listening to,' " the little teacher with the pageboy hairdo echoed, "I suppose that means something you agree with."

"I'm tired of hearing a bunch of crap about how that kid isn't responsible for what he did," Farkas retorted.

The teacher's favorite technique was to repeat what others said and put little quotation marks around it, give it an ironic twist that mocked the speaker. " 'A bunch of crap,' " she repeated, her tone speculative, "I don't think I've ever heard that particular phrase before. I'm not at all certain you can actually have a bunch of —"

"I wouldn't mind going home sometime in the next decade," the tall thin man with the goatee interjected.

Mrs. Barstow couldn't remember all their names. Twelve jurors meant eleven names she had to hold in her mind all at once. Mr. Farkas she had no trouble remembering; he was a florid man with a big mouth who reminded her of that actor who always seemed to play generals in 1950's movies. She couldn't remember the actor's name anymore, but Mr. Farkas looked and sounded just like him, all bluster and noise.

Mr. Dundee was black. Well, not black exactly, more like coffee with cream. He worked for the post office and Mrs. Barstow could just see him doing it, could picture him standing behind the counter making little jokes while he waited on people. He was the kind who'd show up during the Christmas rush with a fuzzy Santa Claus hat. The kind who when you asked for a special stamp, he'd open the drawer and look for it, not just snap that they were out of those and couldn't she see there were people waiting behind her.

No wonder Mr. Dundee thought Tyler Baines was innocent. He was the kind of man who thought the best of people.

The others she tended to think of by looks or occupation. There was the schoolteacher and the man with the goatee and the pregnant girl and the two young men with Mexican names; she could never remember which was Hernandez and which was Lopez. One worked in a garage, but she couldn't remember for the life of her what the other one did. There was the bottle blonde — although Mrs. Barstow had to admit they made hair dye a lot more natural now than they had in her day; you couldn't really tell except that this girl didn't have the complexion that went with real blonde hair.

The last three jurors were closer to her own age. One was a widow; the other two, in that strange coincidence that happened on juries, had both worked for Montgomery Ward. They lunched together every day, exchanging stories about people they had known in common. Mrs. Barstow thought one looked familiar from her own shopping days, but she hadn't said anything. The other one looked like somebody she wouldn't have wanted to return something to.

The widow was speaking her mind. ". . . have to remember what that doctor said about Tyler's ability to control his impulses. The boy is just not like other people. We can't forget that."

Farkas snorted and was about to put his two cents in when one of the Mexicans jumped in. "Man, I don't know about them doctors," he said with a shake of his head. "I don't want to sound like I'm ignorant or nothing, but I can't accept that some kid blows his father and sisters away with a shotgun and we gotta let him go on account of what some doctor says."

"But if he didn't know what he was doing," the nice Montgomery Ward lady said, "then he shouldn't be found guilty."

There were too many people talking. Too many egos vying for attention. Mrs. Barstow leaned back on the hard chair and closed her eyes, trying to recapture her sense of herself. She tended to lose herself when there were too many voices in the room.

The sour-faced Montgomery Ward's clerk nudged her. "You have to try to stay awake, dear," she said in a tone that put Mrs. Barstow's teeth on edge. "I know it isn't easy at your age, but you owe it to the rest of us to make an effort."

Mrs. Barstow, at seventy-five, was the oldest member of the jury. She sensed the defense attorney hadn't wanted her, but she was the second alternate and he was probably out of preemptory challenges. She remembered preemptory challenges from Court TV; she was proud of all the things she'd learned from that program. She'd always thought she'd like to be a court buff when she got old, and now she could do it without leaving her couch. She liked watching trials, liked hearing from the lawyers about why they were doing what they were doing. Some lawyers were slick and smart and she felt they weren't to be trusted, although she would certainly want them in her corner if she were ever in trouble. Others were just like regular people, only they talked faster. They were never at a loss for words, lawyers; that was what she admired most about them. They never stood in front of store clerks, groping for the name of the thing they wanted, the thing they knew perfectly well what it was, could draw a picture of, except that they couldn't remember what you called it.

She opened her eyes. She would have liked to tell Miss Monkey Ward to keep her comments to herself, that she hadn't been asleep and wasn't going to fall asleep and didn't need any officious reminders from prune-faced old bats like her. But although she remembered the word "officious" when she was thinking to herself, there was always the danger that what she wanted to say wouldn't be what she actually said when the time came.

Washington, D.C., December, 1994

"If you can give me one good reason — one, count them, *one* — why we need some Wall Street yuppette on this case, I'll —"

Max Jarvis sawed the air like an old-time actor as he paced the tiny office on Wisconsin Avenue. The walls were lined with towers of cartons whose weight lay heavy on the bottom box, which bent under its load. The desks were littered with legal papers, cardboard coffee cups with logos of Greek diners on the side, computer printouts listing cases spewed out by the legal research program in the corner. On the wall behind Max's desk a hand-lettered sign read "Cruel and Unusual, Attorneys at Law."

"— cool down, Maxwell," the lazy Southern voice drawled. "I got a favor comin' from a friend up North, and this is what he's givin' me for Christmas. A nice shiny WASP who can argue our case without the old farts on the bench goin' 'Here come those crazy death penalty fanatics' the minute she opens her mouth. Someone who can help us lift Tyler Baines from the mire of all the other boys scheduled to die this year. Someone who can get us a little ink and won't look half bad on Court TV. A new face, Max, that's what she is. And a new face is what we need on this one."

Max Jarvis fixed his partner and friend with the look that had earned respect on the streets of Bensonhurst and said, "And what's wrong with our faces? You make a good appearance on the tube, Ren. Those wide blue eyes, that John-Boy Walton accent. The six o'clock news bunnies eat it up like shoo-fly pie."

Renshaw Craley leaned forward, his large bony hands clasped in an attitude of prayer. "We agreed once upon a time, old buddy, that we would do whatever it took to save our clients from the chair. *Whatever* it took. And if it takes us using a Wall Street designer suit with real pearls and a head of hair that cost more than our monthly salaries combined, then so be it. So be it, for Tyler's sake." Ren's horsy face was dead serious, his blue eyes bored into Max's as he repeated, "for Tyler's sake, Max."

Max took in a lungful of dusty air and whooshed it out. "Okay, I get the point, Ren. Tyler Baines is gonna fry if we don't pull a rabbit out of our hats. And you think our hats are empty and we need a new face. Well, I think we've won our share of cases — big cases, newspaper cases, not just penny-ante shit — and I know we've got more knowledge and experience with the death penalty than anyone else in this country, so —"

"A slight exaggeration, Maximilian," Ren interrupted. "The ACLU has a few good lawyers working on Death Row, the NAACP Inc. Fund are no slouches, and even Amnesty International —"

"All right." Max lifted an exasperated hand. "Jeez. Let me finish my point, okay? Which is that no Wall Street hotshot, male or female, white, black or green, can come in here and do anything like the job on this case that we can do. So what the fuck do we need her for? And don't give me that we suddenly need a pretty face instead of good lawyering."

Ren Craley spun around in his swivel chair, pointed to a picture on the wall. It was an ordinary family picnic — at first glance. When you looked closer you saw that two of the boys were Asian, one girl had tiny crutches under her arms, and the beaming blond parents couldn't possibly have given birth to all the children of various colors and ages that surrounded them at the picnic table.

"The Baineses were mighty special people," he said, his Southern accent deepening as he spoke. "Folks thought highly of them, even the ones who didn't think it was right for them to adopt outside their own kind. Face it, partner, Lonnie and Dora Baines were nigh onto saints in West Hamburg, Wyoming. And Tyler blew them away. Just picked up his foster daddy's shotgun and sprayed shot all over that little house with the picket fence. Got two of his sisters as well, one nine and one twelve. And the mother maimed for life. Add to that the fact that people out West don't hold much with the insanity defense, and you've got Tyler practically sitting in the electric chair even as we speak. He's dead, Maxeleh, dead meat. Unless we can pull that rabbit from our hats. And yes, I'm counting on a fresh face, a female face. To get people thinking that a nice-looking young woman wouldn't take a case like Tyler's if she didn't think the boy was seriously screwed up."

"Like using a woman on a rape case," Max said. He'd slowed his pacing and said the words as though thinking out loud. "Yeah, it could work. It's sexist bullshit of the worst kind, but it could work."

"So you're with me, finally? You'll help show our new associate the ropes?" When Max didn't answer at once, Ren repeated his earlier plea. "For Tyler."

Max nodded. "For Tyler."

Cody, Wyoming, June 1987

The man with the goatee was the foreman. Mrs. Barstow knew Mr. Farkas thought he should be the foreman, and was bitterly disappointed when the others chose the bearded man instead. She herself had voted for Mr. Dundee, who after all was trusted to run an entire post office.

"Perhaps we should take another vote," the goateed man said, trying vainly to infuse a little enthusiasm into his voice.

"What for?" Farkas demanded. "It will just come out the same way it did last time and the time before that and the time before that. Six for conviction, six for acquittal."

"They were such a wonderful family," the pregnant girl whispered. "I saw them on television once. A real inspiration, that's what they were."

This was true, but it didn't stop Mr. Farkas from giving the girl a hard glare. "That kind of talk isn't helping one bit," he blustered. "Who cares what kind of family they were? Lonnie Baines and those two little girls are dead and that no-account Indian kid of his did it, and that's all she wrote."

Both Mexicans and Mr. Dundee opened their mouths to protest and Mrs. Barstow couldn't blame them one bit. Whatever Tyler Baines had or hadn't done, it had nothing to do with his being an Indian.

Or did it? The schoolteacher began to talk about Fetal Alcohol Syndrome and how it was more prevalent among children of Native American ancestry. Mr. Farkas's red face wasn't the only one to scowl at her terminology; here in Wyoming, most people still said Indian, even if they said it with a hint of defiance, as if daring those Eastern liberals to make something out of it.

"I don't give a good goddamn how much rotgut whiskey that little brat's momma drank when he was in the womb," Mr. Farkas exploded at last. "He killed Lonnie Baines and those children in cold blood, for God's sake."

"I don't see how this discussion is furthered," the widow said in a shaking voice, "by taking the name of the Lord in vain."

"Oh, Christ," Mr. Farkas muttered, wiping his brow with a limp handkerchief. "Haven't we got more important things to talk about?"

Mrs. Barstow could see that the widow had every intention of telling Mr. Farkas that in her view there was precious little that was more important than respecting the Lord.

Mommy was afraid Tyler would get the gun, like he did before. That was what Melissa, the ten-year-old, had said. Melissa was born without a foot, but you'd never know it to watch her walk. They could do such wonderful things these days, Mrs. Barstow thought, but then she thought about Tyler and how nobody could do anything for him, and she decided maybe things hadn't changed all that much.

What could it have been like, Mrs. Barstow wondered, to be a little ten-year-old with only one foot and a brother who might find the shotgun and blow the whole family to bits?

Why did a family with a son that hard to handle keep a gun anyway?

The answer to that one was easy; it came to Mrs. Barstow unbidden. *This is Wyoming; we need our guns.* That was what her late husband had said every time she begged him to get rid of the gun that stood for thirty years behind the kitchen door, in the little hallway they called the mudroom. He needed a gun, he said, in case a coyote came prowling around the garden, or in case a cougar attacked their dog, or in case — well, just in case.

In case mad killers came out of the mountains and tied them both up and slit their throats with her carving knife. Like that farm family in Indiana that funny little writer wrote the book about.

Thinking about the funny little writer brought back images of Junior: blond and elfin, not at all like her or her husband. Some people joked that Junior had been left by elves, with his wispy golden hair and pointed ears and heart-shaped face.

Tyler found my money and stole it, the Vietnamese boy named Peter had said. *I hid it, but he always found it.*

Mrs. Barstow could sympathize with that. Hadn't her big cousin Annie always found things she hid? Annie came to the ranch in summer; she was two years older and shared Mrs. Barstow's room. She seemed to think that gave her the right to take anything she fancied, so Mrs. Barstow took her most precious things and hid them in places she didn't think Annie would look, but Annie always did. She always did, and she always found them, and she always broke or ruined them.

Ma said it was okay because Annie was their guest and you had to be nice to guests, but Mrs. Barstow never thought it was right, and when she became a mother she knew she would never let anyone steal from Junior no matter what. Guest or no guest, her child would come first.

Did Dora Baines feel the same way? She and Lonnie had two children of their own, two blood-children in addition to the adopted family. Did they make a distinction between their own children and the little guests?

She couldn't blame them if they had, especially when it came to Tyler. It was one thing if your own blood-child turned out bad, but when you had a bad one and he wasn't really yours, you couldn't be blamed for wishing he'd never come into your life.

A fragment of testimony came back to her. Just a little wisp of a phrase; for a moment, she couldn't even remember who'd said it. ". . . considering bringing a suit to compel the agency to resume custody due to a failure to disclose a material fact."

Long words. Legal words. Thank goodness for Court TV; Mrs. Barstow knew that *compel* meant to make somebody do something, and that *failure to disclose* meant that someone had kept something a secret. *A material fact* meant that it was a big secret, an important omission — like the agency not telling the Baineses their adopted boy might have been born with Fetal Alcohol Syndrome.

Had the Baineses been trying to send Tyler back to the orphanage?

It didn't sound as if the orphanage wanted him back.

Washington, D.C., February, 1995

"The first trial ended in a hung jury in 1987, Your Honor," Avery explained. "One of the jurors was taken ill during deliberations and the alternates had already been discharged. On retrial in 1988, the State of Wyoming managed to convince twelve jurors that Tyler Baines was legally sane within the meaning of Wyoming law despite a documented history of Fetal Alcohol Syndrome."

Ren Craley leaned over the makeshift judge's bench and stepped out of character. "I'd watch that hint of sarcasm if I were you, Avery," he said. "You know, that part about the state 'managing to convince twelve jurors.' That kind of stuff's been known to piss off the Supremes."

Max Jarvis nodded; he looked about to add something, but Avery glared at him and he shut up. It was bad enough to be lectured by a backwoods lawyer who'd probably read cases by kerosene lamp, but she didn't have to take back-seat lawyering by two guys instead of one.

Still, it made a lot of sense to moot-court the argument as often as possible before the big day. Ren and Max sat at a long table, shooting questions at her while she tried to stick to the argument she'd prepared while at the same time answering their concerns. It was the only way to prepare for appellate argument; pretend you were before the court and field as many questions as your colleagues could come up with.

"Here's a Sandra Day O'Connor question," Max said with a wicked grin. "Counselor, how do you respond to the State's argument that your client received all the due process of law he's entitled to because the jury was permitted to consider the Fetal Alcohol Syndrome in the second trial?"

"Your Honor is correct that the jurors were told they could take into account the medical history of Tyler Baines," Avery replied, trying for the same deferential tone she intended to use on the real Supreme Court, "but the defense contends that the judge's charge effectively undermined the impact of the medical testimony by not directing the jurors to consider Fetal Alcohol Syndrome a form of insanity under Wyoming law."

"Oh, so this case isn't about the Fetal Alcohol Syndrome as such," Ren

Craley drawled. "Instead it's about the precise wording of the judge's charge. Is that your contention, Counselor?"

Avery shot the tall Southerner a sour glance. "Is that supposed to be Rehnquist or Scalia?" she asked.

"Take your pick," Ren replied. "They're both going to stick it to you."

Cody, Wyoming, June 1987

We couldn't have a normal life, Dora Baines had sobbed. She wiped away her tears with a hand that had only three fingers; her adopted boy had blown the others away with the shotgun. *Tyler was getting too big for me to discipline. He got mad at Sarah and broke her arm; she's only five years old.*

Five years old and blind, Mrs. Barstow recalled. A Romanian orphan who'd been left to die in a miserable institution.

"They wanted him dead," Mrs. Barstow said softly to herself. "They needed him dead. It was the only hope they had for a normal life."

Her eyes filled with tears. *A normal life;* that was what she and her husband had had after Junior died. A normal life, a life that wasn't spent caring for a child who demanded every minute of your time and gave nothing in return because he had nothing to give. A child they labeled autistic, a child who would never hold a job or get married or even laugh at a joke.

The gun was hidden where Tyler wouldn't find it.

But Tyler found everything; there was no hiding place he couldn't ferret out.

The gun wasn't loaded. At least Peter, the Vietnamese boy, had sworn it wasn't supposed to be loaded.

What good an unloaded shotgun would be against marauders from the mountains Mrs. Barstow couldn't say, but Peter had insisted the shells were kept in another, quite separate, hiding place.

A hiding place little Melissa had testified Tyler knew about, because he'd found the money she'd been saving for a new Barbie. He'd stolen it only a week before the night of the gun.

The gun was supposed to be unloaded; the shells were supposed to be hidden.

But when Tyler Baines ran for the gun, grabbed it and pointed it at his adoptive family, it had been loaded and deadly.

Why? Mrs. Barstow let the question nag at her while the others argued diminished capacity. Why had the gun been left where the family must have known Tyler could find it? Why had the shells been hidden in a place he'd only recently raided?

Why had a jar of sparkling water been left on the picnic table where Junior could pick it up and drink from it?

She thrust her fist into her mouth to stop the involuntary cry. The sour-faced Montgomery Ward's clerk gave her a suspicious look.

Mrs. Barstow leaned back against the hard chair and murmured something about feeling faint. Mr. Dundee stood up and walked over to the water cooler, where he filled a little paper cup and brought it back to her. She took it gratefully and sipped; the water felt good going down even if it did have a hard time getting past the lump in her throat.

They had set him up. The family had set Tyler Baines up.

That was not a phrase she'd learned on Court TV, but it was a good one anyway.

Mr. and Mrs. Baines had wanted Tyler to go for the gun. They had come to the end of their rope. Everyone knew Tyler's temper; everyone had said it was only a matter of time before he killed someone out there on the ranch.

No one would have blamed Mr. Baines if he'd been forced to kill his son, if he'd defended himself and his family from the boy he couldn't control.

Tyler's gun wasn't supposed to be loaded. He would brandish a weapon and scream at his parents; his father would shoot him in self-defense, then sob as the gun in the boy's hand proved to be empty. It would all be a horrible mistake.

Washington, D.C., April, 1995

"She did a good job, Max," Ren Craley said. "You can't blame her for what the Supremes did."

"Yeah, I suppose," Max agreed. At least, his words agreed. His face said something else. "She didn't have her heart in it, though. If one of us had argued Tyler's case, we'd have shown some passion, for God's sake."

"Do you really think that would have impressed anybody, Maxie?" Ren countered. His blue eyes were sad. "Hell, boy, we feel passion for all the poor fuckers about to die in the chair or the chamber or whatever, and what the hell good does our passion do any of them?"

"Nine-zip," Max said, tossing the *Washington Post* onto the battered desktop. "Not one dissent. Not even Ginsburg, and you know she hates the death penalty. Nine-fucking-zero and our little yuppette is back on Wall

Street making the world safe for hostile takeovers and it doesn't matter to her one bit that an Indian kid with the I.Q. of a turnip is about to —"

Ren held up a large, bony hand. "Peace, Maxeleh. What's done is done. I have here in my hand a case about a girl in Tennessee who met up with the wrong guy and the two of them knocked off a Seven-Eleven. Boyfriend held the gun, but she drove the getaway car and now she's looking at the chair. He's already been fried; you think we got a chance of getting her life without parole instead?"

Max Jarvis' answer held a world of cynicism. "We might if you don't get any of your fancy Wall Street friends to help us out."

Cody, Wyoming, June, 1987

It was a terrible mistake, Mrs. Barstow had told the deputy when he came to the house the day Junior died. She'd told nothing more nor less than the truth, but he'd misunderstood her and kept on misunderstanding her no matter how hard she tried to tell them: it was a terrible mistake.

Of course it was, dear; now don't you worry about a thing. Junior's in a better place now, dear; it was all for the best.

She had grown to hate being called "dear" — it was what people called you when what they really meant was *shut up.*

They thought she meant it was a terrible mistake that Junior drank the Drano thinking it was soda water. This was before they made it blue so children could see it wasn't water; the liquid in the jar had been clear and bubbly and it ate Junior's entire gullet right out and he died a horrible writhing death.

But that wasn't the mistake she was talking about. She meant it was a mistake for her late husband to think that getting rid of Junior would return their lives to normal.

The Baineses had made the same mistake. Life without Tyler was supposed to be normal, but here they were coming into court at Tyler's trial, every one of them lying about the truth, every one of them mourning a husband and father and two little girls who wouldn't have died if they hadn't been so set on becoming normal again.

You couldn't go back to normal once your life was changed by someone like Junior or Tyler; she knew that now.

New York City, April, 1995

Avery Nyquist folded her expensively manicured hands on the cool surface of the ebony desk. She gazed with expectant calm into Harrison Jeffers III's appraising eyes. She pretended indifference to what her mentor at Ambrose, Jeffers was about to say, but inwardly she swelled with pardonable pride.

"I'm pleased to be able to offer you a partnership in this firm," Hal said in his rich voice. "The partners met last night and I want you to know the vote in your favor was unanimous. No dissenting votes. Everyone here knows what you've accomplished here in the last seven years, and we're eager to welcome you to partnership rank."

Partnership. The Holy Grail of Ivy League law graduates turned Wall Street associates. Seven years of working one-hundred-hour weeks, of playing tennis at one a.m. with someone who worked the same gruesome hours at Simpson, Thatcher, of dashing to JFK to meet a client between flights from London to Hong Kong, of choosing clothes, jewelry, hairstyle with one end in view: does it look like it belongs on an Ambrose, Jeffers partner? And now the Holy Grail was hers.

She smiled at the man across the desk from her, the man who had helped make it possible. Helped, not waved a magic wand for her. She'd earned it, but earning wasn't everything in the cutthroat world she worked in. There were, she knew, equally hard-working lawyers at the firm who were in the offices of other partners being told they weren't quite partner material.

As she opened her mouth to thank Hal, her eye caught the headline in the morning's *Law Journal:* HIGH COURT REFUSES TO OVERTURN DEATH PENALTY IN CASE OF WYOMING YOUTH, it read. The subhead went on: Unanimous Court Leaves Issue of Fetal Alcohol Syndrome Defense to Lower Courts; Baines To Die Tomorrow.

Tomorrow? Wasn't there one more stay, one more appeal? She'd have to call Ren, find out what he and Max intended to do now. The Supreme Court had affirmed, but surely another habeas to the District Court, or perhaps a motion for rehearing before the Wyoming Supreme Court . . .

"Avery, are you listening to me?" Hal's tone held an edge underneath its bantering surface; he wasn't used to being tuned out by those lower in the pecking order.

"Sorry," she murmured. "I just didn't know I'd lost that case." She gestured at the neatly folded *Law Journal* on his desk.

"Which case?" Hal asked, then followed her eyes to the newspaper. "Oh, that," he said, shaking his head. "I should have mentioned it. You can go ahead and say 'I told you so,' " he invited. "You said it was a dead loser. Maybe I should have listened to you and sent somebody else to Washington."

When she got home, Avery promised herself, she'd call Ren Craley to commiserate with him about the decision, to bitch about the fact that it wasn't even a real opinion, just a quickie affirmation which would give the State of Wyoming a green light to go ahead and snuff out Tyler Baines' young, meaningless life.

She had a sudden, vivid recollection of the gleam in Ren's deep blue eyes as he talked law, force-feeding her with every nuance of the Supreme Court's vagaries on the subject of the death penalty.

He cared.

That was the difference between Ren Craley and the man across the ebony desk, the man who'd taught her everything she knew about surviving on Wall Street. That was the difference between Ren Craley and all the men she'd ever dated, ever done business with.

Ren cared.

That was the difference between Ren and her, she realized with a suddenness that wiped away the triumph of making partner. He cared.

She didn't. Not really. Not about this man who'd treated her like a precocious child whose achievements reflected well on him, not about the SEC hearing she'd attended earlier that afternoon or about the IRS consultation she was going to have in the morning. She didn't give a good goddamn about any of them.

She didn't even care about making partner. Once upon a time, it had meant everything to her, but now that it was here, all she could think about was that big, stupid boy being strapped into the electric chair. Could he understand what was happening to him and why? He had picked up a gun in rage; could he know that stone-sober people doing their jobs were going to take his life because there was a piece of paper that said they should?

"Avery?" Hal's voice came to her from far away, sounding concerned. "Are you feeling all right?"

She shook her head. No, she wasn't all right. She didn't know why, exactly, but she was far from all right. She got up from the deep leather chair and made her way, with increasingly swift steps, to the ladies' room. She headed into the nearest cubicle, sat down on the commode, and burst into noisy tears.

Cody, Wyoming, June 1987

Mrs. Barstow tuned in to the heated argument still going on in the smoke-filled room. Only two jurors smoked, and they'd voted to separate for smoke breaks, but this was Wyoming, and you didn't tell men they couldn't light up when and where they wanted to out here in the West. Oh, maybe in California, but that wasn't the real West.

Mrs. Barstow didn't mind the smoke; her late husband had puffed himself to death and the smell was a familiar reminder of the days when she'd shared a life with another person. Funny how the smell of something that caused death made her feel alive.

She had to tell them. She had to make them see.

"It all went so wrong," she said, shaking her head. "So terribly wrong."

"It went wrong from the day those do-gooders took that kid into their house," Mr. Farkas said.

"No," Mrs. Barstow replied. "That's not what I mean. The gun was in the wrong place."

"Yes, dear," the nice Montgomery Ward clerk said in her saccharine tone. "If they'd hidden the gun better, Lonnie Baines and the two little girls would be alive today. But that doesn't help us decide about the insanity plea, now, does it, dear?"

Why couldn't they understand, she wondered, as she stared at first one face and then another. They all looked at her with varying degrees of concern on their faces, concern that said they had no comprehension of her words. They knew she was upset about something, and that upset them, but they had no clue what she was talking about.

"It was just like Junior," she said, certain that would explain everything. As the words left, she reached a trembling hand to her mouth as if to recall them; she had never before spoken of Junior to strangers.

She wasn't sure she could do it now. But then she thought about that boy, that hulking dark-eyed boy with his straight Indian hair and expressionless face and dim brain, the boy who was going to be sent back if anyone would take him, only nobody would. The boy who had reached for a gun his parents had made certain would be where he could find it. She had to go on, for his sake.

She tried. She said the words over several times, in several different ways, trying to make the others understand about the gun and about the Baines' terrible need to rid themselves of the boy they'd tried unsuccessfully to tame.

The words wouldn't come the way she'd planned. She got mixed up, too, calling Tyler Baines 'Junior' and trying to explain about the bubbling water that had eaten him up from the inside and how wrong her late husband had been — as wrong as Lonnie Baines.

She began to cry. It had been so long since she'd even thought about Junior, so much longer since she'd said his name, the name that brought back the reality of him.

"This is too much," the little schoolteacher had said. "This is really too much for the poor old thing."

"Yes," Mr. Dundee agreed. "We've got to tell the judge we're deadlocked. It's cruel and unusual punishment to keep us here when we're never going to come to a verdict."

"No," Mrs. Barstow wailed, "let me finish. You have to let me explain." Her breath was coming in little pants; she felt weak and strange. Why couldn't they shut up and listen? Why wasn't there enough air in this little room? Why did juries need twelve people, twelve mouths, twenty-four eyes, too many voices and legs and arms?

Too many.

Dizziness swept over her; the words she needed to say about Tyler Baines crawled into a corner of her brain and fell asleep. She let her head fall to one side and was horrified to realize that spittle dripped down her cheek.

What was happening to her?

"My God, she's having a stroke," the little schoolteacher cried. "Somebody call the guard. We have to get her to a doctor."

Mr. Farkas ran from the room. The others bustled and exclaimed and reached for her as though their touch could restore her. The nice Montgomery Ward's clerk took out a handkerchief and wiped her chin as gently as you would a baby's.

She opened her mouth to tell them, to make them see what she'd seen, but all that came out were gabbled sounds that reminded her, horribly, of Junior.

"Don't worry, dear," the nice Montgomery Ward's clerk said, patting her hand. "It's almost over. We'll get you out of here, dear, don't you worry."

"Cruel and unusual punishment," Mr. Dundee repeated, shaking his head.

Washington, D.C., June, 1995

"If it please the Court," counsel for the petitioner began, "the execution of Rosalee Jenkins Pruitt is contrary to the Sixth Amendment to the Constitution of the United States of America because —"

"Too wordy," Max Jarvis cut in, stabbing the air with a stubby finger. "We need to stay polite but cut that down to the bare minimum."

Avery Nyquist ran her fingers through her hair and turned exasperated eyes on her new partners. "Is he always this nit-picky?" she asked Ren Craley.

The tall, bony lawyer smiled, showing huge horse teeth. "Yeah, he's a real pain in the behind, but you'll get used to him, Ave."

I'll get used to him, Avery thought. And I'll get used to working twenty hours a day trying to keep people alive, and I'll get used to shopping at Penney's instead of Sak's, and using a drugstore rinse on my hair instead of consulting a master colorist, and I'll get used to working in an office the size of a telephone booth instead of one with a view of New York Harbor. And I'll get used to a steady diet of Supreme Court arguments and last-minute stays and visits to Death Rows all across the country.

I'll get used to caring.

But will I ever get used to the idea that a piece of paper, stamped in triplicate, can take a man's life as surely as a loaded shotgun?

No, she wouldn't.

She hoped she never would.

I started this story in my own writing class, having given the first line "the doorbell rang" to the group as a freewriting exercise. Somehow my own scribbled notes became this story, which was first published in Mystery Scene.

CAT LADY

The knock at the door made her jump, nearly out of her skin. She dropped the cracked coffee mug, spilling the dregs of her strong, black coffee on the floor. The family scattered — kittens tumbling under tables, tomcats jumping onto shelves and knocking off knicknacks. Aunt Jemima, the big black longhair, scrunched herself down and crept toward the coffee. When she reached the scalding puddle, the cat lowered a dainty pink tongue and began to lap up the spill. "Don't, baby," the old lady pleaded, hoisting herself out of her overstuffed armchair with a thrust of powerful arms, "Caffeine'll keep you awake all night."

Reluctantly, she plodded toward the door. *Oh, God, who would come here? Nobody with half a brain, that's for sure. Nobody who had a better place to go.*

She stopped, looking around at the mess. "Can't let anyone in," she muttered. "Not till I redd up a bit." She bustled about, emptying ashtrays, hiding her unfinished breakfast under the bed, plopping dirty clothes in the sink. *Oh, God, they couldn't* know, *could they? I was so careful.*

She took a deep breath of cat-odor-laden air and shuffled toward the door. As she went, she mumbled, "I'm comin', I'm comin'. Keep your paws on."

Her sweaty palm reached for the doorknob. She hoped its coolness would calm her somehow, but instead the knob got as damp and sooty as her unwashed hand.

She opened the door a crack, peering out suspiciously. "Who's there?" she asked. *They won't answer. They're too smart for that.*

She was right; there was no answer. *I suppose I've got to; they'll just come back.*

As she pulled the heavy door toward her, it brushed against a gray tabby, big with unborn kittens. The cat stared up at her with unforgiving eyes, then stalked away, tail held high. "Sorry, Cleo," she murmured.

It was a man. A man in a suit! *Oh, God, it can't be the Health!* Her heart thumped wildly, and she clutched at her bosom. *Not the Health!*

"Miz Jasperson," the man said in a rusty voice that evidently hadn't been used in some time, "I'd like to come in, if I may."

"Well, I don't know," she said doubtfully. She looked past him toward the front yard. Maybe there was someplace there they could sit and conduct their business. She looked at the tree, dead from the blight seven years ago. In the lowest branch, crouched expectantly, perched Primrose, her calico cat. The once-painted bench beneath it was rotted and sawdusty, being eaten by termites before her very eyes. The deaf white kitten she called Beethoven lay sleeping in the shade behind it. In the tall, unmown grass next to the rusty lawnmower that seemed to have tired out one day and just stopped stood the back seat of a 1967 Ford. *Maybe we could sit there and talk* — no, she wasn't *that* crazy. People didn't sit in back seats of cars when there wasn't any car there anymore. Even when that back seat didn't house a whole family of Siamese.

They're closing in. My God, they're closing in. Busybody neighbors — I hope they fry in hell.

"Why can't you just go away?" she whispered, talking less to her visitor than to herself.

"Official business, ma'am," the man replied. "I could come back with the sheriff, but I wouldn't want —"

"Oh, all right," she grumbled, turning. "You better come inside. Just don't step on the moggies."

The moggies jumped and scattered, circled and skittered, meowing and hissing and purring like a feline tornado. The man from the Health stepped back, alarm on his face. "How — how many *are* there?" he asked, his fingers plucking at his pants leg.

As if he didn't know. As if those Nosy Parkers didn't tell him everything. Well, I'll go along with it. I'll pretend I'm the fool they think I am.

"Forty-seven," she said in a tone that wavered between defiance and pride. "Andromeda had a new litter last night. One poor darling died, but five lived, so now there's forty-seven all told."

Just then Big Tom came in, making an entrance as always, his huge orange body a pleasure to watch as he strode like a sultan past his harem, his bushy tail brushing her leg. He faced the stranger, challenge in his laid-back ears and swishing tail.

The Health raised a shaking hand. "Nice kitty," he croaked.

"He's a monster," she informed him with relish. "Ate a whole boot once."

The Health, sidling backward, said he could believe it. He bumped into a chair and began to lower himself into it, then jumped up when an indignant squeak told him he'd just sat on a pair of Siamese kittens.

"Frankie and Johnny, you move now," she said in a brisk tone, "and let the man from the Health sit down."

"Ah, Miz Jasperson?" He made it a question, like he'd suddenly forgotten whom he'd come to visit. "I'm not from the Health, I'm from the Internal Revenue Service."

As if I'd believe that! *Those people at the Health must really take me for a porcupine! What business would I have with Revenuers, and me a tee-totaller?*

"It seems, Ma'am," the Health went on, still playing his little game, "you haven't paid your taxes in, oh, seventeen years."

"Well, I make it eighteen," she said affably, "but then maybe I've got it wrong." She reached down without looking and deftly picked up a tiny black kitten. She held it in one strong hand, stroking its tiny neck with huge fingers.

"Uh, ma'am, seventeen or eighteen, it's still a long time, and Uncle Sam —"

"Uncle Sam wants *you*," she said with a deep, throaty chuckle, pointing her catless hand at the man from the Health. He shrank back, then laughed unconvincingly. Worry lines sprang up on his pale forehead, and just stayed there.

"Don't you remember the war? My brother Faron went. He said if Uncle Sam wanted him, then he was going to give the man what he asked for. Got to go to Paris, France and everything. A regular doughboy."

"Oh, *that* war," the man replied, running his hand over his wrinkled forehead and rubbing hard.

They didn't even send me a smart one this time. Never heard of the Great War.
The man reached into his pocket. "I have a paper here," he began.

"Never read 'em," she said firmly. "Ever since they was wrong about Tom Dewey. Newspapers got nothing to say to *me*."

"It's not a newspaper." The man was raising his voice. *Like he was talking to a foreigner or something.* "It's a lien on this property, for back taxes. The Government's going to take your house."

He was looking at the cats, at Big Tom especially. She could almost hear him thinking: what if one of them jumps on me, or claws at me? What if they sink those fangs into my legs? She knew what they said about her in town, called her a witch and her sweet darlings demon familiars. She chuckled inside, thinking of this city slicker falling for that old story. He shrank back in his chair as Asmodeus, the three-legged patriarch of her clan, sidled past in his ungainly way. Then he rubbed his forehead so hard he made red marks on the pale skin.

"Got a headache?" she asked, leaning over and setting the kitten on the floor with a gentle pat on its tiny rear end. The kitten mewed and scampered under the chair in which the man sat. All around him swirled a storm of cats. He watched them uneasily, with the air of a man who had never really *trusted* cats. "Yes," he admitted in a weak voice, "a *bad* headache."

"Let me rub your temples," she purred, walking over to the chair. Just as she moved toward him, the three-legged feline leapt into his lap. The man squeaked, brushing at the animal with ineffectual hands. Stepping behind his chair, she placed her giant fingers on his throbbing head and began, slowly, lazily, to make circles.

"No, really," he protested. "It's all right. I don't need any . . ." His voice trailed off. The lines on his forehead smoothed themselves out.

The man leaned back in the chair, which was covered with a thick layer of soft cat hair. He drowsed, letting his head fall back, as her massaging hands made gentle movements. She felt his muscles relax; he was limp.

I've got him now! Just like the other one. The Health isn't going to tell me how many children I can have!

She snapped his neck with one powerful twist of her thick wrist. Killing chickens on the farm when she was a girl had turned out to be the best training she'd ever had. Asmodeus jumped off the stranger's lap and hobbled toward the kitchen.

She reached into his wallet and pulled out a card. "Oh, my God," she said to Big Tom, "he *was* from the Revenue, after all!" *I can't figure what they'd want with me; Lord knows, there's no still up here.*

"Unless that's just another trick," she continued, addressing her favorite pet. "After all, that last one said he was from the County, but *we* knew better, didn't we, Tomkins?"

I thought sure this one was the Health. I know they're coming; I just don't know when.

Then she shrugged her powerful shoulders and walked into the kitchen. Pausing to take the clothes out of the sink, she reached into the cabinet and pulled out an enormous meat grinder.

She hefted the meat grinder onto the zinc table and took a saw down from the wall.

Cleo came into the room, her swollen body with its pink tits dragging down her spindly legs. Big Tom walked over and sniffed her, biting her ear for old time's sake. Frankie and Johnny tumbled on the floor in an all-out wrestling match. "That's right, babies," she said. "Anything I love to see, it's my sweet ones having a good time."

She lifted the old washtub and set it under the table, directly underneath the meat grinder. She unearthed a meat cleaver and laid it on the counter, ready to hand.

"The Lord," she explained to her family, "helps those who help themselves." *And, the Lord knows, it takes a lot of meat to feed forty-seven cats.*

She was just about finished when there came another knock at the door. *Finally! The Health!*

I was driving cross country when I became The Sister Who Came To Dinner. I stopped in Boulder, Colorado for a day or two, stayed with Marlys Milhiser and her husband, and then put my back out and had to stay longer. Lying in the emergency room of the Boulder County Hospital, my back in spasm, having to use the facilities and not able to get up and walk to the toilet, I began to wonder what my life would be like if I were old and helpless and always at the mercy of someone else to help me meet the basic needs. It wasn't a pretty thought.

ACCIDENTS WILL HAPPEN

I have to go. She knows I have to go. I told her — what, fifteen minutes ago? Why doesn't she come? I watch the second hand moving from little mark to little mark on the clock, a jumpy little movement, ticking away the seconds I lie here in agony, my seventy-five-year-old bladder about to burst.

Why doesn't she come?

Because she likes it when I can't hold it. She likes it when she gets to clean me up and say in that syrupy cracker voice of hers, Accidents will happen.

Only it won't be an accident. It will be deliberate, not on my part, but on hers. She's taking away my dignity, second by second, as she makes me lie here squeezing my legs shut like a toddler being toilet-trained.

A toddler who isn't going to make it to the potty unless she gets that bedpan over here in one more minute.

Two more minutes have passed. I'm shaking with need. Oh, God, I'm so glad no one from my past can see me now. Professor Hofsteader, reduced to counting the seconds before she pees her bed.

Thanks to that peroxided little bitch in the greens. They don't wear white anymore. They wear sickly green pants and shirts, look like they work in a gas station instead of a nursing home. God knows why.

She's here. Thanks be to God.

I leak a little as the bedpan slides under my frail hips. I can't help it; I have to go so badly, and the sight of the bedpan makes it even worse. It's just a few drops, but of course she sees it and giggles, "Don't worry your head none, Teacher, everybody knows accidents will happen. I'll change the bed in no time flat."

I was not a schoolteacher, you cretin, I was a full professor. I taught graduate courses in art; my paintings hung in the Great Hall at the state university. I taught students who went on to win prizes, whose work is shown in museums.

She changes the bed with a sweet little put-upon smile that says she's earning her crowns in heaven by being so extra-nice to a bitchy old lady. It never seems to cross her tiny little mind that she wouldn't be changing it at all if she'd come when I first rang the bell.

And she could have. That's what galls me the most. If she couldn't get to me because someone on the floor was having a heart attack, or worse, I'd understand. If this only happened once in a while, when one of the comatose patients died, I'd understand. I am not an unreasonable woman, after all.

But it happens on average four times a week. Four nights out of seven, I lie in agony, counting the seconds, praying my sphincter muscles are stronger than I think they are, plotting ways to kill that little bitch.

How can I kill someone when I can't even go to the bathroom by myself?

I don't know, but I'm going to. I swear to God I'm going to.

"Why, your radio is tuned to that awful religious station again, Gladys. How on earth does that happen so often?" Mavis, the day nurse, switches back to public radio. She knows how much I love All Things Considered; how classical music soothes me — and how much I loathe the rantings of Reverend Billy Don Shoemaker. I have told her more than once that the night nurse changes my station and then leaves it, so I can't change it back. She even leaves it on all night, low, not too loud, but still there I lie in bed, the hellfire voice of Billy Don in my head instead of Vivaldi and Garrison Keillor.

Oh, I want her dead so badly. As badly as I have to go on those nights when she puts me through the hell of the old. The hell of helplessness, the hell of depending on the kindness of strangers who are not kind, strangers who enjoy the infliction of pain and indignity on those who used to be their betters.

Yes, their betters. There, I said it. I was better than Bobbie Sue Mason, and I don't care who knows it. She is ignorant; I was educated. She has no sense of beauty; I was an artist. She is young and has no compassion; I was —

Well, perhaps my compassion was nothing to brag about. But I would not condemn my worst enemy to the torture she puts me through, four times a week on average.

I would not.

But I would kill. I would indeed. But how?

There is medication. I could hoard my sleeping tablets and slip them, one by one, into the coffee she drinks all night. Coffee whose smell enters my nose and speaks to me of the days when I was alive. Speaks to me of all-night coffeehouses in Greenwich Village, of little cafes on the Rive Gauche, of long nights in Barcelona — of artistic discussions and cigarettes smoked with lovers, and —

And youth.

When she first came on the floor, I asked Bobbie Sue for a sip, just a taste, of her coffee. The smell took me back, even though hers was an indifferent brew held in styrofoam instead of the nectar of the gods I used to drink out of little demitasse cups.

She screwed up her face into a pose meant to make me think she was actually considering the possibility, then said, "Sugar, I can't give you somethin' the doctor might have told you you shouldn't have. You know better'n that, you bein' a schoolteacher and all."

I corrected her. God help me, I corrected the little snip, told her I was a professor of art at the state university. Even added a little lecture on how difficult it was in those days for a woman to achieve full professorship, and how my year at the Sorbonne of course made a difference in the Faculty's tenure vote.

I might as well have been talking to a cat.

Except that a cat wouldn't have held a grudge, wouldn't have referred to me as "Professor" in a drawn-out little simper whenever I couldn't hold my water, as if underlining ever so slightly the difference between the dignity I had then and the complete lack of dignity I possess now.

I must kill her. I must.

How?

"Darlin', I know just what to do about that radio business," Mavis the day nurse says as she waltzes into my room and rids me of the Reverend Billy Don with a flick of her middle-aged wrist. She has the other hand behind her back and pulls out a long wire made out of a bent coathanger. She hands it to me with a flourish that invites praise. I do not completely understand what she means for me to do with it, but then she shows me. I can reach the dial with it. If I'm patient and careful I can turn the dial and retrieve my public station. If I'm less patient, less careful, I can at least hit the power button and turn the cursed thing off.

Of course, she manages the wire with ease, being a healthy strapping woman whose muscles obey her commands. I bend my twisted fingers one by one around the thin wire and, when I finally have a grip that will hold it, I inch it toward the radio.

"There, now, Gladys. You're almost there," Mavis says in a brisk tone. "Now bring the wire close to the dial and give a little push."

The wire is shaking in my hand; it feels as heavy as a gun. But I am determined. If I can do this for myself, I will gain some tiny control over my life — and every bit helps me feel as if I were still alive.

I am exhausted with the effort. I give the "little push" Mavis recommends — and I succeed in knocking the radio right off the shelf. It lands on the wheeled bed-table next to the IV drip and the nurse's bell-push.

I want to cry. But Mavis — dear, unsentimental Mavis — just picks the radio up, puts it back on the shelf, and says, "You'll get the hang of it in no time, Gladys."

I watch her set the wire in place behind my bedframe. It was made from a white wire hanger; it blends with the painted metal of the bedstead and the white of the cords. All I have to do when I want to use it is reach behind me and unhook it from the cord that connects to the bell-push.

I thank Mavis profusely, but at the same time I wish she could supply me with my own bedpan instead. Some needs are more pressing than others; I believe I could live with the Reverend Billy Don if only I knew I'd get the bedpan when I needed it.

I must have dozed; I wake in a fog of oversleep to hear voices outside my room. It is Bobbie Sue and Dr. Fiske.

". . . really do think Miss Hofsteader ought to be diapered before bed, Doctor," Bobbie Sue is saying in a voice she doesn't bother to keep low. She wants me to hear, oh, yes, she wants me to drink in every nasty word she's saying.

"I don't know, Nurse," the doctor says in reply. I go limp with gratitude, but at the same time there is a hint of doubt in his voice. "I hate to put a patient in diapers unless it's absolutely necessary. It tends to make them regress even more quickly."

"But, Doctor," Bobbie Sue says, and I can picture her tossing her peroxided curls at him and giving him her little pout, "she's had three accidents this week already."

I hold my breath. Dr. Fiske lets out a sigh of resignation and says, "Very well. If she has another one, we'll discuss this again."

No. My soul cries out, No. If I truly had lost the power of control, I would submit, not graciously perhaps. Growing old with grace has not been my strong suit. But I would bow to the inevitable and present my shrunken body to be swaddled like a baby's. If I had to. If I was truly unable to control myself.

But I can control my bladder. For a reasonable period of time. I just can't do it for the unreasonable period Bobbie Sue Mason makes me wait.

Why don't I just tell the doctor I don't need diapers? Why don't I just tell him how long Bobbie Sue waits before she brings the bedpan?

You who ask those questions have never been old. You have never been stripped of everything you ever were, reduced to a grumbling bag of bones in a bed. You have never been called by your first name by boys and girls young enough to be great-grandchildren, without so much as a by-your-leave. You have never been denied coffee and fed mush and waked up so you could be given a sleeping pill you don't want and had your favorite radio station switched to something you cannot stand and be unable to switch it back. You have never depended upon the kindness of unkind strangers.

I have. So I said nothing to Doctor Fiske. Doctor, indeed. That boy was playing doctor with the neighborhood girls when I was ceremonially retired from the university, and he has the nerve to tell me I'm going to be placed in diapers if I have another "accident."

I see by the smirk on Bobbie Sue's face that there will be another "accident," probably tonight.

Bobbie Sue comes in, coffee cup in hand. She drinks a long slow pull, savoring it before my face. "I went to this new little coffee place," she says with a sly grin. "It's real cute, has all these fancy coffees. I believe the one I'm drinking is called a latte." She pronounces it wrong, of course, but by this time in our acquaintance I know better than to correct her. But I do conjure up a sense image of how that milky, strong brew would taste on my tongue. I do exactly what the little bitch wants — I envy her.

And to my intense surprise, she lowers the cup to my level and helps me drink. The smell curls around my nose and invites me to partake of its sensuous depths, to savor the rich taste of dark roast beans laced with steamed milk, topped with just a pinch of nutmeg.

That should have told me something right there. Bobbie Sue Mason is not by nature a nutmeg person. If she'd ordered that coffee for herself, she'd have poured a peck of grated chocolate on top and added cinnamon for good measure.

The nutmeg is for me.

I drink. I drink deep. I drink long. I finish the oversized styrofoam container and lie back with a sigh of contentment.

But later, I remember. Coffee is a diuretic.

I don't have to go so badly. Not yet. I can hold it a bit longer.

The Reverend Billy Don is asking me to make a commitment to the Lord. He says I am a miserable sinner and must repent. I find myself hanging on his every word, trying to concentrate on something other than my growing need.

I remember the wire.

I crane my neck as far as it will go and concentrate on the slender line hanging behind my bed. I focus my eyes on it and slowly edge my arm out of its blanket cocoon. I begin clenching my fingers in anticipation of grasping something thin and elusive. I reach toward it, feeling for the cold touch of metal.

My fingers are made of ice and iron. They no longer bend to my will. So it is three minutes by the clock, by the inexorable second hand, before I have the wire in my hand. I lift it carefully from the cord that holds it in place. I hold it as straight as I can, but it wobbles terribly as I reach for the radio.

I'm too tired, too weak, to work the dial. There will be no public radio. The best I can do is hit the power button and turn the ranting voice off.

I lie in bed exhausted, shaking from the effort of reaching for the radio, and the effort of holding my sphincter muscles. I have to go so badly. How can she let me lie here like this, knowing the agony I'm in?

I rang the bell twenty minutes ago. Twenty long minutes I have lain in my bed, squeezing my thighs shut and counting the seconds as they tick by.

Every awful humiliation of childhood, my own and other people's, comes back to me. The time I peed at the county fair, waiting to use the outhouse. The time my little sister wet herself in church, all over her pink georgette dress. The time Sammy Perkins had an accident during a math test; the children behind him in the long rows of desks pointed and giggled as the puddle formed under his chair and his face turned red as a tomato.

If having an accident is a terrible humiliating loss of dignity at four and five and six, what do you imagine it feels like when you are seventy-five?

In the hallway, I hear Bobbie Sue on the telephone, talking to one of her numerous boyfriends. ". . . on my floor used to paint the prettiest little pictures, and now she's so twisted up with arthuritis that she . . ."

Arthur-itis indeed. I did not paint pretty little pictures, you idiot, I made art.

I made art until my hands turned into claws and my shoulders refused to lift my arms. I molded clay and wielded a brush and mixed colors and once I even welded metal into shapes that spoke of my relationship to the cosmos. I never created anything "pretty" in my life, though I like to think I added my share of beauty to the world.

I have to go so badly. I picture a flood coming out of me, a flood of used coffee. A veritable sea of urine, pouring out over the bed, the floor, sweeping the entire building away.

I reach for the bell one more time. I've rung it six times, but still the chattering voice on the phone tells me her majesty will not deign to answer until it is certain I will not be able to hold back the flood.

I am going to burst. I am shivering in the bed, my muscles working so hard to keep the dam from breaking. I have to let some loose. I have to open the floodgates just a little, no matter how awful it will be to listen to her giggle and her promise to "clean up this little accident in two shakes."

She will clean me up. That is the only salvation. She will strip the bed and pull new fresh sheets from the closet and put a new nightgown over my shrunken bones, and bring a pan and a sponge and wash and powder me like a baby.

At least the voice of the Reverend Billy Don will not be there to harangue me about the hereafter. I have no strength left to put the wire back where it belongs. I have hidden it under the mattress, but it is a near-certainty that Bobbie Sue will find it when she changes my sheets. I sigh; Mavis' lovely present will be taken from me, along with my pride in spending my days and nights undiapered.

The floodgates open. I lie in bed with hot urine flowing down my thighs, into the mattress. The sense of relief is overwhelming, yet I sob a little for my lost dignity. Once more "the Professor" has become a baby. And after tonight I will be able to let myself go as often as I need to, for I will be diapered like an infant. I put my fingers to my eyes and blot my tears; how small and helpless I feel. How old.

What does it matter who I was, what I did? What matters is that I can no longer do for myself.

Perhaps a diaper would be a good thing. At least I'd no longer have the nightly battle, the counting of seconds, the desire to kill.

She comes in, looks down at the bed, with its giant wet spot giving me away. She looks at my face, red with tears and humiliation, and she giggles. "I guess that coffee wasn't such a good idea after all, was it, Professor?"

Then her head cocks to one side; her face wears a puzzled look. "Why, whatever happened to your radio? I could have sworn I left it on for you." She reaches for the power button and brings the unctuous voice of the Reverend Billy Don into the room.

She walks to the closet to get new sheets. She pulls out the metal pan and fills it with water and baby soap. Baby soap. There is baby powder, too, which she will sprinkle and then pat onto my shrunken, hairless once-private parts.

She turns me expertly and pulls the sheets from underneath my body. I tremble that she will find my straightened wire hanger, but I managed to work it under the mattress, where she does not see it. I give it a little smile as I lie on my side, letting her pull the soaked sheet out from under me. Perhaps I can survive the night with one blessing intact.

She whistles along with the awful hymn the Reverend's congregation is singing on the radio. She tosses the wet sheets onto the floor in a heap and slips a new, fresh sheet under me. I should be grateful — and I am, really I am — that she does not leave me in my puddle for hours on end. I have heard of such things, and occasionally I wonder why she confines her cruelty to making me wait too long. But then I hear the voice of the Reverend Billy Don and I realize she likes to think of herself as an angel of mercy. She likes reducing me to helplessness, but she would not put me in a position where my suffering would be an affront to her.

She places the big sponge in the warm water and glides it over my thighs. It feels good. God help me, it feels good to lie in bed while someone washes me in places no other human being has washed me since I was a toddler. Some part of me murmurs a prayer of thanks. She blots me dry and sprinkles baby powder — how nice it smells; I do love talcum — and then reaches for a diaper.

No.

No. I will not let her do this.

I have told myself that this is the last straw, that before I let them diaper me I will drink all my sleeping pills at once and go where no one can take away my dignity.

But there is a better way. I look down at the wire that lies under my mattress and I see the better way.

"If you would be so kind," I begin, letting my voice quaver, "as to wash my back a little higher. I think some of the — wet may have —"

I break off with a blush that is all too real. She gives me a smirk of triumph — she has actually reduced me to asking her for something, to talking about "wet" like a toddler — but she reaches for the sponge and places her hands in the basin.

I slide the straightened hanger out of its hiding place and reach for the radio.

No, not the radio precisely. My goal this time is not the dial or the power button, but the cord that dangles behind the bedframe. I let the hook on the end of the wire grab the cord and then I give a great pull, put all my pitiful strength into the movement.

Bobbie Sue is humming her awful hymn, smiling a smile of triumph as she places the baby-pink sponge into the soapy basin that sits like an affront on the bed-table behind my head.

The radio begins to topple on its shelf, wobbles and dances and finally tips right over, just as it did the first time I used my wire.

The radio falls onto the bed-table with a splash.

With a splash!

"What an awful thing, Gladys," Mavis the day nurse says. She's talking a mile a minute and she hasn't even taken off her coat. She sets two cups of coffee on the bed table and shakes her head.

"I mean, I just can't get over you lying there in that bed, helpless as a kitten, while your nurse is dead on the floor next to you and nothing you can do about it. You must have felt just awful."

She takes off her coat and opens one container of coffee, which she holds next to my mouth. "I know I shouldn't let you have this, darlin'," she says with a smile, "but I also know how much you love a good cup of coffee. And after what you've been through, you deserve a little treat."

I take a sip. Pure heaven.

Before I can formulate a reply, Mavis is off and running. I swear, that woman's mouth could win a marathon. But for once I want to know every detail. "Doctor Fiske said he'd never heard of such a thing, a nurse electrocuted when a radio fell into the patient's bathwater. It just goes to show," she said, shaking her head and making a clicking sound with her teeth.

I wasn't sure what it went to show, but I added my own cliche to the ones piling up around us.

"Accidents will happen," I said, trying not to sound as pleased as I felt. I lay back on the bed and let another sip of coffee roll around my tongue.

I had the idea for an anthology of short stories set along Route 66 when I was living in Edmund, Oklahoma. I also had, somewhere in the back closet of my creative mind, an idea for a story about a 1920's beaded dress that changes hands and changes lives. So I put the dress on a Chicago flapper. Then took it along on the Dust Bowl migration, placed it in a thrift store in Elk City, and then — well, to see what happens to the dress in the long run, you'll have to read the whole story.

TOO MANY MIDNIGHTS

West Hollywood, California, 1985

How should a legend die?

As she had lived. With style and taste and that elusive quality called glamour.

There was no glamour anymore. Glamour was dead. When she'd worked in the Business, there were still women who exuded it like expensive perfume. They dressed to kill even for a trip to the Safeway; they always walked in a cloud of scent and wore hats tilted at rakish angles on perfectly coiffed heads, and their heels were never less than three inches.

Stockings had seams, and lipstick was bright red, and those women were bigger than life and so incredibly seductive that it made you feel more alive just to be near them. Bette Davis and Betty Bacall and that dear Missy Stanwyck and nice June Allyson — they'd been like friends, even if they were stars and she a lowly dresser at The Studio, which was always called just The Studio as if there were only one, and it was always referred to in capital letters.

Now they wanted her to die in a squalid nursing home, wearing some unspeakable hospital gown with a slit up the back and no makeup and mules instead of feather-trimmed slippers on feet without nail polish on the toes. They wanted her to die before she was dead, and this Gerri refused to do. She'd take matters into her own hands and do what she had to do in order to die in her own way.

The morning chat show had a feature on the closing of Route 66. Impossible, Gerri thought, a road that famous, in a song even, closed up like an old store put out of business by the new mall. This country had no heart, no sense of history. First they killed Glamour, and now Route 66 was being put out to pasture. Wasn't it appropriate that she, too, should fade away?

But what to wear for her final appearance on this planet? The forties had been a nice period, if a trifle heavy in the shoulders for her taste. She had a lovely Balenciaga evening suit of black cashmere with embroidery around the neckline and rhinestone buttons. A small black hat with a veil and bright red lipstick and those suede pumps — dignified. Very dignified. But was it the right choice? Was it, perhaps, a trifle too Rosalind Russell?

Standing before the walk-in closet with the clothes organized according to period, she reached out a manicured hand and touched the fragile black chiffon number from the 1920's, laden with beads that twinkled in the strong California sunlight.

What stories that dress could tell!

Chicago, Illinois, 1928

"It's the most beautiful dress I've ever seen." Belinda Carlisle couldn't help crushing the crepe to her breast and burying her face in its sheer, bead-bedezened loveliness. "And you're a perfect darling for buying it."

It was her very first grown-up dress. The first dress in her life that would allow her legs, freshly shaved and encased in sheer silk stockings, to be the focus of male attention. The days of middy blouses and black lisle hose under demure long skirts was over.

"Oh, Daddy, thank you. Thank you so much." She gave the dress one more loving squeeze and turned toward her bedroom.

"Now, Belinda," her father said, raising his voice, "I want you to promise you won't do anything foolish tonight."

"Oh, no, Papa, I won't." The lie tripped lightly off her tongue, but the dress itself knew she was fibbing. How could anyone not act foolish wearing a cloud of crepe with beads that would gleam in the soft amber light and fringe that would tickle her rouged knees?

Oh, yes. The knees were rouged and so were her cheeks, and she pasted her hair into spit curls on either side of her face and one in the center of her forehead just like Clara Bow. She made a Clara Bow rosebud mouth at herself in the mirror, then broke into a wide innocent smile that showed the gap between her front teeth.

She clamped her lips shut; It Girls didn't have gaps in their teeth like farmer's daughters. They were cool and aloof and mysterious. And tonight she wasn't going to be Belinda Carlisle of the banking Carlisles. She was going to be a flapper, smoking a cigarette in an ivory holder, sipping gin from a silver flask, swearing and smelling of orchids and staying out all night with a college man. Talking of Paris and F. Scott Fitzgerald and riding in an open roadster with the wind in her hair. She was going to be the kind of woman Daddy wouldn't want her to know.

She loved her father very much, but she wasn't a child anymore, and tonight she was going to prove it.

As she rubbed the rabbit's foot over her face one more time, adding a smidge more rouge, she hummed the new song that was all the rage:

You can bring Pearl,
She's a darned nice girl.
But don't bring LuLu.

LuLu always wants to do
What the boys all want her to.
You can bring Sal,
Or Dottie or Al,
But don't bring LuLu.

When Price introduced her to his friends from college, she said, with a toss of her newly-bobbed head, "Oh, don't bother with that old Belinda. Just call me LuLu."

And they did. As the night wore on, as they drove in Price's shiny new car with its leather seats from speakeasy to speakeasy, she gradually became LuLu, sheddding bits and pieces of her old Belinda self along the way. The gin helped, of course, but it was the dress that transformed her, somehow permeating her very skin with its forbidden desires.

Finally Price's friend Mack said he knew a place that stayed open all night. A roadhouse. A real and true roadhouse, just like she'd heard about from the fast crowd at school. It was called Wicked Wanda's and it was out on the highway they'd just made a national road. Route 66 it was called, and the sound of it thrilled her because it was so strange and so filled with adventure. It went, or so they said, all the way to Los Angeles, California, and she wondered as they made their way to Joliet how it would feel to keep on going and going and wake up with orange trees all around you.

219 Too Many Midnights

West Hollywood, California, 1978

Route 66. Nineteen and forty-four. The Texas panhandle; a town called McLean. Big army base and a POW camp to boot; Army shows with chorus girls from Vegas and a couple comics couldn't have played a full week in Jersey, they were so corny. But the boys ate that stuff up, and the biggest hand of all went to a bunch of soldiers in drag imitating the chorines. It was supposed to be funny, but to Pvt. Gerald Tinsley, it was the thrill of a lifetime — dressing the way he'd always wanted to, and big macho men watching him perform without disgust.

Was it so much to ask? That he be allowed to die — to live until his death — wearing the clothes he loved? The clothes that transformed him from drab, uninteresting, flawed male to glorious, sexual, sensuous, enticing, fascinating She-male — Queen of all he surveyed?

He hated the term "transvestite." So clinical. And "cross-dresser." That sounded like one of those monks with a huge wooden cross dangling on his chest. No, the proper word for him and those like him was Queen. Regal, dignified, wearing only the richest fabrics, the best cut garments made by the foremost designers of the age.

He'd been lucky to own such luxurious gowns, lucky and of course blessed with a fabulous eye. Everyone said so. The movie stars he dressed for their roles all deferred to him (except Crawford, of course, but everyone knew how she was, never listened to anyone in her life, and my God, look at those lumberjack shoulders. Not a speck of femininity there, not like that sweet Loretta Young, who was happy to give him a castoff gown or two and never raised an eyebrow when he said it was for his sister in Duluth.)

He rambled nowadays. He was getting old. Not as old as he'd hoped to get, but, then, everyone had their cross to bear, and how did we get back to that anyway?

What friends he had left in the Industry said it was time for the nursing home. He couldn't live on his own any longer, not with his muscles failing and his eyesight going and even though that little fire in the kitchen could have happened to anybody — anybody! — the truth was plain.

But even in West Hollywood, there wasn't a nursing home that would allow him to take his true identity with him. Oh, they'd been very generous when it came to furniture. Bring your favorite chair, Mr. Tinsley. Bring photographs for your bedside table. And, since it was Hollywood and not, thank the Lord, Duluth, no one would raise an eyebrow if that special loved one's photograph was male instead of female.

But would they let him sit on the verandah in his favorite silk dressing gown with the breeze blowing the skirt about his knees, fur-trimmed mules on his feet? Would they let him come to dinner in his best Chanel cocktail dress, just the perfect basic black, worn with real matched pearls?

No, they wouldn't.

And so he would die. He would pack a little suitcase and check himself into that wonderful pink hotel in Santa Monica, at the very end of Route 66, and he would watch the sunset and sip mimosas until he fell at last into that long, long sleep. And he would wear his absolutely favorite frock while he waited for the pills to take effect.

When they found him the next morning, they would say, She was a Queen to the end.

But which dress? His closet spanned the decades, from his earliest youthful flings to his matronly years. Which dress would most fully express his inner self?

Perhaps the Thirties, the era of Harlow and Ginger Rogers, the sleek lingerie, the long, flowing lines and perfectly draped chiffon with —

Oh, yes. The pink-green fern print bias-cut cocktail frock that showed off his slender waist. The one in which he'd taught the Continental to a movie star no one ever could have imagined as an escort to not-quite-female beauties. He lay the beaded dress on his rose satin bedspread and paraded about the room with the fern print draped over his shoulders, moving slowly and sensously to music only he could hear.

Ah, the Thirties. Hollywood before the Code, before the twin-bed hypocrisy of the Forties and Fifties. When no starlet worth the name owned a pair of step-ins, since underwear was guaranteed to ruin the perfect line of the gowns.

He'd worn lush honey-colored furs and carried an envelope clutch made of baby alligator, complete with head that still had little teeth like razors.

Perhaps this was the dress he should choose for his last appearance. If only he could find that alligator bag and the shoes that went with it. And the citrine earrings and the brooch with the filigree daffodils.

He sobered as he reflected that the Thirties hadn't been a terribly happy decade for everyone.

Goldroad, Arizona, 1938

"I do believe all the Okies in the world is on this road." Ma fanned herself with the paper fan they give out at church when Sister Hattie passed. It had a picture of Sister Hattie on it, wearing her big old black hat with the white roses. T'other side had a picture of Ransom's funeral home, big as life and twice as scary.

Pa grunted and shifted the tobacco to the other side of his mouth. "All the Okies in the world got car trouble, too, same as we'uns."

"What we gonna sell this time, Pa?"

I poked Bubba in the ribs. And I poked him hard. Ain't no call for a boy to be that stupid and him all of ten years old.

We was gonna sell whatever we had to. Whatever we had left.

Ma like to died when we sold her Mawmaw's tablecloth, the one she embroidered with her own hands. It had flowers on it and birds and leaves and it was real pretty on the table back at the home place. When we done had a table.

Table went nigh onto a year ago. When the dust storms first hit our place.

Pa said we'd never leave. Said the folks sellin' up and headin' out west was traitors. Said the land wouldn't fail us. Said the Lord wouldn't fail us.

Now we're on the road, same as the others. Only we didn't sell up; we was pushed out by the bank. Lost the home place anyhow, and no money to show for it.

Only one thing left to sell. Ma knew it. I knew it.

But Pa didn't.

The car trouble was real bad, and that was on account of the road was real bad. We seen dust before, so bone-dry weren't nothing new, but this here Arizona dust was even dryer and dustier than back home. I ain't never seen dry like this, dry and rocky like I pictured the moon.

And the hills. Lord, I done read about hills and mountains in McGuffey's reader, but living in Oklahoma, you don't hardly see none of 'em. The hill we climbed down to get to this here Goldroad town was so high and the road so snaky we had to come down backwards.

Bubba thought that was fun, but I could see the back of Pa's neck getting all red and sweaty and I knew it was real serious so I didn't laugh when we crept our way down like an inchworm.

Along the way you could see cars that didn't make it. Rusty old Model

A's like ourn and one or two newer models with their hoods open and clouds of steam coming out of them like dragons and the young'uns all scrambling around, glad to be out of doors after all that riding.

The garage man told Pa he needed a new radiator and said if he had a family to tote all the way to Californy, he'd get a new set of tires. He said the desert was death on tires, and if we thought we'd seen the worst of the 66 highway, well, we were plumb wrong because the worst was yet to come in the big hot desert that practically fried you like a hunk of bacon and then froze you silly at night.

Bubba wanted an orange Nehi, but I gave him another poke in the ribs on account of we didn't have no money for such folderol and he could stick his head under the pump and open his mouth if he was dry. Which we all was since that hot Arizona air was half-dust and the sun like to pulled all the water right out of a body, so that we hardly even went to the privy the whole time we was driving.

The garage man had a little bitty old general store right next to his car-fixing place. Inside it was filled with a lot of things that made me homesick for Oklahoma. Quilts piled on a wooden table and embroidered tablecloths like we used to have. Family things people sold when times got hard and they was out of gas and out of luck.

I knew what Ma was gonna sell, and I knew she was gonna sneak it out of the cardboard suitcase when Pa wasn't looking on account of he'd feel real bad if he knew, but we had to have them tires. We had to.

"Earlie Sue," Ma said, her voice all sweet like molasses, which told me she was up to something, "Why'nt you take Bubba over to the shave ice stand and see if the man will give you a chunk without a flavor on it. He couldn't be so mean as to charge you if you didn't have no flavor."

Well, I wasn't so all-fired certain about that, since I didn't think we'd met with huge balls of kindness since we left Oklahoma, but I did take Bubba aside and tell him, "You look all nice and wistful, and be sure to call the man sir." He trotted off, happy at the thought of slippery cold ice between his fingers, running down his chin.

The ice sounded mighty fine to me, too, but I had to see what Ma was gonna do with Aunt Pearl's dress. See, that was what she was gonna sell, and that dress was meant to go to me when I got big enough. Pa always said so. Said I was the spit and image of Aunt Pearl, who was his baby sister and died young and tragic, and I wanted that dress ever since I first laid eyes on it, even if the little beads all over it was winking at me like nasty little crows eyes.

I wanted to be like Pearl and take the train up to Chicago and make me a new life. A new life without any chickens to feed or chickens to bury when the dust got 'em. And if I was goin' to Chicago, I was gonna need that there crows' eye dress so's I could pass for a city gal.

But on the other hand, if we never got those tires and never got to Californy, then I might just die out here in Goldroad, which sure as blazes didn't have no gold in it that I could see, and believe you me, I looked.

I stood just barely inside the general store, trying to grab onto a little bit of shade. Pa was kneeling on the griddle-hot hard ground, looking at them tires of ourn like he never seen them before. Ran his fingers over what was left of the tread and shook his head. I could almost see his thoughts over his head like Orphan Annie's. Them new tires was three dollar and fifty cent apiece, and we needed all four. I pulled the times tables out from the back of my brain and went to work a-calculating. Four times three makes twelve and four fifty-cent pieces makes two dollar and that was fourteen, which was about ten dollars more than we had left in the kick. Not to mention that we'd need gasoline and oil and bread to eat on the way.

That old dress wasn't gonna be worth ten dollars to the garage man, however much it might mean to Pa. Mawmaw's tablecloth was only good for a fillup of gas; the man at the Red Head gas station in Flagstaff wouldn't even give us an extra can to tote.

There was a sound inside the store; I turned and shaded my eyes and peered inside. A woman walked slow and swishy, like a movie star, and the light glanced off the beads on Aunt Pearl's dress, but who —

Did the garage man's wife want to try it on before she bought it?

But then the light hit the woman's face, and I fell back with the biggest shock of my entire life. The woman was my Ma, and the last time she tried to wear that dress, it wouldn't go over her big hips. Now it hung on her like she was a broomstick. But that weren't the real shocking part. My Ma, chief deaconess of the Jesus Saves Through Faith Alone Baptist Church, had her face all painted like a Jezebel. Red lipstick and powder and black rims around her eyes. She looked spooky and pretty and scary and plumb straight-out determined all at the same time.

Well, we got the fourteen dollars and the tires and a can of gas to boot.

And when we needed more, Ma sent Bubba off somewheres, which wasn't never too hard to do, and had Pa take the car over to a garage to check on something or other, and she came back with enough to keep us on the road.

I was in a mortal fright the whole rest of the ride, all the way to Victorville, Califorcy, where Pa finally got some day work, figuring that if he found out what Ma was doing, I'd be a motherless child for certain sure. But as the years have rolled on and I look back on them days, I come to believe that my Pa knew but didn't know.

He didn't want to know, 'cause if he knew, he'd have to kill Ma. So they both kept the family together in their way: Ma by doing what she had to do, and Pa by not letting himself know what she was doing.

They was both heroes of Route 66, you ask me, which you did, come to think of it — but you hadn't better print any of it, because Ma died in the sanctity of her church and wouldn't want any of this told to strangers.

But I sure do wish I could have one more glimpse of her the way she looked in that there crow's eye dress that was meant to go to me but never did.

West Hollywood, California, 1978

The Forties wasn't his favorite decade. The women were too masculine for him, all those suits and shoulders. And the shoes! He could weep for those shoes — although he had rather enjoyed the open-toe look, since it gave him a chance to paint his toenails bright red.

Come to think of it, the Forties hadn't been a bad time in which to grow mature. Which was to say, he'd lost his peachfuzz innocence and replaced it with a sophisticated woman-about-town look that suited his external rather than his internal age. Roz Russell with style, he called it.

The purple Chanel suit with the black velvet collar and the black buttons?

Too Eve Arden.

The copper crepe dress with the drop waist and the beaded flower at the pleated fall? Lovely, but he wasn't at all certain he could still fasten that side zipper. His medication had added a spare tire around his middle even as the rest of him grew skeletonlike from loss of flesh.

The Nile green shantung Anna May Wong number with the embroidered dragons and the slit up the sides? With real silk stockings like only whores could get during the war? Or should he wear nylon in memory of the war effort?

But did he really want to paint his toenails?

As he box-stepped his way back to the closet, the rose dress with the full,

full skirt and no straps caught his eye. Oh, he'd been far too old to carry that one off, but he'd decided to ignore the mirror and dress to suit his inner self. He'd bought a blonde wig and pulled his face back with tape (a homemade facelift), and learned makeup tricks from his friends in the business. Kim Novak was his ideal during this time, although he also loved dear Loretta. But the brunette wig added ten years to his face, so blonde and rose were the colors he chose for his Fifties look.

The long skirt covered bony knees, and the bare male shoulders could always be minimized by the furriest of angora sweater-tops, the ones that curved over the bustline and just barely reached to the waist. With pearls and beads in elaborate designs, made to match the little evening purse and shoes.

The Fifties had made him feel young again, after the business girl Forties.

He'd felt like a prom queen in that rose dress.

Elk City, Oklahoma, 1958

"If that isn't the ugliest dress I've ever seen in all my born days," the woman exclaimed in a loud hog-calling Oklahoma twang. "It's perfect. It's utterly and totally perfect."

She turned to the man in the ratty little shop. "How much do you want for me to take that old rag off your hands?"

"If it's such an old rag, why'd you want it in the first place?" The man shifted his pipe from one side of his mouth to the other; he didn't sound put out, just curious. And not a bit as if he intended to lower the price either.

"We're doing *Private Lives,*" the woman replied. "That dress would be the absolute making of the production. It's so very Twenties. So dated. So passe. So gin and —"

"That there dress sells for fifteen dollars, ma'am. Fifteen and not a penny less."

"Oh, you can come down to ten, surely. It's for charity, after all. The Kiwanis donate all the proceeds to the Children's Hospital."

The Kiwanis of Elk City, Oklahoma, doing *Private Lives?* Taking dear Noel's words and twanging them to death with those god-awful accents?

It wasn't to be borne. So Gerard Tinsley stepped up to the man in the shop and said, "I'll pay twenty. Don't bother wrapping it."

The bulky little woman with the tight pincurled hair and the look of outrage on her Helen Hokinson face drew herself up and said, "You do realize you're taking this dress away from a charitable institution."

"Madame," he'd replied with an echo of dear Noel's charming hauteur, "I consider the rescue of this dress from the Elk City Kiwanis to be an act of charity unparalleled in the history of this squalid little town."

He left her standing open-mouthed as he carried the dress into the wide blue sky day and sped away in his Nash Rambler, heading straight for Hollywood. He felt so good that he raced the Rock Island train that ran parallel to Route 66. He was doing all right, too, until a huge truck pulled out ahead of him.

The dress would be perfect. A Hollywood song-and-dance man was about to hold his annual dress-up party, and Gerri would make a wonderful flapper. He wondered if dear Noel — whom he'd met only once — might deign to drop by.

Santa Monica, California, 1978

He smiled as he pulled the beaded flapper dress from its plastic casing and held it over his torso with hands that barely felt the tissue-thin fabric. He preened in front of the mirror, pantomiming an awkward, old man's version of the Charleston. In his mind, he was at the ball, his very first ball, where all the men wanted to dance with him, to take him into the gardenia-scented garden for a midnight kiss.

As he danced before the mirror, Gerard McEvoy Tinsley became once again, at least in his dreaming mind, the fabulous Gerri.

Joliet, Illinois, 1928

Oh, the music was hot at Wicked Wanda's, and she shimmied like Sister Kate and flirted like LuLu in the song she'd chosen for her anthem. She tossed back gin fizz like it was birch beer and inhaled cigarette smoke without coughing and she sat on a man's lap and let his hands slide up underneath the sheer crepe skirt of her beaded dress.

And the man wasn't her beau.

Price was disgusted with her, but she only laughed at the pinched look on his square-jawed face. He'd started out the evening with prissy little Belinda Carlisle and he was ending it with LuLu, who fascinated men and reveled in their frank admiration of her.

It was the dress that did the flirting, Belinda realized. The dress loved to be ogled and touched, liked the feel of rough masculine hands on its delicate, hand-beaded beauty. The dress wanted sex and gin and music and life with a capital L. It wanted adventure, and as long as she wore the dress, she wanted it to.

If she stripped the dress off right here on the sawdust-strewn floor at Wicked Wanda's, would LuLu turn back into pumpkin Belinda, her Cinderella evening ending in the miserable realization that she'd lost Price and her own self-respect? Or would she laugh and throw her arms around the nearest man and beg him to do what she'd wanted a man to do since the night began? Was it the dress that was making her act this way, or had the dress only released an inner fire she'd kept banked since her girlhood's end?

She would never know.

Price brooded. She'd known that about him, but she'd thought it was essentially a bloodless habit of rumination and calculation. She'd seen him as a man wooing the boss's daughter in hopes of rising at the bank. She hadn't seen him as a passionate lover, hadn't realized he was keeping his own flame of desire under wraps for the sake of a girl he saw as a delicate virgin to be gradually initiated into the magic of physical love.

The delicate virgin lifted her skirts and showed her garters, shimmied her black beaded bottom like a common tramp, and smiled the lusty smile of a girl just begging for it.

He couldn't stand it one minute longer. He jumped up and stepped into the dance floor, grabbing Belinda by the hand and twisting her toward him.

But was it Belinda or LuLu?

Which one did he want?

Was he enraged that his beloved Belinda had become lusty LuLu — or was he jealous of the men who'd brought out the LuLu in her when all he'd been able to do was woo Belinda?

Thirty seconds later, it no longer mattered. His massive football-player's hands reached to her white neck and squeezed. She shook like a rag doll, her legs kicking so hard her shoes fell off. Men grabbed him from behind, but it was too late. He held on like a terrier, pushing his strong fingers into her vulnerable flesh, hating and enjoying the way her tongue popped out of her mouth and her eyes bulged red with blood.

Santa Monica, California, 1978

"Una momia, una momia," Lupe screamed, running into the hallway with

her apron flapping like a crazy bird.

"What you talkin' about, girl?" That was Tasha, the head maid, who doesn't like to hear no Spanish on the job.

"She says there's a mummy in there," I translated. Then I turned to Lupe and said in Spanish that she should stop talking crazy because there wasn't no mummy in that room and she knew it.

She pointed to the room with a shaky hand and I went inside, not being afraid of no mummies or anything else that you could find in the Surf Motel.

Well, I crossed myself right away when I seen it, but I knew it wasn't no mummy. It was just a dead lady was all, a lady in a black dress with lots of shiny beads all over it. An old lady, with big hands and feet like the gringos got, and too much makeup on her papery old face.

She had a glass of champagne next to her on the little table and she looked to me like she went out happy.

It was a minute or two before I remembered that the party who checked into this room yesterday afternoon was a man instead of a woman. A man who gave me a nice tip and said to leave him alone.

I looked a little closer at those big hands and feet and understood. Then I reached out a hand and touched the dress, all filmy and heavy with the beads. It was a pretty dress, old-fashioned, and I wondered what it would feel like to put it on.

In a dress like that, I could get Roberto to look at me, even if it did make Carlos jealous.

I wondered if there was any way I could get the cops to let me have that dress when they was finished with it.

The title is from Have His Carcase *by Dorothy L. Sayers, a story featuring a straight razor. It began for me in an antique shop very much like the one in the story. It wasn't clear to me at first that the protagonist was the same little boy who suppressed the truth of murder in "Tales Out of School," the first story in this book, but then all at once it was his story and I was glad. I would like to see Moondog Evans again some day, but I have no new story for him as yet.*

THE METAL BLESSED TO KILL

Who the hell wants a straight razor these days, anyway?

Safety blades. Electric razors. Everybody was so goddamn safety conscious. Worried about pollution from tap water, about diseases from cats. Spending millions stripping asbestos out of the schools — the same asbestos he'd counted on to save his life when he was a kid.

When he was a kid, there'd been a school fire. A terrible fire at a parochial school named Our Lady of some-damned-thing. He was too young to read the newspaper, but he'd worked his way through that article, sounding out the hard words just like Miss Roth taught him. Reading about kids screaming and hurling themselves to horrible deaths on the concrete playground.

He'd been damned glad when his dad told him about asbestos.

Of course, She made a big goddamn deal about what a baby he was to wake up screaming in the night, dreaming about burning to death in his second-grade classroom.

He was getting old. People who walked around the streets muttering to themselves about schoolkids who'd died 40 years ago were old. People who bitched all the time because nothing was as good as it used to be were old.

Where the hell could he get a straight razor?

In an antique shop, he realized, the thought hitting him with a suddenness that brought him to a stop in the middle of Main Street.

Where else would you go for something outmoded, for something that had outlived its usefulness? Where else but a place that sold the past, preserved as if in amber?

"Nobody uses these much anymore," the chirpy lady behind the counter said. Her voice was edged with wistfulness, a wishful quality that said she often made inconsequential little remarks to her customers, remarks that were meant to stimulate a conversation and a sale, but which more often had the result of driving the customers out the door without exposing their wallets to the musty air of the shop.

"But I have one in the back," she went on. "At least I think I do. My sister may have sold it without telling me."

She turned toward the doorway, which was separated from the main part of the shop by a lace curtain depicting Greek vases and flying birds and grape leaves in an improbable arrangement. The little lady, as plump and squat as a teapot, brushed the curtain aside and stepped out of view.

Randall glanced around the overstuffed store, which was full to bursting with items no one in his right mind would want. Stuffed deer heads loomed overhead; the sun glinted off silver-backed military brushes and turnip watches. The theme was one of Victorian excess, with no section of wall undecorated, no table top uncluttered. Death was a sub-motif; there was mourning jewelry in jet with locks of real hair inside, and funeral paintings of weeping willows and urns. Fringed shawls were artfully tossed over tiny tables and a big ostrich-feather fan was unfolded on one counter. A pincushion full of lethal-looking hatpins sat on the other end of the glass counter, which was filled with smelling-salt bottles and lorgnettes. There was a man's top hat perched rakishly on a mannequin with the figure of the late Mae West.

But did they have a razor?

Only a razor would do. Poetry was everything.

"May I help you?" The voice was irresistible, a whisky baritone redolent of cigarettes smoked after sex, of amber liquid swirling in blown-glass snifters, of full lips coated in bright red lipstick.

He turned. She stood on the stairway that led to the second level of the store. It had, he realized belatedly, once been a bank. High marble columns topped with carved leaves dominated the cavernous space, and a wrought iron staircase led to a mezzanine level.

The woman who stood at the bottom of the elaborate staircase was as solidly built, as classy, as the turn-of-the-century building that housed the shop. "Built like a —" would be the first words any red-blooded male would use when describing this vision in a forties suit that hugged her figure.

She exuded sex. The way She used to do, whenever she was around a man that was not his father.

He felt the same stirring in his pants. The hardness he'd hated when She was the woman who aroused it. What kind of woman produced that hardness in her own son, and then laughed at him?

The woman in the shop had a mocking smile; she stood waiting for him to answer her question as if she knew the words stuck to the roof of his mouth like peanut butter.

Before he could answer, the dithery little woman reappeared, holding an ivory-handled straight razor. "I thought we had one, and here it is. Only a small nick on the handle, and the blade might need sharpening. I used to have a leather strop, but I don't know where —"

"I sold the strop," the sexy one interrupted. "To that awful man who works on the Morgan place. I was certain he intended to use it on his children, but . . ." She let her voice trail off, shrugging a padded shoulder as if to disclaim any responsibility in the matter.

"Sybil," the older lady said with a gasp, "you didn't. You know that child comes to school positively black and blue, and you deliberately sold him our strop?"

Randall's fingers closed into a tight fist. He squeezed hard, as if the sexy woman's neck were between his strong fingers. As if he held her scrawny neck in his clenched hand, wringing the life out of it as if wringing excess water out of the wet wash.

He drew in a deep breath of the musty shop air and unclenched his fist, finger by finger.

There would be no squeezing, no wringing of the chicken-scrawny neck. That would be wrong.

It was a razor She wanted. A sharp straight razor like the one his father had owned, had used for years in the face of her mocking disdain. Why can't you use a Gillette Blue Blade like everyone else, Marvin? Because you're stuck in the past like an old stick in the mud, that's why.

And his father had picked up his well-used pighair brush and lathered his face with lime-scented soap and picked up the straight razor and given it a lick or two on the strop and lifted it to his face and just as straight and true as a railroad track he'd glided the sharp blade down the planes of his face.

And Randall knew the secret of his father's patience. He knew it unspoken, from the earliest years of his life to the day his father Finally Did It in the barn. He knew that with every movement of the blade across his face, his father pictured the selfsame blade dancing across Her neck, creating a permanent smile beneath Her chin.

The gray little woman handed him the razor she'd brought from the back room, placed it in his hand like a sacramental wafer.

It wasn't bad. Better than the one his father used, truth be told. His had a bone handle bleached to look like ivory, but this one was real tusk.

"I'll take it," he said. "No need to wrap it up, just put it in a bag."

The little woman beamed; it was clear she hadn't made a sale in a month of Sundays. The sexy one, who hadn't moved from her place at the foot of the stairs, who stood blocking it so that if he wanted to go up to the mezzanine, he'd have to brush close to her pointed breasts, teasing him under their '40's suit jacket —

Enough!

She opened her red lips in a smirking smile and said, "And who do you plan to kill with it?"

"Sybil!"

He lifted his eyes to hers, gazed deliberately into her mocking face and said, low enough that the little clerk couldn't hear, "A bitch like you."

He smiled a slow lizard smile as the blood drained from her face, as she looked into his too-pale blue eyes, the eyes of a killer She always said, and read the truth of his intention.

He walked to the cash register, handed a twenty-dollar bill to the gray woman, took his plain paper sack and walked out of the store into the August afternoon.

Moondog Evans crept into the barn like a thief. He hadn't been out to the Toller place since — since who knew when? Ma Toller wasn't a woman who invited company, and he and Randall had never been close even though they'd sat in the same classroom in school for twelve years.

It was a small school, not quite a one-roomer, but grades did sit double and triple in a classroom. Which was how Moondog came to be in the room on the famous day Randall Toller came to school and said Bobby Olson "wouldn't be in school today."

That was how he'd said it, just like that, simple and straight. And so Miss Roth had told them to get out their readers and had taken the second-graders through their lesson while the first-graders worked in their work-books.

Later, much later, the sheriff had come by to talk to Randall about what he'd seen when he'd stopped by the Olson house that morning to walk Bobby to school.

Bobby Olson would never be in school again. He and the rest of his family were dead, killed by the crazy uncle who'd been let out of the state hospital too soon.

Randall Toller became a legend. "Bobby won't be in school today" followed him through eleven more years of public education.

The Toller family's isolation from the community was cemented by the father's suicide when Randall was thirteen. "In the barn," the kids whispered to each other during math class. "He Did It in the barn."

Barns were the centerpiece of kid life in those days. You played in the barn; the hayloft became pirate ship or spaceship or theatre as the spirit moved. You went out to the hayloft after a whipping and had a good cry where your sisters couldn't see. You read Tarzan and Huck Finn and the Hardy Boys propped up against the sweet dry hay. You did your first chores in the barn, maybe feeding the barn cats or sweeping the stalls or bringing lunch out to the hands.

A barn was a safe place, a good place. Until Randall Toller's dad Did It in the barn.

And now here he was in that selfsame barn, investigating a second suicide on the Toller place.

"Randall," he said by way of greeting.

"Herman," Toller said, startling him. No one had called him Herman since his great-grandmother died. He'd been Moondog after that guy in the movie for almost forty years, and here was Randall Toller still calling him by his Christian name.

"Where is she?"

The smell told him, really, but he waited for Randall to lead the way, like a guest being shown the bathroom and given a set of matching towels.

Moondog had been too young to be told the whole truth about Pa Toller's suicide, but once he'd taken the job as deputy he looked up the old reports. A hanging, pure and simple. Pa Toller stood on a milking stool and draped a noose around his neck like a Sunday cravat, then kicked the stool away and dangled till he died.

The boys had whispered to one other about the size of Pa Toller's organ when they cut him down. "Blood drains downward," Donny Harris said. His father was a vet, so he knew more about anatomy than any other kid in school. "It collects in the feet and legs and —"

"And the third leg," someone would finish with a leer. "I heard he had a hardon like an ox."

"Like a bull."

"Like an elephant."

It was a hell of a way to get hard, Moondog had thought.

Randall Toller had been a quiet kid before his dad Did It in the barn, but afterwards he was practically invisible. He twitched whenever the teacher looked at him. He sat slumped in his seat, his cornsilk-blond hair barely covering his scalp, which had lots of scars and cuts on it. From where he fell, Ma Toller told anyone who'd listen. That Randall is so clumsy, she'd say, shaking her head. Just like his father.

And now Ma Toller lay in precisely the same spot where her husband's body had been found by their son. Her throat was cut, not quite from ear to ear; they lose the strength to finish the job once the blood starts gushing. A straight razor lay by her side; she'd apparently dropped it before she fell like a stone.

Moondog bent over and peered closely at it. He made no move to touch it. "Your dad's?" he asked, his voice neutral.

Randall nodded. "See that little nick on the handle?" He pointed a shaking finger at the obscene thing in the pool of blackening blood. "I remember when Pa dropped his razor on the bathroom floor."

"Why'd your mother keep it around after — ?" He didn't finish. He didn't have to; Randall would know what he meant.

Randall shrugged a thin shoulder. He'd been a weedy kid and was now a weedy man; he looked like a stiff breeze could blow him down even if he did stand six feet.

"I wouldn't have thought she was the type to kill herself," Moondog remarked. He shifted his weight onto his other leg; standing in one place really played hell with his bad hip.

"She never really got over what Pa did," Randall replied. "Kept on about it, talked about it every day. I guess maybe I should have seen it coming, but . . ." He let his voice trail off like fog over an evening river.

Moondog looked into his old classmate's pale blue eyes. He remembered those eyes with a suddenness that took him right back to Miss Roth's classroom. Rabbit eyes. Scared eyes. Eyes that had seen horror but kept the secret. Eyes that were sometimes rimmed with black and blue smudges; he'd fallen in the barn, he told Miss Roth. Or he'd let himself get kicked by the mule. Or he'd —

There was always an excuse. Always a reason for the bruises and the cuts and the broken bones.

The hunted look was gone now. Randall matched his gaze with a touch of irony behind the faded blue irises. His lips parted in what might have passed for a smile.

"She watched my father shave every day of his life," he said. "Never got over his using a straight razor. I guess she was what you'd call fascinated by it."

"Fascinated," Moondog echoed. He knew there was a truth in this barn, a truth to be found out and paraded before the town and the engines of justice. But it was a truth that would have to be unearthed without him. He looked over at the corpse of the old woman and then at the man who had once been a rabbit child, the man who had looked upon bloody death as a small boy and kept the secret for reasons known only to himself.

He pulled a stubble of pencil out of his shirt pocket and prepared to write "Suicide" in his detective's notebook under Cause of Death. As far Moondog Evans was concerned, Ma Toller had finally Done It in the barn, just like her husband.

CAROLYN WHEAT: A CHECKLIST

NOVELS:

Dead Man's Thoughts. St. Martin Press, 1983; Dell, 1984; Bantam, 1987.
Where Nobody Dies. St. Martin's Press, 1986.
Fresh Kills. Berkley Prime Crime, 1995.
Mean Streak. Berkley Prime Crime, 1996.
Troubled Waters. Berkley Prime Crime, 1997.
Sworn to Defend. Berkley Prime Crime, 1998.

SHORT STORY COLLECTION:

Tales Out of School: Mystery Stories. Crippen & Landru, 2000.

ANTHOLOGIES EDITED BY CAROLYN WHEAT:

Murder on Route 66. Berkley Prime Crime, 1999.
Women Before the Bench. Berkley, forthcoming, 2001.

SHORT STORIES:

"Crime Scene," *Sisters in Crime*, ed. Marilyn Wallace. Berkley, 1989.
"Flake Piece," *City Sleuths and Tough Guys*, ed. William McCullough. Houghton Mifflin, 1989.
"Cousin Cora," *Sisters in Crime II*, ed. Marilyn Wallace. Berkley, 1990.
"Three-Time Loser," *The Armchair Detective*, Autumn 1990.
"Life, for Short," *Sisters in Crime IV*, ed. Marilyn Wallace. Berkley, 1991.
"Cat Lady," *Cat Crimes II*, ed. Martin H. Greenberg and Ed Gorman. Donald I. Fine, 1992.
"Ghost Station," *A Woman's Eye*, ed. Sara Paretsky. Delacorte, 1992.
"The Black Hawthorne," *Danger in D.C., Cat Crimes in the Nation's Capital*, ed. Martin H. Greenberg and Ed Gorman. Donald I. Fine, 1993.
"Undercover," *Murder is My Business*, ed. Mickey Spillane and Max Allan Collins, 1995. Dutton, 1995.

"Accidents Will Happen," *Malice Domestic 5*, presented by Phyllis A. Whitney. Pocket Books, 1996 (Agatha Award and Macavity Award winner).

"The Adventure of the Angel's Trumpet," *Holmes for the Holidays*, ed. Martin H. Greenberg, Jon L. Lellenberg, and Carol-Lynn Waugh. Berkley, 1996.

"Cruel and Unusual," *Guilty as Charged*, ed. Scott Turow. Pocket Books, 1996 (Anthony Award winner and Macavity Award nominee).

"Tales Out of School," *Ellery Queen's Mystery Magazine*, June 1996.

"Love Me for My Yellow Hair Alone," *Marilyn: Shades of Blonde*, ed. Carole Nelson Douglas. Tom Doherty Associates, 1997 (Shamus Award winner).

" 'A' Is for Adams," *First Lady Murders*, ed. Nancy Pickard. Pocket Books, 1998.

"On the Take," *Midnight Louie's Pet Detectives*, ed. Carole Nelson Douglas. Tor Books, 1998.

"The Time of His Life," *Death Cruise*, ed. Lawrence Block. Cumberland House, 1998.

"A Bus Called Pity," *Mom, Apple Pie, and Murder*, ed. Carole Nelson Douglas. Pocket Books, 1999.

"The Case of the Rajah's Emerald," *More Holmes for the Holidays*, ed. Martin H. Greenberg, Jon L. Lellenberg, and Carol-Lynn Waugh. Berkley, 1999.

"Show Me the Bones," *Diagnosis Dead*, ed. Jonathan Kellerman. Pocket Books, 1999.

"Too Many Midnights," *Murder on Route 66*, ed. Carolyn Wheat. Berkley, 1999.

"Oh, To Be in England," *Malice Domestic 9*, presented by Joan Hess. Avon, 2000.

"Remembered Zion," *Unholy Orders*, ed. Serita Stevens. Intrigue Press, 2000.

"The Only Good Judge," *Women Before the Bench*, ed. Carolyn Wheat. Berkley, 2001.

TALES OUT OF SCHOOL

Tales Out of School by Carolyn Wheat is printed on 60-pound Turin Book Natural (a chlorine-free and acid-free stock) from 11-point AmeriGarimond. The cover painting is by Victoria Russell. The first printing comprises two hundred twenty-five copies sewn in cloth, signed and numbered by the author, and approximately one thousand softcover copies. Each of the cloth-bound copies includes a separate pamphlet, *Life, For Short* by Carolyn Wheat. The book was printed and bound by Thomson-Shore, Inc., Dexter, Michigan, and published in November 2000 by Crippen & Landru Publishers, Norfolk, Virginia.

CRIPPEN & LANDRU, PUBLISHERS
P. O. Box 9315
Norfolk, VA 23505
E-mail: CrippenL@Pilot.Infi.Net
Web: www.crippenlandru.com

Crippen & Landru publishes first edition short-story collections by important detective and mystery writers. Currently (November 2000) available are:

The McCone Files by Marcia Muller. Trade softcover, $15.00.

Diagnosis: Impossible, The Problems of Dr. Sam Hawthorne by Edward D. Hoch. $15.00.

Spadework: A Collection of "Nameless Detective" Stories by Bill Pronzini. Trade softcover, $16.00.

Who Killed Father Christmas? And Other Unseasonable Demises by Patricia Moyes. Signed, numbered clothbound, $40.00; trade softcover, $16.00.

My Mother, The Detective: The Complete "Mom" Short Stories, by James Yaffe. Trade softcover, $15.00.

In Kensington Gardens Once . . . by H.R.F. Keating. Trade softcover, $12.00.

Shoveling Smoke by Margaret Maron. Trade softcover, $16.00.

The Man Who Hated Banks by Michael Gilbert. Trade softcover, $16.00.

The Ripper of Storyville and Other Ben Snow Tales by Edward D. Hoch. Trade softcover, $16.00.

Do Not Exceed the Stated Dose by Peter Lovesey. Trade softcover, $16.00.

Renowned Be Thy Grave by P. M. Carlson. Trade softcover, $16.00.

Carpenter and Quincannon, Professional Detective Services by Bill Pronzini. Trade softcover, $16.00.

Not Safe After Dark by Peter Robinson. Trade softcover, $16.00.

The Concise Cuddy by Jeremiah Healy. Trade softcover, $17.00.

All Creatures Dark and Dangerous by Doug Allyn. Trade softcover, $16.00.

Famous Blue Raincoat by Ed Gorman. Signed, unnumbered overrun clothbound, $30.00; trade softcover, $17.00.

The Tragedy of Errors and Others by Ellery Queen. Trade softcover, $16.00.

McCone and Friends by Marcia Muller. Trade softcover, $16.00.

Challenge the Widow Maker by Clark Howard. Trade softcover, $16.00.

The Velvet Touch by Edward D. Hoch. Signed, numbered clothbound, $40.00; trade softcover, $16.00.

Fortune's World by Michael Collins. Signed , numbered clothbound, $40.00; trade softcover, $16.00.

Long Live the Dead: Tales from Black Mask by Hugh B. Cave. Signed, numbered clothbound, $40.00; trade softcover, $16.00.

Tales Out of School by Carolyn Wheat. Signed, numbered clothbound, $40.00; trade softcover, $16.00.

Forthcoming Short-Story Collections

Stakeout on Page Street and Other DKA Files by Joe Gores.
Strangers in Town: Three Newly Discovered Stories by Ross Macdonald, edited by
    Tom Nolan
The Celestial Buffet by Susan Dunlap
Kisses of Death: Nate Heller Stories by Max Allan Collins
Adam and Eve on a Raft: Mystery Stories by Ron Goulart
The Reluctant Detective and Other Stories by Michael Z. Lewin
The Dark Snow and Other Stories by Brendan DuBois
The Old Spies Club and Other Intrigues of Rand by Edward D. Hoch
The Spotted Cat and Other Mysteries: The Casebook of Inspector Cockrill by
    Christianna Brand
Nine Sons and Other Mysteries by Wendy Hornsby
The Adventure of the Murdered Moths and Other Radio Mysteries by Ellery Queen
Kill the Umpire: The Calls of Ed Gorgon by Jon L. Breen
One of a Kind and Other Mysteries by Eric Wright
Problems Solved by Bill Pronzini and Barry Malzberg
Cr

T Hoch
L

    stitutions who
publications.